Jackie Ashenden writes 
heroes who've just got th
have it blown wide apart
lives in Auckland, New
inimitable Dr Jax, two k
torturing alpha males an
found drinking chocolate martinis, reading everything she
can lay her hands on, wasting time on social media or
being forced to go mountain biking with her husband. To
keep up to date with Jackie's new releases and other news
sign up to her newsletter at jackieashenden.com.

Clare Connelly was raised in small-town Australia among
a family of avid readers. She spent much of her childhood
up a tree, Mills & Boon book in hand. Clare is married to
her own real-life hero, and they live in a bungalow near the
sea with their two children. She is frequently found staring
into space—a surefire sign that she's in the world of her
characters. She has a penchant for French food and ice-cold
champagne, and Mills & Boon novels continue to be her
favourite ever books. Writing for Mills & Boon is a long-
held dream. Clare can be contacted via clareconnelly.com
or her Facebook page.

SEXY BEAST

JACKIE ASHENDEN

BURN MY HART

CLARE CONNELLY

MILLS & BOON

First Published in Great Britain 2020
by Mills & Boon, an imprint of HarperCollins*Publishers*
1 London Bridge Street, London, SE1 9GF

Sexy Beast © 2020 Jackie Ashenden

Burn My Hart © 2020 Clare Connelly

ISBN-13: 978-0-263-27753-1

Printed and bound in Spain
by CPI, Barcelona

SEXY BEAST

JACKIE ASHENDEN

MILLS & BOON

To the lady in the University of Auckland library staffroom

who used to blatantly read romance every lunchtime despite the sneers.

This one's for you.

CHAPTER ONE

Freya

I HATED EVERETT'S launch party.

It wasn't really his fault. It was just that my dress was too tight, making me feel like an overstuffed sausage, and when you're nearly six foot, built on the Amazonian side—not to mention a redhead—an overstuffed sausage is not how you want to feel. Plus there was the whole being a Clydesdale in a room full of Arabian Thoroughbreds thing going on, what with the room being full of tiny women in glittering dresses, all prancing around.

But that wasn't unusual for me. As a mechanic from a tin-pot little Texan town whose best friend just happened to be a billionaire, I was often in situations where I didn't really fit.

I was way more comfortable in my garage, lying under a car in grease-stained overalls, than I was at fancy fundraisers like this one.

My friend Everett Calhoun and his two friends Damian Blackwood and Ulysses White were launching a special foundation that they'd set up with the backing of the giant multi-billion-dollar company the three of them had started years ago. The fundraiser had all the fancy trappings of a really big event, with famous people and designer outfits, jewellery auctions and a really amazing venue—the British Museum—in a gallery with lots of sculptures from ancient history.

Not my idea of a good time. I preferred hanging with friends at a low-key bar or pub, with a beer.

But then, I wasn't here because I liked glitzy parties.

I was here because Everett's business interests took him all over the world and I very rarely got to see him. He'd needed a date for this party, and so he'd asked me. He never asked for help; he was more usually attempting to help me—not that I'd ever let him—so it was nice to be able to do something for him.

I'd always wanted to see London and since I'd taken on Casey at the garage I was able to leave the business without worrying it might fall over if I missed a day or two.

Resisting the urge to rub my sweaty palms down the dress I'd hurriedly picked up at a store along Oxford Street that afternoon, I craned my neck trying to spot where Everett was. He'd told me he was going off to find me a drink and he was taking his time about it. Not that I was unhappy about that.

Because there was another reason why the party was getting to me. Why I was feeling antsy and restless and more than a little distracted. Everett might have needed me to be his date tonight, but I also needed something from him. Something I'd been considering a lot on the flight to London that I hoped wouldn't change our friendship, but maybe would, and whether that was a good idea or not was anyone's guess.

But I couldn't start talking to him about that because he wasn't here, which was super annoying. Especially when I really needed the margarita he was supposed to be getting me.

He shouldn't have been that hard to spot considering he was six-four and built like Superman, but I couldn't see him anywhere.

I could see Damian Blackwood, phenomenally good-looking and radiating charm like a Hollywood movie star, talking to a bunch of people and making them laugh, his beautiful voice and Australian accent making him easy to pick out in the crowd.

Ulysses White was there too, striding around grim-faced, his black eyes full of ice, his assistant trailing after him—another of those thoroughbred women—looking exasperated.

But Everett Calhoun? My best friend in the whole wide world? Where the hell was he?

'Little,' a deep voice from behind me said.

Only one person ever called me 'Little'.

I turned and there he was, and right on cue my heart starting beating faster, the way it always did around him. The way it had been doing ever since he was sixteen and I, two years younger, was adjusting the bow tie on the suit he'd hired for prom.

He'd been gorgeous then and he was gorgeous now, especially in a tux, the tailored black fabric highlighting his height and the width of his shoulders and powerful chest.

Back in Texas, before the military, he'd worn nothing but jeans and T-shirts and always looked hot AF. But in the suits he now wore? Oh, man, flat out delicious.

His dark blond hair had once been shaggy and I'd always wanted to push it out of his eyes. Now he wore it cut army-short and, even though I missed the length, I liked the way the short cut highlighted his amazing face.

He wasn't classically handsome, like his friend Damian. His features were blunter, harsher, intensely masculine. His jaw was strong and square, and his nose had a bump in it from when it had been broken while he'd been on deployment somewhere. His brows were heavy, his eyes deep set and blue as the ocean, with a tinge of green. He'd never been much of a smiler, which was a shame since his mouth was the perfect shape for kissing and—

Stop.

Everett was staring at me, blond brows pulling down into his usual frown, the one that made him look like a very stern Viking. 'What's up? I got you the margarita you wanted.' He held out the drink while I tried to ignore my physical response to him.

It wasn't usually this noticeable. Then again, I wasn't usually at a party trying to get up the courage to ask my best friend if he'd help me out…sexually.

Not that I wanted actual sex. I just wanted an orgasm. No biggie.

First, though, I needed a drink.

Shoving thoughts of orgasms aside, I gave him a grin. 'Took your time. What did you do? Make the tequila yourself?'

'Had to help Damian with a problem.' Everett was characteristically short on detail. 'You want this or what?'

Still grinning, I grabbed the glass and took a large gulp, the alcohol burning on its way down. I probably needed to be careful, especially considering it had been alcohol that had put the thought of Everett and orgasms in my head in the first place.

It had been my twenty-first birthday and my first time in a bar. Too much beer and late night conversation about relationships—or, rather, my lack of one. And by 'relationships' I meant 'sex'. Or, rather, me rambling on to Everett about how sex wasn't that great for me, because men didn't seem to know how to get me off. I couldn't quite understand how the conversation had ended up where it had, but the result was Everett telling me that if I wanted an orgasm that badly to come and see him, and he'd give me one.

I'd forgotten about it the next day—mainly because I'd been drunk as a skunk—and he hadn't mentioned it either, and so the offer had gotten lost in the mists of my own drunken memory.

But a week or so later the memory had popped back up, my embarrassment complete when it reminded me that while I might have been drunk during that conversation, Everett had been stone cold sober. Of course my brain had instantly frozen, the briefest burst of hope flashing through me before I could stop it. The hope that maybe the offer meant he was as interested in me as I was in him. Stupid brain. I knew he wasn't. He'd never treated me as anything more than a friend and I was sure his orgasm proposal had more to do with friendship than it did with any kind of sexual attraction.

Which naturally had ensured I would *never* take him up on it. Ever. I didn't want pity orgasms from Everett, because that was what it felt like, no matter what his intention had been in offering to help.

I didn't need his help. Never had. And that had *nothing* to do with the fact that I'd been crushing on him since for ever and had always nurtured secret thoughts that maybe one day he'd suddenly turn around and see that his best friend was a woman, not just a tomboy in grease-stained overalls.

Except then Tiffany's wedding had come along. She was my favourite cousin—I was brought up with her after my mother died—and I'd been asked to go, but the thought of enduring a hen party full of sexual innuendo, when I had no decent sex life to make innuendos about, seemed sad. My aunt and her family—Tiff excluded—thought I was pretty sad as it was, and I was a little sick of it. Being nearly thirty and not having had an orgasm with a partner seemed wrong, and I was a little sick of that too.

I could have pretended, I guess. Made up some story of wild, no-holds-barred sex with some amazing guy. But the truth was that I'd always had a nagging doubt that the problem lay with me. That there was something wrong with me, that I wasn't much of a woman somehow.

I hated that feeling since I knew exactly where it had come from: my very critical aunt who never failed to comment on my faults, especially on my height and how unfeminine I was. And even though I was totally fine with myself these days, her comments had stuck, echoing in my head when I was at my lowest. Whispering to me that I'd never be able to have a fulfilling relationship, that I'd end up being alone for ever.

I didn't want to be alone for ever. I didn't want her comments in my head any more. I didn't want to feel like a lumbering Clydesdale in a room full of pretty fillies. I didn't want that doubt about myself.

So I'd changed my mind about Everett's offer. I wanted to feel like a woman and if anyone could do that it was him. Sure, it might be a pity orgasm, but hey, at least then I'd know that the problem wasn't me.

He had his hands shoved in his pockets now and was staring at me, still looking every inch the stern Viking with his steely gaze, hard jaw and powerful build.

An intimidating guy, Everett Calhoun.

But he'd never intimidated me. I'd known him since I was eight and he was the boy next door who'd seen me crying in the backyard. He asked me if I wanted to shoot some hoops with him, because he wanted to be a basketball player when he grew up and that I should be too, since I was tall.

He'd been the first person to see my height as an asset not a drawback, and that was how he'd treated me ever since. He was a good guy who looked out for people even though life had dealt him a shitty hand.

Or at least it *had* been shitty. Now it was pretty good, though he'd worked very hard to get where he was today, and I admired him for that.

Still wasn't intimidated, though.

'You didn't answer my question,' he said patiently.

'What question?'

'I asked you what was up.'

So he had.

'So "what's up" in the general sense?' I said. 'Or maybe "what's up" in the literal sense, as in some balloons escaping or…'

Everett remained silent, his blue gaze unwavering. How had he picked up that I was nervous? Admittedly, I tended to run at the mouth when I was uncertain, but I was sure I hadn't been babbling before.

I needed some more margarita. Stat.

'Jet lag,' I said, gulping at my drink. 'It's a bitch.'

'Jet lag,' he echoed, those two words somehow encompassing an entire universe of scepticism.

'Yeah, man. Flying cattle class is no joke. You've probably forgotten.'

Everett's brows twitched. 'I offered to pay for business class.'

'Which was generous, but unnecessary.' I could have used the extra legroom, but it was just such a waste of money. A plane was a plane. 'Anyway, so this is fun. Not. Why didn't you ask one of the fillies over there to be your date?' I waved my glass in the general direction of the Thoroughbreds. 'I'm not ungrateful, believe me. Just…puzzled.'

'Because Morgan said we had to bring someone who mattered to us,' Everett said, turning to glance out across the crowded gallery.

Morgan was the little woman I'd seen trailing after Ulysses. His PA and Damian's baby sister, apparently. She was the one who'd organised this launch for the new Black and White Foundation, which was something to do with disadvantaged kids. A great project, I thought, and it was very Everett to put all his considerable money behind a very good cause.

He was a man of action rather than words, but that was what I liked about him. He never spent a lot of time talking about what he was going to do. He just went ahead and did it.

'Plus,' Everett went on, clearly reading my mind, 'I hate shit like this and it's good having someone around that I don't need to talk to all the time.'

I grinned, a small glow of pleasure sitting just behind my breastbone. It was always nice to be appreciated by him, especially since he didn't often say stuff like that out loud.

All of this is going to change when you ask him for your favour—you realise that, don't you?

Lifting my glass, I took another healthy sip, watching the swirl of the crowd in the gallery and shoving that thought aside to an unused corner of my brain. Operation Orgasm didn't have to change anything, not if I didn't let it. And I wasn't going to let it.

All I wanted was to turn up at Tiffany's hen party with the knowledge that my clitoris and/or vagina were in perfect working order, and that I was just as much a woman as my perfect, delicate cousins were, despite what my aunt thought. And hey, once I knew for certain that the issue wasn't me, perhaps I could move on from my hopeless crush on my best friend and find someone who might want to crush on me instead.

'Thanks E,' I said. 'Best friends who are also billionaires rule.'

He grunted, which was Everett-speak for thank you.

I knocked back more margarita, only slightly disturbed to see I'd had nearly all of it in the couple of minutes since Everett had brought it to me. But if downing a whole margarita in the space of five minutes was what was needed to get this request out, then that was what was needed.

There was a silence. An uncomfortable one.

I was painfully conscious of his massive, powerful figure standing next to me, and for a second I didn't know what would be worse, him saying, 'Yeah, sure, I'll give you an orgasm' or, 'Not if my life depended on it'.

'You're nervous.' His deep voice was a rumble, his gaze still on the swirling crowd. 'Why?'

Dammit. Of course he'd come back around to that. He never let anything go, the asshole. And I still wasn't ready to tell him the reason.

You're never going to be ready.

That was, unfortunately, true. In which case, I needed to suck it up, get on with it and stop pretending it mattered. Hell, if the worst came to the worst, I could always pay someone to give me one. I wouldn't be the first woman to pay for an orgasm, surely?

Ignoring his question, I downed the rest of my margarita and put the empty glass on a plinth supporting some ancient Greek sculpture. Then I glanced around to make sure there weren't any other groups of people near us, because the last thing I wanted was an audience.

Luckily, there was no one in our immediate vicinity, so I turned to face him. I was aware of the small thrill that hit me every time I had to look up at him, because I generally had to look down at people, not up. 'I…uh…need to ask you something.'

He raised one blond brow.

Okay, Freya. It's now or never.

It should have been easy. I owned a garage and was around men all day. I'd never had any problems talking to them before. I'd never had any problems talking to Everett either. But suddenly it wasn't easy. Suddenly it felt like the hardest thing I'd had to do for years and years.

Perhaps it was because I preferred to give help rather than receive it. It definitely had nothing whatsoever to do with the sex.

'So, uh, remember the night of my twenty-first birthday?' I began awkwardly.

His gaze narrowed. 'Some.'

'Right, well, you know you made me an offer that night?'

His gaze narrowed still further. Did he remember? Part of me hoped he didn't, even though it would mean me having to explain the whole thing out loud.

'About orgasms, yes?' He didn't hesitate with the reply or stumble over the word. As if he said 'orgasms' every day in just that tone of voice.

So. Clearly, he remembered. Which was great since I didn't have to go over the whole thing again, but also…awkward.

'Yeah.' I willed my cheeks not to flush, because red on red was never a good look. 'And you said that—'

'If you wanted an orgasm, you could come to me,' he finished, his face disturbingly expressionless.

'That's about the size of it.' My hands were somehow in fists at my sides so I opened them, trying to relax. 'So, I guess that's why I'm a little…nervous.' I took a breath. 'Because…uh… I'd like to take you up on your offer.'

CHAPTER TWO

Everett

I'D BEEN RIGHT in thinking she was nervous. I'd picked up on it the moment I'd met her at the gate at Heathrow that morning, and it had only seemed to get worse as the day had gone on.

But I'd thought it must have something to do with the Black and White Foundation launch. Like me, she hated formal parties, and I'd assumed it was that.

But apparently it wasn't the party.

It was me and the orgasm offer I'd made her years ago.

I'd thought she'd forgotten about that, especially since she'd been drunk at the time. She certainly hadn't mentioned it the next day, or even since, and so I'd left it, because if there was one thing Freya was it was stubborn as hell. And if she didn't want my help then she didn't want it.

In fact, 'No, thanks' was her stock answer to all the help I'd offered her over the years. *No, thanks* to the finance for her garage when she'd first set it up. *No, thanks* to a loan for a house when she'd finally got sick of her aunt's constant criticism and decided to move out. *No, thanks* to a vacation at one of my properties in Hawaii after working her ass off the first year she'd owned her garage. *No, thanks* to talking to the bank after she'd fallen behind on some of her repayments.

It pissed me off. Mainly because I liked doing things for the people who mattered in my life, and Freya mattered. But she was adamant in refusing me every single goddamn time, and so I'd stopped offering, because I wasn't a fucking idiot.

Except, for some reason, my help was exactly what she wanted this evening.

Interesting. What had made her want it now?

She was looking pretty damn embarrassed. Her face was bright red, which was startling against the vivid green of the pretty gown she'd bought on a lightning fast trip down Oxford Street, and her fingers were splayed stiffly at her sides, as if she was trying to relax her hands and not doing a very good job.

So, nervous and embarrassed, which meant something had to have pushed her into asking me.

'My offer,' I repeated, studying her. 'That you've never mentioned before today. Not even once.'

She gave me a forced grin. 'Yep. That's the one.'

'Why?' I asked. 'And why now?'

'I'm super glad you asked me that question, because yes, there's definitely a reason.' She let out a breath. 'It's Tiffany's wedding in a couple of weeks and I didn't want to turn up dateless yet again. Plus the hen party is going to be a nightmare. So I thought if I knew for sure that the problem wasn't me—'

'The problem is never you,' I interrupted, because I didn't like it when she talked herself down. She didn't do it when it came to fixing engines, so I couldn't understand why she did it in relation to her love life.

She rolled her eyes the way she always did whenever I tried to tell her she was wrong about something. 'Yeah, well, I don't actually know that it's not me, do I? Because if I did I sure as hell wouldn't be embarrassing myself by asking you for help.'

My usual irritation at her insistence on not letting me do a single thing for her shifted, getting sharper at her obvious annoyance at having to ask me for help at all.

But I didn't let it show. I never let anything show.

'So nothing's changed then?' I ignored her eye roll. 'You haven't even found one guy who's managed to get you off?'

Annoyance glittered in her dark jade-green eyes. 'No, and not through want of trying, believe me.'

'No need to be defensive. I'm just trying to work out why I'm your last resort.'

'You're not my last resort.' She shifted on the strappy high-heeled sandals she'd bought with the dress, teetering only slightly. 'Sex just isn't something you'd ask your best friend for help with, okay?'

'Not necessarily,' I disagreed, still annoyed for some reason. 'But then, you're not asking me for sex, are you?' I lifted a brow. 'Or are you?'

She flushed, going the same shade of fiery red as the fat plait that hung down her back. 'Uh, no.'

'So, just an orgasm then?'

'Yes. Look, you don't have to do it if you don't want to. I'd rather it wasn't something you got mad about.'

How she knew I was irritated, I had no idea, but then Freya often picked up on my emotions with uncanny accuracy. Which only irritated me further.

Why are you getting mad about it, anyway?

I wasn't mad. I was just…irritated.

I'd made her the offer because I didn't like seeing her unhappy, and that kind of vanilla sex wasn't a big deal. Fixing her sex life for her wasn't any different from her fixing my car for me. And besides, I was good at it. Getting a woman off was easy when you knew what you were doing, and I certainly did. But she hadn't mentioned it again and since that was pretty much par for the course with any help I offered her, I'd left it at that.

I hadn't thought it was still a problem, but obviously it was.

'I'm not mad,' I said aloud, to remind myself. 'And I haven't said no. I'm just disappointed you didn't come to me sooner.'

'Yeah, well, I didn't.' She gave a little shrug and for some reason I found myself staring at the way the silky fabric of her gown pulled across the curves of her generous breasts. 'Like I said, I don't usually think of orgasms in conjunction with my best friend.'

There was no reason that she should either, since I'd never seen her as anything more than a friend who happened to be a woman. Sure, I'd checked her out, because I was a man and not blind, and she was gorgeous. Who wouldn't notice a nearly six foot tall redhead with an athletic body and the kind of curves to keep a man very happy indeed? A round, pretty face, cute button nose, full pouty mouth and enough freckles to fuel the girl next door fantasies from here to fucking kingdom come.

Freya wasn't a pocket Venus. She was the literal, actual, life-sized version.

But, even so, I'd placed her very firmly in the friend zone. She was the single most important person in my life and I didn't want to compromise our friendship with sex. Especially given the kind of sex I preferred. I'd always tried to be the good guy in her life, the person she could count on no matter what, and the last thing I wanted was to put that at risk because I couldn't control my own stupid dick.

I wasn't looking for more even if I'd wanted it. My legacy would be the Black and White Foundation for disadvantaged kids, the one that Ulysses, Damian and I were launching that night, and I was more than happy with that. A family of my own wasn't on the cards and never would be, not with the kind of shitty genes that I had. But I wanted to do something with my wealth, otherwise what was the point in having it?

Damian liked to spend his money on fast cars, parties, jewels and women, while Ulysses preferred tech. I spent my hard-earned cash on protecting those who couldn't protect themselves—initiatives for the homeless, women's refuges, anti-violence campaigns, addiction centres and various other things, especially in my home town.

Which all sounds very virtuous and sacrificial, but it wasn't. My friends were born good guys, though they spent their money trying to make themselves look bad.

I'd been born bad and spent my money trying to make myself good.

So far it was working, but who knew for how long?

Won't be for long if you tell Freya what you really like when it comes to dealing out orgasms.

I scowled at the thought. Yeah, that wasn't happening. Not on any planet. The last thing my decidedly *un*-kinky best friend needed to know was that I got off ordering other women around and punishing them.

Freya frowned at me. 'And now you're scowling. This is going well.'

Firmly shoving aside thoughts of the dominance games I liked to play, I concentrated my attention on her instead. 'Be straight with me, Little. What exactly are you asking for?'

She only just missed another eye roll. 'I thought I was clear, but okay, apparently not. I'd like just one orgasm that isn't self-administered before having to go to Tiffany's hen party in a couple of weeks. There.' She drew herself up, her chin lifting. 'That straight enough for you?'

How are you going to do it? Put her on her knees? Get her to suck you off?

I had no idea where the thought came from. Maybe from the glitter of challenge in her eyes, because a challenge from a woman always got me interested. Or, rather, it got my inner dominant interested.

Yet it had never happened with Freya before. Never ever. And it wasn't because she hadn't challenged me before, because she certainly had. She constantly poked at me, but it was always in a very easy-going, good-natured way that amused me rather than anything else.

Maybe that was why the Dom in me stirred. She hadn't ever given me a look quite as direct as that before. Or maybe it wasn't her directness but her request to help her sexually that had got me thinking about how to give her what she wanted in a way that would be the most intensely satisfying for her.

Either way, I found myself looking at her closely, studying how the green silk of her gown clung to her figure, outlining curves a goddess would have been proud of. Beautiful, full tits. An elegant waist. Curvy hips. Long, long legs.

Normally, I didn't much care what kind of body a woman had, because it was all about the way they submitted to me that got me off. But I had to admit that, thinking about it, Freya had one hell of a sexy figure.

She could take anything you gave her.

The thought wound through my head and I wasn't sure I liked it. Because although I could give Freya what she wanted, it would be vanilla all the way. I didn't need to subject my friend to the kinds of games I liked to play. Hell, if I wanted that, there were plenty of clubs that could meet my needs. In fact, I already knew of a couple in London that I could head to after the party.

'Yeah, that'll do,' I said, shoving all those thoughts away. 'Though I don't know why you need to prove anything to Tiffany.'

Tiffany was the cousin she liked the most and the only one out of all that family who wasn't a total dickhead. I'd always hated the way they treated Freya—her aunt especially—but Freya had never let me intervene. It was her problem to deal with, apparently.

'I'm not proving anything to her,' Freya said firmly, giving me a warning look. 'I'm proving it to me, okay?'

Stubborn Little. She could give a mule a run for its money. 'Understood. Though you don't need to—'

'Oh, for God's sake, E,' she interrupted. 'Just tell me whether you will or not.'

I ignored the small electric jolt that her interruption sent straight down my spine, making the beast in me want to put her on her knees and punish her for it.

She was always so impatient. I preferred to collect all the available intel before I made a decision and this situation was no different. 'Why me?'

'Seriously? You know why you. You offered, remember?'

'Yeah, but you'd clearly rather do anything else than be here right now asking me for an o—'

'Okay, okay.' She flapped her hands at me yet again then took a little breath, giving me the look she always gave me when she was being serious and straight up, which wasn't very often. 'Look, you said you were good at it. You said you always got a woman off. That your failure rate was zero percent.' Her forehead creased. 'Or is this a fisherman situation?'

'This is not a fisherman situation. Why would I lie about it?'

'Men do.' Her gaze was very serious. 'All the freaking time.'

Of course, I instantly wanted to know who'd lied to her and why, but now wasn't the time. I'd have to ask her about it later.

'I do not have a failure rate,' I said flatly, 'because I've never *not* got a woman off.' It wasn't a brag. Just a straight-up fact. 'And yes, I can get you off too, if you want me to.'

I'd never been going to refuse her. Not helping her when she finally asked me for help was simply not an option.

An expression that looked like relief flickered across her face, though there was something else there that looked a little like uncertainty. 'Oh, well, that's, uh, great. But it'll be a challenge. Not gonna lie. I'm a tough nut to crack.'

I gave her a look. Because Freya might act tough and make like she was one of the boys, but she was definitely a woman underneath all of that. And I knew how a woman's body worked. I knew how a woman's mind worked too—at least when it came to sex—and I had no doubt at all that using both to get Freya off would not be a problem.

'You won't be.' I allowed myself a slight smile. 'And besides, you know I like a challenge.'

'You've definitely got one.' She turned to look over the crowd once more.

'Little,' I ordered, letting a thread of steel wind through my voice, just to see what she'd do.

She turned to look at me pretty much instantly.

She's responsive.

Oh, hell, no. Not going there, remember?

I held out my hand to her. 'Come on. Let's go find somewhere more private.'

Her eyes went very round. 'What? You mean here? Now? But I—'

'No point in waiting.' I grabbed her hand and turned, tugging her along with me. There wasn't much point in hanging around, and once I'd made up my mind I acted. And the part of the launch where various items were going to be auctioned off for a fundraiser, including some of Damian's jewellery collection, was going to be starting soon and I had to be present for it. Might as well get this over and done with right now.

CHAPTER THREE

Freya

EVERETT'S HAND WAS WARM, his fingers firm as he took my hand in his, and I found myself being tugged along behind him as he strode from the gallery, heading for one of the exits.

For a couple of seconds I was too shocked to resist. I was too shocked to do anything much but stumble after him, my brain flailing around trying to work out what was going on. Because he couldn't be serious. He couldn't mean this orgasm stuff *now*. Could he?

You know he is.

But of course he was. Everett was nothing but serious and once he made up his mind about something he didn't mess around. When he had a mission he was on it and nothing and no one would come between him and accomplishing it.

It was unexpectedly scary, and my heartbeat was suddenly ten million times faster than it had been a moment ago. I found it difficult to breathe and there appeared to be a whole roomful of butterflies fluttering around in my stomach. I wished I'd had another margarita because, holy shit, I needed one.

What if I couldn't do it? What if he couldn't? What if Everett Calhoun and his zero percent failure rate actually failed? Where would that leave me?

Perhaps there's something wrong with you after all.

I tried to ignore that thought, tried to pull myself together as Everett tugged me out of the gallery and into a quiet corridor, where there was no one around.

Then he dropped my hand and turned, his palms settling on my hips—his big, *hot* palms—as he pushed me gently, but very firmly, into a small alcove off the corridor and up against the wall.

I blinked.

Everett was a big guy, tall and broad and muscular. And of course I'd noticed, because there weren't many men around who were taller than me. But I'd never thought I'd like just how much taller he was, and how much broader. How it felt like he was towering over me, his wide shoulders blocking out the view of the corridor, his body a wall of hard granite right in front of me.

A wall of *hot,* hard granite.

Holy shit. My mouth had gone dry and I was abruptly very, *very* conscious of his hands on my hips, and how the heat of his palms was burning through the silk of my stupid tight dress.

His hands were so big. How come I'd never noticed that before? And how come I'd never noticed just how hot he was either?

I looked up and had to tilt my head back just to meet his gaze; the butterflies in my stomach fluttered harder. My breathing had gone AWOL and the atmosphere was suddenly crackling with a weird sort of electricity that seemed to be solely generated by Everett's intense blue stare.

The way he looked at me, like I was the sole interesting thing in the universe, was…disturbing. And the way he loomed over me was disturbing as well, because it was making me feel…small. His big hands made me feel almost…dainty.

He was so very, *very* male and for the first time in my entire existence I felt very, *very f*emale.

I didn't like it. I'd come to terms with my height and my build. To the subtle slights my aunt sent my way about how I was a 'big girl' and that I had to be careful with overly feminine dresses because they would look strange on a 'woman of your size'.

She meant well. She wasn't being deliberately cruel. But I wasn't like her or her three daughters, my cousins. I wasn't small and slender. I didn't like dolls or tea parties as a kid, and I didn't like shopping as a teenager. I preferred hanging out with my uncle as he worked on his old Chevy, where there was no pressure to act or look a certain way. Where I wasn't being picked at or told to be more like my cousins.

Where all I had to do was hand him a wrench now and then.

So yeah, I didn't *want* to be frilly and feminine. And I didn't want to feel small and dainty, or any of the other female kinds of things I hadn't measured up to. Especially not when I was supposed to be trying to settle Operation Orgasm.

So what are you going to do? Push him away?

I couldn't do that, not now I'd asked him to help me out. And anyway, he was still my best chance. Zero percent failure rate, right?

So I tried not to think about his hands on my hips or his granite chest in front of me. Or how much he was towering over me right now. Instead, I went for my usual response: a joke.

'Whoa there, tiger,' I said breathlessly, pushing at his chest a little. 'Give a girl some air.'

He didn't move. Not even an inch. 'Am I making you nervous?'

His voice was a dark, deep rumble, his blue eyes glittering with sparks of green, and I had the sudden sense that maybe I'd bitten off more than I could chew.

But that was crazy. This was Everett. My best friend Everett. And yes, I'd been lusting after him since I was a teenager, but I wasn't a teenager anymore. I'd been with plenty of guys and pretty much they were all the same. They were either intimidated by me and tried to make up for it by being extra aggressive and douchey, or they wanted me to make all the decisions for them. Or, in the case of my last date, they started off confident and then, when I failed to get into it, they blamed me for not being sexy enough.

Everett wasn't like any of them, it was true, but would he really be that different?

I was afraid I already knew the answer. And I was afraid because if he was different this would make everything so much more pressured. What if he couldn't do it? Or, even worse, what if I couldn't?

And what if he could?

One warm hand gripped my chin, forcing my head back, and I found myself looking into his eyes. 'Answer the question.' There was a steely note in his voice, one I'd never heard him use with me before.

'W-What question?' I asked, stammering for no good reason other than the heat of his fingertips on my skin was making every thought in my head fray and shred like wet paper.

'Do I make you nervous?'

'No, of course not.' My response was automatic and also a complete lie, because yes, he was making me nervous. He was making me very nervous indeed. 'I mean, come on, E. You're you. I've known you since you were ten years old and you'd cry when you missed a hoop—'

Unexpectedly, his thumb pressed down over my mouth, shutting me up.

I blinked, momentarily stunned silent.

'You talk a lot when you're nervous,' he said. 'You

turn everything into a big joke, because that's easier than being afraid, right? So what are you afraid of, Little? Tell me.'

Afraid? Ha! As if. At least not of him. But I didn't want to tell him all about the stuff I *was* afraid of. Such as how I was worried that there was truly something wrong with me. That the reason I couldn't come had something to do with a defect in me. Because I was supposed to be fine with myself the way I was. I was supposed not to care.

So, in lieu of answering, I opened my mouth and bit his thumb instead.

At least, I tried to. Because the second I was about to bite down, he murmured, 'Uh-uh. Little girls who bite don't get what they want.'

It was honestly so stupid that I should have laughed. Little girls who bite? Come on. Yet I'd never felt less like laughing in my entire life.

I was very conscious that the tip of his thumb was in my mouth and that he tasted salty, the flavour of his skin on my tongue making me both hungry and thirsty for something I didn't know how to ask for.

'Good girl,' he said, when it became obvious to both him and me that I wasn't going to bite down. He removed his thumb. 'Now, answer the question. What are you nervous about?' There was no doubt he expected to be obeyed. No doubt at all.

And instead of laughing, of telling him what a dick he was being, I heard myself say, 'That I can't do this.'

He didn't laugh. He didn't even smile. He only frowned slightly. 'Why would you think that?'

I didn't want to go any deeper into all the insecurities I'd thought I'd shrugged off over the years, that were all apparently still there, so all I said was, 'We're in a hallway and there are people around. And it's not even like I can get naked or anything.' I let out a breath, suddenly miserable. 'It's not going to work.'

Everett arched one blond brow, as if he'd never heard anything so stupid in all his life. 'First, you're assuming you have to get naked to come. And second, you're assuming that I don't know what I'm doing. And I do.'

Man, he could be arrogant sometimes.

'Oh, yeah?' I didn't hide my scepticism, because this was all starting to feel a little ridiculous. 'How?'

He tapped me lightly on the forehead. 'You use this.'

I scowled. 'Hate to break it to you, E, but my clit is not in my forehead.'

Ignoring my joke, he only gave me the most intense, stern look, that made me want to squirm. Then, very lightly, he trailed his finger from my forehead down the centre of my nose to the tip, and then further down, pressing gently in the dip at the top of my lip, before brushing over the curve of my bottom lip, a brief touch on my chin, and then away.

I froze, my heartbeat roaring in my ears like it did after a particularly hard workout at the gym.

It felt like he'd drawn a stripe of fire right down

the centre of my face. Like he'd picked up one of the arc welders I had in my garage and turned it on my skin, searing me. My skin burned, my mouth incredibly sensitive.

What the hell had he done? With a single touch. Other guys had touched me before, but it had never felt like that. As if I'd been burned. It was almost too much, too intense. Like if he kept going, kept touching me, I'd break apart or collapse in a puddle of liquid metal at his feet.

'Oh, yeah,' he said, nothing but utter certainty in his eyes. 'This is going to work.'

I swallowed, weirdly unable to look at him. Sure, I'd always had the hots for Everett Calhoun, but I hadn't expected to respond this strongly to him and I didn't understand it.

It made me want to shove him away and go back to the hotel, and then maybe get the next plane out. Run straight back to Texas and retreat into my garage, hide under the Maserati someone had brought in last week, lose myself in fiddling with engines. They, at least, were simple.

I couldn't do that, though. I might have opened a can of worms with this dumb orgasm idea, but closing it now was pointless. Especially since all the worms had escaped.

'What was that for?' My voice had gone oddly husky.

Fascinating sparks of green glittered in his blue eyes. 'Reconnaissance.'

I reached for another joke, trying to put some distance between me and my weird reactions. 'Well, you know, I've been calling this Operation Orgasm in my head so I guess reconnaissance works. I'm kind of on a mission, right?' I tried to grin. 'You gotta plan strategy and tactics, that kind of stuff.'

'Uh-huh,' Everett said.

A silence fell, yet all I could hear was my voice echoing around the hallway, saying stupid things and trying to be funny. Trying to cover the fact that I was deeply unsure, and failing. And Everett only stood there, an implacable wall in front of me, staring at me, the tension around us getting more intense and electric.

I flushed and tried not to squirm under the pressure of that stare, my head filling up with all kinds of stuff I should say to make the moment less intense. To make myself feel less embarrassed and exposed. To make myself feel less vulnerable. Which was odd when I'd never felt this way around him before.

But my mouth wouldn't work. He was so…big. His hands had come to rest on my hips again, and they were so hot. And I could smell the familiar scent of his aftershave, fresh and outdoorsy, like a forest on the edge of the sea. I'd always liked the way he smelled. It was sexy and familiar, and it made me feel good.

Except, the kind of good it was making me feel now was almost overwhelming. My heart was beating even faster, a heavy feeling between my thighs.

You're getting hot for him. Way too hot.

Yeah and getting way too hot for him had never been part of the plan.

'Dude, looking at me isn't going to get this orgasm show on the road.' I tried to sound casual and not at all like I was on the verge of a panic attack. 'You have to actually do something.'

His stern gaze didn't even flicker. 'You're talking too much again. Which is a good sign. Because if you weren't nervous, I'd be worried.'

'Yeah, I don't think nervousness is a good thing when it comes to coming, if you know what I mean.' I pushed playfully at his chest. 'Come on, you're crowding me here.'

He didn't move.

'E.' I pushed at him again, but it was like trying to move a mountain. A huge, hot mountain. 'Dude, seriously. I need some air.'

Again, he didn't move, that intense stare burning right through me. 'No, you don't.'

'Yes, I do. There's—'

'Plenty of air. You only feel like there isn't because you're breathing very fast.'

'Yeah, because you're standing right there and I don't like—'

'You do like it.' He cut me off, his gaze on mine like a searchlight, shining into all the dark corners of my mind that I never went to. 'You're turned on by it. And you don't want to be turned on, do you?'

'Wow, who knew there'd be this much talking?' I

tried for yet another joke, desperately uncomfortable with the turn of the conversation. 'Geez, E. Can't you just go for my clit like a normal man?'

He completely ignored me. 'You're fighting it. Why?'

'I'm not.'

'You are.' He shifted and my entire attention was caught by the way his big body moved, the pull of his tux across his shoulders, the stretch of the cotton over his muscular chest. 'Why don't you want to be turned on, Little? Is it me? Is it the situation? What?'

I glanced away. The intensity of his gaze was too much, so I tried concentrating on a spot just over one of his powerful shoulders. 'I told you, I'm a challenge.'

He shifted again and then one of those big, hot hands slid down between my thighs, coming to rest directly over my pussy through my dress.

I went utterly still, shocked. Not so much at how he was touching me, but at my own intense reaction. I stared at him, trembling. Hard.

His thumb moved, exerting a slight pressure on my clit.

'Holy shit,' I choked out, the words coming out of me before I could stop them. Because I had no idea what the hell was happening. I was hot, burning up, all the heat concentrated where his hand was, where his thumb was, and on the pressure that was way too much and yet not enough.

'A challenge?' Everett murmured, his blue gaze

gone turquoise as it searched my face. 'No, Little. Far from it. You're seconds from coming already.'

'I'm not.' The denial was automatic, because it couldn't be true. It normally took ages for me to feel good with a guy and I'd usually turn my attentions on him, since that was easier. Sometimes, I could get myself to at least enjoying the proceedings, but I'd never, *never* got to trembling point at one touch, not like this.

'Yeah, you are.' Everett's gaze was like a laser and I knew he could see my shock, my disbelief. 'And you thought you were a tough nut to crack, hmm? Too easy, Little. Too easy. So, I'm going to make it harder.' His focus intensified, making it harder to breathe, my pulse getting faster and faster. 'You're not allowed to come, okay?'

I couldn't move and I couldn't look away. It was like his stare was a tractor beam, holding me completely immobile. 'B-But,' I stuttered, my voice thick and hoarse. 'Isn't that the whole point?'

'Don't argue. Just do as you're told.'

'E—' I broke off, gasping as his thumb shifted minutely between my thighs, the slight pressure on my clit sending the purest, most exquisite bolt of pleasure radiating through my entire body.

'Don't come.' He virtually growled the order out, shifting again, moving closer so he was almost pressing against me, surrounding me with his heat. 'If you do, I'll be very disappointed.'

I barely heard him, too shocked at how my body

was reacting and so turned on I could hardly speak. Because he was right. I *was* seconds away from coming right here in the hallway. All he'd have to do was move his thumb again, and that would be it. I'd be gone.

How was this happening? What was it that was making me feel this way?

Not what. Who.

I stared up at him, unable to do anything else, looking into his fierce blue-green eyes. It *was* him, wasn't it? It was him, Everett, making me feel this way. With his height and his power. With that stern Viking stare. With the weird electricity that was crackling between us.

I'd always known I was attracted to him. I'd just never guessed that he would have this effect on me. And if I had…

You would never have come to him for help.

The thought arrowed through me at the same time as voices echoed down the hallway as a group of people came out of the gallery.

I tensed, but Everett didn't move and neither did that maddening hand between my thighs. 'E…' I said shakily. 'There are people coming.'

'So?'

'But I—'

'Eyes on me, Little.' He moved even closer as the voices got nearer, not looking away from me, shielding me with his body. And then his thumb moved again, a light touch, sending another bolt of pleasure pulsing along every nerve ending I had.

I bit down on the desperate sound that threatened to break free, trembling harder, going hot, then cold, then breaking out into a sweat. There was a thudding ache between my thighs and a tension coiling right down low inside me.

The group of people was moving past us, but I barely paid attention. The entire world was made up of Everett's blue eyes looking down into mine, the heat of his body radiating into me, and his hand pressing lightly between my thighs, driving me half out of my mind by doing nothing more than just resting there.

'E...' I whispered, not even sure what I was asking for. 'E, please.'

'What do you want?' His thumb moved again, and I shuddered helplessly against the wall. 'Because if it's to come, then I'm sorry but the answer is no.'

'But I...' I was panting and I must have lifted my hands to his chest at some point because my fingers had curled into the white cotton of his shirt, holding on as if I was about to fall down.

'No,' he repeated, iron in his deep voice, a hard glint in his eyes. 'Don't you dare make this easy for me.' And then the bastard moved his thumb once more.

I shuddered, white-hot pleasure almost blinding me. This was insane. I'd spent years trying to get off with guys and now, here I was, in a hallway with my best friend's hand between my thighs and all I could think about was *not* coming. Because I wanted to do what he said. I wanted to please him.

'S-Stop touching me then,' I stammered.

The green in his eyes glittered like sparks of emerald in a churning blue sea. 'Try harder.'

But his thumb was pressing down and the pleasure was building, and it becoming impossible to resist. Telling me not to come was like telling a starving woman not to fall face first into a chocolate cake.

I couldn't drag my gaze away from his, couldn't stop myself from moving restlessly against the wall, every part of me wanting to press against him, relieve the relentless ache that was building higher and higher. 'I… I…' I began.

Everett leaned in, his mouth near my ear, his breath warm on my sensitive skin. 'Naughty, Little. You can't stop yourself, can you?' Then he pressed his thumb down firmly on my clit.

A lightning bolt of pure sensation hit me, sizzling down through my head, along my spine and out through my feet, and my mouth opened, a scream of raw ecstasy trying to escape as the climax hit me, ripping me apart.

But Everett turned and put his lips on mine, capturing my scream, silencing it. And his arms came around me, holding me as I burned to the ground where I stood.

CHAPTER FOUR

Everett

I HAD FREYA pressed up against the wall, her entire body shaking, her scream vibrating against my mouth. Dimly, I could hear the people who'd passed us still talking as they made their way down the other end of the corridor—they hadn't heard a thing. Not that they were important right now.

What was important right now was that I didn't flip up Freya's pretty green dress, rip her panties off and sink my cock inside her. Or, alternatively, force her to her knees and order her to suck me off.

I was hard. Seriously fucking hard. And on edge in a way I hadn't been in years. And I didn't know what the hell was wrong with me.

Getting Freya off should have been simple, and in the end it had been. She was the most responsive woman I'd ever touched so whatever guys she'd been sleeping with, they must have been the stupidest assholes ever to walk the earth. A few easy questions would have been enough to figure out that she had major performance issues, and those could have been solved easily enough.

Hell, I'd solved them within a couple of minutes. And after that...

My groin ached and the heat of her mouth was insanely distracting. She tasted of the margarita she'd had earlier, sweet, with a bite to it, and something else, something delicious that I wanted more of. The scent of Freya and aroused woman was heady in the air around me, and it was a major turn-on. In fact, everything about this was a major turn-on and it shouldn't have been.

Giving an orgasm was no problem. But getting hard myself? Almost getting lost in the way her eyes widened and darkened when I told her what to do? When I saw how nervous she was with me? And how turned on I'd made her?

No, I hadn't expected that. At all. Not a problem in the normal run of things, but this was not the normal run of things. This was Freya, one of my closest friends. The person who knew me best, better even than Ulysses and Damian. And I couldn't afford to get myself on edge around her.

No, so you'd better take a fucking step back, hadn't you?

Yeah, that was an issue. She was still trembling and I still had my hand on her pussy, my thumb on her clit. The silky fabric of her dress was thin, and I could feel her heat against my palm. I wanted to keep it there, play with her more, see how far I could push her. Maybe give her another orgasm right here and now. She was so responsive, it wouldn't be difficult.

Yeah, and what would she think about all the orders you've been giving her? What would she think if you told her to suck you off?

A cold feeling trickled like ice water down my back. Dominance games were all well and good in the club. But I didn't play them outside it. And I *definitely* wasn't going to play them with her.

I had some of my dad's darkness in me, some of his potential for violence, and when I got on edge it showed. Easier to deal with that edge in a club, with a stranger. With someone I wasn't connected to on the same level as I was connected to Freya. Someone who didn't matter as much to me.

So. Get. The. Fuck. Away.

It took far more willpower than it should have to lift my head and shove myself back from her. She stood pressed to the wall, her jade-green eyes almost black, her cheeks deeply flushed. Her mouth was all full and red, and I could taste her... Fuck, she was delicious. But this whole thing had been nothing but a mistake.

I expected her to say something light and funny the way she normally did, to normalise everything, but she didn't. In fact, for the first time in the history of our friendship, she only looked at me and said nothing at all.

You've fucked up, friend.

My chest tightened. 'Are you okay?' I asked, the words coming out harsher than I wanted them to.

She nodded, but again didn't say a word.

The silence thickened around us, full of a tension that had never been there before.

Christ, I needed to get out of her vicinity. And fast.

'The auction is in ten,' I said shortly. 'Meet me at the entrance to the museum after.'

I didn't wait for her to respond. I simply turned and strode back out into the gallery.

It seemed as if a decade had passed out there in the hallway, while back in here everything was the same. The crowds were doing what they'd been doing before I'd pulled Freya outside, and I swear the music—some classical shit—was exactly the same piece that had been playing before.

I couldn't get my head around how everything here was going on as normal, and yet my entire personal universe felt like it had tilted on its axis.

So you got hard for your friend? Big fucking deal. Handle it.

Yeah, shit, I was turning this into something it shouldn't be. Making a rookie error in thinking that a simple fucking orgasm would change things.

So, I'd made Freya come and it had been pretty good for her. And I'd gotten hard in the process. So what? Where was the issue? Well, there wasn't one, not if I didn't want there to be, and I didn't want there to be.

I would treat it like I treated sex in general, which was as a release valve that helped me get on with the important shit in my life.

Such as managing this auction.

Shoving away the inappropriate sexual thoughts that were lingering in my head, I made a point of checking on my staff, dotted here and there amongst the knots of people. Then I went over the security plan in my head yet again, concentrating on the details to keep from thinking about how much Freya had liked me standing over her and holding her chin. How nervous she'd been of me, and how that had turned her on, because, oh, yes, it had. And how, in the end, she'd tried to hold off that orgasm just because I'd told her to—

'Everything in place for the auction?' Ulysses' cold voice came from behind me, mercifully derailing my thoughts.

I didn't look around. Instead, I shoved my hands in my pockets and stared grimly out at the crowd, trying to get my dick under control. 'Yeah, should be.'

'Damian's wondering if the security team is in place.'

I glanced down at my watch to check the time. Right on target. 'Any minute…now.'

As soon as I said it, the members of my security team in the crowd began to move, gathering people to urge them down to where a podium had been set up for the auction. The secure van containing the jewels from Damian's collection that were to be auctioned

off tonight would be pulling up now too, with more
security to keep the jewels safe as they were taken
into the museum.

Which reminded me...

I scanned the crowds, checking out where Damian's date—the sneaky little thief who'd managed
to breach my security in Hong Kong—was. But I
couldn't see her.

'Looking for Morgan?' Ulysses asked, obviously
thinking of other things. 'She's dealing with—'

'No,' I said curtly, conscious that my temper was
showing. 'I'm looking for Damian's date.'

Ulysses shrugged, noticing neither my tone nor,
apparently, caring very much about Damian's date.
But that was Ulysses all up. He didn't do people.
Patterns and tech and money were his thing, which
made it kind of incredible that he'd managed to be-
friend Damian and me. We'd met online as teenagers, connecting with each other over shitty childhood
experiences.

Then Ulysses, one of the most driven men I'd
ever met, had had some cryptocurrency success,
and he'd roped Damian and me into it, and before
we knew it we were the proud owners of a multi-
billion-dollar company.

Give or take ten years of hard fucking work, of
course, since making money required drive, determination and a certain amount of arrogance. Which
we all had. In spades.

I glanced at Ulysses, but he wasn't looking at

me. His gaze was firmly pinned on the pretty little woman with long black hair who was down near the podium, holding a tablet in her hands and directing people. Morgan, Damian's little sister and Ulysses' PA.

Interesting. Did Damian know his friend was watching his sister like that? Since Ulysses obviously still had his head attached to his body, I was thinking that probably Damian didn't.

'Five minutes,' Ulysses said, then abruptly strode off in the direction of the podium, the crowds parting around him like the Red Sea before Moses.

'So,' another, more feminine voice said hesitantly from behind me. 'Are you going to tell me what that was all about or am I going to have to guess?'

A heat I definitely didn't need or want shot through me as I caught a hint of her scent, sweet and feminine and musky.

Freya.

Fuck. I didn't want to talk to her right now, not when I had to be on deck with this goddamn launch. And definitely not when I was still as hard as a teenage boy looking at *Playboy* for the first time.

'The auction is starting.' I tried to be less curt with her than I had been with Ulysses and failed. 'We'll have to continue that later.'

There was a small silence, then she said, 'Um… was it me? Did I freak you out?'

Something tight shifted in my chest—the memory of her voice, all small and uncertain, telling me that she was nervous because she thought she couldn't do it. As if not being able to come was somehow her fault and not the clearly fucking awful men she'd been sleeping with.

I might be an asshole, but I didn't want to be one of those men. I didn't want to be an asshole to her.

So I turned.

She was standing at my elbow, her eyes dark, her usual sunny smile absent.

You bastard. Did you even think about what walking away so suddenly might mean for her?

Of course I damn well hadn't. I'd just wanted to get away from her before I did something stupid, like put my hand around her throat and take everything I wanted from her mouth.

Because the truth of the matter was, the problem *was* her. Just not in the way she thought.

'No.' I held her gaze, letting her see if not the truth then as much of it as I could show her. 'It wasn't you, I promise.'

An expression I couldn't read passed over her face and then she nodded, the tightness around her mouth relaxing. But she still didn't smile. 'Okay, well, that's good.'

I could tell she didn't believe me.

Without thinking, I reached out and took her chin in my hand the way I would have done with any submissive in need of reassurance, holding on firmly and making her look at me.

Surprise flickered through her eyes, then, unexpectedly, all the tension bled out of her, her gaze turning dark as she stared back at me. Responding to my authority.

Holy shit.

My breath caught, my inner dominant waking up, and I said, before I could stop myself, 'It's not your job to doubt me, understand?'

'But—'

I pressed my thumb over the velvety softness of her mouth, silencing her. 'Quiet,' I ordered, and her eyes went wide. She didn't say anything though, and a small electric pulse bolted down my spine at her instinctive obedience. 'I meant what I said. It wasn't you. Do you understand? Nod if you do.'

She nodded, making no attempt to pull away from me, only watching me as if she couldn't drag herself away.

'Good,' I murmured, that electricity coiling deep inside me, heating me up. 'We'll have to talk about this later, because right now I have an auction to manage.'

She blinked and I suddenly wanted to kiss her again, nip that full bottom lip, make her jump. I wanted to make her wary of me, so she wouldn't see me as the safe friend I'd always been to her…

Except no. What the fuck was I thinking? I wasn't going to put that shit on her. We were friends and giving her an orgasm didn't change that, no matter how hard I'd got in the process.

Letting her chin go, I turned away so I didn't have

to see the slightly glazed expression on her face. 'Get yourself another drink,' I said. 'I'll come find you after the auction's over.'

I left her to it, forcing her out of my mind and whatever the hell I was going to say to her later, concentrating my attention instead on the whole reason for the party in the first place: the launch of the Black and White Foundation.

This was important to me for a number of reasons, but mainly because the foundation was to help disadvantaged kids, and I'd once been one of those kids. My mom died when I was very little and my dad wasn't able to hold down a job, since he preferred drinking and knocking the shit out of people to working. So we were poor. And when you're poor the opportunities for changing your situation are few and far between. I wanted to change that for the kids affected by poverty. I wanted them to have opportunities, a chance to better their lives and find a way to get out of the poverty trap, and that's what I hoped the foundation would achieve.

Good thing, then, that the auction turned out to be a massive success. The funds we managed to raise were enough to give the Black and White Foundation a great start. And I was expecting both Damian and Ulysses to be pleased by this, but Ulysses seemed preoccupied and Damian was drinking and smiling like he didn't give a shit about anything. Except I knew he did because he kept scanning the crowd, looking for someone. I suspected it was for his date, but when I asked him where she was he said she'd gone home with a headache. Clearly it hadn't been her he was looking for, in that case, but I didn't press him.

I was a little preoccupied myself. Mainly with Freya.

The whole rest of the evening my attention was consumed with her, aware of her in a way I'd never been before. And not in the way a friend would be, that was for fucking sure. I kept glancing around to see where she was and who she was talking with, her presence like an itch I couldn't scratch.

My brain kept going back over that episode in the hallway, replaying the way she'd looked at me, the heat of her pussy against my palm and the taste of her mouth as she'd screamed out her climax. And then, out in the gallery, the warmth of her skin as I'd taken her chin in my hand, the way her eyes had darkened as I'd told her to be quiet…

Yeah, I did not need to be thinking about any of that. At all.

Yet it was damn difficult not to when every time I looked up she seemed to be almost…glowing. Because there was no other word for it. Her skin was luminous, a pretty flush to her cheeks, and her eyes had gone as brilliant as the emeralds in one of Damian's pieces. She looked fucking gorgeous, radiating heat and sex appeal, giving people that warm, generous smile of hers.

She was talking to some tool now who was looking at her with obvious interest, and who could blame him when she was glowing like that? No doubt from the effects of the orgasm, since I was pretty sure that was why she was looking so damn sparkly and happy.

The orgasm *I'd* given her. Me, not the asshole who was talking to her right now.

I'd never been possessive my entire life, certainly not of a person, not after the way my bastard of a father had treated people. And I'd never felt anything like that for Freya. Protective, yes. Wanting to smash some fool in the face for daring to talk to her? No.

Except that was what I wanted to do right now. I wanted to stride over there and get up in his grille and tell him to fuck off home and leave Freya alone.

I was good at controlling myself. My military training had helped keep those darker urges in check, as did driving myself hard at work, along with the occasional club visit. So there should be no reason for that possessive urge to rise up inside me, almost choking me. No reason *at all*.

But that didn't stop the fact that it was happening, and if I wasn't careful I *was* going to go over there and make a complete dick of myself.

It was like that orgasm had tripped a switch inside me and I was damned if I knew how to turn it off.

I ignored the urge as long as possible and then, when it started to distract me more than was safe, I went and found Morgan and asked her to keep Freya company for me. Morgan gave me a suspicious look,

but I didn't explain and luckily she didn't ask any
further questions, walking off muttering something
about 'dumb alpha males'. And next time I looked
up, the asshole was gone and Morgan was chatting
to Freya instead.

Better. Much better.

The auction finished late and there was a definite high energy in the gallery afterwards; people
had obviously enjoyed themselves, many of them
appreciating the excitement of watching expensive
jewels going for outrageous sums of money. Especially since it was for charity, which put the stamp
of virtue on everything.

I didn't want to stay and socialise—like Ulysses, I
hated small talk with a passion—so I left Damian in
charge of wrapping things up since he seemed determined to distract himself from whatever was bothering him, and went to find Freya. She was staying
in my suite in the Shangri-La in the Shard and she'd
probably want to catch a ride back with me.

*Weren't you going to go to a club? Find yourself
a bratty sub to punish?*

Yeah, I'd been going to do that, sure. But that
would be to admit that I couldn't handle myself. That
I couldn't flick off that switch. And I had to. Because
there was no way anything else was going to happen
with Freya, no fucking way.

My temper was touchy by the time I found her
waiting for me near the gallery exit, and it was *not*
helped by the fact that the asshole who'd been talk-

ing to her earlier was talking to her again. And that she was smiling up at him as if he was the best thing she'd seen all week.

I tried to lock my baser instincts down hard, but when she spotted me coming towards her she flushed. Beautifully. And the possessive urge I'd been trying to ignore all fucking night rushed to the surface. Because it didn't take a genius to figure out why she'd blushed.

Me. And the orgasm I'd given her.

That guy was still in her face and I wasn't in any mood to be polite when I got to them. I slipped an arm around her waist and pulled her firmly against me. 'Ready to go?' I asked, giving the guy trying to chat her up a 'What the fuck are you looking at?' glance. 'Limo's out front.'

She frowned down at my arm. 'Brian and I were just talking about—'

'It's not going to wait,' I interrupted, knowing I was acting like an asshole, yet apparently unable to stop myself. 'We have to go now.'

The guy she was talking to took one look at me, then gave her a weak-looking smile before sidling away. A wise decision on his part.

'Excuse me?' Freya demanded, turning and pushing my arm away from her. 'What the hell is going on, E?'

I only just stopped myself from reaching for her. 'What the hell is what going on?'

'What you did just then. With Brian.'

'I don't give a fuck about Brian.' My temper pulled at the leash I'd put on it, which was a bad sign, a very bad sign. I turned towards the exit before she could see how pissed off I was. 'Come on, it's time to go.'

And I strode out before she could say a word.

CHAPTER FIVE

Freya

EVERETT'S LIMO WAS waiting at the kerb and I followed him into it, more than a little annoyed—not to mention weirded out—by his strange behaviour.

Then again, I'd been weirded out all evening, so I guess that wasn't anything new.

That moment with Everett out in the hallway had changed everything I'd thought about myself and I honestly had no idea how to handle it.

Sure, I'd often wondered whether it was the guys I'd been with who were the issue rather than me, especially when I could come perfectly well on my own. Yet those doubts about myself, about my femininity, had lingered. One guy had even told me straight up that the problem must be me, since he'd never had an issue getting a woman to come before. And even though I'd shrugged it off the comment had somehow stuck in my heart, along with all the other criticisms that my aunt had levelled at me. More proof that I didn't measure up in some vital way.

But…it wasn't me that was the problem after all, was it? Not when all Everett had had to do was touch me a couple of times to make me come in seconds flat.

I really didn't know what to think about that. What was clear was that apparently, with Everett, I had no problem getting turned on and no problem coming in a public place, simply with him touching me through my dress.

In the hazy aftermath, all I'd been able to do was lean against the wall, trying to find the power of speech since it appeared to have vanished along with my thinking processes. And when Everett strode away back to the gallery I hadn't stopped him, needing a couple of moments to get myself together again.

But then, as soon as I went back into the gallery, I'd felt all strange. Kind of exposed and a bit vulnerable. And I'd had half a thought that perhaps I'd done something to make Everett walk away from me, so I'd gone in search of him, wanting to know straight up if it was me.

Except he'd told me it wasn't. And when I'd expressed my doubts, he'd taken my chin in his hand and he'd looked at me, pinning me with the same stare as he'd used out in the hallway. As if he could read every thought in my head, see all my niggling self-doubts. And then those doubts had fallen silent, everything in me going quiet and still.

I'd no idea why that had happened. No idea why I hadn't pulled away, offended at him being a bossy, arrogant bastard. But offended had been the last thing I was. He'd told me I wasn't the problem and when he looked at me like that I believed him. Completely.

Then he'd gone and spoiled it all by acting like a possessive dickhead in front of Brian, the guy I'd been talking to just before.

Everett didn't look at me as I settled into the soft black leather of the seat, only muttered something about the hotel to the driver before subsiding back into silence.

But it wasn't a comfortable silence. Even though his hands were in his pockets, his long legs were stretched out in front of him and he looked like he was relaxed, there was tension in every line of his big body.

He was angry about something, I could tell, but I had no idea what it could be about. He'd told me I wasn't the problem, but if it wasn't me then what the hell was it? The auction? Brian? But no, surely not that. He'd never had issues with any guys I'd talked to before, so why would it be a problem now?

It was all very strange because Everett was normally a very level kind of guy. He kept his emotions buried deep—hell, sometimes it was difficult to tell whether he even had them since he only rarely let them show. And I knew why that was. His father was a grade-A asshole who spent most of his time taking out his frustrations on Everett and his mom, and so Everett had spent most of his time trying to do the opposite.

Sometimes I wanted to tell him that he didn't need to try so hard because he'd never be like his father in a million years, but since conversations like that always ended up rebounding on me and my family issues I tended to steer clear of them.

Though we were going to have to have some kind of discussion, that was clear. Especially after what had happened out in the corridor.

Outside, the lights of London slid past the windows of the limo while inside the silence deepened.

Everett made no attempt to break it, sitting silent and tense until I eventually lost patience. 'Talk to me, E. What's going on? Why were you being such a tool back there?'

'No reason.' The words settled into the quiet like hard, flat stones thrown into a pond. 'Nothing to do with you.'

'I didn't say anything about me.' I frowned. 'Or were you lying when you said it wasn't before?'

His head turned, his gaze a brilliant slice of sharp blue. 'No.'

He didn't need to elaborate. The flat authority in the word told me all I needed to know: of course he wasn't lying. But he wasn't telling me everything either.

'Look,' I said, trying to be reasonable. 'You're not the world's politest guy, but you're generally not rude. And you don't tend to look at people like you want to kill them. So I'm guessing there's a reason you were such an a-hole to Brian. Unless you are actually an a-hole and sorry, E, but you're not.'

The sharp blue of his eyes got even sharper, but he didn't say anything. Then he turned his attention back to the seat in front of him, a muscle twitching in his hard jaw.

Oh, yeah, he'd gone from stern Viking to pissed off Viking and I didn't know why. What the hell had set him off?

So I waited. Because sometimes with Everett if you waited he'd spit out what had got him riled.

'It's fine,' he said eventually, his voice deep and vaguely gritty, and I could almost see the effort of will it took for him to ease the rigid line of his jaw. 'I've just got a few things on my mind.'

'What things?' I raised an eyebrow. 'Anything I can help with?'

'No.'

'E, come on. You've never been this strange with me before.' I paused, knowing I was going to have to say it. 'Is it the orgasm thing? Because maybe I shouldn't have asked—'

'It's not that.' He shifted slightly in his seat, making me very aware of the fact that his muscular thigh was right next to mine, and that I only needed to reach out and I'd be able to put my hand on it. I'd be able to feel how hot he was and how hard.

My mouth dried as a pulse of heat went through

me and I was suddenly very glad he wasn't looking at me because it probably would have shown
on my face.

Hell, what was I thinking? I hadn't considered
what would happen after my 'Give me an orgasm'
request. Only that he either would or wouldn't give
me one and then we'd go on our merry way, happily
being friends till the end of time.

And if it got a little complicated, then it wouldn't
be anything we couldn't sort out ourselves. Because
yeah, we were friends and nothing was more important to me than that.

Except this had already become more complicated than I'd expected. I hadn't thought he'd have
this effect on me. I hadn't thought he'd get weird
with me either.

You didn't really think about him at all, did you?

Yet another wave of heat washed through me,
though this time it had more to do with shame than
desire. Because no, I hadn't thought about him and
how he'd handle this. Not one single iota.

Good going, Johnson.

'I'm sorry,' I blurted out before I could think better of it. 'I didn't think about what this might mean
for you. And it's obviously weird and you're probably regretting—'

Everett's hand shot out suddenly, his fingers gripping my chin again. Then he turned my face towards
him and closed the gap between us, stopping anything I'd been going to say with his mouth.

This kiss wasn't anything like the one he'd given me in the corridor, where he'd silenced my scream of release. That had been a simple stopgap measure to prevent me from being heard. But this...this was different.

This kiss was deliberate, intent. And this time he was kissing me because he wanted to.

It was so unexpected that all I could do was sit there in shock. Then his hand slipped to the back of my neck and he gripped me tight, his tongue pushing into my mouth, exploring, demanding. It was so freaking hot I couldn't breathe.

The kinds of kisses I'd had from guys before had either been timid and hesitant or straight-up aggressive, without any finesse or technique, all clashing teeth and wet, probing tongue.

Everett's kiss had as much in common with those kisses as a crappy sedan with a high performance super car. He took my mouth with a focused, highly controlled aggression, and yet with a delicacy that left me trembling. There were no clashing teeth, no accidental biting of tongues. No awkwardness at all.

He kissed me as if he never expected anything but for me to give him everything he wanted, and I found myself doing exactly that. Opening my mouth to him, letting the kiss deepen, get hotter, wetter. I moaned softly, unable to help myself because this was the kind of kiss I hadn't known I'd wanted. Where I wasn't worried about whether I should be more demanding or more hesitant. About whether

I might taste strange or whether they wanted me to take the lead, or perhaps I should let them take it instead. Whether the way I kissed wasn't quite right and maybe they wouldn't like it.

I didn't worry about any of that because Everett didn't let me. He took charge of the kiss completely, leaving me with no other choice but to respond to him.

And I did, whimpering as the kiss got even deeper, hotter. Harder.

His hand on the back of my neck held me in place so I couldn't have pulled away even if I'd wanted to. But I didn't want to. I wanted to stay right there, kissing him for ever, the taste of him like coffee and dark chocolate and all the things I particularly loved rolled into one.

Shit, if I'd known how well Everett could kiss I wouldn't have bothered with anyone else.

Then, just as I was reaching out to him to pull him closer, he let me go.

My heartbeat roared in my ears and my mouth felt swollen and achingly sensitive. There was a pulse between my thighs, heat in my blood. I couldn't seem to catch my breath.

He stared at me the way he'd stared at me back in the gallery, intent, focused, and even though he'd taken his hand off the back of my neck I couldn't seem to move. There was so much power in that look, so much authority. I was hypnotised by it.

'You want to know why I'm in such a pissy

mood?' His voice was deep and rough. 'It's because of this.' He reached for my hand and, before I had a chance to move, he pulled it towards him, bringing it over his fly and pressing my palm down against the zipper.

I inhaled sharply, shocked. Because I could feel his cock through the wool and he was hard. Very, *very* hard.

Holy crap. Holy freaking crap. Was that what kissing me had done to him? Or was he kissing me because he was hard?

'No,' he said, the Texas drawl he'd almost lost suddenly sounding very pronounced as he lifted the thought right out of my head. 'I've been hard all fucking night and it's because of you. Because of you coming all over my hand.'

I could feel my cheeks go bright red as heat poured through me, and I stared at him like a complete idiot. I had *not* expected him to get turned on by what we'd done together. It might have been naive of me, but I hadn't.

No, because you didn't think of him at all, remember?

That was true. But…this was only a hard-on and a hard-on wasn't feelings. He was a guy. They got erections at the touch of a stiff breeze, so it might not be *me*. It might just have been a very natural physical reaction to how he'd touched me.

I blinked, the heat of his hard-on soaking through

the wool of his pants and into my palm. 'Oh,' I said stupidly. 'Uh, I was not expecting that.'

'Didn't think you were.' He closed his fingers around my wrist. 'You'd better stop touching me now.'

But I didn't want to, because it didn't seem right. I'd wanted something from him and he'd given it to me, and now it seemed like he wanted something from me and it was only right that I should give it back. Especially when I hadn't thought of how this would affect him, not once.

Nothing at all to do with how badly you want to keep touching him.

And I did. The feel of him beneath his zipper was incredible. He was long and thick and…oh, yeah, very large.

My heartbeat accelerated and I had to clear my throat before I could speak. 'Or I could keep on touching you,' I said huskily, meeting his gaze. 'Seems fair, right?'

CHAPTER SIX

Everett

I SHOULDN'T HAVE HESITATED. I should simply have taken her hand off me and told her no, that this wasn't a quid pro quo and she didn't owe me anything.

But I didn't want to. What I wanted was exactly what she'd suggested: her touching me. My hand on the back of her neck, pushing her head down so she had to take my cock in her mouth. Winding her plait around my wrist and pulling it tight so I could direct her. Telling her what to do. How hard to suck. And then swallowing every bit of my come.

Poor Little. She was probably thinking of a short, discreet hand job, not that. She had no fucking idea.

'No,' I growled, tightening my grip on her wrist.

She gave me a small grin and waggled her eyebrows. 'Oh, come on, surely one good orgasm deserves another?'

Really, she was so cute and so very sweet, and the last thing I wanted was to unleash myself on her in full-on Dom mode. I guess I could have said yes and gone vanilla, but I had a feeling I'd only end up even more pissed off than I was already.

She'd responded to me back in the gallery, responded to my authority whether she knew what she was doing or not, and the Dom in me was now awake. And it didn't want her any other way.

Fuck, I shouldn't have kissed her. Shouldn't have shown her what she was doing to me, but I hated not being straight with her. That had never been the kind of friendship we'd had and I didn't want to start lying to her now.

I didn't want to tell her about the possessiveness, but I could tell her the main reason for my pissy mood and that was the fucking hard-on for her that wouldn't leave me alone.

Unfortunately, though, that hadn't cleared things up between us. No, it had only made it worse.

'You don't owe me anything.' My bad temper prowled through my voice though I tried to keep it locked down. 'I'm not keeping score.'

'I know, but—'

'No.' I took her hand off me.

She looked stung. 'I'm sorry. I'm not trying to push you or anything. I just thought you might want…you know.'

The note of hurt in the words was a direct hit straight to the centre of my chest. Shit. I ground my teeth, the slight pressure of her hand lingering, mak-

ing me very aware that I was still hard and that this
conversation was not helping.

In fact, all it was doing was making me think this
conversation needed to end and I knew just how to
end it. By grabbing her again, taking away her hurt
and giving her something else in its place, something
much more pleasurable.

Except that wasn't going to happen.

'I know you're not.' I tried to moderate my tone
and failed. 'But the answer is still no.'

'Oh, okay, well, fine.' She gave a negligent shrug
and looked away abruptly. 'It's no big deal. Just an
orgasm.'

*Yeah, and that's what you thought right at the be-
ginning. No different from her fixing your car, right?*

That was true. But I'd based that entirely on the
fact that I'd never seen her as anything more than a
friend, and I'd seen no reason for that to change. Yet
it had changed. I was seeing her in other ways now,
ways that I shouldn't be, that would make things difficult, if not cause irreparable harm.

I wasn't a man she could give casual orgasms to
because there was nothing casual about the hard-on
in my pants, or about all the things I was starting to
want to do to her.

I glanced over at her.

She had her head turned away, looking out the
window, and she'd folded her arms across her chest.
The fat red plait she habitually wore her hair in was
lying over one shoulder, curving around one full

breast and nearly reaching her waist. The colour looked intense next to the green of her dress and the pale expanse of her skin. Fucking beautiful. But her jaw was tight and her shoulders were hunched and she was radiating hurt.

No big deal? Who was she kidding? Who were we *both* kidding? Of course this was a big deal. The entire situation was a massive fucking deal, because essentially I'd just rejected her.

I wanted to tell her it wasn't personal, but that would be a lie. It was very, *very* personal.

'Little,' I began, wanting to say something to make it better, but what I had no idea.

'I told you, it's fine,' she said before I could finish, still keeping her gaze averted. 'You don't have to say anything.'

'It's not fine, though.' I didn't bother to make it a question since it was pretty clear it *wasn't* fine.

There was a silence and I thought she wasn't going to say anything more. Then she turned and looked at me, challenge in her green eyes. 'I have one question and then I don't want to talk about it ever again. What if I was someone else? Would you let me then?'

Jesus Christ. What could I say that wouldn't hurt her any more than she was already hurt? Because the answer was 'Yes, I would'.

'Little,' I repeated.

But it was too late. She knew what my answer was already and another flash of pain crossed her face. 'Is it because I'm your friend? Am I not good enough? Not experienced enough…what?'

You really thought she wouldn't think any of this? You know what her upbringing was like. How her aunt treated her.

I did know. And of course she'd think that the problem was her because for all that she acted like she was fine with who she was, she really wasn't. Not deep down.

I couldn't bear that. I just couldn't fucking stand it.

I reached out, even though I knew I shouldn't, and I closed my fingers around the base of her plait and I pulled her in towards me.

Her breath caught and her eyes went wide but she didn't resist, staring at me as though she'd never seen anything like me before in her entire life.

'The problem isn't you,' I said, my voice husky and edged with temper and a heat I couldn't disguise. 'The problem is me and what I want.'

Her gaze was inches from mine and I'd never noticed how the jewel colour of her eyes was threaded through with gold. It was the most beautiful goddamn thing I'd ever seen. She smelled good too, of that light feminine musk that made my cock even harder, and she was warm.

Goddammit, I had no idea what I was doing.

And yet I didn't let her go.

'What do you want?' she asked.

'Things that I shouldn't be asking you for.'

'Like…what?' She was breathing very fast. 'Tell me.'

I didn't want to. But it was too late now.

'I want to be in charge, Little. I want to tell you what to do. I want to make you take my cock in your mouth, then wrap that plait of yours around my wrist and use it as a pair of reins. Pulling on it when you suck too hard or not hard enough. Using it to punish you.' I kept my voice flat and I didn't look away, letting her see the dark thing that lived in the core of me. 'And then, once you'd done that to my satisfaction, I'd fuck you from behind. Hard.'

Freya stared at me wide-eyed, shock darkening her brilliant green gaze.

Did you expect anything different? She thinks you're a good guy and you're not and you never have been.

Of course I hadn't expected anything different, so why disappointment should collect so painfully inside me I had no idea.

I let her go and instantly she sat back, as if she wanted to put as much distance between us as she could. I pretended I hadn't noticed and that it didn't make the disappointment inside me sharper.

'Um…' She blinked. 'Well, okay. That's unexpected.'

'Yeah,' I said, embracing my simmering anger because that was easier than dealing with the disappointment. 'So now you know why I said no.'

She glanced away, biting her bottom lip, which didn't fucking help matters, and then glanced back. 'So, what? You like to be in charge. That's not…

unheard of. And hey, given the kind of guy you are,
I'd be surprised if you didn't like that kind of thing.'

'You did hear what I said, didn't you?'

This time her gaze didn't even flicker. 'Of course
I did. I'm just trying to figure out why you didn't
want to tell me that.'

'Because you're my fucking friend, Freya.' I held
myself rigidly in my seat, fighting the hot lick of
anger, trying to lock it down. 'And I don't want to
put all that shit on you.'

'Why not?' She said it like there wasn't a problem,
like there was nothing for her to be frightened of.

So what is *the problem? You're the one who's
making it a big deal.*

I could feel a muscle flick in my jaw, tension
crawling through me. I wasn't ashamed of my dominant urges. I accepted them. But they were a side
of me that I didn't want her to see. I wanted to protect her, that was all. I wanted to preserve the image
she had of me as a good guy, because when times
got tough it was her vision of me that grounded me.

I might not ever be that man, but at least it gave
me something to aim at.

'Because fear is part of it,' I said, giving her another little bit of the truth, but not the whole. 'I like
it when a woman is afraid of me and yet turned on
too. And I also like it when she's nervous.'

She frowned slightly. 'So you must have really
liked it when I was nervous in that hallway, right?'

'Yes.' I bit the word out, not sure why I was letting her have this discussion with me when I should have said I didn't want to talk about it.

'I don't get why that's a problem.' Her frown deepened. 'Or the orders part. Or any of it really. So you're a bit kinky. That's okay. Lots of people are.'

'I know it's okay,' I snapped. 'But the big deal is when you want to do all of that to your best friend and she has no fucking idea what it's all about, because she's never tried it.'

She gave me a searching look. 'Is that the only thing that's bothering you? That I might not be into it?'

It was not the only thing that was bothering me but I'd already turned this into a much bigger issue than it needed to be, so there was no need to make it any worse.

'Yes,' I said flatly.

'Well, let's try it, then.' She said it like that was the most logical, reasonable thing in the world. 'I mean, why not? I might be into it…you never know.'

I just stared at her. 'This is not a causal thing, Freya.' I used her name so she understood the gravity of the situation. 'At least not with me. It's fine to have that attitude within the context of a club, where there are rules, but this is not a club situation and we're not strangers. We're friends. And no, a casual orgasm won't change things, but this could. And that's not even considering how I've actually never wanted to do this with you before.'

'But you do now?'

'What do you think?'

She gave me a quizzical look. 'Why now? Was it the orgasm you gave me? Or have you not had sex in a while? Or was it—'

'I'm not talking about that right now. I need you to know that this could completely fuck things up between us.'

She shrugged. 'Sure. But only if we let it.'

Frustration coiled inside me. 'Why are you so hell-bent on doing this? If it's just a case of one orgasm deserving another, then surely it doesn't matter to you whether I say yes to it or not?'

Colour flooded through her face then, making her eyes look even greener than they were already. 'Well, I guess I lied then. I guess it does matter.'

'Why?' I demanded, wondering why the hell she was blushing.

She swallowed, her throat moving, drawing my attention to her frantically beating pulse. 'Because it's not a case of me owing you anything or feeling like I do. It's a case of me wanting to touch you because I want to. Because I…I want you, E.'

I went very still. Very, *very* still. 'You want me?'

'Yes.' Her chin lifted slightly even as her blush deepened. 'I've wanted you for years.'

CHAPTER SEVEN

Freya

EVERETT'S GAZE WAS like a laser boring into me, a bright, intense blue, and I wanted to look away. But I made myself hold it because he'd told me something about himself that he'd obviously found difficult, which meant I needed to do the same. Even though telling him I'd wanted him for years wasn't something I actually wanted to admit to.

'Years?' The word sounded very neutral. Too neutral. 'How many are we talking here?'

'Uh…since I was about sixteen.' My cheeks felt like they were on fire.

He looked at me searchingly. 'You never said anything. Not one damn word.'

'No, I didn't.' Because I was a big, garish redhead in a family of small blondes. Who had to tie her hair back in family photographs and stand in the background because the colour drew attention and so did her height. Who was too tall for hand-me-downs so had to put up with whatever cheap clothing her aunt could get her. Who was supposed to be part of the family and yet never felt like she was.

My aunt had pointed out all my flaws from an early age, so why would a guy as handsome and smart and driven as Everett want someone like me?

'Why not?' he asked.

I wasn't going to tell him all of that, no way. It was too sad for words.

Instead, I said, 'You never gave any sign you were interested in me that way, so I decided it was better not to say anything. You were more important as a friend to me.'

He said nothing to that, only studied me as if I were a stranger he'd only just met, while all the secret little hopes that he'd maybe had a crush on me the way I'd had on him died stillborn. It was obvious he hadn't. And I tried to tell myself I wasn't disappointed.

But he wants you now though, remember?

Yeah, he did. And that was something. Though it probably wasn't me so much as the fact that I just happened to be the last woman he'd had a sexual encounter with. Still, it would have been nice if he'd said something, but he didn't. He just kept on looking at me in that unnerving way.

'So, where does that leave us?' I asked when I couldn't bear the silence any more.

He tilted his head, the light coming through the windows of the limo highlighting the incredible bone structure of his face. Strong jaw, broken nose and deep set, shadowed eyes. The most beautifully shaped mouth…

'What exactly are you asking for, Little?'

The question was casual-sounding but I didn't make the mistake of thinking it was casual in the slightest.

I swallowed, my heart beating faster. 'You seemed like you wanted something from me and, like I said, I can provide it. I *want* to provide it.'

'No, you're going to have to be more specific than that.' He shifted minutely in his seat and, just like that, I was even more painfully aware of him than I had been before. Of the sheer size of him, taking up all the space in the limo, not to mention most of the air. 'Is it just an orgasm you're promising or do you want more?'

'What more?' I asked, conscious that my voice had gone husky.

'Sex.'

The word fell into the electric silence between us like a stone thrown at a glasshouse, smashing through the panes and spraying shards everywhere.

Sex. With Everett.

It's nothing you haven't thought about before. A lot.

I didn't think it was possible for my cheeks to get any redder, but apparently it was. I wanted to look away from his relentless predator's gaze, but I didn't want to be a coward. I'd been the one to push him,

to get him to tell me his secrets; I couldn't be reluctant to bear the consequences of those secrets now.

Those secrets excite you, face it.

Maybe they did. And maybe I wanted to find out
more about them. More about him, because this was
a side to my old friend that I'd never guessed at. And
yes, it excited me.

'Sure,' I said as levelly as I could. 'Why not?'

Sparks of green glittered in his eyes. 'Say it. Give
me the words. So there are no misunderstandings.'

I swallowed yet again, trying to moisten my dry
mouth. 'Yes. I want to have sex with you.'

Another silence, so full of unbearable tension that
it felt like I'd gone deaf, the only sound my frantically beating heart.

Then, strangely, it was Everett whose gaze flickered and who glanced away from me. 'Fuck, Little...'

This time it was me who reached out, placing a
finger on his mouth before I was fully conscious of
what I was doing. 'Everett.' I used his name to get his
attention. 'I want you. I want this.' His lips against
my finger were hot and unexpectedly soft, and I felt
them tighten as he tried to speak so I pressed a touch
harder. 'It's my fault that I made this happen between
us, but I can't change what happened out in the corridor. And I don't want to either. I gave you my truth.
Why don't you show me yours?'

He was silent another long minute, his eyes glittering in the light as they searched my face. What he
was looking for I had no idea, though he must have

found an answer somewhere because he reached up suddenly and wrapped his fingers around my wrist, pulling my finger away.

But he didn't let me go. Instead he brought my palm to his mouth and kissed it, watching me all the while. I shivered.

Then he bit the soft flesh at the base of my thumb very, very lightly.

It didn't hurt yet electricity pulsed through me, all the way down my spine to coil in a tight, burning knot between my thighs.

And everything changed in a split-second.

It wasn't my friend sitting opposite me but someone else. A tall, powerful, devastatingly sexy stranger, with definite hunger in his eyes. With an intense, forceful presence, a dominance that made me want to bow my head to him.

He wasn't so much Viking now as an emperor.

The energy between us changed too; it was very clear that the control he said he wanted he'd simply taken. And that I was okay with it. More than okay with it.

It felt like I'd handed him something precious and he'd closed it in one of those big hands. I knew it would be safe with him. Knew it down to the depths of my soul.

He lowered my hand but he didn't let it go, threading his fingers through mine. 'Here's how it's going to work,' he said calmly as if now we were in this space there would be no more doubts and no more indecision. 'You will have a safe word. You know what that is?'

'Yes,' I said huskily. 'I've heard a little about… that stuff.' A *very* little. Like *Fifty Shades* little.

'Whatever you've heard or read, nothing will be the same as the reality. Just remember that, okay? So your word will be red. You can say that and it will stop everything.' He paused, the look he was giving me sharpening. 'You trust me that I'll stop? Because I will. Tell me you understand.'

This was getting very real. Maybe a little too real. What the hell was he going to do to me that I'd need a safe word for? Would there be whips and chains? Gags and gimp suits?

Getting cold feet?

Maybe. But I wasn't going to change my mind. I'd decided I wanted to do this and there was no going back.

'I understand,' I repeated, only sounding slightly shaky.

If he saw my uncertainty he gave no sign. Instead he went on, 'Good. So you won't speak unless I give you permission. The only thing you can say without my permission is your safe word. You will also do whatever I ask you to do. I'll allow some hesitation to start with, but I will expect complete obedience.'

My heart fluttered around in my chest like a bird shut inside a house flying frantically around trying to get out.

I wouldn't be able to speak. I'd have to do everything he said. Shit, he was really throwing me into the deep end. Was I ready for this?

He was watching me closely, obviously gauging my reaction, then his fingers around mine tightened in reassurance. 'All I'm going to do is what I told you I'd do just before, okay? Nothing else. You're new at this and, even though I like to push a sub, I'm not going to do that with you. But if you're going to trust me, I have to trust you too, understand?'

I opened my mouth to ask him what that meant and then, remembering, shut it again and nodded my head instead.

The look in his eyes flared with obvious pleasure that I'd obeyed his 'no speaking' rule and I felt stupidly pleased with myself. 'Okay,' he continued, 'I'm trusting you to tell me if it gets too much for you. I don't want you trying to be brave or trying to prove a point by not saying your safe word. And I sure as hell don't want to end up hurting you. So you have to be straight with me. Does that make sense?'

It did, so I nodded.

'Also, remember this. I'm not going to give you anything I think you won't be able to handle.'

But how did he know what I could and couldn't handle? He might be my friend and know me better than anyone else alive, but still.

'And if I get it wrong,' he added, obviously knowing exactly what I was thinking, 'you have the safe word, okay?'

I nodded again.

Everett stared at me a long moment, then he glanced away as the car began to slow. 'We're here. Last chance to change your mind.'

But I'd already decided I wasn't going to. I wanted him. I wanted to see what else there was to him besides him being my friend.

It might change things too much. It might be something you can't come back from.

No, it wouldn't be. I was confident that however the sex changed things between us, it wouldn't be for the worse. We knew each other and we trusted each other and anyway, once we took this step, perhaps we could put all the weirdness behind us and get back to being actual friends again.

So I didn't move, merely squeezed his hand to let him know I wasn't going anywhere.

The limo pulled up outside the Shard, its jagged silhouette reaching high into the sky, and Everett got out, holding the door for me with an old-fashioned gallantry that I might have teased him about if the situation had been different. But I wasn't allowed to speak and I wanted to show him I could do this, so I didn't say anything, letting him take my hand again as he led me into the building.

It was a super fancy hotel and not my thing at all. I'd tried to tell Everett that I'd stay in a hostel while I was in London, but he wasn't having a bar of it. He told me that his suite had a free bedroom, so why the hell didn't I just stay with him? Plus he didn't want to be worrying about me in a hostel.

I didn't want him worrying about me either, so I'd swallowed my discomfort about the hotel and told myself that I didn't care that it was too expensive and too fancy for a plain old mechanic from Texas like me. That it was kind of like a super-overpriced hostel in many ways and, besides, I'd have to suck it up because it made Everett happy.

I did the same now as the doormen pulled open the doors for us and Everett strode in as if he owned the place, tugging me with him. We didn't have to wait for an elevator and within seconds we were up on the top floor where Everett's suite was.

The trip in the elevator might have been odd and uncomfortable for me but, because I wasn't allowed to speak, I couldn't say anything. And for some reason that helped me just relax into the moment, since there wasn't much else I could do. Not when Everett didn't say anything either.

He didn't say anything when he opened the door to the suite and ushered me inside either, though the nerves that had been sitting in the pit of my stomach since I'd gotten out of the car suddenly tightened, tangling like wet yarn.

The suite was one of the biggest in London apparently, and the views over the city were amazing. Earlier, I'd looked around with amazement at the massive plate glass windows and discreet low furniture upholstered in varying shades of gold and cream, overwhelmed by the understated luxury of the place.

There was a dining table down one end, where Everett had been working that afternoon, his laptop and papers still scattered on the table-top. I stood in the living area as he strolled over to it, taking out his phone and his wallet as he went, and putting both down calmly on the tabletop. Then he turned to me, catching my gaze with his.

He held it as he shrugged his jacket off and put it over one of the chairs, then lifted one hand to the bow tie of his tux and pulled it free, dumping that on the table. Then he undid the top couple of buttons on his shirt, revealing the tanned skin of his throat.

I took a shaky silent breath, pinned by the intensity of his gaze.

He began to undo his cufflinks, the movements slow and measured, and then, once they were off and deposited on the tabletop as well, he began to roll his sleeves up, exposing sinewy forearms and strong wrists.

I'd had no idea that a guy simply taking his jacket off and rolling his sleeves up could be so insanely sexy. But, oh, my God, it was. The lights of the city illuminated him, highlighting the way his shirt pulled across his muscled shoulders and chest, turning his short blond hair silver and shadowing his eyes.

He looked mysterious and powerful. A beautiful stranger. Not the man I'd known for over twenty years. Not my friend.

My skin prickled, my breathing coming faster and

harder and, despite my nerves, I could feel an ache beginning between my thighs. It was insistent and normally I'd be trying to hold on to the feeling for all it was worth, trying not to let it escape the way it always seemed to.

Yet this felt different. This felt like it had out in the corridor in the museum, a steadily growing sensation that would overwhelm me rather than the other way around. Something I couldn't escape from even if I wanted to. Which was a frightening thought, yet also exciting at the same time.

God, what was my brain doing?

'Seems like you're overthinking,' Everett murmured as he finished with his sleeves, strolling casually over to where I was standing. 'Perhaps you need something to occupy yourself with instead.'

He seemed even taller now and I had no idea how that had happened. Not to mention more muscular. It was almost like I had to tip my head back even further to meet his gaze and, when I did, his height did that strange thing again, making me feel small and dainty next to him.

I wanted to ask him what he meant by me needing something to occupy myself, but then I remembered that I wasn't allowed to speak and had to catch my breath instead.

His relentless blue gaze turned approving. 'Good girl. See? You can be quiet when you want to.'

Again, a weird warmth glowed in my chest, something in me liking that I'd pleased him. But then maybe it wasn't weird. He was my friend and I liked doing things for him.

He's not your friend now.

No, he wasn't. Yet the warmth filled my chest all the same and somehow my nerves settled. Perhaps it was good I wasn't allowed to talk. Not speaking meant I didn't have to try and think of things to say, to be funny to ease the mood. I could stand here and not say anything, and it would be fine.

One corner of Everett's mouth curved slightly and I found myself staring at it, fascinated, wondering what on earth was making him smile since he smiled so very rarely.

But he didn't explain. That fascinating almost-smile played around his mouth, his blue eyes glittering. Then he said, 'Strip for me, Freya.'

CHAPTER EIGHT

Everett

HER EYES WIDENED in shock then immediately darkened, and for a second there was a moment where I wondered if she'd actually refuse. I wasn't sure what I would have done if she had, but then it didn't matter because the moment passed and she was stepping back slightly, reaching behind herself for the zipper of her dress.

I didn't say anything and I didn't offer to help. I wanted her to take her clothes off for me of her own free will, unwrapping herself like a present just for me.

She had a bit of difficulty but then the zipper came down and she was shrugging the straps off her shoulders, the green silk sliding down, over her breasts and hips, down her thighs before pooling at her feet.

The lights of the city bathed her body, making her skin look pearlescent and the freckles scattered across it like gold dust.

It wasn't anything I hadn't seen before. I had seen her in a bikini after all and she was still wearing a nude bra and a pair of lacy panties in the same colour. This felt different though. Because now that underwear was the only thing between me and her naked body, and soon she would be taking that off too.

My cock ached, hard as a fucking rock, but I'd had a lot of experience in ignoring it and so I had no problem ignoring it now. In fact, nothing was a problem now. All the damn issues and dramas of before seemed to have vanished the moment Freya had looked into my eyes and told me that she wanted me.

Perhaps it had been a stupid decision to agree to this. Perhaps we'd regret it later. But I knew the moment she'd put her finger on my mouth that I was going to do this. That I was going to have her.

The dominant in me wanted her and, even though she had no idea what she was getting herself into, she'd given me her consent. It was something she'd only find out by experiencing anyway, and maybe afterwards she'd change her mind. But we weren't at that point right now.

We were in the moment and that was exactly where I wanted to be. No future or past. Just me and her. Where I was in charge of her and where I could give us what we both wanted.

Complete control. It was a good feeling. A calm, settled feeling.

We'd both crossed the line and now there was nowhere to go but onward.

'Nice,' I said softly, letting my attention linger on her curves and making sure she noticed me look. 'You've got a beautiful body, did you know that?'

A blush washed through her and her lashes swept down, veiling her gaze, though she didn't move.

She wouldn't agree and I knew it. She was probably thinking of her aunt and her cousins, and their narrow standards of beauty. How she wasn't little and blonde and girly like they were. About how she wasn't supposed to care about that, and yet somehow did.

Silly, Little.

It was time she learned just how good this lovely body of hers could make her feel.

'Take off the rest,' I ordered.

She hesitated a second, then began to take her bra off.

'Slower,' I murmured. 'Tease me some.'

Again she flushed, but her movements slowed, the straps of her bra slowly falling, one arm holding the cups to her tits, while the other reached around to unclip it. She gave me a look from underneath her lashes and, whether she'd meant it to be or not, it was insanely sexy.

'Very nice.' I let her see how it pleased me. 'Keep going.'

She glanced away again, but the tightness around her mouth eased as she let the fabric fall away, her bra dropping to the floor.

Beautiful. Sheer fucking perfection. Her breasts

were full and round, and perfect for my hand. Her
nipples hard and pink, all ready for my mouth.

Oh, yes, I was going to spend a lot of time with
those pretty tits of hers.

'Panties, please,' I reminded her when it seemed
like she'd stopped.

She blinked then pushed her hands into the waistband of her underwear and eased them over her hips,
and down her thighs to her ankles. Then she stepped
out of them and straightened up, finally and glori-
ously naked.

My breath caught, my fucking dick aching.

And for a second all I could do was stand there
and look at her. Because she was gorgeous. Tall and
athletic, and with curves to die for. Pale, silky skin
and a pretty nest of bright red curls between her
thighs.

Fuck, she was amazing. I'd known she was built
like a goddess, but whenever I'd admired her it had
always been in a detached, intellectual way. As a
friend, not a lover. Tonight, though, it was different.
Tonight, I could admire her in a way I never had before, a wholly sexual way.

And I did. As though the embers of attraction had
always been there, glowing hot, and all it took was
a breath to make them burst into flame.

I gritted my teeth, desire gripping me even tighter
than before, and it took me a second to control my
breathing, to get myself locked down.

Once I had myself back in hand again, I moved

over to her. She stilled, and I could see that she was
shaking a little. Which wasn't a bad thing, because
nervousness could make pleasure more intense for
some people. Certainly, out in the corridor at the
museum, she'd been shaking like a leaf. Just before
she'd come all over my hand.

So I let her get nervous of me, let her get wary. Intruding into her physical space and letting her get a
feel for how much bigger than her I was. Because the
dark part of me loved to intimidate, loved to make
someone feel small and vulnerable and exposed.

I watched her as I did so, studying her to make
sure arousal was in her eyes alongside the fear and,
sure enough, it was there. I hadn't been mistaken
back at the museum. She did like me looming over
her physically.

I got even closer so she could feel my heat, and
then very slowly I circled her, watching her, letting
her get a taste of the predator in me.

She stood very still, her breathing getting faster
and more audible in the silence, and her skin was
deeply flushed. I could smell the musky scent of her
arousal, see the shivers that chased over her skin,
goosebumps rising in their wake.

Oh, yeah, she was finding this all very arousing.
You knew she'd like it. You knew she'd be into it.

I hadn't known, not really. But I did now. Fuck,
yes, I did now.

I stopped behind her, very close, and then I
reached up and wrapped my fingers around the base

of her plait, holding on to it. 'You like me looming over you, don't you? You can speak.'

'I'm not sure—'

I tugged lightly on her plait. 'Honesty, Little.'

She caught her breath. 'I…guess I do. Yeah. I like it.'

'Why?' Slowly, letting her feel it, I wound the silky mass of her hair around my wrist.

She shuddered. 'What are you doing?'

'Answer the question.'

'W-why do I like it?' Her breathing had become ragged. 'Because…because you're tall. And you make me feel…small.'

I'd already suspected that was the answer, but it pleased me to hear her say it, pleased me that she was being honest, because we'd always been honest with each other.

'And you want to feel small?' I leaned in so my breath brushed the shell of her ear, sending another shudder through her. 'Is that what you like to feel?'

'I didn't think I did, but…yes. I suppose I do.'

'Why is that?' I tugged on her hair again, hearing her breath catch.

'I…don't know. Maybe it makes me feel…' She faltered. 'I didn't think it mattered. I thought I was over it.'

I tightened my grip on her plait, frowning at the note of hurt in her voice, a dark, possessive feeling uncurling inside me because I didn't like the sound of that, not one fucking bit. 'Over what?'

'It doesn't matter.'

Without warning, I wrapped one arm around her waist and pulled her against me. At the same time, I tugged hard on her plait, jerking her head back against my shoulder so she was looking straight up at me. 'It matters,' I said flatly. 'Tell me.'

She trembled, her naked body warm and pliant, her eyes wide and dark with arousal. 'Okay, okay. I like it when you make me feel small because it…it makes me feel more like, I don't know, more kind of f-feminine.'

I should have felt satisfied that I'd been right, but I wasn't satisfied. I was just fucking pissed off. Because I knew where this had come from. 'Your fucking aunt, right?' I demanded, staring down at her, holding her tightly.

'Don't be angry with her, E. Please. It's not her fault that—'

'It is her fault,' I said sharply, the anger on Freya's behalf making me feel a little bit savage. 'Do you think you're any less female? Any less of a woman because you're tall? Because you're built like a fucking goddess?'

Her mouth opened as she searched my face and I let her see the heat in my eyes. Then I pressed my aching dick against the softness of her ass, my fingers spreading out on her stomach and holding her there. 'You feel what you're doing to me? That hard cock is for you. *Because* of you.'

Colour swept over her skin and her throat worked

as she swallowed, staring at me as if she was looking
for lies. But there were none. I'd demanded honesty
from her and I gave back the same. 'I like you tall,' I
growled. 'I like you strong. I like your body exactly
the way it is. And you know what else?' I pulled on
her plait tighter, drawing her head back further, exposing her throat. Forcing her to rise on her tiptoes
to prevent it from getting painful. 'I like it because
I'm a big man, Little. And you're built to take me
and that's fucking hot.'

She blinked up at me, a whole raft of emotions
flickering over her face, gone so fast I couldn't read
them.

'Can you?' I demanded, tightening my grip to
make her aware of how I held her and how restrained
she was by me. 'Can you take me, or am I wrong?'

If I'd thought in any depth about how badly I
wanted to hear her agree, it might have disturbed
me. But I didn't think about it. I simply held her gaze
with mine, letting my authority do the work.

'No,' she whispered, her green eyes darkening
still further. 'You're not wrong.'

A deep satisfaction unwound inside me, the pleasure of knowing I'd got it right, that I'd read her responses correctly. And I liked that she'd trusted me
enough to tell me too.

And that trust was her gift to me.

If she only knew the real you...

Yeah, but she didn't. And she wouldn't. The only
dark part of myself that she'd ever see would be the

one I'd show her tonight. The one that would give her the most pleasure. And that was my gift to her. To tap into her deep desires, give her pleasure beyond anything she could imagine for herself. Pleasure she didn't even realise she was capable of.

God, I wanted to show her that. In fact, I hadn't realised how much until now, until I had her naked and in my arms, under my control.

'Good,' I murmured. 'In that case let's take this further.' Tugging on her hair, I eased her head to one side, exposing her neck. Then I bent and kissed the silky skin just below her ear. 'Remember what I told you in the car? About how I was going to pull your hair while you sucked me off? And then I was going to fuck you from behind?'

'Yes,' she said breathlessly.

'And you thought it was a joke, didn't you?'

'I didn't—'

'Well, it's not,' I interrupted, then bit her, my teeth grazing the delicate cords at the side of her neck, the taste of her skin both salty and sweet in my mouth. Fucking delicious.

She gasped, trembling, and I nuzzled down the side of her neck to the sensitive place where it met her shoulder. Then I bit her again to prove my point, harder this time. Giving her a hint of pain. Showing her I was serious.

'Ohhh…' She exhaled sharply, squirming against me, her soft ass grinding against my hard dick. 'Yesss…'

I grinned. And because I was an asshole and I loved making her break, I said, 'Naughty, Little. You weren't supposed to make a sound.'

She froze. 'But you said—'

I let go of her hair, then smacked her on the ass at the same time as I gave her another bite, the sound of my palm connecting with her flesh echoing in the room.

She made a half-choked noise, jerking in my grip, and I grabbed her hair again, pulling it back so I could see her face. See what that small taste of punishment had done to her.

There was shock in her eyes, but it was clearing, giving way to heat and...yes, *fuck* yes, challenge. She didn't speak and I waited, allowing her a moment to say her word if she needed to. But she remained silent, the deep green spark in her gaze daring me to do my worst.

She was brave to push me like this. But then that was Freya, wasn't it? She always pushed me. Teasing me, giving me shit, not letting me take myself too seriously. Not letting me brood too long when things got dark. Cutting through my ego when I got too full of myself, being honest with me when other people were too afraid. Grounding me.

I'd had no idea she'd bring all that to what we were doing now, but she was and it made everything that much hotter.

'That's what will happen when you disobey,' I said softly, looking down into her eyes, letting my own challenge meet hers. 'Punishment. And I like giving out punishment, so by all means feel free to test me.'

She didn't look away, only bared her teeth, which sent a jolt of electricity crackling down my spine.

Pretty, brave Little.

I tightened my grip on her plait, making sure she couldn't move. 'Time to get on your knees.'

She gave me a look that was nothing but fire. Another challenge, if I wasn't much mistaken. Then, slowly—because I still had a grip on her hair—and not a little gracefully, she went down onto the floor in front of me.

Heat streaked through me and my dick was so hard it hurt, but I took a couple of moments to appreciate the view because she was so fucking fine. She was naked, her skin pale and lovely, the tips of her breasts pink and hard, the curls between her thighs glowing fiery red.

I could see her pulse beating fast in the hollow of her throat and the light coming through from the windows showed how flushed she was.

You don't get that this is even slightly wrong? Making your best friend kneel before you?

Oh, yeah, it was fucking wrong. And maybe it was that wrongness that made it so damn hot. But I was in it now and there was no going back. Who knew if we could recover our friendship from this? All I could do was keep going, make sure that this was the best damn experience she'd ever had in her entire life.

'Get my dick out.' I kept up the tension on her plait, watching the flames leap in her eyes and her jaw get tight.

She didn't like me ordering her around—or rather she did, but she was just annoyed that she did. And she was going to make me pay for it, I suspected.

Good. Bring it on.

Her hands came to my belt buckle and I could see her fingers trembling slightly as she pulled it open.

'Not scared?' I murmured, wanting to push her, get her into challenge mode because it was fucking turning me on in a major way. 'Too much for you, huh?'

Her gaze flicked to mine, full of emerald flames, letting that speak for her. And I read her answer loud and clear.

Fuck you, asshole. I'll show you how scared I am.

I grinned as her fingers found the button on my pants, flicking it open, letting her see how much I was enjoying her challenge. Because I had one of my own. 'You know how I said you were built to take whatever I give you? Well, you've been good about not making a sound and I'm impressed. But I'm going to make it harder for you to stay quiet.'

I could see the muscle in her jaw flex as she bit down on whatever it was she was going to say and grabbed the tab of my zipper. I was expecting her to jerk it down roughly, but she didn't. Instead she held my gaze as she drew it down slowly, so achingly slowly. Her knuckles brushed over my insanely hard cock, sending sparks scattering though me and I was aware, suddenly, that I was hanging by a thread.

And that she'd put me there.

How the hell did she do that?

I had no idea. I didn't ever let myself get too on edge, not given how dangerous that was for me. Yet my best friend strips naked and brushes her hand over my dick and apparently I was holding onto that edge by the skin of my teeth.

Perhaps I should have pulled away, but it was too late for that and I knew it. I couldn't have walked away from her if I'd tried.

My breathing was loud and getting louder and Freya's gaze held a hint of triumph, as if she knew just how close to the boundaries of my control I was, not to mention her role in it, the hot little witch.

She was spreading the material of my pants wide now, fingers brushing over the ridge of the hard-on pressing against my boxers, and clearly very satisfied with what she was doing to me.

I needed to get control of this situation and fast.

I flexed my wrist, pulling her hair tight, and she let out a hissing breath. 'No playing,' I said flatly. 'Get my cock out and suck it like you mean it.'

She was breathing fast, the quick rise and fall of her tits showing me how much. But the flames in her eyes didn't lessen one iota.

She did as she was told, pulling down the front of my underwear, her fingers reaching inside the cotton, circling my dick, and it was all I could do not to make a sound. Because the feel of her touching me just about blew the back of my head clean off.

I gritted my teeth as she got me out and even though it was stupid given that I was a damn adult and didn't need any kind of validation, I couldn't stop the burst of satisfaction that went through me as her eyes widened.

I was not a small man.

Her fingers tightened around me and she squeezed, running her thumb up the length of my shaft and then over the slick head.

A growl rumbled in my chest, pleasure licking straight up my spine.

'I said no playing,' I murmured. 'Which means you just earned yourself another punishment.'

She lifted one red brow, giving me a plain 'Bring it on' look.

Oh, she had no fucking idea, did she?

'Open your mouth,' I growled.

CHAPTER NINE

Freya

I COULD BARELY hear anything over the sound of my own heartbeat, chills chasing themselves all over my bare skin.

I was on my knees in front of my best friend, his cock was in my hand and I was naked.

He was giving me orders. He was talking about punishments. He was pulling my hair and biting me. He was telling me I was built to take him.

He was so fucking hot I swear I was seconds away from coming and he'd barely touched me.

Holy crap. What was wrong with me?

Everett's cock was hot and smooth in my hands and a whole lot goddamned bigger than I was expecting. Though why I should have expected otherwise, I had no idea. Not when, as he'd said, he was a big guy anyway.

I'd never thought of that part of a man's anatomy as beautiful. A little bit comical, a little bit ridiculous, kind of vulnerable maybe. But not beautiful.

Everett's was though. He felt warm and smooth and hard, like the metal of a car sitting out in the hot sun. Yet not quite like a car because his skin had a velvety feel to it, making it silkily touchable. His dick curved up towards his stomach, giving me a glimpse of the chiselled lines of his six-pack beneath his shirt.

My mouth went even drier than it was already and I wanted to push his shirt up, lick my way up that fantastic abdomen, find his chest and stroke him there too, explore all those beautiful muscles.

'What did I say?' His voice was low and rough, scraping over me deliciously. 'I gave you an order, Freya.'

Oh, yeah. Open my mouth, right?

I took a shaky breath, conscious of his hand holding my plait tightly, sending delicious prickles of pain over my scalp. I'd never thought that someone holding my hair like that would be so hot, but it was. And part of me wanted him to do it harder. The weird part of me that wanted to push him, make him do… more somehow.

I had no idea why I wanted that, but there was something in me that found it exciting to challenge him. That was thrilled with the leap of green in his eyes in response. Because he liked it when I did that too. I knew him well and I knew when he was excited about something.

You. He's excited about you.

Heat washed over me at the thought, making the pressure between my thighs become even more intense than it was already. But I didn't want to think about that too much and, anyway, he was getting impatient. And even though part of me didn't want to do what he said purely to mess with him, I wanted to taste him more.

So I opened my mouth.

He didn't hesitate, thrusting forward, his dick sliding into my mouth.

I groaned, I couldn't help it, the salty, masculine taste of him hitting me with a vicious punch of lust. So. Damn. Good.

'You like that?' His grip on me tightened, sending more prickles of pain over my scalp. 'You like having my cock in your mouth?'

I couldn't speak so I just nodded, panting almost.

'Look at me, Little.'

I didn't even think about disobeying him this time and I looked up. He was so fucking tall from this angle. So fucking intimidating too, all power and authority. All blazing blue eyes, a ferocious expression on his handsome face.

I loved it.

'I like this,' he said roughly. 'I like seeing my cock in your mouth. It's fucking hot.' He reached down with his other hand and stroked my cheek, his fingers unexpectedly gentle. 'You know what to do now.'

Oh yes. I did.

Tightening my hold on his cock, I lifted my other hand and gripped one of his powerful thighs for leverage.

Then I proceeded to blow his fucking mind.

At least that was the idea. I'd never had particularly strong feelings about blow jobs one way or the other. Sometimes they were fine. Sometimes they weren't. But they were, without exception, never hot.

Everett was now the exception.

I sucked him, teased him. I ran my tongue along his cock, licking around the sensitive head, teasing the tip, tasting his raw, masculine flavour. I heard the deep, rough sounds I drew from him, felt the grip in my hair change, become even tighter. Felt the muscles in his thigh get rock-hard. And an intense satisfaction filled me.

Yeah, I could do this to him. I could make my best friend the billionaire groan and shake. I could make him curse. I could push him.

I could give him pleasure.

Me, the big, awkward redhead. The elephant in a family of gazelles.

'Deeper,' he ordered roughly. 'Harder.'

So I opened my mouth wider, took him deeper so he was brushing the back of my throat. I didn't care. I just wanted more. I wanted to make him come.

Increasing the pressure of my mouth, I sucked harder, glorying in the feel of having him in the palm of my hand. Of giving him as much pleasure as he could handle.

Except it wasn't only him who was getting off on this. I was too. I could feel the pressure climb inside me, and I couldn't stop from reaching down between my thighs to touch myself.

'No.'

The word crashed over me even as he pulled my hair hard, tugging my mouth away from him, leaving me panting and aching, and weirdly empty.

His gaze was fierce as he stared down at me. 'Did I say you could touch yourself? No, I fucking didn't. I own that pussy tonight, understand? And it's mine to touch, not yours.'

I was breathing so fast I thought I was going to pass out, and again, like so much of this, I had no idea why the blatant ownership in his voice was so freaking hot, but it was.

You've always been his. You know that.

Maybe I did. Certainly, in this moment I was more Everett's than I'd ever been anyone else's. Not the family I'd been brought up with, that was for sure.

I looked up at him, all authority and possession, and the devil in me wanted to keep on pushing, to see how far I could go. Because I loved that look on his face and I wanted more of it.

So I held his gaze and deliberately circled my clit with one finger, sending streaks of white heat through my veins. God, I'd never thought I'd find touching myself while he watched so hot. I'd never thought of touching myself in front of someone else, period. Yet I was doing both now, and it was so erotic I knew I'd come in seconds flat.

He growled, his grip on my hair tightening even

more, making me gasp, and then he reached for my hand and pulled it away. Keeping his gaze on mine, he then lifted my fingers to his mouth and sucked them inside.

I shuddered as wet heat surrounded my skin, his tongue licking my fingertips like they were his favourite flavour of popsicle. His teeth grazed my skin and I was lost in the pressure of his mouth as he sucked. And he watched me the whole time, sending the heat level inside me into the stratosphere.

'Fucking delicious,' he said after he'd given my fingers a last lick, his voice rough and raw and gritty. 'I'm going to taste that pussy of yours soon. But you didn't do as you were told, Little. And you know what that means?'

I was panting, the ache between my thighs so insistent it was all I could do to keep still. Not that I could have moved anyway, not with the grip he had on my hair. It hurt. And yet it felt so good. My heart was going double-time, adrenaline careening through my central nervous system…

Of course I knew what that meant.

Everett gave me a feral grin. 'My favourite part. Punishment.'

I could have said no. I could have stood up and walked away, and he would have let me go. I didn't have to kneel here and take it.

But I'd pushed him, knowing full well what it would lead to. Which meant some part of me wanted this. Wanted my best friend to give me whatever punishment he usually meted out to his lovers in the clubs he frequented.

Some part of me wanted to know what it would feel like, because I was sure I was going to like it.

Besides, if I walked away now it would make all this line-crossing we were doing weird and point-less the next morning.

It's already going to be weird tomorrow.

I didn't want to think about that, though, so I shoved it away.

Everett was doing that intense searching look again, probably checking to see I was still on board with him, so I lifted my chin and gave him another 'Bring it on' look. The green glitter in his blue eyes became pronounced, which thrilled me right down to the bone. Oh, he liked me challenging him. He *really* liked it.

Without hesitation, he urged me to my feet. I felt a bit unsteady and he must have noticed because, as he walked me over to the couch, his free hand was on my hip, steadying me. Ready to catch me if I fell.

He sat down on the couch, pulling me down with him, arranging me face down over his knees. I was breathing so fast and I could feel his cock, hard and ready, pushing against my stomach.

'Keep still,' he ordered. 'And don't make a sound. Take your punishment like a good girl.'

He didn't give me any time to wonder what he was going to do, though, given the way I was lying across him, I kind of knew. And it was weird. I wasn't exactly a small girl and I would have felt entirely self-conscious with another guy, no matter how dominant.

I didn't with Everett though, because he was so big. His thighs were muscular and powerful beneath me, easily taking my weight, and when he released my hair finally and put one hand in the small of my back I could feel how large it was in comparison to myself. And I could feel how strong he was as he held me down. Making me feel small. Making me feel delicate.

At least until his other hand came down on my butt. Hard.

I gasped because even though a part of me was expecting it, I didn't know quite how it was going to feel. And it hurt. Because he wasn't holding back.

'Take it,' he growled, low and rough. Then he gave me three smacks in rapid succession, leaving me barely any time to breathe, barely any time to react. Making my body jerk in helpless response, my skin turning to fire as the pain spread out.

His hand came down a fourth time, but this time he stroked me, his fingers trailing over the curve of my ass, lightly massaging my stinging skin.

And I didn't know how or why, but like the way he pulled my hair, the pain began to morph into something else, turning pleasure on its head and giving it teeth. So I was squirming in his lap, unable to keep still, wanting more, wanting something I couldn't name. Something I ached for, something only he could give me.

There were tears in my eyes and I didn't know why.

'Please, E,' I heard myself plead hoarsely. It was breaking his rules but I didn't care. 'Please.'

He squeezed one butt cheek gently, making my ass sting and me shudder, pushing everything higher. 'Are you begging me, Little?'

'Yes.' My hands found the couch material and I was gripping it like it was a lifeline, my hips lifting against his massaging hand. 'Oh, please.'

The heavy, warm hand in the middle of my back pressed down, holding me still again, and I groaned.

Then he slipped his other hand between my trembling thighs, his fingers finding my pussy, stroking through my folds. I squeezed my eyes shut as the pleasure ignited every raw nerve ending, tearing a desperate sound from my throat.

'Scream for me, Freya,' he ordered quietly.

And then his finger found my clit and he pressed down.

The orgasm came like a thunder clap, annihilating me, crushing me under the weight of the pleasure it brought with it.

And I opened my mouth and screamed and screamed.

CHAPTER TEN

Everett

SHE WAS SHAKING across my knees, her screams of pleasure echoing around me, and all I could think of was that we had to do this again. We *had* to.

Because she was so fucking magnificent. Responsive. Obedient, yet challenging. Pushing back when I pushed her, letting me know what she wanted without having to say it. We were so in tune. I could feel the high that dominance gave me hurtling through my veins. It didn't happen that often—in fact, I couldn't remember the last time it had—because, for it to hit, perfect trust had to be attained. The sub giving me her trust while she took mine, each of us knowing what the other wanted instinctively. It only happened with people who knew each other very well or, very occasionally, with a stranger who just happened to be compatible.

I'd never found that perfect partner and deliberately so. I loved the high, but I'd never felt comfortable giving myself to someone so completely.

But right now, right here with Freya, somehow I had.

And even though she was the one doing what I told her, even though she'd just taken her punishment like a champion, and then come like a fucking super-star, screaming her pleasure to the heavens, it was me who was on the brink. Me who suddenly wanted, more than anything in the entire goddamn world, to lock her in my bedroom for the next month at least.

What the fuck have you done?

The question broke through my Dom high, the calm and intense focus draining away, and I was suddenly aware that my breathing was way too fast, my jaw aching. My dick was pressed to the softness of her stomach and I was on a knife-edge.

I wanted to fuck her so badly I couldn't speak.

She shuddered across my legs, her beautiful body trembling with the force of her climax, and her ass was the most gorgeous red. I hadn't gone easy on her, but I hadn't been too hard for a newbie. And I'd delivered the spanking fast to get it over with so she didn't have time to get too concerned.

I groped for my calm, for the high that had been there before, but it was gone. There was only the roar of my own need pounding in my head.

Get a fucking grip.

Yeah, I had to. And there were only two ways to deal with it: get up and leave, handle my dick myself in the privacy of my own bathroom. Or I fucked her and got it over and done with.

Fucking her, though, felt like giving in, admitting I was on the edge of my control, and I couldn't afford that. Control was the only thing that separated me from my old man and I wasn't giving that up for anyone. Yet what the hell else could I do? I couldn't get up and leave immediately, not without seeing if she was okay and giving her some aftercare. Some people needed it more than others, and usually I was pretty good at it, though I kept myself at a distance, obviously.

Except I couldn't do that with Freya. And being distant with her, walking away, would hurt her far more than any spanking would.

Christ, I was screwed. Or, rather, I would be. Soon.

'E?' Freya asked in a croaky-sounding voice, beginning to shift on my knees.

That decided me. I didn't want her to see how close to the edge of my control I was, and if she got up she would. So I held her down, my hand on her back. 'Stay there,' I ordered curtly. 'I haven't finished with you yet.'

Then I moved, shifting her so she was lying face down on the couch before kneeling behind her. I pulled out a condom and rolled it down over my cock with hands that were shaking far too much for my liking. Then I pulled her up on her knees so that perfect ass was facing me, still reddened from where I'd spanked her.

Fucking gorgeous.

I wanted my high back, wanted the calm so I

could focus on her more, but it had gone and there was no time.

'E?' She shifted, trying to turn her head toward me. 'Are you okay?'

Jesus. After spanking her, *she* was the one wondering if *I* was okay.

I didn't answer. Instead I gripped my dick and fitted the head to her perfect little pussy. I'd wanted to tease her, make her beg for this, make her beg for me, but the feel of her blew the last shreds of my control sky-high.

'Going to fuck you now,' I growled, letting her know where I was at, and then I shoved myself home.

She groaned, her back arching. 'Oh…yes…' Pleasure vibrated in her voice and when I shoved deeper she trembled.

The heat of her wiped every thought from my head, the clutch of her pussy around my cock like nothing I'd ever felt in my life. She held me so tightly, so completely. Like the way she hugged me, it felt like she was grounding me.

I found myself stroking her ass, her skin like warm satin, and I couldn't stop myself from moving, sliding out of her and then back in. Deeper. Harder. Faster.

She panted, lifting her hips to my thrust, taking me as hard as I was taking her. And I'd been going to lean forward and take that silky plait in my hands, wind it around my wrists and use it to tease her, edging a little pain, but all thought of more teasing was gone. Completely.

Instead I put my hands on her hips and gripped her tight, thrusting hard into her. She felt so good, so fucking good. Too good. As if our friendship had been a jigsaw puzzle that had always been missing a piece and this—sex—was it. The final piece that made an entire picture.

I shouldn't have done this. I shouldn't have had her. I should never have touched her. But now it was too late. Now, I was going to come and hard, and way before I was ready.

Jesus, when had that ever happened? Fucking never.

She was moaning, her whole body trembling, and I wasn't going to last, not the way I wanted to, so I reached around and slid my fingers down between her thighs, finding her swollen clit. Then I stroked her as I thrust.

A cry broke from her and her pussy clenched hard around my cock as she came, and then I was thrusting harder, deeper, driving myself into her as the pleasure swept up my spine and exploded in my head like a fucking firework.

I think I might have roared her name. I definitely shouted something as it hit, and it was all I could do to hold myself together as it annihilated me.

As the pleasure bounced around on the inside of my skull, echoing and re-echoing, I slumped forward over her, barely aware of where I was. She was all softness and sweet musky heat beneath me and I wanted to nuzzle against her skin, lick her all over, then take her again. Harder this time.

Make her yours.

The thought glowed in my head like a neon sign and for a second I couldn't do anything but stare at it, because what the hell? Make her mine? She already was mine. My *friend.* And a friend she needed to stay.

I didn't want to move but I forced myself to pull out of her, getting off the couch and heading straight into the suite's bathroom, shutting the door.

My hands shook as I dealt with the condom and then I stood there, holding the basin, my head bent, trying to pull myself the fuck together.

Because I had to. I was the Dom. I had to be in control, always.

And I wasn't now, because she'd got to me. She'd got under my fucking skin. She'd given me that Dom high, made me think things about making her mine, and that wasn't supposed to happen, not with her. This was a one night only deal and we weren't going to do this again.

So what are you going to do? Leave her out there alone? Not touch her again tonight?

I couldn't do that, not after what I'd promised her. She deserved more. And she definitely deserved a man who was in control of himself, not losing it like—

I shut my eyes, my dad's face and his pleased smile replaying itself in my memory. To this day I don't know what made that night any different from all the others, because Dad got drunk every Saturday night and he always took it out on me. I usually tried to make sure I was in my bedroom with the door locked, but that night I went downstairs to get a drink of water, thinking that he was passed out on the couch, that I was safe. But I wasn't safe and he wasn't passed out on the couch. He was in the kitchen and he cuffed me around the head, starting in with his usual litany of bullshit, about how hard it was being a single dad and all the opportunities he'd missed because he'd had to look after me. He usually lost interest after a couple of punches, but that Saturday I realised something: I was bigger and stronger than he was.

And something in me snapped.

Rage poured out of me, years of putting up with his shit coming to a head, and I turned around and punched him in the face before I could stop myself. And after that I kind of lost it. The next thing I knew, Dad was on the floor, blood all over his face, and just before he fell into unconsciousness he smiled, like he was proud of me, and said, 'Real chip off the old block, aren't you, son?'

He saw it in me even then, and I'd felt it in the rage that had nearly eaten me alive, the potential to be like him. So, control it had to be. I had to keep a tight rein on my temper, keep everything locked down, because I never, *ever* wanted to turn into him.

So far, I'd never had a problem keeping my shit together. Never had anything that would threaten it.

Until tonight. Until Freya.

Overreacting much? You fucked her once and it was good. That doesn't mean anything.

True. Perhaps I was overreacting. It was just a night after all. It wasn't going to happen again. Besides, I certainly couldn't go back in there and pretend none of this had happened, or walk out like a fucking coward. That wouldn't be fair on her, not when she'd been so into it.

And so into you and what you did to her.

I gritted my teeth against the wave of intense satisfaction that thought brought me. Yeah, I didn't need that kind of temptation in my head right now.

We'd had sex, just like I'd promised, and maybe if I'd been less concerned with her feelings I would have told her it was over and we needed to go to bed. Separately.

But I couldn't do that with her. I couldn't spank her, fuck her, then have everything return to normal immediately. Perhaps I could have if she'd been a stranger, or an experienced sub, but she wasn't either of those things. She was my friend, who'd trusted me to introduce her to a new experience, and I couldn't tarnish it by being a dick about it now.

I couldn't let her down like that.

Pushing myself away from the basin, I went back out into the suite.

Freya had found a throw from somewhere and was sitting on the couch wrapped up in it. She gave me a wary look as I came back, and I could see the worry in her eyes. Of course she had no idea why I'd walked away like that and naturally she'd be questioning herself.

'What's up?' she began. 'I'm sorry, I didn't—'

'Why are you covering yourself?' I held her gaze, letting her know that nothing had changed, that I was resuming my Dom role. 'I didn't tell you that you could.'

A flush moved through her skin, turning her the most delightful shade of pink. Her eyes glowed, the tension in her body gradually bleeding away. 'Oh, but I—'

I grabbed one end of the throw and jerked it away from her, leaving her naked on the couch. 'Much better.' Taking a step towards her, I raised a hand to the collar of my shirt, beginning to unbutton it, liking how her gaze dropped to watch as the fabric parted. Hunger rose in her eyes and satisfaction coiled deep inside me. I could find that high again. With her it would always be within reach. And maybe I'd let myself have it for tonight. It would make it much better for the both of us—no, not just better. It would make it phenomenal.

And if there was one thing that my Little deserved it was phenomenal.

Tomorrow could take care of itself.

'Now,' I murmured, shrugging out of my shirt, 'where were we?'

CHAPTER ELEVEN

Freya

I CRACKED OPEN an eye the next morning and for a second couldn't work out where I was. It looked like a hotel room—a very *nice* hotel room—with views across a city—a familiar city…

Recognition hit me, along with the memory of everything that had happened the night before. The orgasm that Everett had given me in the hallway at the British Museum. The orgasm he'd given me back in the living area of his hotel suite. The orgasm I'd had with him deep inside me…

So. Many. Orgasms.

Heat washed through me and I had to close my eyes again, more than a little overwhelmed. By everything Everett had done to me the night before. By my own reaction to him. By the sheer amazingness of the sex.

By the weirdness of doing all of that with my best friend.

We'd done a whole lot more out in the living room after he'd come back from the bathroom, and I had to admit to being more than slightly exhausted by the time he'd picked me up in his arms and taken me into the master bedroom, where he was sleeping. Then he'd laid me in the bed and got in beside me, wrapped his big, warm arms around me and told me to go to sleep.

And I had. Instantly.

But now I was awake and the morning was here, the next day beginning and... I opened my eyes once more and turned my head on the pillow.

There was no one beside me. I was alone.

My throat felt a bit achy, which was weird, and I told myself it didn't matter that he wasn't here. We'd said it was only for the night and the next day we'd go back to normal. Put it behind us, no harm, no foul.

Yet I had a sneaking suspicion it wasn't going to be as easy as that. Not when last night had been... well...were there enough superlatives in the world to fully describe it? Amazing. Phenomenal. Incredible. But even that didn't cover the way Everett had made me feel.

It went beyond simple physical pleasure. He'd made me feel good about myself in a way I hadn't felt for a long time. And that brought a little bit of pain with it, because I'd always thought I was fine with being the big Clydesdale in a room full of show ponies. But apparently I wasn't all that fine. Because with a burning look and a few simple words of praise, Everett had nearly made me cry.

He'd always accepted me as I was, liked me as I was. So to know that he also lusted after me as I was had flicked a switch inside me. Last night, even though I'd followed his orders, I'd felt powerful and sexy and strong, not to mention intensely feminine.

I'd never felt that way before and it was…pretty damn good.

And now it's over.

The ache in my throat deepened. Yeah, of course, it was over. One night, that was what we'd said. And I didn't want anything more. Everett was my friend, and a friend was more important to me than anything else. Relationships were more hassle than they were worth, especially when the shine wore off, as it always did. At least a friend stuck by you, no matter what.

On that rousing thought I pushed myself out of bed, wincing slightly as unfamiliar muscles pulled, reminding me of everything Everett and I had done the night before. Hunger for him gripped me suddenly and sharply, and I had to stop and take a steadying breath to force it back.

He'd given me what I'd asked for and it seemed like he'd enjoyed himself too, but now we'd satisfied our curiosity that was it. I'd successfully achieved Operation Orgasm and I was certain it would happen again. With another guy.

Yeah, are you sure about that?

Ignoring the niggling doubt, I slipped into the massive bathroom and treated myself to a hot shower. A part of me didn't want to wash the scent of him and of sex away, but keeping that on my skin would have been weird so I gave myself a decent scrub. Might as well start as I meant to continue.

There was a thick white towelling robe hanging from a hook near the shower, so after I'd got out I put it on and belted it firmly. I had no idea what time it was, but it was clearly full morning and I was starving.

Breakfast and caffeine were needed, stat.

I wandered out into the living area of the suite, only to come to a dead stop as I spotted Everett sitting at the dining room table. He had his laptop open in front of him and he was clearly in the middle of some work. It would have looked very professional if he hadn't also been wearing only a pair of jeans.

My mouth went bone-dry, my brain helpfully replaying memories of the night before in my head. Him, unbuttoning his white shirt. Him, unzipping his pants. Him, naked. Golden skin. A scattering of crisp blond hair on his powerful chest. Sharply defined, rock-hard muscle. The way my stern Viking was built was enough to make Thor jealous.

I couldn't stop looking at him now, the way the light fell on him through the windows gilding his smooth skin, turning his blond hair bright gold. He was frowning at his computer screen, his profile all intense concentration, and something inside me clenched hard.

You're never going to find another man like him and you know it.

I swallowed. No, of course I wouldn't. Everett Calhoun was one of a kind. There wasn't anyone else like him, and if I wanted anything resembling a future sex life I was going to have to adjust my expectations.

Pushing aside the way my stomach dipped, in what I told myself definitely wasn't bitter disappointment, I strolled over to the table, pulled out a chair beside him and sat myself down in it.

He didn't look up, which was probably for the best, since looking at him close up wasn't any better for my peace of mind than looking at him from far away. In fact, it was worse because there was a mark on his neck that I knew I'd given him, and there was one on my inner thigh that he'd given me in punishment.

And then thinking of punishment set off another train of memories that I didn't need right now, making my butt suddenly feel hot and my pussy throb and every other inch of skin feel achingly sensitive.

Goddamn it.

'Hey,' I said into the silence. 'So, is there breakfast?'

He nodded over to a trolley that I'd somehow missed seeing, covered in various silver-domed platters. There was a basket of rolls and pastries and also—blessedly—a steaming carafe of coffee.

'Oh, great,' I said, staring at him. 'Thank you.'

He still didn't look up. His blond brows didn't even twitch.

'A "Good morning, how are you today?" might be nice.' I probably shouldn't have pressed the issue, but I couldn't help it. I just wanted him to look up and make eye contact.

Finally, his gaze lifted, his direct blue gaze meeting mine. There was nothing of the heat that had been in there the night before, nothing of the hunger or the intensity. There was only slight exasperation, the look he always gave me when he was in the middle of doing something and I was interrupting.

Clearly we were back to being friends again.

'Good morning, how are you today?' he said without inflection. 'There. Happy now?'

I should have been happy. I should have been really pleased that we were back to normal. But I wasn't.

I forced a smile. 'Ecstatic. Want a coffee?'

He looked back down at his computer. 'Yeah, that would be great.'

My gut dipped again, a sudden lurch that I couldn't deny this time was nothing but disappointment. Though I didn't know what I was expecting from him, not after we'd promised each other that a night was all it would be.

He was only doing what we'd agreed. What the hell was my problem?

Annoyed, I pushed myself out of the chair and

went over to the breakfast trolley, picking up the covers over the food and taking a look at what was inside. Bacon and eggs and a fluffy omelette. Blueberry pancakes. All my favourites in other words, and that needled me too, though again I had no idea why.

My annoyance morphed into anger and I found myself putting the covers back on the food with slightly more force than was needed.

Stupid—I was being stupid.

Trying to get it together, I busied myself with getting coffee for us both, ladling Everett's up with sugar since he liked his coffee black and sweet, before turning to bring it back to the table.

Only to find him staring at me, his blond brows pulled down.

It was so like the stern look he'd given me the night before, as he'd told me what to do, that everything in me tightened, my breath catching.

God, he was hot. Why had I liked the way he'd ordered me around? No, not just liked it. I'd *loved* it.

'What's the matter?' The question was brusque, with an edge of command to it that I wasn't sure was intentional or not.

What I did know was that I found it unbearably exciting.

'Nothing,' I said, equally brusque, even more pissed off than I was already.

His gaze narrowed, his focus intensifying. 'Bullshit.'

Heat prickled over my skin, something in the heart

of me responding instinctively to that edge inside him. I tried to ignore it. 'You want this coffee or what?'

'Little.' There was a warning note in his voice.

'No,' I snapped. 'You don't get to do that now. I'm not taking your orders any more.'

Something that looked like surprise shifted in his gaze, as if he hadn't realised what he was doing. Then, slowly, he leaned back in his chair, his gaze flicking back down to his screen. 'Yeah, fair enough. And sure, I would like that coffee.'

Him backing down should have mollified me. But it didn't. If anything it made me feel even grumpier.

Get a fucking grip.

I gritted my teeth and tried to get a fucking grip, moving back over to the table with the mugs of coffee I'd poured for us. Of course, I put his down with a little more enthusiasm than I should have and it slopped over the rim of the mug.

Everett stared at the brown stain on the tabletop and then looked up at me. 'Nothing, huh?'

I could feel my face getting hot. 'I'll get a cloth.' I put my mug down and turned away.

Only to feel Everett's strong fingers wrap tightly around my wrist.

'Hey,' I snapped, turning back. 'What are you doing?'

His blue gaze bored into mine, his grip unrelenting. 'And you don't get to do that either. If you're not taking my orders, don't start behaving like you're desperate to be punished.'

My cheeks flamed and abruptly I was trembling. The heat of his touch and the way he was holding me, the slide of light over his bare skin, outlining every muscle—it was all too much. It was all making me intensely aware that maybe one night wouldn't be enough, that I'd want more than that. And that maybe he didn't want to give it to me.

'Or do you want some punishment?' His voice turned hard, his gaze blue lightning. 'Is that what you're trying to say?'

Heat streaked through me. He wouldn't be talking to me like this if he didn't want it as badly as I did, surely? No, he wouldn't. And he wouldn't be looking at me so intently either, the way he had last night, as if he was reading every thought in my head.

I pulled against his hold deliberately, watching the flames in his eyes leap. 'Punishment? Why the hell would I want that?' I lifted my chin and pulled again, harder this time. 'Let me go, asshole.'

But he didn't. Instead he shoved back his chair and rose to his full height, making excitement buzz in my veins and a wild thrill ripple all over my skin.

He jerked me close, right up against his chest, his hot skin like a furnace burning through the material of my robe. He looked down at me and there was nothing of the friend in his eyes. Nothing at all.

Holding me tight, he tugged at the tie of my robe, pulling it undone and letting the material gape open. Cool air whispered over my skin, closely followed by the heat of his hand as he slid it blatantly between my thighs.

I shuddered as his fingers stroked over my sex, and instantly I was wet. Already I was on the verge of coming and it shocked me how ready I was for him. 'We said only one night,' I forced out, a moan escaping me as he found my clit with one finger and began to circle it lightly. 'I…d-didn't think you wanted more.'

'I'll tell you what I want and what I don't. You don't get to assume anything, understand me?' Staring down at me, he slid one finger inside me, making me shake. 'Fuck, you're wet. You want my cock? Is that why you're so pissy? You want my cock and you don't know how to ask for it?'

I could barely speak as pleasure began to uncurl inside me, slow and liquid. 'Yes,' I breathed. 'I want it. But not just for a night.'

He eased another finger inside me, stretching me gently, and I gasped. 'I see. Well, perhaps I'm in a generous mood. And perhaps I'd like to give you what you want. But you have to take some punishment first, because I don't like lies.'

This was probably a bad idea. No, not just bad. It was the worst idea in the history of the world. One night we could have chalked up to curiosity and moved on. But more than one…? Yeah, I wasn't sure we could do that.

Yet right now I wasn't thinking about that and I was pretty sure neither was he. Because he'd responded so quickly to me, and so intensely, he must have wanted this as badly as I did. And he'd been waiting for a sign from me.

I tipped my head back and looked up into his stern blue eyes. 'I don't want to be punished,' I lied. 'And I'm not turned on. Not even a little.'

Everett grinned. Then, before I could move, he turned me around and pushed me down face first over the table.

CHAPTER TWELVE

Everett

I SHOULDN'T HAVE done it. I shouldn't have pushed her down over the table. I shouldn't have pulled the robe off her. I shouldn't have spanked her ass bright red. I shouldn't have turned her over and fucked her hard right there on the table-top, making her scream even louder than she had the night before.

And I definitely shouldn't have picked her up, thrown her over my shoulder and carried her into the bedroom, where we did it all over again.

No, what I should have done was keep on with my spreadsheet and ignore the increasingly annoyed looks she was sending me. Ignore the fresh scent of her skin, undercut with the musk of her growing arousal. Ignore the flashes of skin that her robe kept showing me. And yeah, I should have ignored the way she'd snapped at me, making it perfectly obvious what she wanted from me, even though she really didn't understand it herself.

But I didn't ignore it.

I gave her what she wanted, what we both wanted, and now what should have been just one night included a morning, and still my goddamn cock wanted more.

Freya was lying beside me on the bed and both of us were naked. The sheets were on the floor. She was on her front, hugging a pillow, while I lay on my back, staring at the goddamn ceiling, trying to figure out where the hell we went from here.

One night, I'd said. And what had I done the second she'd come into the room, all warm and sexy and freshly showered?

The control I thought I'd mastered was lying in shreds on the ground along with the fucking sheets.

'So,' she said quietly, her voice husky. 'What now?'

It was a very good question and one I didn't have an answer to. 'It was supposed to be a night.' I didn't look at her, though I could feel her gaze resting on me.

'Yeah, I know.'

A small silence sat between us.

'Do you still want more?' I asked, because I had to know where this was going, and I thought I knew the answer.

'I mean...do you?'

I turned my head.

Her eyes were the green of a forest as they looked into mine, the freckles dusting her nose golden. Her hair had dried into thick waves over her shoulders and it had turned to fire in the sunlight coming through the windows.

My God, but she was beautiful.

'Yes.' I let her see the truth in my gaze. 'I do.' And I did.

I'd tried keeping her at a distance that morning, but that had lasted all of five seconds. And sure, I could draw a line under it now and really make an effort to keep everything locked down. But, by taking her this morning, we'd crossed yet another line and it seemed stupid to try and cross back over it again. She wanted more and so did I, so why not? Why not keep doing this until we'd both finally had enough, and then move on? She could get me out of her system and vice versa. And, besides, admitting that she was getting to me would mean accepting that my control wasn't as perfect as I thought it was.

True, it hadn't been last night, but perhaps that was me being a pussy about it. Perhaps I just needed to harden up. And wouldn't carrying on doing this with Freya be the perfect way to go about it?

What about your friendship? How is that going to work?

It was going to work how it had worked before. We'd put this aside and go on as if nothing had happened.

'You're here for another five days,' I went on, calmly blasting all the plans for this week to smithereens in favour of my dick. 'So let's keep doing this until it's time for you to fly back to the States.'

It was only five days. What harm could it do?

Something that had been tight before relaxed in her face, her green eyes glittering. 'I…would be very okay with that.'

'Just five days. No more.'

'And then we go back to the way it was before, right? Just friends again.'

'Yeah.' I turned onto my side and propped my head on my hand, looking down at her. 'Just friends. And afterward we draw a line under this. We won't talk about this again.'

She nodded, her gaze already dropping to my chest. 'That's fine. I can deal with that.'

I put out a hand and stroked my fingers over the satiny skin of her shoulder, allowing them to trail down her side, watching as she shivered gratifyingly. 'Are you happy with me taking charge?'

'Yes.' There was no hesitation at all in the word. 'Why do I like it so much when you do?' Her brow wrinkled. 'Is it weird? Does it mean there's something wrong with me?'

'Why the hell would you think there's something wrong with you?' I frowned, not liking that she'd think that way, though, knowing Freya, it wasn't any wonder.

She gave a small shrug. 'I dunno. Perhaps it's weird.'

'If it makes you weird, then it makes me even fucking weirder.'

'You're not weird, E.'

I stroked back up her shoulder again, relishing

the feel of her silky skin against mine. 'No, I'm not. And there are lots of other people just like me and just like you that get off on it too. So no more talk about how it's wrong, understand?'

'Oh, I don't think it's wrong really. I just... I'm surprised by how much I like it.' She had a very serious look on her face. 'But I think it only works with you. The thought of doing this with another guy leaves me cold.'

The same satisfaction I'd felt the night before shifted in my chest again. As if I was pleased she didn't want to do this with another man. As if I'd punch anyone in the face who even dared to think they could do the same thing with her.

Dangerous.

I tried to ignore that thought. Yes, the urge to punch someone *was* dangerous, but what Freya did or didn't do with another guy shouldn't affect me. Because what the hell did I care if she wanted to follow someone else's orders? Have someone else's hand spanking her perfect ass?

A growl caught in my throat at that particular image and I had to shove the urge away hard before it got out.

Perhaps you shouldn't be thinking about her with other men?

Yeah, no. Definitely not. It didn't bode well for the five days we'd just agreed on, but shit, if I couldn't control myself for five days then there was no fucking hope for me. This would be a test.

'You don't need to do it with another guy,' I said. 'You have me for the next five days and what we do together during that time is no one's business but ours.' I lifted my fingers from her shoulder and trailed them over the curve of her cheek instead. 'I don't think you're weird. And I don't think what we're doing is wrong. You like it. I like it. That's enough.'

Freya's lovely mouth curved, the serious look vanishing. 'Yeah, that's true.' She lifted her hand, her fingers reaching to stroke my chest. 'I mean it, E. I don't think you're weird either. But...' She gave me a questioning look. 'What do you get out of orders and punishments?'

I'd never been asked that before but, since I'd demanded honesty from her, I couldn't give her anything less than honesty myself. 'Control.' I turned my hand over, letting the backs of my fingers brush against her cheek. 'That's what it's about. You giving me control, you making me responsible for your pleasure, is a gift. I like making people feel good, I like helping them out, and I get off on anticipating a woman's needs. I get off on pushing her too, showing her what her body is capable of, what *she* is capable of.' I let my hand drop away and put it over hers where her fingers brushed against my chest, holding her fingertips against me. I'd never articulated this to anyone before and for some reason I really wanted her to know. It was a part of myself I hadn't shared with anyone. 'There's a moment when it's all really good, where I'm just in the moment. Intensely focused.

Powerful too. I'm completely and utterly in control of everything. It's…like a drug high, only better.'

Her eyes were wide. 'That sounds awesome.'

'Submissives can get a high too, when it's really intense. Basically, a massive endorphin rush.'

She blinked. 'Really?'

'Sure.' I eyed her. 'You might have had a taste of it last night.' There was no 'might' about it. I'd recognised that glazed, spacey look.

Her eyes went even wider. 'Was that what it was? A high? I mean, it did kind of feel like that at the time.'

'Well, that's what it is. I like taking control…you prefer to give it up.'

'Huh.' She gave a slow nod. 'Maybe I do. But why is taking control so important to you?'

Freya knew about my dad, and what he was like, but we never talked about it because I didn't like discussing it. Especially not with her. Back when I was younger, being with her was the only time I could get away from him, so talking about him made me feel as if he was intruding where he didn't belong. Freya made me happy and I didn't want to taint it by talking about that old bastard.

I let out a breath, not wanting to talk about it now either. But she was looking at me so earnestly I couldn't not give her a straight answer. 'You know what Dad was like. Always drinking. Always having to fight something. Fucking angry at everything, with not an ounce of self-control. I didn't want to be like him.'

'But you're not like him.'

She had no idea. She hadn't seen me punching the old prick in the face and kicking him to the ground. Or seen the recognition in his eyes as he'd lain on the floor, looking up at me standing over him with my knuckles bloody. And she definitely hadn't heard that note of smug satisfaction in his voice as he'd told me how much like him I was…

'There's always that potential.' I kept my tone noncommittal, hoping she'd get the hint and not ask too many more questions. 'Alcoholism runs in families, and violence goes along with it, so I thought practising a little self-control myself wouldn't hurt.'

Her palm was warm against my chest, unwavering as her support of me had always been. 'Yeah, I suppose that's fair enough. But, for what it's worth, I don't think you'd ever do that.'

The conviction in her voice was unshakeable, as was the certainty in her gaze. She'd always seen something in me that wasn't there and I didn't have the heart to tell her she was wrong. Besides, I liked it when she looked at me like that. It made me feel like there was hope for me after all.

I said nothing, but I squeezed her hand, letting her know I appreciated the statement.

She smiled. 'So…that high. Does it happen every time?'

I shook my head, holding her palm tight against my chest. 'No. It's only happened to me a handful of times. You have to have a certain level of trust with someone before it works like that, and it really involves absolute trust. Trusting your partner and them trusting you. And trust can only really be found in the clubs if you're not in a permanent relationship.'

'Oh? Why is that?'

'Because clubs have rules and people monitoring them. It's once you go out of a club, where no one is checking up on people, that things can get dangerous and scary.'

Freya's green eyes searched my face. 'I… Did it happen with…uh…us?'

I'd known she was going to ask and though something in me wasn't happy giving her the truth, I couldn't lie about it either. 'Yeah,' I said.

Her eyes went wide. 'It did?'

'Last night. This morning.' I shouldn't have gone on, but I did. 'It felt like I could read your mind, Little. Like I knew exactly what you wanted, without you having to tell me. And you knew exactly what I wanted from you too. I could feel your trust in me and how absolute it was, like you'd trust me with anything. Anything at all.'

She nodded, her gaze still wide. 'Yes, I would.' Her throat worked as she swallowed. 'It's not like that with everyone?'

'No. No it's not.'

We stared at each other for a long moment and I could feel something thickening in the air between us. Something that really shouldn't have been there.

And it was clear she felt it too, because she suddenly looked down at my chest again. 'Why me then?' The question came out sharply, as if she hadn't meant to say it. 'Why is it different with me?'

'I think because you're my friend and we have a level of trust in each other already.'

'So…the other women this has happened with… You had the same level of trust with them?' That sharp note was still in her voice, as if the idea of other women bothered her. Almost as if she was… jealous. Which was odd, because she'd never been jealous before.

You've never slept with her before.

Another thread of emotion twisted inside me and I didn't like it. Complications. Christ, if I needed a reminder of why this whole thing had been a bad idea then here it was.

'Those other women are in the past.' I reached to take her chin in my hand, to tilt her head back so I could see what was in her eyes. 'You're the one in my bed right now.'

'Yeah. Yeah, I know.' She pulled away before I had a chance to take hold of her, tugging her hand out from under mine and turning away. 'You know, I didn't have breakfast and I should really have something to eat.'

Then, before I could stop her, she'd slipped off the bed and headed out the door.

CHAPTER THIRTEEN

Freya

AS SOON AS I went back into the living area of the suite, belting the robe I'd grabbed to wear around me again, I knew I'd made a mistake. I'd succumbed to a stupid burst of jealousy about the other women Everett had gotten his 'high'—or whatever the hell it was—with.

It was dumb. I knew I was special to him. I knew it. I was his friend and that meant a lot. But…somehow, knowing he'd felt that high with other people, knowing he'd had that experience with someone else…

I don't know. I guess I wanted to be even more special. I wanted him to have it with *only* me. I had lots of other things he shared only with me—that mention about his evil old man, for example—so why not this? But saying that to him would make what had happened to us into something more than it was. And we weren't doing that.

Five days. That was all, and hell, that was fine by me. More than fine. The moment he'd pulled me to him this morning, all hot, sexy authority and dominance, I knew I wanted more. That one night wasn't enough to explore what we'd discovered. And doing this again over the five days I was in London, before I left for home and Tiffany's stupid wedding…yeah, that was perfect.

So, no more making a big deal about the sex. And no more getting jealous or possessive, right?

Yes. Right. I'd enjoy what we had here and now and once I left we'd both draw a line under it like he'd said.

In the meantime, breakfast.

The food had cooled, but I didn't care. I got myself a plate of bacon, scrambled eggs and some pancakes, then I sat down at the table and started to eat.

Everett wandered out a few moments later, wearing jeans and nothing else, which was more than okay by me, though I preferred him naked.

He was frowning, giving me a gauging look, and I knew if he asked me what was wrong yet again I'd probably scream. I didn't want to have to explain my reaction to the thought of those women. I didn't want to have to admit to him that I was jealous. Because then everything would become a big deal and that was not what this was about.

So, instead, I swallowed my mouthful and said, to pre-empt him, 'Hey, so I'm not in London all that long and I'd sort of planned to do some sightseeing.

Go and see the Tower of London, Big Ben, Buck-
ingham Palace—all that stuff.'

It wasn't a lie. I had wanted to go and do all that
stuff and I still did. I also could use a break and some
fresh air to calm myself down, get rid of the sex hor-
mones clouding my brain with stupid things like jealousy and wanting to be special to him in some way.

Plus, maybe it would be good for us both to put
on some clothes and be just friends again for a while.

He stood there watching me, rubbing at his chin
with one hand, the other buried in his jeans pocket.
He had some golden morning beard running along
his jaw and it looked good on him, made him look
even more like a Viking than normal—a disreputa-
ble one—and I wanted to touch it, to see if it felt as
soft as it looked. I also wanted to touch him, to run
my fingers over his golden skin, trace the muscles of
his powerful chest and stomach…with my tongue…

No, bad Freya. I wanted to do some sightseeing
and that was sightseeing of the city, not yet more of
Everett's glorious body.

I tore my gaze away from him and shovelled some
more bacon into my mouth.

'Sightseeing,' he echoed, as if the word didn't
mean anything to him.

'Yeah, you know. As in seeing the sights. Doing
touristy stuff.'

There was a silence.

Then he came over to the table and pulled out one
of the chairs where he'd been sitting before, sitting

down fluidly in it, his long legs stretched out before him. His blue gaze swept speculatively over me.

I held up a hand. 'Don't do it.'

One fair brow arched. 'Don't do what?'

'Do that Dom thing. Looking at me like you're trying to read my mind.'

Instantly he frowned. 'I wasn't.'

'Yes, you were. I don't want to talk about anything, E. I said I wanted more and so that's what we're doing. But I'm in London and I don't want to spend all of it in bed, okay? So stop analysing my every reaction.'

He said nothing, the look on his face unreadable. And for a second tension gathered in the air between us the way it had before, and I knew that all I'd need to do was throw out a challenge and we'd end up back in bed again.

But that wouldn't get me seeing the sights of London and right now I needed out of this hotel room. So I didn't throw out a challenge. I ate some of my pancakes instead.

Eventually, Everett let out a breath. 'Okay, sightseeing it is. I've got a few things organised for you anyway.'

I felt the usual combination of irritation and pleasure that always went through me whenever Everett 'organised a few things'. He was a thoughtful guy, and often did things to help me out. But it was always a double-edged sword. I liked that he thought of me, yet I preferred to handle things myself. Especially after Aunt Helen used to make such a big deal of it. 'You're a big, strong girl,' she'd tell me whenever I asked her for something. 'You should be able to handle it yourself.'

And so I had. And I continued to do so. And though I might have needed Everett's help with the orgasm stuff, I could handle looking around London on my own.

'Thanks,' I said, 'but you know you didn't need to do that. I was planning on having a look around myself.'

A muscle flicked in his impressive jaw, a subtle tension gathering around him, and when he spoke his voice was gritty with irritation. 'Can't you let me do just one fucking thing for you?'

I blinked at him, surprise washing over me. He'd never got angry with me when I refused his help before. Never even got irritated. He would simply shrug one of those impressive shoulders and say stuff like 'Well, the offer's there'. He'd never seemed bothered one way or the other.

But he was definitely bothered now. Which in turn bothered me.

I put my fork down. 'Hey, I didn't ask you to organise anything. I was happy to look around on my own.'

'Yeah, you're always happy to look around on your own. You never want anyone to do a single fucking thing for you.' He put his hands on the arms of the chair and shoved it back forcefully as he stood up. 'Fine. We'll do it your way.'

Then, before I had a chance to reply, he strode from the room.

I watched him go, open-mouthed, shocked. He'd never before let me know that my insistence on standing on my own two feet bothered him. Never.

But shit. What did he expect? I couldn't go running to him every time I needed something. He was very generous, I knew that. And he always wanted to help.

So why don't you let him?

I frowned, because I had no answer to that. I just didn't let him. He'd offered me money and support and all kinds of things over the years and I'd never accepted any of it—well, definitely not the money anyway.

The business was mine to deal with and I wanted to deal with it my way. It was the only thing I had that was wholly mine, the one place in the world where I felt at home and I didn't want to be reliant on anyone else.

Not the way I'd been reliant on my aunt and uncle after my mother had died. Coming into their house with nothing, knowing my aunt in particular didn't want me there, even though Mom was her sister. Knowing that if Mom hadn't been killed, they wouldn't have had a grief-stricken eight-year-old to bring up, because my dad was long since out of the picture.

But…Everett didn't know that, did he? I'd never talked in any great detail about growing up with my aunt and uncle, though he'd picked up on quite a bit.

Perhaps he should know why you're being a jerk? Especially after what he told you just before.

Yeah, when I'd asked him about what he got out of ordering women around and taking charge. Because I'd been curious. It hadn't surprised me when he'd talked about control, especially in relation to his dad. Though Everett was nothing like his dad and never would be. I hadn't been surprised when he'd mentioned that having control was less about the power he had over other people and more about giving them what they *really* wanted. Of course he'd see it in terms of giving to people, about helping them, because that was what Everett had always been about.

And he's always offering to help you and you keep refusing.

Yeah, but he'd never said it bothered him before, so where did he get off suddenly being all angry at me about it?

Annoyed with him and feeling guilty for being annoyed at him, the pancake I was chewing on suddenly didn't taste very good.

Come on, he was trying to do something nice and you flung it back in his face.

That was true. And then I'd snapped at him when he'd been irritable about it. Perhaps I needed to go and explain my position to him, so he understood. Hell, maybe I could even let him do whatever things he had 'organised' for me. It wasn't a big deal and it would make him happy, so why not?

Irritated with myself, I got up from the table and went to find him.

He was in the bedroom and he must have had a lightning-fast shower because he had a towel wrapped around him and his golden skin was glistening with moisture.

God, he was gorgeous.

I couldn't help simply standing there to watch him as he leaned down to pick up some underwear that he had on the bed, the towel dropping from his hips to reveal his magnificent naked body.

Leaning against the doorway, I tried to moisten my suddenly dry mouth and find my voice. 'Hey... uh... I didn't mean to snap at you before. I'm sorry.'

He gave me one searing blue glance, then turned away, beginning to dress.

There was a thick silence.

Oh, yeah, I'd really offended him, hadn't I? Shit.

'I didn't know it bothered you so much that I didn't accept your help,' I said quickly, hoping it didn't sound defensive. 'You should have told me.'

Stepping into his jeans, he tugged them on, doing up his zipper. 'It's not your problem.'

'Well, you've kind of made it my problem now.' I swallowed. 'I don't want to upset you, E.'

He turned to pick up the dark blue T-shirt that was lying on the bed. 'I'm not upset.'

I snorted. 'Now who's talking bullshit?'

He went still, his back to me. Then he turned abruptly, and there was something fierce burning in his blue eyes. 'I've got all this fucking money. And if I can't help anyone with it, then what's the fucking point of it? What's the fucking point of *any* of it?'

Surprise rippled through me. I'd never thought that much about his money, about him as a billionaire. I mean, I knew he was loaded and I knew he worked hard for it. But I hadn't thought about what he did with that money, other than donate to charitable foundations and stuff, plus helping out worthy causes in our small town.

I never thought he'd have definite feelings about that money either.

Are you sure this is just about the money?

Good question.

Frowning, I folded my arms. 'What has helping me got to do with "all this fucking money"?'

He ignored that, staring at me, an expression I couldn't interpret on his face. 'Why won't you let me help you?'

An uncomfortable feeling shifted inside my chest and I was conscious of the wood of the doorframe digging into my shoulder. I didn't really want to talk about this, but it was probably something he should know, given how much it was pissing him off.

Sex is really dealing out massive truth bombs all over the place, huh?

Oh, that was crap. Telling him this had *nothing* to do with the sex. Nothing.

'I don't know,' I said. 'I think it's got something to do with losing Mom. With having to go and live with Aunt Helen, and having to rely on them. And I was so different to them. Not just physically, but in other things as well. My cousins were into girly stuff and I was more interested in cars and fixing things.' I folded my arms, not sure why I was finding this difficult to talk about. 'I had to be given things. And my aunt always kind of made a big deal out of having to buy me clothes, and stuff I needed for school. Not in a bad way, just…in a way that made me not want to ask her for things.' I bit my lip and looked away from him, the way he was looking at me making me feel weirdly exposed. 'I didn't like mentioning when I grew out of my clothes because she always made some comment about how big I was getting and how tall, and how expensive it was to have to get me new clothes all the time.'

'So that's why you kept wearing those sneakers that were way too small for you and jeans that were always too short?'

Oh, God. He'd seen that? How embarrassing.

I glanced away again. 'I didn't want to tell her.'

'Because you wanted her to notice, right?'

I could feel my face getting hot. 'No, of course not.'

'And the more she didn't notice, the more you wore clothes that were too small, shoving it in her face.'

He's right. You were punishing her for that.

I kept my gaze on the windows behind him. 'How do you know?'

'Because I noticed,' he said. 'I noticed everything about you, Freya.'

My cheeks burned and I kept staring at the city glittering in the sunlight beyond the glass. I didn't know why I felt so weird about the fact that he'd noticed my stubborn rebellions. Perhaps because it had felt petty. Aunt Helen hadn't had to take me in after Mom's death, yet she had, saving me from going into the foster system.

But still. I'd got a certain satisfaction out of seeing her eventually take notice of the fact that my T-shirts were way too tight and my jeans too short. That I winced when I walked because my feet hurt. She'd huff, irritated, and then make noise about having to buy me more and what a shame it was that I couldn't get hand-me-downs from her girls because I was too big.

'Yeah, well,' I said, deciding this conversation needed to get back on track. 'Me not wanting to accept help wasn't to do with you, okay? It was my deal. Plus…the garage is mine. It's kind of the only thing that really is and I didn't want anyone coming in and taking over.'

'I wasn't taking over. I was only offering you some financial help.'

'Sure.' I glanced at him again. 'But you're a take-charge kind of guy, E. So forgive me if I was trying to protect myself from that.'

'You don't want to be protected from it,' he shot back, staring hard at me. 'You like it. And you're strong enough to push back if it's a problem for you.'

He's not wrong.

No, he wasn't. Damn him. I really liked it in the bedroom after all.

Shifting restlessly yet again, I couldn't work out why this conversation felt so difficult when it was supposed to be about him, not me. Which, on reflection, was probably why this conversation was difficult. 'Look, I just wanted to explain why I didn't want you to organise sightseeing stuff for me. And to say sorry. And also that if you *had* organised a few touristy things for me—' I steeled myself and met his relentless blue stare '—then I'd like to take you up on them.'

CHAPTER FOURTEEN

Everett

I STARED AT FREYA, my T-shirt still gripped in one hand, forgotten about.

Hell, was this her actually accepting something I'd done for her for a change? She'd accepted my help the night before about the orgasm stuff, but then she was the one who'd come to me.

This was different. This was about me offering, wanting to do something for her, and her refusing, the way she always did.

It shouldn't have affected me the way it had out there in the living area. Sure, I found it frustrating normally, but she was right. I'd never told her how much it bothered me. Mainly because I didn't want it to bother me.

Yet it had really fucking bothered me just before and, for some reason, my patience with it had just snapped.

Nothing at all to do with the fact that you crossed the line and started screwing her.

I shoved that thought away. Sex had nothing to do with this. It wasn't supposed to have any impact on our friendship and I wouldn't let it.

You need to stay in control, man.

That was true. Yet I hadn't. I'd let myself get pissed off, then I'd snapped at her and stalked off. I hadn't expected her to follow. And I hadn't expected her to explain or apologise. And now here she was, doing both.

She leaned against the doorframe, looking sexy in the white towelling robe, her hair flowing, long and thick and tousled, over her shoulders. Her arms were folded and she was giving me a defiant look, as if daring me to argue with her.

As if I would.

I'd been offering her things for years and she'd never accepted any of it, and now I finally got why. And I understood. I'd seen her stumbling around in too small shoes and too small clothes and wondered why she'd never just asked her aunt to get her new ones. She'd never really explained why not and because we'd both been young I hadn't pushed for more of an explanation. And afterwards I'd kind of accepted that it was just part of Freya being stubborn.

But it wasn't. It was Freya wanting to be noticed. Freya wanting to be cared about.

Unwanted emotion sat on my chest like a stone, sympathy for her and yet more anger at her goddamn family who had been so reluctant to take her in after her mom had been killed, and who'd never made any attempt to hide how much of an imposition it had been for them.

I couldn't do anything about that, couldn't change the way her aunt especially had treated her. But I could make her feel noticed. I could make her feel beautiful and special, and all the things she truly was.

I could make her feel cared about. And perhaps this time she'd let me.

'Good,' I said gruffly. 'I appreciate it.'

Her expression softened. 'I know you do.'

I wanted to pull her into my arms in that moment, kiss her, take her over to the bed and make slow, sweet love to her, show her how appreciative I truly was. But slow, sweet love wasn't our dynamic, and it sure as hell wasn't mine. And, besides, it would have been changing something that was already working well, and since everything already felt like it was in a state of flux I ignored the urge.

Instead I said, 'You'd better get some clothes on. Can't have you running around London bare-assed.'

She grinned. 'You'd kind of like that though, wouldn't you?'

I gave her a measuring look. 'Keep pushing and you might just find yourself on the receiving end of a few punishments. Such as taking a naked stroll, sure.'

'You wouldn't.'

This time it was my turn to grin. 'The question isn't whether I would or wouldn't. The question is whether you'd obey me or not.'

She flushed, which was interesting, then pushed herself away from the doorframe. 'I'm going to… uh…go get dressed.'

I let her go, finishing getting ready myself then going back out into the living area to complete a few tasks. Ulysses had left me a couple of texts and more than a few voicemail messages, asking me where I was because we needed to meet to go over the funds we'd raised at our event the night before, and also where the fuck was Damian, because he wasn't answering his texts.

I did care about the fundraiser, but it didn't require ten texts and five missed phone calls about having a goddamn meeting right the hell now. I cared even less about whether Damian was answering his texts—given his preferences, he was probably still asleep in some woman's bed. And I cared even less than that about Ulysses being pedantic about all this shit.

What I cared about was that finally Freya was letting me do something for her and I was going to take that opportunity with both hands.

So I ignored Ulysses, made a few other phone calls, arranged a few things, then I turned my phone off.

And waited for her.

The things I'd arranged were a private tour of the Tower of London so we didn't have to wrestle with the crowds, including a look at the Crown Jewels and a visit with the Ravenmaster who looked after the ravens. And after that I took her for a special lunch at a historic London pub, where she had a pint and a ploughman's lunch and then made me laugh at the face she pulled at the packet of pork scratchings I'd also bought for her to try.

Afterwards, I took her up in one of the Black and White helicopters—I'd flown in the army and I liked to keep my hand in—and we took a sightseeing trip over London by air. She loved that, I could tell, though I thought she was at least as interested in the helicopter as she was in the city below us, which made sense: Freya loved machines.

Back on the ground, we went back to the hotel and got rid of some of the steam we'd built up over the course of the day by indulging ourselves for a couple of hours in the suite. Naked.

Then I took her out for dinner on the Thames, on one of the company's luxury yachts, motoring slowly under a beautifully lit up Tower Bridge.

She stood on the deck, leaning against the rail, and I watched her tip her head back to look at the bridge as we went under it, the lights shining on her face. She was grinning, her eyes alight, and the tight feeling I'd experienced back in the suite that day returned.

It felt good to make her smile like that. To make her happy. Because if there was one thing Freya deserved it was to be happy.

'This is great, E,' she said as the lights slid over her skin. 'Thank you.'

Simple words and yet I knew she meant them. And that meant something to me too.

I didn't speak. I just reached out and took hold of her hand, lacing her fingers with mine, and for a moment I felt like I had the night before, when I'd pushed myself inside her. As if the final piece of a jigsaw puzzle had been found and locked in, revealing the entire picture. A picture I'd never seen the whole of before.

Why are you thinking about goddamn jigsaw puzzles? And, more to the point, why are you holding her hand?

Shit.

I glanced at her to see if she'd noticed, but she was still looking at the bridge. Yet her fingers were tight around mine as if holding hands was something we did every day.

It wasn't, of course. Because holding hands wasn't something friends did.

But I didn't pull my hand away and neither did she.

After the boat trip, we went back to the hotel and I had her on her knees in the elevator as we went up to our suite, ordering her to get me off by the time the doors opened or else there'd be trouble.

Little witch was damn near successful too, but I'd had years of controlling my physical responses and I managed to hold off until we got back to our suite. Which naturally meant I could dole out a few punishments, which she loved.

We didn't get to sleep until exceptionally late and that involved another sleep-in the next morning. I'd arranged a few more trips that day too, another helicopter ride, this time to Windsor Castle, and then a private tour around a wizard theme park based on one of her favourite books as a kid. She squealed a lot about that and even let me buy her a few souvenirs.

But I'd saved the best—or at least what I considered the best—till last. I knew she didn't like shopping and wasn't much into clothes, and part of that was because she just wasn't interested. But I wanted to show her how beautiful she was. That I noticed her. And so I'd booked a private couple of hours in one of London's most exclusive sex stores. It wasn't sleazy, catering only to ultra-high net worth clientele, and you couldn't just walk in off the street. You had to make an appointment.

It was tucked away in a historic building in an alley near Oxford Street, and Freya was still talking about the wand I'd bought her as the limo stopped outside it and I got out, holding the door open for her.

'Where to now, Jeeves?' she asked in a terrible faux English accent, looking around at the old buildings surrounding us.

I took her hand and pulled her to the entrance of the store and pushed the buzzer. The door opened and a small, delicate Bambi of a woman pulled it open, smiling at us both. 'Mr Calhoun, Ms Johnson, please come in.'

Freya was frowning now as I pulled her through the door and into the plush interior of the store.

The floor was dark, ancient-looking wood polished to a high sheen and covered with silk rugs. The walls were painted dark blue with lots of medieval-looking paintings in heavy gold frames. Thin stainless steel rails held hangers on which were positioned bits of silk and lace in every kind of colour there was, as well as long negligees and nightgowns. All very pretty and all very vanilla. As long as you didn't see that the rails also contained all sorts of very expensive and exquisitely made fetish-wear too.

Freya looked around, her eyes getting rounder and rounder as she took in the glass cases on the walls with all the jewellery in them—jewellery you wouldn't find in a normal jewellery store, that was. Rings and chains and studs for all kinds of piercings, plus clamps and plugs in various different metals, studded with gems or plain. There was a variety of vibrators and dildos and lots of other fancy sex toys too.

I tended to go for plain and functional when it came to toys, though I did prefer the materials to be of the highest quality.

'What the hell is this?' Freya hissed in my ear as the shop assistant made herself scarce, as per my instructions.

Once she'd vanished out the back, I turned to Freya and said, 'I wanted to buy you something.'

'Buy me what?' Her face had gone very pink. 'Because if you're thinking that rubber mask thing over there then—'

'I want to buy you something pretty and frilly and sexy,' I said very deliberately. 'Something feminine. Something that's just for you. I'd also like you to choose something that we can both find pleasurable.'

She blinked, glancing at the rails of pretty lingerie and then the cases full of jewellery. At the crops and whips displayed on the wall, and the leather restraints displayed nearby. 'Um…'

I watched her face, saw the doubt and anxiety flicker across her familiar features. 'I don't go for hardcore stuff,' I said, addressing the anxiety at least. 'So don't worry about that. This needs to be something you'd like too.'

She looked back at me. 'And if I don't like any of it?'

I'd prepared for her refusal and I knew what I was going to say. 'Then you don't have to. But—' I paused, holding her gaze '—I would love to see you in something pretty, Little. Because I think you would love it too.'

She shifted on her feet, clearly uncomfortable. 'I don't like this kind of stuff, E, you know that. I don't like shopping and girly things…' She faltered, her gaze sliding to the rails again.

'Yeah, I think you don't like it because of all the bullshit your aunt put in your head. I think you'd love to put on some pretty lingerie for me, to get yourself feeling all sexy and hot just to tease me.'

She continued to stare at the clothing on the rails, the flush in her cheeks deepening. 'None of these things are going to fit me...'

It was strange how much I wanted her to do this for me. Or maybe it wasn't strange. Maybe I only wanted her to be able to see herself the way I saw her—tall and strong and beautiful. A complete fucking goddess. I wanted to get all that shit her aunt kept telling her right the hell out of her head.

'Yeah, they will. All the lingerie in the store right now is your size.'

That made her look sharply at me. 'What?'

'I made certain that everything on the rails right now is stuff that fits you.' It had been a precaution; I wanted nothing in here that might potentially get in the way of her enjoyment of this. And I knew if she allowed herself this she *would* enjoy it.

And so would I.

Her gaze narrowed. 'How?'

'I asked them to.' I allowed myself a slight smile. 'One of the benefits of being a billionaire.'

Freya snorted, but when she looked around again her gaze was more appraising.

'Well?' I didn't want her to know how much I wanted her to say yes. Shit, I didn't know how much *I* wanted her to until this moment. 'Or will I have to order you to do it?'

She turned that appraising look on me. 'You'd like to see me in something like this? Pretty lingerie?'

'Yes.' I shoved my hands into the pockets of my jeans. 'In fact, right now, there's nothing I'd like better.'

'Hmm.' She gave me another look, making everything inside me draw strangely tight. 'I guess I could try something on.'

CHAPTER FIFTEEN

Freya

HE LIKED THAT. I saw it in his eyes, the familiar blue spark of desire catching alight. And that made me feel good too.

In fact, the past couple of days had involved nothing but pleasing him by going on the trips he'd organised for me. And when I knew I'd pleased him I felt pleased too. It was a little closed circuit of pleasing each other, the good feelings flowing back and forth between us in perfect harmony.

Of course, it wasn't only about pleasing him. I'd really enjoyed the trip to the Tower and Windsor Castle. And it had been super cool to be on the yacht at night, watching the lights of Tower Bridge move overhead as we went underneath it, feeling his fingers close around mine as he held my hand. And the theme park had been amazing. I'd decided I'd let him arrange the trips, but under no circumstances was he to buy me anything and…well, I'd caved as soon as I'd seen some cool wands. They'd been expensive—nothing I'd normally buy for myself—and he'd been very pleased to get them for me and so I… simply hadn't objected.

But this…this felt different. This wasn't a souvenir of a cool place or tickets to a tourist attraction, but something I would wear. Something specifically designed to make me look sexy. Oh, yeah, and pretty and feminine too.

I didn't know why I felt uncomfortable about it. Actually, no, I did know. It was all exactly as Everett had said. It was about the bullshit my aunt had put in my head about my size and my height. How unlike a woman I was, as if that was something to be ashamed of. And I'd thought I'd got over that years ago, that I was comfortable with myself, but…yeah, I wasn't. And the thought of putting on lingerie, of trying to be pretty and sexy for Everett…

The way Everett was looking at me was very intense. He'd said it would make him happy and I could see that he hoped I would do this.

I didn't want to make a big deal of it. We only had another couple of days to go anyway so…why not? And the truth was I was kind of excited to do it. Everything here was in my size, which meant I wouldn't have the humiliating experience I'd had as a kid of being way too big for their biggest size, and my aunt rolling her eyes as I told her nothing here fitted me. 'You'll need an adult size then,' she'd said. 'That's going to be expensive.'

That was me. The size of an adult woman at twelve and 'expensive'.

Breaking his intent stare, I turned and went over to one of the rails, looking through the sets on the hangers. They were…pretty. Very pretty. In lots of different colours, some lacy and some not. Silk and satin and velvet. Bows and hearts and sequins.

I liked them, I realised. And more than that, I wanted to wear them. I wanted to put them on and see what I looked like. And then I wanted to turn around and watch Everett's face as he saw me in them.

A hot streak of desire spiked in my blood, my mouth going dry at the thought. Would he like what he saw?

You know he will.

Yeah, he liked my naked body and he'd never made any secret of how much. The way he looked at me, the way he touched me, making me feel beautiful and sexy and feminine…

Oh, hell. Why was I hesitating? He was going to *love* this.

My hesitation disappeared and I gave him a flirty look from over my shoulder. 'Anything in particular you want to see?'

His blue gaze burned as it met mine. 'Something really skimpy. And lacy and frilly.'

'They're all lacy and frilly.'

'Then anything.'

Guys. They were all the same.

Smiling, I turned back to the rail and took a handful of hangers off, then headed toward the very luxurious-looking fitting rooms. Each of them had stained glass doors that cleverly hid most of what was going on behind them, while revealing enough to be a little sexy and provocative.

There was a couch opposite, upholstered in rich gold velvet, and Everett sprawled down in it, stretching his long legs out, his gaze on me. 'You don't need to close the door,' he suggested. 'I told the shop assistant to take some time off. It's just you and me in here.'

I grinned, stepping into the fitting room. 'Bold of you to assume that I'd be into just you and me being here.'

He gave me a very intent look. 'Fortune favours the brave.'

A shiver went down my spine. A very good shiver. Because if there was something I knew about Everett Calhoun it was that he was both brave and bold and, given that we were alone in here, I was thinking he wasn't going to let me leave without at least ordering me to do something to him.

Well, I was more than okay with that.

Firmly closing the door—he could use a little anticipation—I stripped off my clothes and held up the first piece of nothing. Green silk and gold lace that hid precisely zero. I pulled a face but telling myself nothing ventured, nothing gained, I pulled it on.

It fitted beautifully, just as he'd promised. But it was very revealing. It was mostly just lace so my nipples were clearly visible and so was my pussy, the bit of string between my butt cheeks not covering a damn thing. The waistband had a frill, which seemed utterly pointless, and for a second I caught myself wondering what the hell I was doing putting this crap on.

But I shoved the thought aside. I was doing this for Everett, because he would take pleasure in it, and not for any other reason.

There was a full-length mirror inside the fitting room but I didn't look at it. I wanted him to see me first.

Taking a breath, I pushed the door open and stepped out into the store.

As soon as he saw me his eyes went wide, the blue spark igniting into flame, and the doubts that had settled in my head were abruptly gone. His hands went to the couch cushions as if to push himself up and out, but I held up a finger. 'Uh-uh,' I murmured. 'You stay there.'

I didn't expect him to do as I said, yet he froze, staring at me. Then, after a second, he relaxed back against the cushions, his gaze moving in a slow, steady sweep over my body. 'Are you gonna tease me, Little? Push me? See how far you can take me with that sexy body of yours?'

There was so much appreciation in his look, in the husky sound of his voice that any remaining shreds of doubt vanished.

I took a couple of steps toward him then stopped.

'Oh, dear, I think I dropped something,' I murmured. Then I bent down, letting my plait fall over one shoulder, giving him a really good view of my cleavage, before straightening again.

He was sitting there, ostensibly relaxed, but I could see the tension in his posture. I could also see the rapidly growing bulge in his jeans.

I smiled, slow and sexy, coming close to him before moving around him, reaching out to trail a casual finger across his chest and then, as I walked behind the couch, across his shoulders. 'Is this frilly and sexy enough for you?'

He turned to watch me, tracking my movements as I circled around the other side of the couch. There was a hungry expression on his face and he reached out as I came to stand in front of him again, his palm possessively cupping the back of my calf. His skin was hot, the touch sending electricity crackling through me.

'Tease,' he growled. 'There'll be trouble if you keep doing that.'

Anticipation had begun to coil deep inside me, making my breathing get faster. I could see how much he was enjoying this and it made everything feel so much more intense for me too. And it was becoming very, very clear how much I enjoyed pleasing him. Because in pleasing him I was pleasing myself.

'Uh-uh, no touching,' I murmured. 'Not unless you don't want the blow job I have planned for you.'

He gave another growl but let me go, and I grinned, backing away toward the fitting rooms again.

Once the door was closed I took a shaky breath, feeling the burn of excitement coursing through me. Then I turned around and looked at myself in the mirror, trying to see what he saw.

A tall redhead in frilly green and gold lingerie, pale skin, pink nipples and the flash of red curls between my thighs. My cheeks were flushed and there was a definite sparkle in my eyes.

I looked… Yeah, okay, I looked sexy. I certainly felt sexy, especially remembering how intensely Everett had stared at me.

Reaching behind me, I pulled the elastic band out of my plait and shook out my hair, letting it fall in thick red curls down my back. I didn't need my hair down to look sexy, I realised, but it was nice to have it free, nice to have the brush of it on my skin, enhancing all the other sensations.

Excited now, I carefully took off the green and gold silk, then reached for a teddy in deep blue silk. Again, it was basically lace, my body completely visible beneath it. There must have been some kind of silver thread in the lace because there was a slight shimmer to it, a sheen that followed my curves as I moved.

Holy crap, Everett was going to love this one as well.

I turned once more and pulled open the door, putting my hands on my hips and striking a sexy pose that for once wasn't ironic.

He was sitting forward on the couch, his fingers loosely linked between his knees. It looked casual but the way his gaze raked over me was anything but.

'Fuck,' he muttered and there was even a note of reverence in his voice.

I strutted over to him, getting right up close, daring him to touch me. And he did, putting out one of those big warm hands and sliding it up my hip and along my side, his fingers brushing the underside of my breast.

'Oh, dear,' I murmured, shivering under his touch. 'That's not allowed. Do that again and there'll be no blow job for you.'

There was fire in his eyes, the dominant nature I'd grown to adore rousing—and rousing hard. But he was obviously getting off on me teasing him because he did what I said, pulling his hand back. 'Doesn't work that way, baby,' he said roughly. 'Giving me orders is only going to end in a spanking.'

I blew him a kiss. 'Promises, promises.'

Beginning to back away toward the fitting room again for the next change, I was brought up short by his hand wrapping around the back of my knee, his gaze bright and blue and sharp. 'You don't need the fitting room. Change right here in front of me.'

Another streak of heat shot through me, but all I did was raise an eyebrow. 'Haven't you ever heard of the benefit of anticipation?'

Apparently, though, I'd come up against one of his boundaries because he only shook his head. 'Do it.'

In spite of myself, I looked toward the door of the store because, even though we were the only ones here, it was still a store. And people could come in at any time. The windows were curtained, but still...

'Don't worry about them,' Everett ordered in a low voice. 'The only person you have to worry about is me. And how to please me. And right now what would please me is to watch you strip naked in front of me.'

My breath caught and I was pushing the straps of the teddy off my shoulders before I knew what I was doing, easing it down and stepping out of it.

Everett leaned back on the couch, his gaze sweeping over me and lighting fires wherever it rested. 'Beautiful. Absolutely fucking gorgeous.' He didn't take his eyes from me. 'On the rail closest to the fitting room is a sexy gold playsuit. I want you to put it on for me.'

I blinked. Okay, it was something I hadn't picked up yet he'd obviously had it in mind for me.

Over the past few days he'd conditioned me into obeying him so I turned without protest and went over to the rail, conscious of the air moving over my bare skin and the silky rugs on the floor under my feet.

It was instantly clear which particular item he was talking about.

It seemed to be made of nothing but gold ribbon

that fastened behind the neck and travelled down the body in a kind of harness linked by gold hoops. Delicate golden chains adorned with crystals were fastened between the ribbons, clearly designed to highlight a woman's curves.

It was beautiful and delicate and I was sure I'd break it the second I stepped into it.

'I can't wear that,' I said, holding it up and looking at the delicate structure. 'I'll destroy it as soon as I put it on.'

'No, you won't.' His voice was a deep rumble of sound behind me.

'E, come on. I'll—'

'I had it made especially for you.'

The words fell into the space around me, each one echoing weirdly. He'd had it made…for me? This beautiful, delicate thing was actually for me?

Slowly, I turned around, forgetting entirely that I was naked, meeting his intense blue stare. 'What?'

His stare didn't even flicker. 'When I said everything is in your size I meant they were made for *your* measurements. And that includes the playsuit.'

I didn't know why that felt confronting, but it did.

'E, that's stupid. Come on—'

'Bring it here.'

There was no resisting him when he was in full-on Dom mode, at least not for me, and I found myself walking over to him before I could even think twice about it.

When I reached him, he took the playsuit from

me, divested it of its hanger and held it up for me to step into. There was something about the way his strong capable hands held it, carefully and delicately, that made my whole body tighten.

He was looking at me with that challenge in his eyes, the one I recognised whenever he gave me an order he knew I wouldn't like. Daring me to do it.

And the tight feeling in my body crept all the way up to my heart.

He'd done this for me. He'd filled this store with pretty, frilly things that were made just for me. Not for anyone the same size as me, but for *me*. They were mine.

I'd never had anyone do that for me before. Not one single person. Not since my mother had died.

My eyes felt scratchy, like there was sand underneath my lids, and my throat ached. It was stupid how a store full of tailor-made lingerie made me feel this way, but it did. And of course it would be him, because he was Everett and he'd always cared.

Then something in his expression softened, as if he could see the ridiculous emotional moment I was having. 'You're going to look so beautiful in this,' he said quietly. 'I can't wait to see it on you.'

Still, I hesitated, desperately trying to swallow the massive lump in my throat.

And this time Everett didn't issue any orders. He only said, 'Please, Freya. For me.'

It was the 'For me' that did it. Because, of course, I'd do anything for him.

'Give it here,' I said thickly.

Everett shook his head. 'Let me.'

How could I say no to that?

Trying to pull myself together, I let out a breath and put my hands on his shoulders to steady myself as I stepped into the delicate structure of chains and ribbons and crystals. His hands were gentle, smoothing the ribbons against my skin and adjusting the chains, handling me this time as if I was just as delicate as the playsuit he was dressing me in, and for some reason that made my eyes prickle. Those hands could be rough and hard, delivering both pain and pleasure, yet I hadn't thought they could be gentle too. Holding me as if I were a precious thing.

I blinked hard, trying to ignore my flailing emotions as he settled the metal bits against my skin, then adjusted a few things before fastening the ribbon that connected it all together behind my head. Then he sat back and began to carefully arrange the chains so they framed my breasts and curved around my hips, before spinning me around and arranging them to drape over the curve of my butt.

Then he spun me around again so I was facing him and leaned back on the couch, his gaze travelling over me achingly slowly, from my knees all the way up my body until he was looking straight into my eyes. 'You,' he said simply, 'are a fucking goddess.'

CHAPTER SIXTEEN

Everett

I KNEW THE moment we'd walked into the store she was going to look fantastic. And she did. The chains lay against her pale skin, beautifully framing her perfect tits and the curve of her hips and thighs. The crystals glittered in the light and the chains gleamed, drawing attention to every female part of her, from her hard, pointed nipples to the fiery curls between her thighs, again framed by the chains and ribbon that circled the top of each thigh. Red hair cascaded over her shoulders and her eyes gleamed like emeralds.

Sensual. Beautiful. Powerful. Intensely female.

But she was more than that. She'd put that bodysuit on, even though she didn't want to, even though I hadn't ordered her to, and she'd done it for me. Because I'd asked her to.

I was so fucking hard I ached, but that wasn't the only thing aching as I'd carefully adjusted the bodysuit against her skin. There had been tears in

her eyes when I'd told her that everything in this
store was for her, and I could see how much that
had meant to her. It had made my chest ache, and
it shouldn't.

We only had another couple of days together like
this and afterwards that would be it. We'd go back
to being friends again. But the way she'd looked at
me, those tears in her eyes... Shit, could we ever go
back to being just friends?

You don't want just friendship from her, admit it.

I forced that thought away and ignored the aching sensation in my chest. Because it was a moot
point anyway. I couldn't offer her anything more
than friendship and that was the bottom line. It had
always been the bottom line.

She might think I wasn't my old man's son through
and through, but she didn't know what I'd done to
him. And she'd never know, because I couldn't bear
her to look at me differently. I couldn't afford for her
vision of me to change, because then I'd have nothing
to aim for. Nothing to aspire to. Nothing to live up to.

I needed her to believe that I was a good man,
because if she didn't then all that was left for me
was that potential, the seed of violence I knew was
planted deep inside me. That would grow if there
was nothing to keep it at bay.

'See?' I said roughly, looking into her pretty face,
letting my total and utter admiration and appreciation of her show. 'It didn't break. And you look incredible.'

She flushed, the chains glittering along with her heightened breathing. 'I'm a bit afraid to move in case they do.'

'But they won't.' I nodded toward the fitting room. 'Go and look at yourself in the mirror.'

'E—'

'Please.' I didn't often say that word, but it came all too easily with her. 'I want you to see what I see when I look at you.'

She let out a breath, clearly reluctant. But then turned toward the fitting room and walked slowly into it. Yeah, she was doing all of this for me, making the pressure in my chest get even worse.

I wanted to see what was in her eyes when she finally saw her reflection, so I pushed myself out of the couch, coming to stand behind her as she looked at herself in the fitting room mirror.

A crease appeared between her brows as she stared at it, and she bit her lip, the crease deepening the more she stared. I took another couple of steps until I was close and then I trailed my fingers down her sides, disturbing the chains and making them glitter, sending the crystals swinging. 'See how the ribbon and chains outline and frame your curves?' I murmured. 'And here…' I lifted my hands to her breasts, cupping the warm weight of them gently. The chains pulled over her nipples and she shivered. 'See how they frame your breasts too? You look stunning.'

Moisture glittered on the ends of her lashes, powerful emotions shifting in her green eyes as she met my gaze in the mirror.

I stilled. 'Little…'

'No one ever did anything like this, E,' she said, her voice soft and faintly hoarse-sounding. 'No one ever did anything that was for *me*, to make *me* happy. To make *me* feel good. Aunt Helen only did things for me when she was forced to and she was always pissed off about it. And I know why. She didn't want her sister's kid forced on her and I don't blame her. She already had three kids of her own, and then she got lumped with me.'

My chest felt like a boulder was sitting on it, because the pain in Freya's face I could feel inside myself too, a stab right through my heart.

She'd always told me she didn't care about her aunt's opinion of her, but I'd known how much bullshit that was. So I'd tried over the years to do things for her so she knew that I fucking cared about her and that her aunt's opinion mattered for shit. But it was hard to help someone who kept insisting there was no problem.

Except right now, here, that insistence was gone, and the fact that she cared, and cared deeply, was written all over her face.

I settled my palms on her stomach, pulling her close, holding her against me so she was in no doubt. So there would never be any doubt ever a-fucking-gain. 'Well, you didn't get lumped with me,' I said flatly. 'I chose you to be my friend, Freya Johnson.

And I will always choose you. Every single fucking time.'

Her eyes were liquid, glittering like the jewels on the chains against her skin. 'Why? Why would you do that?' She sounded like she genuinely didn't know. 'Why the hell would anyone want me?'

I stared at her, a hot, fierce sensation sitting in my gut. 'Haven't you been listening? Haven't you heard a single word I've said to you over the years? What your honesty and your humour and your loyalty have meant to me?'

Red crept through her skin. 'I…'

'No, you haven't. Because you're too busy telling yourself you're fine. Too busy telling yourself you don't give a shit. Too busy listening to other people who don't care about you when you should have been listening to the people who do.' The words were far too strong and far too vehement, but they were out now and I couldn't take them back.

Freya stared at me in the mirror a second longer, her green eyes shimmering. Then, abruptly, she turned in my arms and looked up at me as if she didn't trust the reflection she saw in the mirror. 'E—'

'You ground me, Little.' I cut her off because I couldn't seem to stop the words from pouring out. 'You give me shit when I need my ego checked. And you stand by me when I need support. And you're sexy as fuck.' I lifted my hands and cupped her face. 'The question isn't why would I want you. The question is why *wouldn't* I want you?'

She took a short, sharp breath, the expression on her face full of some powerful emotion that I didn't understand. Then, without warning, she rose on her toes, her hands sliding to the back of my neck, and she brought my head down so she was kissing me, hot and deep and desperate, pressing that gorgeous body of hers against me as if she'd die if she didn't touch me.

This wasn't about simple friendship any more, and I knew it. Could taste it in her kiss and in the craving that suddenly gripped me tight. A craving that demanded more, far more, than that. A craving that demanded nothing less than total and complete possession.

I should have pulled back then. Put her from me and walked away.

But I didn't, because I couldn't. The only thing I wanted was her and so I took her, pushing my fingers into her silky hair before I could stop myself, cradling the back of her skull. Then I kissed her back just as desperately as she was, my tongue in her mouth, tasting, exploring. Demanding. She gave a moan and the kiss turned even more desperate, feverish. She kissed me like she was starving, like she couldn't breathe and I was her air, and that wouldn't have been a problem if the dominant side of me had stepped in to control the situation.

The problem was, I didn't seem to have a dominant side any more.

I was *all* dominant. I wanted to be that air. I

wanted to be the one who gave her fucking life, the one she turned to, not only for fun and friendship, but for help and for comfort. For pleasure and release.

For everything.

I wanted to be everything for her, the way she was everything for me.

I wanted her to be mine. Mine and only mine.

Something roared to life inside me in that second, something I'd been trying to keep locked down and under control, that simply burst the chains I'd kept on it and tore through me like a fucking wildfire.

I picked her up in my arms and took her back to the couch outside the fitting room. I sat down with her in my lap, kissing her desperately the whole time as I reached for my wallet in my back pocket and the condoms that were in it. Her hands were already dealing with the button and zipper of my jeans, clawing at them, because apparently she was as hungry for me as I was for her.

I ripped open the condom packet with my teeth and slid one on. Then I gripped my cock in one hand and put the other on her hip, adjusting her so her pussy was right where I wanted it. Then I thrust in hard, watching her face as I did so, her green eyes going wide and dark, a sharp breath escaping her as I slid in deep.

She felt so good. Hot. Tight. Wet. The muscles of her pussy clenching around me, holding me to her. Her face was flushed, the colour of her eyes so vivid, and she stared at me as if I was the only thing in her entire universe.

And I wanted to be the only thing in her entire universe. I wanted nothing and nobody else to be there but me.

Freya, my best friend. My lover. *Mine*.

I took her mouth hard, my fingers digging into her hips as I thrust up into her, and she tried to move with me, her hands gripping my upper arms for balance. It should have been slow and sensuous—at least that was what I'd intended it to be. I'd wanted to play with those sexy chains, scrape them over her nipples and press them against her clit, drive her wild. But the fire blazing in my veins wouldn't allow it.

My fingers were gripping her so tightly I knew I'd leave bruises on her delicate skin, but I lifted her up and brought her down hard on my hungry cock. The sound of her flesh meeting mine was loud in the silence of the store, and she was panting. I brought her back down on me harder, at the same time as I thrust up, angling her hips so she could take me deeper. The feel of her around me was indescribably good and yet it wasn't enough.

There was a roaring in my head, the ache in my chest getting worse and worse even as the pleasure built higher and higher, a bonfire inside me. The raw possessive need for her was suddenly overwhelming.

She was mine. All mine. And I would make sure of it.

I moved, needing her beneath me, pulling out of her and pushing her off my lap and onto her back on the couch. Then I hooked one leg then the other over my shoulders, shoving myself inside her again. She gasped, her hands moving to my chest as I leaned forward to grip the arm of the couch, sliding as deep into her as I could get. Then I began to fuck her—and not gently, because the feeling inside me wasn't gentle.

It was a raw and savage need that I couldn't control like I knew I should have, and I was blind to everything but the desire to possess her utterly.

Another woman might have protested, but Freya didn't. Her hands slid to my shoulders, her nails digging into my skin, and she shifted and bucked beneath me, trying to fuck me as hard as I was fucking her. There was a wild light in her green eyes, her teeth bared, and she was panting.

I'd never seen anything so beautiful.

'You're mine,' I growled down at her, pinning her with my weight to keep her still. 'You're fucking *mine*.'

'Yes,' she gasped, her body straining as she tried to move. 'I am. Always.'

The satisfaction was so intense I leaned down and stopped her mouth with mine, kissing her, biting at her lower lip as I shoved myself inside her, deeper, faster. Because of course she was mine and now she knew it too.

The pleasure was becoming unbearable now, and

I only just had the presence of mind to slip my hand down between her slick thighs to find her clit, to apply some pressure and some friction, making her stiffen and arch upwards as the orgasm hit her.

Then it was hitting me too, like a fucking freight train, and I was shoving myself into her as the pleasure exploded like a bomb in my head, my hands hard on her as I proceeded to lose what was left of my goddamned mind.

I lost myself for long minutes afterwards, feeling like I'd been hit with a baseball bat, my head ringing, my heart shuddering inside my chest.

What the hell happened to you?

I'd lost control of myself. That was what had happened. And it hadn't been anger that had been the catalyst, not this time, but good old-fashioned lust.

No. It wasn't lust.

A cold thread wound through me because I knew deep down that of course it hadn't been lust. We'd done nothing but have sex for the past three days and I hadn't lost it like this before.

You know what it is.

But I didn't want to think about that, so I shoved it aside as I felt her squirm beneath me, pushing myself back to give her some room and also so I could see her.

She was looking up at me, her gaze brilliant, her face flushed. But the delicate bodysuit of hers was a wreck. Some of the chains had broken and the ribbon had snapped. A few of the crystals had come loose and were embedded in her soft skin, leaving marks. Scratches. All signs of the control I'd lost.

What the fuck were you thinking? You know how dangerous that is.

The cold thread wound tighter, the boulder sitting on my chest getting heavier and heavier.

'Wow,' Freya breathed, looking up at me. 'That was...' Then she stopped and frowned. 'Hey, what's up?'

I was good at controlling my expressions, but clearly not good enough. Shit. The last thing I wanted to do was explain any of this to her. Not the heavy feeling sitting in the centre of my chest, the knowledge that something was wrong. Something I should have held tight to, that I'd let go.

And I knew what happened when I let go. My dad, bloody on the floor and smiling at me like he'd finally seen something in me that pleased him, that made him proud.

'Real chip off the old block, aren't you, son?'

The ache in my chest became a crushing pain that I dealt with by ignoring it completely.

'Nothing,' I said shortly. 'I'm afraid I ruined your pretty playsuit.' I began to ease myself away from her, only to have her reach for my wrist, her fingers circling around it to hold me where I was.

'E, you said you wanted honesty from me.' Her grip on me tightened, her gaze searching my face. 'But you need to be honest with me too. What's going on?'

Ah, shit. What the hell was I going to do now? I

didn't want to talk about this crap with her. Not here, not now. Pretty much never.

Gently, I disengaged her fingers from my wrist and moved off her, getting up off the couch and getting rid of the condom in a wastebasket near the counter. 'I'm pissed off that I ruined your suit.' I kept my attention on doing up my jeans. 'That's all.'

'No, that's not all.' She pushed herself off the couch, seemingly not at all bothered by the remains of the playsuit that left her pretty much naked. 'What's the problem? The suit presumably you can replace. It's not as if you're strapped for cash.'

I finished doing up my jeans then looked at her. 'I'm not having this discussion now. I'm going to get all of this packed up and sent to the hotel—'

'E,' Freya interrupted and there was a note in her voice that stopped me cold. 'Why are you lying to me?'

'I'm not lying,' I snapped, knowing I sounded petulant but unable to help it. 'What the fuck does that matter, anyway?'

'It matters because you matter, Everett.' Her gaze was as direct and honest and brave as she was. 'And I know something's wrong. I saw it in your eyes just before. So why don't you tell me? Please.'

CHAPTER SEVENTEEN

Freya

THERE WAS A hot gleam in Everett's eyes that looked a hell of a lot like anger and I had no idea why. What I did know was that, whatever was going on, his reluctance to talk pissed me off too.

He couldn't demand total honesty from me and then not tell me what his deal was. And anyway, hadn't we done this already a couple of days earlier back at the hotel?

It felt especially raw after what he'd just given me in the fitting room, the way he'd put his hands on me and told me he'd always choose me, possessiveness flaming in his blue eyes. I had loved that, even as part of me hadn't wanted to accept what he'd said, that I wasn't as fine about my aunt's treatment of me as I'd made out.

But then I hadn't wanted her to matter. I hadn't wanted her to hurt me. And I hadn't wanted to accept the things Everett had done for me or listen to the nice things he said about me, because if I had that would have felt like admitting I'd been hurt. And that I did care.

Yet I couldn't look into his hot blue eyes and keep on insisting that I was fine either. I couldn't keep on denying the emotion clogging in my throat and making my eyes prickle. Because to do so would have meant denying all Everett had done for me, saying it meant nothing. And the fact was, it didn't mean nothing. It meant everything.

Because *he* meant everything.

I'd had no words for it in that second, hadn't been able to speak even if I'd wanted to, so I'd kissed him instead, hoping my body would say what I couldn't.

He'd taken me hard and desperately, with no orders this time, and no control. Just him, savage and raw and wild. It had been unbearably exciting to be pinned beneath him, held down and taken furiously, as if he was so starved for me he hadn't been able to help himself. Then he'd growled out that I was his and I knew in that moment that I was. And that I didn't want to be anyone else's.

Nothing had seemed to matter then. Not my aunt. Not the fact that she'd never cared for me the way I'd wanted her to. Not how I'd always felt too tall, too big, too out of place all my life.

Nothing mattered but Everett calling me his.

Until, of course, he'd pushed himself away from me and started lying about why.

'It's not you,' he said flatly.

'You know, for once I don't think it's me, either.'

And I didn't, not given how many times over the past few days he'd proved it wasn't. 'So what is it?'

He shook his head and turned toward the door. 'Let's talk about this later. Why don't you get dressed?'

'I don't want to talk about this later.' Because I knew what would happen. We'd get back to the hotel and Everett would distract me in some way, and then the opportunity would be gone.

'Too bad.' He kept on moving toward the door.

Asshole.

I quickly went around the couch and put myself between him and the exit. He stopped, glowering. 'Don't push me, Little. I'm not in the mood.'

'And I'm not in the mood for you being an evasive dick.' I squared my shoulders and lifted my chin. 'I said please.'

Tension gathered in the air around him. He was mad. I could see the hot blue spark of anger glowing in his eyes. 'Like I said. I don't want to talk about it.'

'After you basically pushed me into baring my soul to you in front of the mirror just now? How is that fair?'

He looked away. 'I have my reasons.'

My stomach dipped, disappointment aching inside me. I didn't want to push him if it was going to hurt him to tell me, but I couldn't deny that it hurt he didn't want to. It felt like he didn't trust me the way I trusted him.

'Okay,' I said, trying not to let that hurt show. 'I won't insist. But if you won't tell me what the issue is, you could at least explain why you have to keep it such a big secret.' I hesitated. 'You can trust me, E. You know that.'

Everett muttered something filthy under his breath. 'It's not about trust.' He lifted a restless hand, running it through his hair in a gesture I'd almost never seen him make before, glancing down at the floor. 'I just…don't want you to see me differently.'

I frowned, puzzled. 'See you differently…to what?'

He didn't reply, though his hand dropped and abruptly he looked at me, a fierce expression in his eyes. Then he took a sudden step forward, his gaze dropping down my body, to the ruined playsuit, and he put out a hand, his fingers brushing over one of the marks on my side, where a crystal had pressed against my skin. I shivered.

'I hurt you.' His voice had thickened, full of an emotion I didn't recognise.

I frowned and put my hand over his where it touched my side. His skin felt warm underneath my fingers, but that expression on his face…it was pain.

'E,' I said softly, my heart constricting, 'you didn't hurt me. Honestly. And anyway, those times you spanked me hurt worse than that.'

He lifted his attention from my skin and met my gaze. 'That was different. I meant to do it those times. And I was in control of myself. I was…not in control just then.'

'So? I liked it. I liked that you were kind of desperate. It was exciting. And I would have told you if I hadn't been into it.'

Something shuttered in his face, like a light going out or a door closing. 'I can't be like that, Freya. Not with you. It's too risky.'

There was a heavy note in his voice. A kind of finality that made me feel cold inside. 'What are you talking about? What do you mean, "too risky"?'

He was silent, and for a long moment I thought he wasn't going to speak. Then he said, 'Remember years ago? When my dad got beaten up? I told you he'd got into a fight while he was out drinking.'

I did remember, dimly. It had been years ago and I'd thought it was only what the asshole deserved. Everett hadn't said much about it, but then he never talked about his father much as it was.

'Yeah,' I said. 'I remember.'

Everett's gaze was very blue and very direct. 'The fight he had was with me. *I* beat him up. He was drunk again, and he cuffed me around the head and I…I snapped. I got so angry. I punched him, and then I punched him again, and then the next thing I knew he was on the ground.'

A wave of shock passed over me. Cool, controlled Everett snapping and punching his father? I could barely imagine it. Then again, if anyone could have pushed him to the limit it would have been his horrible father. Only he'd never said a word about this to me, not one single word. I'd simply accepted what he'd told me as the truth, that his father had got into a fight. I'd never even had a suspicion that it would be otherwise.

'That wasn't the worst part, though,' he went on, his gaze dropping from mine, back down my body to the little dents in my skin the chains had left. He trailed his fingers over them, making me shiver yet again. 'The worst part was when he was lying on the floor, and I was standing over him. And he looked at me and he just…smiled and told me I was a "chip off the old block". As if he was proud of me. As if I was just like him.'

My heart was a big ball of hurt in my chest—hurt for him. While another part of me was furious at him for not telling me this, for keeping this from me for so long, especially when it had clearly been eating him up inside. But this wasn't about my anger, so I tried to sound neutral as I asked, 'Why didn't you tell me about it?'

His fingers trailed over another set of dents at my hip and again he was silent. Then he looked at me again. 'I didn't want to talk about Dad with you. Being with you was the only time I could escape him and even talking about him made it feel like he was intruding. But mainly…I didn't mention it because I didn't want you to see me differently. I didn't want you to look at me the way Dad did, as if I took after him.'

My throat closed up. 'Oh, E. I would never look at you that way. Never. Why would you think I would?'

'Because I never told you I'd hurt Dad. You didn't

know.' He looked away again, his hand dropping from my body, every line of him tense. 'And I decided you couldn't know, because you were the only person who didn't see him in me. You thought I was a good guy and I just…I needed someone to believe that.'

The shock deepened, widened. I'd never pushed Everett about his father because he hadn't wanted to talk about it. And since I didn't talk about my aunt, it didn't seem fair to bug him. But maybe I should have. Because then I could have done something for him, so he didn't have to deal with this alone. Except I'd been too wrapped up in my own stuff, too busy telling everyone I was fine, to be bothered paying attention.

I swallowed, pushing back the regret that was choking me. 'Yeah, well, I know now, don't I? And nothing's changed. You're still a good guy.'

But he just stared at me. 'Am I?'

'Of course you are, you idiot.' I reached out a hand to his chest, resting my palm against the hard width of it, wanting to touch him, offer comfort. 'You're not a drunken, abusive asshole, for a start.'

He glanced down at me, his body wound tight as a spring. 'I got angry, Freya. And I just lost it and I shouldn't have. I should have controlled it, should have kept it locked down, but I didn't. I lashed out at him and I fucking nearly knocked him out.'

'Yeah, and? He deserved it. Hell, if I'd been there, I would have put in a few punches myself.'

Everett's gaze burned with a fierce, cold light.

'You don't understand. Of course he deserved it, but I shouldn't have lost it the way I did. And I can feel that anger inside me, Freya. It's still there. It's like a bomb waiting to go off, a little piece of him I can't get rid of. All I can do is make sure I stay in control enough that it doesn't.'

I stared at him, shock radiating through me. I hadn't known he thought that way, hadn't even guessed. Sure, I knew he'd always been a fairly locked down kind of guy, but I hadn't known the reason. 'Look,' I said, wanting to reassure him, spreading my fingers out on his firm chest, 'I get why you might feel that way. But there's no bomb, E. There's no piece of him inside you. There's only you. So you lost your temper one day. Who hasn't? That doesn't make you magically turn into him.'

'So me on the couch, losing control with you, tearing that suit off you? Scratching you? Wanting to own you? That doesn't have any potential to turn toxic like Dad did?'

I frowned, searching his handsome face, because he seemed committed to this and I didn't know why. 'But that's got nothing to do with your father being a violent drunk, Everett.'

He put his hand over mine where it rested on his chest. 'It's all about control. Dad had none, which means that if I don't want that potential to become reality, I have to have it all.' Gently, his fingers closed around my hand and he pulled it away from him. 'And I don't have that with you.'

Something cold settled inside me and I let him drop my hand. 'What?'

There was a hard edge in Everett's gaze now and I knew what that meant: he'd made a decision. 'We have to stop, Little. You and me. It has to end.'

That hard edge was sharp and it cut me, and it hurt. So much that I caught my breath. 'What?' I repeated, like an idiot. 'What do you mean, it has to end? But we've only got another couple of days—'

'No.' There was no arguing with that word. It was heavy and final like a rock fall over a mine shaft, closing off all possibility of escape. 'It's better if we stop sleeping with each other now.'

The hurt deepened, which was strange because this was only supposed to be about sex. We hadn't promised each other anything more than that. Just a few days and then we'd go back to being friends.

You don't want to go back to being friends, not now. You want to be his.

But I ignored that thought. Ignored it completely. Sure, I liked sex, but I could go out and find it with someone else. It wasn't a big deal. Everett had shown me a few things about myself and I was grateful for it. I could find that with another guy.

'So, what?' I didn't know why I was pushing, but I couldn't stop myself from asking. 'You lose control once, rip an expensive item of clothing, put a few scratches on me, and that's it?'

A muscle in his jaw flicked. 'It's not the bodysuit, Freya. Or the scratches. It's you.'

'Me?'

'Yes, you.' His voice had turned rough. 'You're the one who tests my control. You're the one who makes me lose it. And I can't have that. Our friendship is too important to risk.'

'Oh, bullshit,' I snapped, not sure why I suddenly felt so angry, so hurt, but unable to stop the words coming out all the same. 'This isn't about our friendship. And it's not about me either, so don't make it all my fault.' I lifted my hand from his chest then poked him with my finger. 'This is about you, E.'

His expression grew suddenly cold. 'Okay, fine. It is about me. It's about me not wanting to be the man my father was. Is it so fucking wrong not to want to turn into a violent drunk?'

'It is when it's a complete goddamn lie,' I shot back. 'You know you're nothing like your dad.' I poked him again. 'I've known you for years and years and there's nothing bad in you, Everett Calhoun. So all of this—the bodysuit, the scratches, not wanting to turn into your dad… You know what I think? I think it's just an excuse.' My throat closed, but I forced out the rest. 'You're looking for a reason to stop this, aren't you?'

He ignored my poking finger and went very still. 'And if I was?'

There was a pressure inside me, around my heart, squeezing tight. 'Then you need to be straight with me. You need to tell me it's over.'

'I thought I just did.'

Of course he had. So why was I arguing? Why did this hurt so much?

'It's just sex, Freya.' His voice was hard and cold. 'It wasn't supposed to be anything more.'

But it is.

Yeah, it was. And I knew why. If I looked deep in my heart, I absolutely knew why. The answer had been there all along, sitting inside me for years.

I was in love with him. I was in love with my best friend and that was why this hurt so much. That was why it felt like I was breaking in two.

Just sex, he'd said. That was all it was for him, and if he was looking for excuses to end it then that was all it would ever be for him.

It felt like something was tearing apart inside me, but I turned away so he wouldn't see it because I didn't want him to know. I didn't want him to give me platitudes and soothing, or even his own brand of hard understanding. I didn't want him to do anything for me at all.

I didn't need him. I never had.

'Okay,' I said, trying hard to sound as if I didn't care. As if I didn't give a shit. 'I'll just go and get dressed.'

'Freya,' he said.

But I didn't want to hear it. I'd heard enough already.

I went into the fitting room, shut the door hard and then I locked it.

And then I sat on the floor and cried.

CHAPTER EIGHTEEN

Everett

I SAT AT the dining table in the hotel, staring hard at the laptop in front of me, trying to concentrate on my spreadsheet instead of the sounds of Freya getting her stuff together in preparation for her trip back to the airport.

I wasn't going with her. She'd been adamant she didn't want me to come and I hadn't argued. Seemed like it would be better for us both if I didn't.

Especially given how tense the past couple of days had been.

Your fault, asshole.

Oh, I had no illusions about that. I knew it was my fault. I'd been the one to make the decision to stop sleeping together and I'd known that that decision would hurt her. And it had. She'd tried to hide the pain that had glittered in her green eyes, but I saw it anyway. I always knew when she'd been hurt, no matter how many times she insisted she was fine.

She'd been insisting she was fine for the past couple of days too, pretending nothing was wrong. Pretending we were the same kind of friends we'd always been. But we weren't. I'd organised a couple more touristy things for us to do before she left, and we'd carried on with them. But the magic was gone. There was a tension between us that hadn't been there before and, quite honestly, I didn't know if it would ever go away.

I didn't know what to do about that, either. I couldn't keep sleeping with her, I couldn't give in to the possessive need to make her mine, not if I wanted to stay in control of myself and my emotions. Not if I wanted to stay being the man I'd made myself into. Because, shit, what other options did I have? I could keep her, sure, but I knew what would happen if I did. That need I felt for her, that desperation, was too close to the anger that burned inside me, the anger that was still there, even though my dad had died years ago. Anger that he'd turned to drink after Mom died. Anger that he hadn't been able to control himself. Anger that he'd taken it out on me, that he'd made my childhood miserable.

Freya had accused me of looking for an excuse to end it when I'd told her we couldn't sleep together any more and I guess she wasn't wrong. Because it wasn't so much the control that was the issue, as it was the feeling behind it. The boulder sitting on my chest. The need for her that had only been growing

the past few days, a need that went beyond friendship, that wanted something more.

Something I didn't want and had never wanted.

It was why I preferred the clubs and the strangers in them. Why I liked the rules and conventions
that went along with them. I could keep my distance
and not give too much of myself to any one person,
because the trust I shared with people in the clubs
wasn't based on emotion. Emotion was dangerous,
and I knew exactly how dangerous. And if anger
could shake my control then surely I would be more
at the mercy of something deeper?

I couldn't risk it. I wouldn't risk it.

There was badness in me, no matter what she said.

She deserves better than you, anyway.

I stared, unseeing, at the laptop screen, the pain
that had been sitting just behind my breastbone, the
pain I'd been telling myself I didn't feel for the past
few days, deepening.

Yeah, she really did deserve better. Because I had
a feeling I'd fucked up our friendship too, probably
beyond repair.

*Come on, did you really think things would go
back to normal?*

I muttered a curse and pushed back my chair,
getting out of it and walking to the windows, then
walking back to the table again, restless and antsy,
unable to sit still.

No, I knew they wouldn't, not deep down. But
I'd hoped.

Freya's footstep sounded from behind me and I swung round to face her. She was standing in the doorway, the duffel bag—which was the only thing she'd brought with her—slung over one shoulder. In jeans and a T-shirt, she looked tough and together and so goddamned sexy I was hard instantly. Which was the state I'd been in constantly for the past few days because although my head was clear where we were at, my dick disagreed.

Freya gave me one of those awful forced smiles that didn't fool anyone, least of all me. 'Thanks for the past few days.' She slid her hands into the pockets of her jeans. 'It's been…really great.'

My jaw ached and the pressure in my chest felt like a vice, slowly winding tight. 'Good,' I bit out. 'You sure you don't want me to come with you?'

'Uh, no. Thanks.' Her teeth sunk into her bottom lip as if she'd wanted to say something and then had thought better of it. 'Okay. Well, I'd better go. Guess I'll see you when I see you.' Avoiding my gaze, she began to turn.

'That's all?' I didn't know why I spoke. I shouldn't have, but I couldn't seem to stop myself. 'A thanks and goodbye?'

She turned back, an emerald spark of anger bright in her eyes as she glanced at me. 'What else did you expect?'

Anger coiled inside me, at myself for the way I wanted more when I knew I shouldn't and, irrationally, at her for making me want it. Another sign that ending it had been the right decision.

'Nothing,' I said roughly. 'Forget I said anything.'

Something about her tensed in that moment and she looked away. I wanted to close the distance, take her chin in my hand and force her back to look at me. Because she was hurt and I...

What? What are you going to do? Kiss it better? Take her in your arms and tell her everything will be okay?

I couldn't. Because I knew it wouldn't be.

After the briefest of hesitations, she turned back to the door. 'Okay. I'd better go.'

'Freya.' I couldn't help myself. My hands were in fists in the pockets of my jeans and I wanted to reach for her so badly it was all I could do just to hold my ground. 'I'll see you back in the States, yes?'

She stopped, her back to me. 'I don't know if that's a good idea.'

The vice in my chest squeezed so tight I couldn't breathe. 'What do you mean, you don't know if that's a good idea?'

Her back was to me, tension in every line of her shoulders. And everything in me wanted to grab her, get her mouth under mine, kiss and stroke away that tension so it would never bother her again.

But I didn't and the silence in the room got deeper, wider.

'Because I...' She stopped then turned abruptly

again to face me and I saw what she'd been trying to hide: the tears tracking slowly down her face.

I took an involuntary step towards her, the tears on her cheeks like a knife to my heart, but she shook her head. Hard.

'You know,' she said huskily, 'I thought if I pretended hard enough that I was fine then I would be. But I'm not fine, E. I'm not. And I'm not because I've decided that I can't have you as a friend any more.' She lifted a hand, wiping at her face and blinking furiously. 'I want to be more than that to you. Because you're more than that to me. I'm in love with you, Everett.'

A part of me must have already figured out how she felt, because it didn't come as a surprise. But it hurt all the same.

'It's okay,' she said before I could open my mouth to reply. 'You don't have to say anything. I know you don't want what I want and honestly, it's fine.' She gave me a brief watery smile that broke my heart. 'I'll be okay. But…we can't be friends at the moment. I can't do it. In fact, I'm not sure if I'll…' She stopped and swallowed, wiping away more tears. 'I'm not sure if I'll ever be able to do it. I hope you understand.'

It felt like she'd put her hand on the hilt of the knife in my heart and had twisted it brutally hard. Making agony seep through me. Her friendship was worth more to me than anything in the whole goddamn world. More than the billions sitting in my bank account. More than the company my friends and I had spent years building. All that stood between me and my fucking father.

And now she'd just taken it away.

You've got nothing to live up to now, have you?

No, I didn't. There was nothing between me and Dad now, so what was the point in pretending? Why was I bothering to be someone I wasn't? Live up to an ideal that didn't exist?

She thought I was a good guy, but I wasn't. A good man would have told her that he loved her in return, would have dried her tears and held her, never let her go. But I wasn't a good man.

So all I did was ignore the knife shredding my insides and said coldly, 'I understand.'

Freya gave a little nod, as if I'd just confirmed something for her, and then she turned back to the door once again and walked through it and out of my life.

It was better that way. It really was.

I kept telling myself that for the next few hours after she'd gone, as I circled the suite, walking around and around, unable to sit still or concentrate, the pain in my chest getting deeper, growing wider. Along with my fury.

The pain was fine, because pain was the easiest thing in the world to control. But anger had always been different. It seethed and boiled away inside me like lava, as if I was a volcano about to blow, and I couldn't get a handle on it.

I stopped in front of the windows eventually, staring out as dusk now settled over the city, and I realised I must have been circling the suite for hours.

Yet all that walking and the pain and the fury hadn't changed. I felt just as furious and full of agony as I had in the seconds after she'd gone. Because, of course, I only had myself to blame.

I was the one who'd ended it. I was the one who'd hurt her. I was the one who'd stayed silent after she'd told me she loved me.

My jaw ached. My shoulders ached. Everything fucking ached. And I could see myself reflected in the glass, fury written all over my face.

And it was my dad looking back at me.

You'll never be the man you wanted to be. Not when all you see is your father.

I reached out and touched the glass, touched that reflection, the anger inside me choking. Because he'd been right. He'd always been right. I was exactly like him.

'I've known you for years and years and there's nothing bad in you, Everett Calhoun.' For some reason Freya's voice from the other day floated back to me, exasperated and angry and full of impatience. *'You know what I think? I think it's just an excuse...'*

I stared at my reflection, the words echoing inside me.

Yeah, it had been an excuse. Because I hadn't wanted the feeling inside me, the growing, insistent craving for her. A feeling too big for me to deal with. It was desperation and ecstasy and need and pure happiness rolled into one. Friendship and sex and trust, and too many others to name.

A feeling that pushed me to the edge.

A feeling I didn't want to acknowledge.

But she did. What's your excuse?

It felt like a bucket of ice water had been dumped suddenly over my head. I had excuses—I had plenty of excuses, just like she'd accused me of. But that was all they were. Just excuses.

Because I was afraid. Afraid of the feeling inside me, the one I couldn't deny.

I was in love with her. I was in love with my best friend and I didn't want to be. Because what did I know about love? My dad had never shown me any affection at all, let alone love. All I'd got were fists to the face and empty beer cans strewn everywhere, and that wasn't what I wanted for Freya.

She'd lost her mother, then been dumped with a family that didn't want her. Had been brought up by an aunt who hadn't cared for her. And now she'd been rejected by a friend who should have supported her, a friend that, despite all of that, she loved. And she deserved better than that.

She deserved someone who would love her completely and without reservation. Without control. Without fear. A man who had a good heart instead of a dark one.

The feeling inside me, the intense, possessive one,

wound its fingers around that dark heart of mine and squeezed. It was agony.

At that moment my phone buzzed in my pocket and it was only reflex that had me answering it. 'What?'

'Where is Damian?' Ulysses demanded, apparently not noticing my tone. 'He's been gone for days and we need to get this meeting—'

'I'm not interested in your meeting,' I growled. 'And I'm even less interested in where the fuck Damian is.'

'This is important, Everett.' His voice was its usual cold, flat self. 'I need to get this foundation off the ground and I need you two to—'

'I don't care.' I hit the disconnect button, for once cutting him off rather than waiting for him to do it.

However, almost immediately, my phone started to buzz again and this time—naturally—it was Damian.

I did *not* want to speak to him, but I knew if I didn't answer he'd just keep calling, so I answered it. 'Ulysses is trying to find you and he's pissed off,' I said before Damian could speak. 'So you should be calling him rather than me.'

'Nah, I don't want to speak to him.' There was something in Damian's voice I hadn't heard before, a note of…warmth maybe? 'I don't think he'd understand.'

'Understand what?' I wasn't in any mood for whatever games Damian was going to play.

'I'm going to be in Italy next week, bro. And I don't want to be disturbed, okay? I thought I'd call and let you know you'll both have to do without me for a while.'

'What? Why? What are you doing in Italy?'

Damian hesitated slightly. 'I'm getting married.'

For a second I just stared out the window, not really taking in what he was saying because it was so out of left field I didn't understand. 'Excuse me?'

He laughed. 'Yeah, I know, right? Can you believe it? Biggest manwhore in the fucking world getting married. But it's true.'

This was…surprising to say the least.

'Who?' Oh, but then I knew. It had to be the woman he'd brought with him to the foundation launch the previous week. 'Your jewel thief, right?'

'Yeah, that's her.' This time there was no disguising the heat in his voice. It was like a goddamn fire. 'Don't worry, she's fully background-checked.'

It took me a minute to remember I'd been worried about that before. It felt like a lifetime ago. 'You didn't seem happy with her last week.'

'No. Because she walked out on me. Which was fair since I was being a dick.'

'So, what? She just walked right on back?'

'No.' I could hear the smile in his voice. 'Believe it or not, I went after her.'

That was a first. Damian never chased anyone.

'Why?' I asked, not even sure why I was asking because I didn't care.

'Why?' he echoed, sounding amused. 'Because I realised she was more important than all the bullshit I was telling myself. That's the beginning and end of it.'

I found myself gripping the phone way too tight for comfort, my heart pounding hard in my chest. I couldn't see myself in the glass any more. All I could see was Freya and the tears on her cheeks.

'You okay, man?' Damian asked. 'Did the shock of my impending nuptials kill you or what?'

I barely heard him. All I could hear was her voice telling me she loved me and how loud it sounded, making all my excuses and lies seem pathetic and weak. And they were pathetic and weak. They were bullshit, just like Damian had said.

So why was I holding onto them so hard? What was I so afraid of? Did I really believe my dad was right? Did I really think I was bad right at the heart of me?

Why would you believe him rather than your friend who you've loved and trusted since you were ten years old? She didn't believe it so why should you?

Something crystallised then in that moment. Freya had never lied to me. Had never given me anything but honesty and trust. Yet I'd never repaid her. I'd given her pleasure and friendship, but the Dom had wanted to stay in charge by holding a piece of me back. Because staying in control was more important.

But was it more important than her?

You know the answer to that.

'Bro,' Damian said. 'You are dead, aren't you?'

'No,' I said hoarsely. 'I just realised something.' And I disconnected the call before he could speak, as the truth fell all the way down inside me and settled there, becoming part of me.

Nothing was more important than her. Not my need for control, not my desperation not to become my father, and certainly not my fear that I had nothing to give her.

She was the most important thing in the entire fucking universe and always had been, and she needed to know that. Just like she needed to know that I loved her.

I didn't expect her to change her mind about us, not after I'd hurt her so badly. But the only apology I could make was to give her my heart, darkness and all.

And hope that when I laid it at her feet it was enough.

And maybe, just maybe, she'd want to pick it up.

CHAPTER NINETEEN

Freya

I SAT DISCONSOLATELY at the table in the back of the lame nightclub Tiffany had chosen for her hen party, watching the dancing getting underway.

The party was as dire as I'd been expecting. I liked Tiff, but her friends seemed like competitive types, all of them comparing boyfriends and jobs and shopping habits.

The conversation—as I'd feared a couple of weeks ago—inevitably turned to sex, especially when Tiffany started opening up her presents. There was the usual array of sexy lingerie and very tame sex toys and various other things, but I couldn't help grinning a little as she pulled the wrapping off the present I'd got her and stared at it, wide-eyed.

Stupid Everett had tried to give me a whole lot of things from our date at the sex shop, but I'd refused them. I hadn't wanted things. I'd wanted him. But just before I'd left London, I'd remembered I'd had to get Tiff a gift and so I'd stuck a couple of things in my bag for the journey home.

Now Tiffany was staring at them, her blonde hair falling over her shoulders, clearly not knowing what they were. My two other cousins were peering at them, fascinated, as were her other friends.

'They're nipple clamps,' I said helpfully. 'And these little things here—' I touched the chains hanging from them '—are for added weight.'

'Added weight?' Tiff echoed, looking at me astonished.

So I explained. Several of the other women were staring at me as I spoke, clearly aghast, but more than a few others were interested.

'That sounds like an experience,' Tiff said, a speculative look in her eyes.

I grinned in what I hoped was a mysterious way, even though smiling was the last thing I felt like doing. I really hoped they didn't want me to go into it, because I couldn't bear thinking of Everett and everything we'd done together.

Everything that was now lost.

I probably shouldn't have told him I was in love with him before I walked out of the hotel that day in London. That I couldn't be friends with him either. But I'd known I couldn't go on pretending I was okay. Pretending I didn't need him. Pretending he didn't matter to me.

I'd spent my life doing that with my aunt and I couldn't do it with him. What I felt for him was too

important. *He* was too important. And even though I
knew telling him wouldn't change anything, I had to
say it, even if it was just to admit it to myself. Also,
if I was going to break off our friendship, I needed
to tell him why.

I hadn't expected any dramatic change of heart
from him and he hadn't disappointed. He'd told me
his reasons for not wanting more and even though
I thought they were bullshit reasons I wasn't going
to argue.

I wasn't going to beg either, or settle for anything
less than what I wanted, because if there was one
thing Everett had shown me, it was that I deserved
more than that. There'd be someone out there who'd
be able to give me more than just sex, more than just
friendship. Who would choose me and give me their
heart. Who would love me the way I loved them.

Except you're never going to love anyone but him.

I reached for my margarita, shoving that thought
away hard, because I really didn't need that negativ-
ity in my life right now.

And then, suddenly, everyone in the booth we
were sitting in fell silent, the way women often do
when they spot a good-looking man heading their
way. So I turned my head to see what was happening.

A man was moving through the nightclub, the
crowd parting for him like he owned the place. Tall
and broad-shouldered. Powerful. So goddamn hot in
jeans and a tee my heart just about stopped beating.

My stern Viking.

Everett.

'Wow,' someone murmured. 'Who is *that*?'

'Freya's friend,' Tiff said and then she grinned at me. 'You didn't tell me he was coming back.'

I opened my mouth to tell her that I hadn't known, but my voice seemed to have disappeared because nothing came out. I could only sit there and watch as Everett strode up to the booth, his sharp blue gaze on mine, as if all the other women sitting there with me didn't exist.

He didn't bother with a greeting. He only said, 'Little, I need to talk to you.'

I wanted to shake my head and tell him to leave, because if he thought he could just waltz back into my life after I'd told him we were done he had another think coming.

'Hell, no,' I snapped, finding my voice. 'You can damn well—'

'Fine. I'll say it here then.' His gaze was blazing, the expression on his face intense, and he didn't look anywhere but at me. 'I shouldn't have let you walk away from me in London. I shouldn't have let you walk away, period. But I did, because I'm a fucking coward. Because I didn't want to admit that you're more important to me than anything else in my entire goddamn life. Because I didn't want to acknowledge the truth.' Utter silence had settled over the table, but Everett didn't seem to notice. 'Because the truth is I love you, Freya Johnson.'

I stared at him, blindsided, my heart feeling like it had been given an electric shock. 'W-what?'

He reached for me then, taking hold of my hand where it sat on the tabletop and pulling me up and out of the booth. And I went, unresisting, still in a state of shock as he walked fast through the night-club, tugging me along behind him until we were in a quieter, darker part of the club. Then he pushed me up against the wall and caged me against it, all heat and ferocity, the intensity he always kept locked up inside himself flooding out.

'I told myself I was only going to say those things to you and then walk away,' he said fiercely. 'Let you choose for yourself what you wanted. But…fuck, Freya. I don't think I can walk away from you. I know I should but I can't.'

'I don't understand.' My voice sounded thick and hoarse, and I didn't know what to do with my hands. I wanted to touch him so badly, but I knew if I did I wouldn't be able to stop. 'You said you couldn't—'

'I know what I said,' he interrupted. 'But I was wrong. I was so fucking wrong.' He shifted one hand, cupping my cheek in one large palm. 'I told myself that letting you go was about staying in control. But you were right that day in London. It was an excuse. It was bullshit to make myself feel better about the fact that I was in love with you and I was fucking terrified.' His thumb stroked my cheek gently, even though the look in his eyes was anything but gentle. 'I don't know anything about love, Freya. Dad sure as hell never told me he loved me, never showed it either, so I have no goddamn idea how to love you. But…' He stopped as his voice got rougher, the look in his eyes becoming even more intense. 'You're the most important thing in the entire fucking universe to me and so I want to try.'

I swallowed, my mouth dry, my heartbeat hammering in my head, my eyes prickling with stupid tears. 'You know I can't do friends, E. I thought I made that clear.'

The blue glow in his eyes deepened. 'Why would you think I'd want friends? Especially when I can have this.' His fingers firmed on my jaw and then his mouth was on mine, and he was kissing me. Not hard and desperate this time, but deep and sweet and slow, a gentle exploration, a taste. And a question.

A question I already knew the answer to.

When he finally drew back and looked at me, his heart was in his eyes. 'I'll beg if you want me to,' he said. 'On my knees if you need it.'

I could have made him wait. I could have been angry and yelled at him for hurting me. For making me cry the way he had. And part of me wanted to, wanted to see him on his knees too.

But my heart had no patience for anger and it was tired of suffering, so I lifted my hands and put them on his chest and pressed hard, soaking up his heat and his strength. 'You're a bastard, Everett Calhoun. And you deserve a punishment for hurting me the way you did.'

'Anything,' he said hoarsely. 'Anything. Just name it.'

'Okay.' I swallowed, looking up into his eyes. 'Your punishment is that you have to bring me coffee in bed every morning for the rest of our lives.'

His expression became even more fierce. 'Only if the bed you're in is mine.'

'Yes.' My heart was tender and sore, and it was the most beautiful feeling in the entire world. But not quite as beautiful as the feel of his hand on my skin. 'I don't want to be in anyone else's.'

'Little…' Both his hands cupped my face as he moved closer to me, pinning me in place. 'You know I'm not just talking about sex, right? I want more than that. I want to keep you. I want you to be mine. And not for five days. I want you for ever.'

I couldn't swallow this time, emotion choking me. 'What made you change your mind?' I forced out, because I had to know. 'You were so adamant before.'

He let out a breath, easing his body closer to mine so we were pressed up against each other. 'I just kept thinking about what you told me, about how all of that control stuff was excuses. And in the end it was really just a simple choice. What was more important—my excuses or you?' He leaned down, his mouth brushing over mine. 'That's when I realised it was you. It will always be you.' He pulled back, giving me one of his rare, beautiful smiles. 'I don't know if I'll ever be a good man, Little. I'm possessive and controlling, and no doubt I'm going to be jealous as hell. Plus I've got a temper. But you make me want to be better. You make me want to be the man you see when you look at me.'

My stupid eyes prickled harder. 'You idiot,' I managed to force out. 'How many times do I have to tell you? You already are that man. And shit, you think I don't have any flaws? I'm prone to being a martyr and pretending everything's fine when it isn't. I'm too damn stubborn for my own good. And you know I've got a temper too. Oh, and I—'

But he didn't let me finish, his mouth covering mine and silencing me. And then, when he finally pulled away and we were both panting, he said, 'Don't be my friend, Little. Be more. Be mine. Be my wife.'

I blinked, my heart filling up and overflowing. 'Is that a proposal?'

He gave me a feral kind of grin. 'No, that was an order.'

'Oh, no,' I breathed, happiness stealing all my air. 'Forced to marry the hot billionaire who loves me, who'll give me all the orgasms I might ever want, and who'll keep me in the manner to which I shall certainly become accustomed. Will no one save me?'

No one saved me.

I was cursed to live out the rest of my days with a stern, hot, dominant Viking who loved me beyond all reason.

Too bad I loved every second of it.

EPILOGUE

Everett

'You've got to be kidding me,' Ulysses barked down the end of the phone. 'You're spending the next week on some island?'

'It's not just some island,' I said patiently. 'It's Capri. And it's for my honeymoon.'

'I can't get hold of Damian and now you think you can just go off to Capri?'

I lay back on the sun lounger and slid my arm around the very beautiful and very naked goddess who was lying on it with me, and who had her hand around a very sensitive, not to mention hard, piece of my anatomy. 'Yes,' I said. 'Sorry.' Even though I wasn't sorry.

'Don't give me sorry.' Ulysses sounded as furious as I'd ever heard him. 'You know I need you two here to handle the trustees. That's the one thing I can't do myself.'

'Too bad.' I didn't care about Ulysses and his issues. They could look after themselves for a week or two. 'You've got Morgan to help you.'

'But I—'

I disconnected the call then threw my phone in the pool.

'Are you sure that's a good idea?' Freya murmured.

'Hanging up on Ulysses or throwing that in the pool?'

'Uh, both?'

'He can deal.' I lifted a brow. 'Or do you need to get back to the garage?'

Her fingers moved on me, making me hiss. 'No, Casey can keep handling it. Though I guess we need to figure out what happens next?'

We did. In fact, there were a whole lot of things we needed to figure out, such as where we were going to live, given how I travelled a lot, and what that would mean—if anything—for her garage. She wouldn't want to give that up, and hell, I wouldn't make her. But there was a whole wide world out there for Freya, and I wanted to show her all of it.

Still, that could wait. There were other more important things to do first.

'Sure.' I gave her a stern look. 'But that's not where your attention should be now, wife.'

Her green eyes glowed and she gave me a smirk. 'Make me, husband.'

If that wasn't a challenge I didn't know what was.

But then that was totally Freya. She challenged

me, excited me, aroused me. Loved me. She wasn't only my friend and my lover.

She was my for ever.

She was the good in my heart.

* * * * *

BURN MY HART

CLARE CONNELLY

MILLS & BOON

PROLOGUE

SHE'S BEAUTIFUL. BUT that's not why I notice her. In a sea of men wearing tuxedos, she has Titian-red hair, long and wavy to halfway down her back, and she wears a dress of green silk that makes her pearly skin glow.

But beautiful women are a dime a dozen in my world, so it's more than that.

Holden.

Our conversation rings in my ears and I know I would do anything to blot it out, to blot out the pain of the past. Sex, in my experience, is an exceptional way to silence memory and thought.

Do you remember that morning? When Dad dumped your mom? Don't you remember the way she screamed?

Remember it? It's burned inside of me, her wounded, animalistic cry of disbelief. Jagger and Holden were numb to it—they'd seen this often before. But for me, I've never forgotten that. My mother screamed as though her body was catching fire and my father did nothing but stare at her with contempt.

The memory is like the devil at my heels. I want to silence it. To conquer it in the only way I know how.

She lifts her head, her eyes latching onto mine. The flame transfers out of my body, across the room and ignites something within her. I see it in the flaring of her eyes, the lift of her lips into the sexiest smile I've ever seen, the hint of pink blossoming in her cheeks. My attention is dragged back to the conversation I'm in but, for the next hour, I'm conscious of her on a cellular level. I could pinpoint exactly where she is in the room at any time.

'Hey.' She's right behind me. I turn around slowly. We're both alone for the first time all night. Speculation lifts.

'Hey yourself.'

'Having fun?' Her voice is soft and musical. Desire sparks in my gut.

'Sure. I love this kind of thing.' My tone is replete with sarcasm.

'Same here.' She responds in kind but her conspiratorial smile lightens her words.

'Do you want a drink?'

She tilts her head to the side, considering that. 'I think I've had enough to drink.'

The words sit between us, the implied invitation unmistakable. 'Do you want to get out of here?'

Her eyes sharpen with something unmistakable and then she's nodding. 'Absolutely.'

I haven't had sex in about a billion years. Okay, not quite that long, but a really long time. I'm too busy and there's something about being Asha Sauvages that makes it hard to meet people I can trust.

So I have no idea what's overtaken me tonight, nor why I propositioned this guy. Except I do. I mean, he's hotter than Hades, and in this crowd of buttoned-up suits he stands out like a real-life Greek god. His hair is long, but pulled up into a messy man bun. His jaw is covered in a fine coating of stubble and his eyes are permanently narrowed, whether in disapproval or assessment. Either way, the effect is stunning. On his wrist he wears a couple of fine leather bands, and on the other an expensive wristwatch. Yep, he's gorgeous, but that's not why I propositioned him.

Today is the anniversary of my mother's death— also known as my birthday—which means my father, brother and I go to the cemetery and then have lunch together.

And every year it's the same thing. *'We weren't supposed to have any more children.'* I'm the 'any more'. *'If only we hadn't fallen pregnant again.'* With me.

My brother's sole purpose at these lunches is to rein my father in, but the longer the lunch goes on, the more wine he drinks, the more apparent it becomes that he really wishes, with all his heart, that I hadn't been born.

Happy birthday, me!

Don't get me wrong. This isn't a self-esteem issue, it's a *fuck my family, I want to do something for myself* mood. I have dedicated my life to our family business, to being someone my dad could be proud of, and tonight I just want to have really great sex and push everything else from my mind.

And Theo Hart is, if the rumours are to be believed, the king of great sex. He's renowned in Manhattan for his phenomenal business skills—last month *The Times* ran an article about the Hart family and the fact their wealth increases by five million dollars every hour—but he's just as revered for his devoted bachelorism. I've heard rumours about him for years, but this is the first time we've met and I have to say, for a night of mind-blowing no-strings sex, he's exactly what the doctor ordered.

So I promise myself this: I'll have one night with him and I'll enjoy it fully so this day won't be about my mother's death while she was giving me life; it won't be about the fact my dad is disappointed in me; it won't be about anything except me and Theo Hart. He's the birthday present I'm giving myself.

I had no way of knowing, though, that one night with Theo Hart wouldn't be enough. That this would be the beginning of something bigger, something fun and intoxicating and something that would ultimately bring about more pain than I've ever known in my lifetime. If I had, would I have stepped away from him?

Probably not. Theo Hart has been my kryptonite from the moment we met and there's simply no escaping that.

CHAPTER ONE

Six months of very hot, no-strings sex later...

You're late.

I READ HER text message with mixed feelings. Desire, impatience, need.

Frustration, because my brother Holden needs me and if I were anywhere near decent I'd put Asha off till another night so I could give Holden my undivided attention. But the thing is, where Asha's concerned, I'm ruled by one particular part of my anatomy.

One hour. Max.

I tap the reply quickly, then jam the phone in my back pocket. 'The wedding's in a month, man.'

Holden's grey eyes fix me with a level stare, the kind of stare that would scare the shit out of someone who didn't know Holden like I do.

'I'm aware of the date.' His lips are grim.

'So? Get your shit together. Jagger needs us.'

He turns his head away, his square jaw covered in more than stubble. It looks like it's been months since his skin has seen anything approaching a razor. In fact, it looks like months since his liver has seen anything other than alcohol. I shift my gaze around his apartment warily. 'You need to move on.'

'Sure.' His shrug reeks of sarcasm. 'Done.'

I grind my teeth together. 'How many times and in how many ways do we have to say it? You're our brother. I don't give a shit what some goddamned paternity test shows. No one does. You were raised a Hart, you'll always be a Hart.'

'But I'm not.' The words are emphatic. 'And with all due respect, you don't know what the hell you're talking about.'

'Don't do that.'

He stares at me.

'Don't act like you have a monopoly on the whole "fucked up by your parents" thing. We're all by-products of our father's approach to life.'

Holden turns away from me. 'He's not my father, remember?'

'You think biology is the only definition of family?'

His back is ramrod-straight.

I expel an angry breath. 'So what, man? You want to just turn your back on us? Walk out on Jagger and me, like we mean nothing?'

'No.' It's an angry denial. And then he angles his

face back towards mine, his eyes like ice chips. 'I just need time.'

'It's been months.'

'There's no statute of limitations on this. I'll get over it if and when I'm ready.'

'Fine. But just—don't block us out, okay? I'm here for you. So's Jagger.' We're not much into the touchy-feely stuff—no one who'd lived our childhoods would be—but I feel like I need to say to Holden what I've never said to another person in all my adult life. 'I love you, man.'

His brows lift in surprise and for the briefest moment there's a grin on his face, so familiar that my stomach clenches because I catch a tiny ghost of my brother, my real brother, the guy I grew up with. He reaches for a pair of socks that are balled up on the bench beside him and throws them at me. 'You're turning soft in your old age.'

I laugh, reassured for now, glad to have sighted him and convinced myself he hasn't drunk himself into a catatonic stupor. 'Yeah, yeah. I gotta go. See you Sunday?'

'Sunday?'

'Pick-up. At the hotel. Don't be late.' I throw the socks back at him. They land between his eyes. I laugh as I leave, but there's a heaviness inside me, a heaviness I can't shake.

'You're late.' I pull the door inwards at his knock, and a familiar rush of longing assaults me. Theo Hart in any guise is one of the hottest guys on the planet. I mean, he could basically be Jason Momoa's body double. Fewer tats, but every inch of delicious rugged hotness. I swear a little drool escapes the corner of my lips.

I love him in a suit, all buttoned up and conservative, every detail immaculate, but I love him most like this, because this is so perfectly suited to the man he is. In low-slung, faded denims and a black T-shirt, he is casual and hyper-masculine.

'Sorry.' He grins and my stomach flip-flops. His eyes drop from my face, scanning my body slowly, so sensual heat licks my flesh as though he's touching me. The gown is couture, a gift from a designer friend. I traded her a signature Fleurs Sauvages luggage set for the entire Spring-Summer collection. This piece is black silk and it hugs my breasts, hips and falls to just above my knees. It's a simple slip but the detail is in the design. The cut of the fabric enhances curves without being overstated. 'You look beaut—'

'No time.' I reach for him, pulling him inside. He kicks the door shut with his booted foot, stepping out of them shortly after so his feet are bare. He lifts me against his body, all his hard planes and muscles making my insides turn to mush. 'Where were you?'

He kisses me and my hands tangle in his hair. It's styled into a messy man bun on top of his head. I dislodge it unapologetically.

'Got held up. Doesn't. Matter.' He's pushing at my dress but I shake my head.

'I have to go out soon. I literally have twenty minutes.'

'Fuck.' The word makes me smile because it speaks volumes regarding our mutual desperation. It's unsurprising. It's been two weeks since last we saw each other—the longest since we started this bizarre and mutually satisfying agreement. 'Cancel your plans.'

It's easy to forget that Theo is one of the wealthiest men on the planet. There's something low-key about him that puts me at ease, then he fires commands like that at me and I remember he runs the shipping and maritime branch of the behemoth that is Hart Industries, that he's used to commanding tens of thousands of employees.

'I can't. You're going to have to go fast.'

His grin widens. 'I don't think that'll be a problem.'

I laugh, because where a mere mortal might feel the need to insist they could *never* come quickly, Theo is secure enough in his manhood, and has given me more than enough orgasms, to know that the ability to render pleasure quickly isn't a bad thing.

He's only been to my apartment a couple of times before this but he remembers the way to my bedroom easily. We kiss and walk and stumble a bit as we move quickly through the penthouse, shouldering our way through the doorway and falling onto the bed in a tangle of limbs and fabric. He pulls at my underwear, a lace thong, gliding it from my legs with reverence even as he moves quickly, then pushes my dress up. I lift onto my elbows so he can guide it over my head.

'Don't let it crumple,' I instruct, laughing because Theo is the last person on earth to give a crap about preserving clothing. But I have to wear the dress tonight and wrinkles will kind of be a giveaway as to what I've been doing.

With a droll expression, he drapes it at the foot of the bed but I don't watch. I decide I don't really care about crinkles. I don't really care about anything in this moment except him and this.

His fingertips caress my flesh and I tremble, pleasure bursting through me. My hair is long and red. I used to hate it and dye it black, but somewhere in my early twenties I gave myself over to its natural colour and let it grow. It falls to the small of my back in thick, voluptuous Titian curls, and I love how obsessed by it he is. His hands fist the lengths and he drops his head, kissing my mouth, holding my hair, the weight of his body on mine a pleasure beyond compare. My hands fumble at his belt, undoing it, pushing his zip down, freeing his cock, my fingertips curling around his length hungrily. I release a jagged sigh of relief. It's been way too long—a mistake of circumstance. His life is busy, and mine is the same. Coordinating our schedules is hard but, oh, so worth it.

'Protection,' he grunts, pushing his clothes off impatiently at the same time he pulls a condom from his wallet and slides it over his dick. He's impressively efficient with this stuff and never forgets the practicalities, which I love, because sometimes I'm so caught up in what's happening between us that I can barely recall my name.

'I will move heaven and earth to avoid having children,' he joked one time, when I thanked him for always being so prepared with his condom supply.

He said it as a joke but I felt the undercurrent and knew not to push it. He's dropped enough little comments like that over the last few months for me to get the picture: he had a shit childhood and is a committed lone wolf.

His body is back on mine in two seconds and I wrap my legs around his hips, pulling him towards me.

I don't need to ask twice. There's no mystery to this—we both know why he's here, and it's far from our first time. He thrusts into me and my body trembles in silent but powerful recognition. Thank God. It's been too long. He moves slowly at first so I drag my nails—painted our newest shade of red, *Ruby Rose*—down his back and dig my fingers into his buttocks. He laughs, that deep, husky tone of his voice sending a *frisson* of desire along my spine.

He thrusts deeper, harder and I tilt my head back, pleasure exploding through me. His mouth drops to my breasts, his stubbled jaw providing a sensual contrast on my flesh—his mouth is warm and soft while his jaw is almost painful on my sensitive skin. He sucks a nipple deep in his mouth, rolling it with his tongue the way he knows I like, his fingers tormenting my other breast as he drives deeper and I arch my back, welcoming him, needing him.

My first orgasm is mind-blowing. I dig my nails in harder, only stopping when it occurs to me, in the back of my desire-flushed mind, that I might draw blood. I let my hands fall to my sides and I ride the wave, pleasure contorting my face, satiation making my breath husky.

As my breath starts to return, I push up so we roll over and I'm on top. His eyes are laced with heat, his sculpted cheekbones slashed with dark colour, and I know his own orgasm is close at hand. With my body on his, I begin to rock on my haunches, pushing up and easing myself down, slowly, tormenting him in a way that's seriously unkind given how quickly he just got me off.

But the power of this is addictive and I love that he doesn't fight me, I love that he submits to my brand of torment, letting me take control even when I suspect he wants to grab my hips and hold me down. I lean forward so my breasts brush his chest and he growls my name in the back of his throat so it reverberates from his body to mine. *Ashaahh*. I love the way he says that, deep and guttural. It's so primal.

I keep moving my hips, rocking back and forth, the pressure of his cock inside me and his body against mine making my temperature skyrocket. Pleasure builds again so I know I'm going to come once more, and hard. I'm trembling all over, an orgasm on the periphery of my awareness, and then he's kissing my lips. His hands grab my hips and he moves me in time with his own thrusts, so he's buried deep inside of me again and again until finally he explodes just as I tip over the edge of the earth. Our bodies fall apart in unison, our voices mingled as pleasure wraps around us both, fervently demanding our surrender. And we give it willingly, urgently, the speed of this coming together unusual for us, but nothing I'm going to complain about.

Sure, I prefer the nights when we have hours and hours to kiss and taste and explore—I'm already itching to go down on him, to take his cock in my mouth and drive him to the point of insanity with the things I can do to him, but there's no time. My body is still on top of his, he's deep inside me, when my doorbell buzzes and the faintest hint of a male voice comes to us.

'Shit.' I push up onto my elbows, casting a glance at the diamond-encrusted wristwatch I always wear. 'He's early.'

Beneath me, Theo's expression is laconic. He's the cat that got the cream, but there's no time for post-coital bliss. I roll off him and pick up my dress, my knees a little wobbly as I stand and pull the fabric over my head.

My brother's voice comes through the door again. 'Shit,' I mutter. Then, louder, 'Just a second.'

I turn to Theo, who's watching me with a curious look. 'You have to hide.'

He bursts out laughing. 'Hide?'

'Yeah. Hide.' I reach for him, grabbing his hand at the same time I bend down and scoop his clothes off the floor. I thrust them at his chest, a warning look on my face. 'In there.'

He shoots a look over his shoulder in the direction I've pointed, then shakes his head. 'I'm not hiding in your closet.'

'My brother's here.'

'So? Aren't you going to introduce me?' He's teasing but I instantly reject the suggestion, even when it's not a suggestion made in earnest.

'Er…sure. "Hey, big brother! Here's the guy who's been fucking my brains out the last six months."'

'You could just use my name.'

'And say what? That you're my very convenient fuck buddy?' I draw my brows together. 'Just—stay in here.' The words hold a warning. 'Shit! Where's my—?'

He's holding my thong on the tip of his finger. His look is pure molten seduction. Damn it, I want him again and he knows it. I snatch the thong and pull it on a little awkwardly, then run my fingers through my hair.

'How do I look?'

'Like a woman who's just been ravished.'

Great, I was afraid of that. 'Just...don't make a sound. Shut the door behind you when you leave.' I press a harsh kiss to his lips and move to my bedroom door but, before I walk through it, I rush back to him. 'Thanks. You were great.' I wink and squeeze his butt before turning and leaving.

Joshua, dressed in a tux, looks exactly like our father. 'Hey.' His eyes scan me and show the exact opposite reaction to the one I saw on Theo's face fifteen minutes ago. I don't mean I'd expect my brother to look at me like he wanted to rip my clothes off, but where Theo looks at me like I'm the most beautiful woman he's ever seen, Joshua's expression always shows a hint of disapproval. He strides past me, presses a perfunctory kiss to my forehead, then moves into the kitchen.

Which is seven paces closer to my bedroom.

I look down the corridor betrayingly, and note the outline of Theo's body through the crack of the door. He's pulled his boxers on, at least, but if Joshua happened to look down the hall he'd see a half-naked billionaire smiling smugly back at him.

'Shouldn't we be going?'

'We've got a few minutes if you want to fix your hair, Charlotte.'

I bite back a pithy retort. My hair is fine, though probably a little wild after Theo's ministrations.

'Fine, help yourself to a drink.' I wave my hand towards the kitchen then clip back towards my bedroom, tempted to give Theo a piece of my mind. But when I walk in he's nowhere to be seen. I click the door shut, my eyes scanning the room. Where is he? I stride into the en suite bathroom and reach for my hairbrush, gliding it over the soft waves a few times before Theo comes up behind me, pressing his body to mine. The touch sets off a thousand and one fire-works in my bloodstream.

But that's nothing to when he catches the hem of my dress with his fingertips, pushing it up so his fingers can brush my sex, his palm cupping me and pulling me back against him. I swallow a moan, my eyes locking to his in the mirror.

'No time,' I mutter, dropping the brush into the sink with a clatter.

'Wanna bet?'

Oh, help me. Theo *loves* a challenge. I know this about him, and I love this about him, but in this mo-ment… 'It's my stepmother's birthday,' I murmur, making no effort to move away. 'I can't be late.'

His eyes flare with amusement. 'You won't be.' His hand moves faster; a finger pushes inside of me. I buck backwards and moan. He laughs, spinning me around and kissing me, swallowing the sound. Plea-sure ricochets through me, volcanic and urgent. A beautiful, hot delight that lashes my core and makes me tremble. I brace myself on the vanity as pleasure sears me, red-hot and fierce.

'Charlotte?' he murmurs into my mouth, his thumb padding my sex.

'Long story.' I find his lips. 'You started this. Don't you dare stop.'

'Charlotte? Are you done?' My brother's voice is a very unwelcome intrusion. I rip my head away from Theo, but his grin is my undoing. I hold Theo's eyes, lifting a hand to his shoulder, and shout towards the door, 'Just a sec. I'm coming.'

And I am. Seconds later, I'm spiralling completely out of control, his mouth swallowing my frantic cries, his hand holding me together and driving me apart at the same time. My fingers are in his hair, tangled in its length, and then, almost as soon as I've crested over that tsunami of sensation, he's pulling away, rearranging my dress around my thighs. 'It's good to know we can add quickies to our repertoire.'

My breath is rushed. 'For sure. Next time you have five minutes between meetings, call me.'

'Will do. Charlotte,' he adds as an afterthought, a teasing smile on his face. But there's something in his eyes, a seriousness, a question I don't want to answer. A question he doesn't really want to ask— because we don't do that. We don't really talk about anything other than how much we want each other, and that suits us both.

'Only my brother calls me that.' I poke my tongue out. 'See you soon.'

I feel his eyes on me as I slip from the room and knowing he's watching me brings a huge smile to my face, just like always.

* * *

I look around the en suite bathroom with curiosity. It's nothing out of the ordinary. Toiletries, make-up, and a lingering scent of her that makes me want to go out into her kitchen and announce to her brother that actually she won't be coming with him at all because she and I aren't done yet.

We didn't plan to keep seeing each other for so long. She's busy, I'm busy, and sometimes our schedules are such that we can't manage to catch up as often as we'd like. But that's the best part of this no-strings situation. It's no big deal. There's never any drama with Asha. We agreed to that from the start, and for the last six months it's been working perfectly. In fact, I'd have to say I think I've cracked the code for the perfect relationship. Keep it physical and keep it light.

That's it.

Et voilà.

I wonder whether, if my dad had worked this out, he might not have married every woman he slept with. Briefly, my chest tightens, as it always does when I think of my father. No, that's not right. He's the man who gave my mother sperm but he was never really much of a dad. Not to me, not to Jagger, and definitely not to Holden. Darkness descends for a moment and I close my eyes, the hatred I feel for him rushing through me.

Asha's muffled voice brings me gratefully back to the present. I can hear their voices but not clearly enough to know what they're saying. Curiosity has me moving closer to the door.

'I organised the diamond necklace,' Asha is saying, her eyes sliding to the door so she sees me and I grin. She blanches and jerks her head back to her brother. His back is to me, so I only have the impression of a tall, slim man dressed in a dark tuxedo.

'She'll love it. What's happening with Angel Pie?'

Angel Pie? I frown.

'We're just waiting on FDA approval for the mascara. The packaging is almost finalised—we're down to two box designs. Market testing is showing amazing strengths across the whole product line.'

The brother nods. 'You're happy with it?'

'Are you kidding?' Asha's face lights up. My gut punches. She's so gorgeous. 'I've only been working on this for four years.'

Her brother nods again, slower. 'Good. I'm proud of you, Char.'

She hesitates for a moment, in a way that has me holding my breath for no reason I can think of. Then she smiles. 'Let's go.'

'I guess we have to.'

'It won't be that bad.'

'Sure it won't be.'

They share a look that is purely conspiratorial and a twist of longing spears me. I miss Holden. I know I literally just came from his place, but I don't mean in a physical sense. I mean I miss him as part of our family, as someone who looks at us like brothers and grins. He's a part of our fabric and I don't care what any DNA result says. He's a Hart as much as I am, as much as Jagger is.

The front door clicks open. I move nearer her bedroom door so I catch the moment she pokes her head back in the corridor to meet my eyes. She's glaring at me but I see amusement in her features and I shrug my shoulders, pulling her bedroom door wide open. Her brother's out in the communal corridor; there's no risk of being seen. But nonetheless, she quickly withdraws her head, slamming the door to her apartment behind her.

It's only the third time I've been in her apartment, and it's the first time without Asha. Charlotte. A small frown smudges my face. My curiosity is natural. We've been sleeping together for just over six months but I know hardly anything about her beyond the basic biographical details. That she's the MD of her family's luxury cosmetic and lifestyle brand, that she works her beautifully shaped rear end off, which explains why she's twenty-eight and, up until she and I happened to meet, hadn't had sex in almost a year. She's fiercely intelligent and doesn't take shit from anyone—two things I respect enormously about her.

I'm tempted to snoop. Just a little. Yeah, yeah, it's kind of a bullshit thing to do but, looking around her apartment, I can't help but notice little details that I would never have guessed at—details that have previously passed me by because I don't notice anything except Asha when Asha is around.

Things like the fact she must enjoy cooking, going by the healthy assortment of cookbooks near the kitchen. I pick one up. It's well thumbed, vegetarian, which she definitely isn't. I replace it, then do a three sixty. Her taste in furnishing is eclectic and bright, not what you'd expect from a woman who runs a company like Fleurs Sauvages. This is fanciful, frothy, feminine. I smile at a pink cushion shaped like a pair of lips.

I'm so tempted to look around, but I don't. Not just because it would be weird and creepy, but because no part of this is about getting to know one another. Our cardinal rule was formed a week after our one-night stand: this is just sex. I don't ask about her life, she doesn't ask about mine.

I've never been in such a perfect relationship.

I whistle as I pull the door shut, already wondering when I can see her again…

CHAPTER TWO

'ASHA, THIS IS Angus Fienes, the son of a dear friend of ours.'

My stepmother puts her hand in the crook of my arm, drawing me away from the conversation I was in the midst of. I dutifully obey, ignoring the glance of disapproval she gives my hair.

'Hi.' I look in his direction, not at all surprised to see a guy who looks like he could have walked off a preppy photoshoot beside her. His teeth are the brightest white I've ever seen, his eyes oceanic blue, his skin a buttery tan, with hair that looks soft and golden. 'My stepdaughter, Asha.' She doesn't pause before she says my name, in the way my father does. To Caroline, I've only ever been Asha; she didn't know me as Charlotte, so it's easier for her to accept my reincarnation.

'Asha—' his smile is one hundred per cent model perfect '—I've heard a lot about you.'

I look at him blankly, knowing I should insert some kind of platitude, and that I would if I really cared. Nonetheless, Caroline is looking at me expectantly and this is her birthday party, so I placate her by offering the man a tight smile.

'Angus is a hedge fund manager. Very successful,' Caroline murmurs, leaning closer towards me. This bothers me on so many levels. I like Caroline. She's a sweetheart. But she is also, unequivocally, a gold-digger. Twenty-four years younger than my father—who she makes sublimely happy, I'll admit— she was working as a flight attendant for an airline when they met. Despite the fact she's got a fortune at her fingertips, and I at mine, she doesn't seem to realise I don't place quite the same value on marrying well as she evidently does. Beyond that, I wonder what she'd say if she knew I'd been sleeping with one of the wealthiest men on the planet for the last six months.

Six months! How the hell did that happen? When we began, I swore I'd only let it go on for a month or so. Just to store up some great sex memories before going back to my somewhat monastic commitment to running Fleurs Sauvages. I hadn't been as sold on the whole 'just sex' thing as Theo—not that I'd tell him that. Not because I want more than that with him—only a masochist would try to turn a committed bachelor like Theo into anything more—but because one day I do want an actual relationship. With someone. A husband. Kids. A familiar sense of nostalgia washes over me because that sense of family is something I've never known. So maybe, in my mind, I'm making it bigger and better than it really is, but all I know is that the sense of belonging which comes from family is something foreign, something that I really want.

Angus laughs quietly—it's a nice laugh. 'It's easy to be successful in this market.'

I give him a point for modesty but take it away again when I realise how false it is. He's preening in front of me, waiting for me to make some comment on his genius. I don't. He's right; it's a soft market right now, not hard to be successful.

Caroline falters a little, her smile dropping by degrees. 'Asha runs the make-up side of things.'

I suppress a familiar flare of irritation. The 'make-up side of things' is actually Fleurs Sauvages and the company is worth over sixty-four billion dollars. It's not just make-up, but a complex range of luxury brands across all industries—handbags, fragrances, jewellery, footwear, lingerie. While cosmetics are my passion project, I'm responsible for everything that falls under the Fleurs Sauvages umbrella. Or, as my family apparently likes to think of it, I 'tinker with pretty things'. That used to bother me a lot more than it does now.

When I first took over, the pressure to prove myself was immense. I went to work every day with a nauseated feeling in my gut that I couldn't shake. I don't know when that eventually gave way. The company's first billion-dollar year with me at the helm? When I finally secured an exclusive deal to have only our products used for Barcelona and Lyon fashion weeks? I don't know. But as I've got older and worked harder, I know I have the experience and skills necessary to do the company justice. In any ordinary family, I'd say I have what it takes to make my father proud, but pride isn't something I've ever known from my dad. That doesn't stop me from wanting it sometimes, though.

'Impressive.' Angus is being sincere now and it occurs to me that, given his line of work, he has a fair idea—a better idea at least than Caroline—what being MD of a company like Fleurs actually entails.

'Thank you.'

'Would you like a drink?' He nods towards my empty glass. I stare at it for several seconds, a frown on my face, consternation rolling through me. I feel *guilty!* Actual guilt! Like I should say no because of Theo. Because I'm fucking him? Jeez, what's wrong with me? He's made it abundantly clear that all he will ever be able to give me is a long line of orgasms and I'm fine with that.

Dating each other is absolutely *verboten*. But other people?

Okay, calm down, Ash. The guy's asked to get you a champagne from a free bar; it's not a marriage proposal. I push a smile to my face. 'Yeah, great. Why not?' It's as non-committal as an acceptance can get but my stepmother doesn't get the memo. She claps her hands approvingly as we walk away.

'She's planning our monogram,' I mutter, shaking

my head, earning a laugh from Angus. His hand in the small of my back feels weird. His hand is different to Theo's. Long slim fingers, somehow slighter and less…confident? Less authoritative, certainly.

'I think you're probably right.'

'So your parents are friends with mine?'

'They play cards.'

'My dad plays cards?'

'I think it's just an excuse to drink whisky, but yeah.'

My smile is over-bright. I shouldn't be surprised. There is an entire catalogue of things I don't know about my father, and vice versa. I've taught myself not to be upset by his disinterest in my life, and I gave up a long time ago on wondering what I could fix within myself to make him love me. Dad's Dad. He's set in his ways, and those ways include keeping me at a distance. This is just another example of the chasm that stretches between us.

The party is taking place in a private room at the Plaza. Waiting staff mill around, distributing canapés, elegant jazz fills the air and the bar is serving only the best alcohol. I accept a new champagne gratefully, finding the anaesthetic properties helpful in getting through this kind of event.

Despite my place in this life, I've never really enjoyed soirees like this. 'I heard a rumour you're in line to become CEO at the next board meeting.'

I slant a glance at Angus. 'I'm pretty sure you heard wrong.' My voice betrays the rivalry, given the way we've been pitted against one another since birth. But that rivalry is only a small part of me. I feel sympathy for Joshua too, sympathy at the expectations that have almost drowned him. It's fascinating to see how differently we turned out, given that he grew up with an excess of expectations and I was diminished by a shocking lack of any.

'Your appointment would make you the youngest CEO of a *Fortune 500*.'

I arch a brow. 'You've done your research.'

His smile is quite charming, in a preppy schoolboy kind of way. 'Always.'

He's flirting with me. I frown as that same burst of guilt travels the length of my spine once more. But I'm not doing anything wrong, and neither is Angus. Theo isn't my boyfriend. He's not even really my lover. We don't linger over long nights together, sensually discovering each other. We appoint a time, meet, screw, then leave. He's a fuck buddy, his purpose in my life as clearly delineated as mine is in his. Besides, talking to Angus gets me out of having to circulate. I catch Caroline's eye about half an hour later—she's watching us with a smug smile on her pouting lips.

I'm tempted to end the conversation just to thwart her expectations, but by now Angus is talking about an archaeological dig he went on in Cairo during his grad degree and, since I'm truly interested in that experience, I stay where I am, ignoring the fact I'm making my stepmother so blissfully happy.

Eventually, though, I realise the crowd has thinned. 'I'm going to have to call it a night.' I look at my watch, surprised to see it's almost midnight.

'You're sure? There's a bar around the corner...'

'No.' I shake my head. 'I have a conference call with Tokyo. It was nice talking to you.' I'm even more surprised to realise I mean it.

'Same.' He lifts a hand to mine and a shiver—not the good kind—runs down my spine. Because this definitely feels wrong. It's not, though, I remind myself. Theo knows the deal. We're not a couple, we're not dating. And Angus is just being friendly.

'I'd love to see you again. Any chance you're free for a drink later this week?'

'A drink?'

He nods. 'You know, a beverage in a vessel. A bit like this.' He nods towards my champagne glass.

I roll my eyes. 'Sorry, I just didn't expect...'

'Seriously?'

'No, I—'

'I'm sorry.' He shakes his head apologetically. 'I didn't mean to make you feel awkward.'

'You're not. I don't.' The sense of guilt is an excellent reason to accept his invitation. What I've got with Theo is a no-strings affair that's going nowhere. I can't pass up a chance at a real relationship because the guy I'm sleeping with might object. It would be weird *not* to accept. Angus is handsome, nice, he's made me laugh a couple of times. Definitely worthy of further exploration.

'So I can call you?'

I reach into my clutch and pull out a card. 'Text me,' I clarify. 'I'm in and out of meetings. It's easier.'

'Got it.' He leans forward and presses a kiss to my cheek. I bristle and hope he doesn't notice.

'Thanks for the company. Your stepmother was right—you're charming.'

He's Greek. Or Greek-American. But the American part of him is almost completely muted by his Greek heritage, which expresses itself in myriad ways: his complexion, dark like burnt butter, with eyes the colour of ebony, a chest that is broad and muscular and covered in a sprinkle of hair, and features that are symmetrical and strong, as though they've been chiselled from granite.

A week after my stepmother's birthday and I'm at Theo's place, pressed against the floor-to-ceiling glass, my body raw with feelings as he holds my hips and takes me from behind, his every shift an intimate possession that sparks fire in my blood, just like that first night. Manhattan twinkles beneath us, bright lights in slender columns, and directly outside on his rooftop terrace is an infinity pool that will be perfect for cooling the day's heat, and passion's tempest, from my body.

But thought isn't possible. Not when his hands come around my front, cupping my breasts, his fingers strumming my nipples so I cry his name again and again and push my hips back, taking him deeper, moaning as he does just what I've wordlessly asked for. One of his hands drops to my clit and he massages me there skilfully so I explode without warning, swearing over the top of his name. He stills, letting me absorb this, letting me feel every single damned sensation before he moves once more, his hands roaming my body, touching every inch of me, each thrust slow at first and building until he's joining me in a powerful crescendo that robs me utterly of breath.

He grabs my body, pulling me to stand, holding me almost straight against him and buries his face in the crook of my shoulder so I hear his ragged exhalation as he loses control and comes deep inside of me.

'Wow.' It's minutes later before I'm capable of speaking. And even then I'm still not really able to articulate anything meaningful. 'Wow.'

He laughs, but I feel his own surrender to this, his own awe at the power of our physical connection. Sex with us is out of this world. 'Yeah, wow.'

Slowly, I move away from him, but he keeps hold of me, spinning me in the circle of his arms. His face is perfection. I stare at him for several beats then smile, kissing his nose and moving to the side.

'Thanks.'

He laughs. 'You don't have to thank me every time.'

I lift a brow, reaching for my camisole. 'But you're *so* good at that.'

He watches as I slip the silk over my head and reach for my thong. 'So, Charlotte, huh?'

It's the first time I've seen him since the afternoon of my stepmother's party. I'm not surprised he's brought this up—I am surprised, though, that I haven't thought of a way to answer it. And yet we don't really do this, talk about personal stuff. I lift my shoulders. 'It's no big deal.'

'No? It's kind of a strange nickname.' He pulls his jeans on and moves to the kitchen, grabbing a beer out and lifting the top. He's so stunning in that moment I give myself a few seconds to drink him in—the caramel of his complexion, the breadth of his muscled chest, a frame that doesn't have an inch of spare flesh.

'It's my christened name.'

He's still and watchful as those words digest. 'You were born Charlotte?'

'I was born a baby,' I correct, teasing, pulling my skirt over my hips and zipping it up. 'My dad called me Charlotte after my mom…' I swallow, the rush of sadness familiar. 'My mom died a little after I was born. Complications from my delivery. Her name was Charlotte.'

He frowns, considering that. 'You didn't like the name?'

'I didn't like the ghost.'

He holds his beer towards me. I take a long sip, then pass it back.

'It's hard to explain,' I say after a moment. 'I just

felt like every time my dad looked at me he saw my
mom. Or, rather, he saw the myriad ways I was nothing like her. Changing my name didn't really change
that but I guess I thought it might.' I paste an over-
bright smile to my face, not really wanting to drag
this shit show into our light and fun relationship.
'Besides, it was during my rebellious teenage phase.
I did a lot of stupid crap back then.'

'So you legally changed your name?' he pushes,
a smile hovering at the edges of his lips.

'Yep.'

'Why Asha?'

'I liked it.' I shrug. 'It means hope. It felt…appro-
priate at the time.'

I feel like he wants to ask me something else, like
he wants to ask me many things, but he doesn't. He
pulls me towards him instead, takes a drink of his
beer and then kisses me, pushing the liquid into my
mouth so I laugh and swallow, my hand pressing to
his naked chest. I love how light he keeps this.

'You free Friday?'

My heart thumps. Guilt slices me. I ignore it.
'Nope. Saturday afternoon?'

'Can't. I'm in Sydney for a thing.'

'A thing?'

'My brother's bachelor party.'

'That's right. He's getting married.'

'Yeah.' He grins. 'More fool him.'

'You don't approve?'

'Nah. It's good. Grace is perfect for him and

he's…the happiest I've ever seen him. But marriage is just…not for me.'

I know this about him. He spelled that out in black and white when we agreed to embark on this whole thing.

'It's really important that you understand what I want, and what I don't want, because I'd never want to lead you on. I'm always clear about my limits and the whole happily ever after bullshit isn't for me.'

'So you've said.'

'You can't do Friday?'

My heart thumps. Because I want to see him again before he goes but I have plans. With Angus. I lower my eyes, making an effort to keep my tone bland. I'm doing nothing wrong. 'Nope.' My mouth feels dry and my pulse is thready. 'I actually have a date.'

'A date?' He laughs and something shifts inside of me, emotions I can't comprehend.

'Yep.'

'You're *dating*?' His smile drops as his eyebrow shoots up.

'I mean, no. I haven't been. It's a first date.'

'You're going on a date with someone?' He strides to the fridge and pulls out another beer, handing it to me. I take it on autopilot and crack the lid.

'Is that a problem?' Is he…*jealous*? This, I hadn't expected.

He frowns, rubbing his palm over his jaw. 'I just didn't realise.'

'We're not... I mean, what you and I are doing isn't a real relationship, right?'

'Hell, no,' he's quick to agree, just as I knew he would. 'Who is he?'

'Just a guy I met through my parents.'

'And he asked you out?'

'Yeah. At my stepmother's birthday thing.'

He nods again. 'So you like him?'

The question is insultingly carefree. He's *not* jealous. 'I don't really know him. But he seems nice. I'm interested in getting to know him better, for sure.'

'What's his name?'

'Angus Fienes.'

He laughs. 'Seriously? *Him?*'

'You know him?'

'I've met him a few times. I must say, I presumed you had better taste.'

I roll my eyes. 'What's wrong with him?'

'Nothing. He's very sensible. You'll be married with two point five kids in a year's time.'

A smile twitches on my lips. 'Apart from the fact that's biologically impossible, it's just drinks at the Four Seasons. Let's not get ahead of ourselves.'

'But you want to meet someone? Like him?'

For six months we've been sleeping together and not once have we needed to have a conversation like this. I guess it was inevitable that at some point we'd have to pop the naïve bubble we've been enjoying and address our situation, but now that we're doing

that I'm startlingly reluctant to alter any of the pa-
rameters of what we are.

'I guess so.' I drink from the beer and lift up onto
the bench, sitting on its edge, angling my body to
take in the view of Manhattan. My shoulders lift
into a small shrug of their own volition. 'I'm twenty-
eight. I feel like, if I'm not careful, I'm going to wake
up in a decade and realise I don't have a life outside
of Fleurs Sauvages.'

I glance at him; he looks terrified, like I'm about
to try to wrangle a ring onto his finger. 'I get why
you're not into the "happily ever after" thing. I respect that. We're just…different.'

He nods, his eyes holding mine for so long I feel
almost as though he's lancing me with his gaze. 'I'm
disappointed,' he says at length. 'But I was never
going to find it easy to let this go.'

His words have a contradictory impact on me. On
the one hand, panic tears me apart at his implication
that he's letting this—me—go; on the other, there's
delight that he's admitted such a prospect isn't easy.
Neither emotion sits well with me.

'You're not proposing we end this?'

His expression shows bemusement. 'I don't see
an alternative.'

'Because I'm catching up with a guy for a drink?'

'Because I'm not going to sleep with a woman
who's sleeping with someone else.'

That's right. We discussed monogamy ages ago.
I didn't remember until now because Theo is more

than enough for my appetites. It never occurred to
me that either of us would be sleeping with someone else on the side.

'It's just a drink,' I say quietly. 'I'm not about to
go home with him.'

He lifts a brow. 'Given how we met...'

'Come on, Theo, I'm giving you my word. I'm
not going to disrespect you like that. We've been
sleeping together for six months and, while this
isn't exactly a conventional situation, it still means
something to me. I have no intention of being with
the two of you at once.'

Silence falls as he mulls this over. 'So what do
you suggest?' he asks after several beats have passed,
my nerves stretching.

'Things between us stay the same until I say otherwise. Or you do,' I hasten to add. 'If it gets serious
with Angus, or any other guy, I'll tell you.'

I don't realise I'm holding my breath until he nods
and pulls me towards him. 'I know we're just fucking, but I don't share well, Asha.' His kiss robs me
of the ability to think and a minute later I'm naked
again, welcoming his body back to mine, knowing
in that moment I'm just precisely where I want to be
most in the world.

CHAPTER THREE

SHE HAS EVERY right to date another guy. Not to sleep with him while we're sleeping together but to date, sure. I know this and in fact I completely support that decision. After all, she's a great woman, a serious catch. Any guy would be lucky to have her. She deserves every good thing in life and I have no interest in giving it to her.

But Angus Fienes is just…not Asha. He's so pretty, always with his hair styled and his collar popped, his dimples showing in an artfully shaved face. The idea of Asha ending up with a guy like him feels completely wrong.

I tell myself that it's simple friendly concern that leads to this: me, sitting at the bar of the Four Seasons on Friday night cradling a glass of eighteen-year-old Macallan, my eyes lifting to the door every few minutes.

Plus, I kind of like the idea of screwing up their date. There, I admitted it. I'm a bastard. But, knowing he's not right for her, I don't even feel a hint of remorse for this. If she wants to date, she should at least choose guys who are in the ballpark of being worthy of her.

They arrive just after eight. She's come straight from the office—I recognise the navy blue suit she's wearing. I know it well. The lining is pale grey, like silver. She's teamed it with a camisole that drapes to reveal her cleavage. She takes the jacket off and places it over the back of the chair, which he holds out for her. She's not wearing a bra. Fuck. My body tightens with desire, a need to hold her close and be with her. Angus's eyes linger on her breasts and I want to punch him. As if he has any right to even occupy the same airspace as Asha.

Her hair is styled into a bun at the nape of her neck. I love it when she wears it loose, long red curls falling down her back like a waterfall made of flame. Angus lifts his hand imperiously and a waiter appears at their table. Angus presumably cracks a joke because Asha laughs and my eyes narrow. She can't seriously be into this guy? He's wearing skinny jeans that finish about an inch higher than his ankle with brogues and no socks. Hipster alert.

Something primal tips inside of me. I want to stalk to the table and lift Asha up, throw her over my shoulder and drag her back to my place, tie her to the bed and drive her wild in all the ways I know she loves best. I don't. I throw the Scotch back then tap the glass, silently requesting a refill.

I didn't come here tonight with a firm plan in

mind. I thought it would be fun, a bit of a joke, but watching some other guy do his best to charm the pants off Asha is, it turns out, far from entertaining. What the hell is she thinking, dating someone like this? Don't get me wrong, she's a free agent. I've never had any interest in pushing commitment on her. The very idea makes my skin crawl. But if I'm going to give up the best sex I've ever had, it's not going to be so she can go out with some kind of painfully trendy heir to a tyre factory fortune. I bet this guy has never even had to make his own bed. Asha will be ridiculously bored by him.

I have no choice but to make her see reason. I grin to myself as I stand, imagining all the ways I can torture her body into submission, and place my credit card on the bar as I prepare to slip out the side entrance. I can't say why but I take one last look at their table at the exact moment Asha lifts her head. Perhaps there's something in my movement that's familiar or maybe it's just a coincidence but she turns towards me and our eyes lock.

Surprise flexes her face and then there's fury, her lips tightening as she glares at me.

Okay, she's pissed off. I guess, seeing it from her side, I probably shouldn't have come here. But, seriously, this guy is a waste of her time. No harm, no foul.

I'm not really surprised when she texts me an hour later.

WT actual F, Theo?

Okay. She's still pissed off. I don't want to go into this via text though so I don't reply immediately. A moment later, my phone buzzes again.

I'm downstairs. Buzz me up.

I reread her message and then stride towards the front door of the penthouse, pressing the button quickly, even as I know it gives me only a few minutes to work out how to play this. Asha's never been angry at me before. We don't really get into any situations that would enable anger. There's no emotion in what we're doing, generally. So this is new for us. I have no idea how she reacts when she's pissed off, nor how likely she is to be calmed down. This is a new side to her and even as I know I have to make this right, I am a little fascinated to see Asha in this frame of mind.

The night is warm, one of those sultry New York evenings that make it easy to remember that the city is built on a swamp. Somewhere between the hotel restaurant and my place she's taken her jacket off and draped it over her arm so all I can think is how much I want to rip that damned camisole off her and erase the lingering hint of Angus's pervy stare.

'I'm so mad at you,' she snaps as a preamble, dropping her handbag inside the door and crossing her arms over her chest.

So, she's hot when she's angry. Her lips are pouting, her cheeks pink, her eyes sparkly. 'Yeah?'

She continues to glare at me but a small frown crosses her lips. She's not wearing lipstick, which is unusual for her. I don't particularly want to think about that waste of space kissing it off her.

'What the hell were you doing there?'

'I wanted to see you on a date.' I shake my head, dragging a hand through my hair. 'I was curious.'

'You had no business showing up—'

'I know that.' My admission momentarily silences her but actually she's right. I crossed a line tonight and I'm surprised I did so. 'I thought it would be funny.'

'Funny?'

It's the wrong thing to say. Her temper spikes and she shoots me a look that is pure venom.

'What, were you jealous or something, Theo? Because we talked about this already.'

'Jealous?' I reject the idea fiercely. How can I be jealous of Asha dating someone when I have no interest in dating her?

'It was just a drink,' she reminds me witheringly, pushing past me into the kitchen.

'He's not right for you.'

She pulls a bottle of wine from the fridge and pours herself a glass. 'You don't know anything about him.'

'I've known hundreds of Angus Fienes in my time, Asha. He'd never make you happy.'

'You don't know that.' But I do and, what's more, I see it in her eyes that she agrees with me. She won't admit it now because she's pissed off with me, but I know she knows I'm right.

I stride into the kitchen and catch her hands, lifting them to my chest. 'You'd always be a trophy to him. You deserve to be with someone who sees you as a person, not just a name.'

She sucks in an indignant breath, her eyes flashing fire with mine. 'I don't even know where to begin with that. First of all, that's one of the reasons I like Angus—there's no way he's into my money. He's rich enough all on his own. I don't think he gives a shit that I'm heir to the Sauvages fortune.'

'Yeah, right.'

Her glare intensifies.

'And secondly, where do you get off telling me who I should be with? What do you care?'

'He's not right for you.'

'Stop saying that!' She takes a gulp of her wine and slams the glass down so hard I'm surprised it doesn't break. 'Damn it, Theo, this is my life.'

I grind my teeth together. 'You're right.' My voice is deep. 'I'm sorry.'

Her eyes widen as she lifts her face to mine. Silence falls around us, prickly and laced with uncertainty. I look down at her face, so beautiful, and I take stock of this situation quickly. It's one of the things I'm best at: summing up the facts and forming a plan of attack.

'You want to meet someone,' I say slowly, thoughtfully. 'And I get that. I'm not going to stand in your way, Ash. We both know we've had a good run but we can't do this for ever.' I grin. 'Well, I could, but we want different things and so, by all means, date. But not pretty boys like Angus.'

The ghost of a smile twitches on her lips and relief shifts through me. Happy Asha I like. 'He's actually really nice.'

I ignore her assertion. 'Nice is fine for about three seconds. You need more than nice. And you sure as hell need more than some spoiled trust fund shit.'

She arches a brow. 'I'm sorry, Mr Hart Dynasty?'

But she doesn't mean it. We both know that my brothers and I, while born with a mass of wealth, have worked our asses off to strengthen our business interests. Trust fund brats we are not.

'Let me help you find someone.'

She snorts and reaches for her wine to drink, shaking her head. When she can speak again, her smile is fully in place and I want to kiss her. Angry Asha is hot but happy Asha is the sexiest woman in the world. 'Erm...no.'

'Why not?'

'Because that's completely creepy.'

'Why?'

'Because we've been sleeping together for six months. It's...weird for you to hook me up with someone.'

'I disagree. I know you intimately. Who else is better placed to play Cupid?'

'And you'd seriously be happy with that?'

I shrug, pleased with this development. There was a tiny part of me that had started to worry about where this was going. Six months of sleeping with one woman is a first for me. I've had lovers for a week or two, but not many. Usually, I'm more of a one- or two-night stand kind of guy. And while I know that nothing will ever shake my distaste for the institution of marriage, it's hard not to worry that the longer we fuck, the more blurred the lines could become. So making this offer, knowing I could help Asha find long-term happiness while walking away whistling, proves to me that I don't feel anything for her besides desire. Which is just the way I like it.

I smile to show her my sincerity. 'Ash, we know what this is, right? I didn't go to the Four Seasons tonight because I was jealous or whatever. I'm not trying to get in your way of dating Angus because I secretly want more with you.' I scan her face for any sign of reaction to my words, but she shows me none. Even better. 'I just think you can do so much better. And I want you to be happy. That matters to me.' And it really does.

That's a first for me too. I've never been with a woman I actually cared about. Don't judge me—I'm following in my father's footsteps, apparently, but at least I'm not stupid enough to marry any of them.

'I just think…'

I lift a finger to her lips, silencing her. 'Listen.' She bites the pad of my finger so I drop my hand and flick one of her nipples. She draws in a shuddering breath. A rush of power shifts through me.

An idea shapes within me, almost perfect in its simplicity. We need to put a stop point on what we're doing. It has to end soon because, while I completely trust my own ability to stick to our rules, I worry sometimes that Asha could mistake what we're doing for more, and I don't want that. I don't want to hurt her. It would kill me to do that.

'My brother's getting married in a month. Why don't you come to the wedding? There'll be a bunch of great guys there, friends of ours, any of whom would be a better fit for you than Angus Fienes.'

Her eyes narrow imperceptibly. 'And you'd seriously be okay with that?'

I shrug. 'Why not? This has to end some time.'

I can't fathom her expression. Her eyes are the most magnificent shade of green but they darken so they're almost grey when she looks at me, a hint of something in their depths, and then she smiles, a teasing smile. 'No stalking at the Four Seasons?'

I lift my fingers. 'Scout's Honour.'

'No way were you a Boy Scout.'

'True, but I mean it.'

She considers this for a moment. 'What about you?'

'I'll be happy for you.'

She's quiet as she mulls this over. 'And then what? Find someone else to do this with?'

'Maybe.' I grin but, in all honesty, the idea of sleeping with another woman holds very little appeal. Yet. I know that will come, in time. It's just that when Asha's in the room my libido has no room for anyone else. 'I'll cross that bridge when I get to it.'

She pulls away from me to sip her wine. 'You were wrong tonight.'

'I know. It was a bit of a dick move.'

Her eyes hold mine. 'A bit?'

I know that look in her eyes. It pulls at me like an invisible string. 'Can I make it up to you?'

'What do you have in mind?'

My laugh is throaty. 'Things that are better shown than described.'

'Oh?' She places the wineglass down more gently now.

'From the minute you walked into the bar, I have been wanting to do this.' I close the distance between us and fist her camisole, pushing it up her body quickly. She lifts her hands so I can sweep it over her head and toss it away from us. It's a warm night but the penthouse is climate controlled, cool and comfortable, and her nipples tighten in response to the air.

She lifts a finger to my chest, holding me at a distance, and there's a line between her brows. I still, waiting for her to say whatever's on her mind, even when my body is thrumming with need.

'You're sure about this?'

I'm surprised to find myself hesitating, as though the words are blocked inside of me, so I grin to dispel that. 'One more month then I'll play Cupid myself. Deal?'

She pulls back to look at me, her eyes flashing with something I don't recognise. 'Deal. Now show me how sorry you are, Theo Hart.'

It's almost dawn and I know I should go. I've never slept the night at his place and I don't plan on sleeping here now. He's asleep, though. I can't say I blame him. For hours he 'apologised' to me, using his clever mouth, hands and impressive cock, until my body was trembling from the number of orgasms he'd given me.

I was livid when I left the Four Seasons. L-I-V-I-D. I mean, we'd discussed this and, even though I had misgivings, I went along on the date because Theo and I had agreed it made sense. And sure, my misgivings had grown once Angus met me outside the bar. I think his appeal at Caroline's party had been that he was a lifeline in the midst of an event I really would have preferred not to be attending at all. Still, he *is* a nice guy, just not my cup of tea, and none of that is Theo's business.

He and I are so black and white in what we're doing. And yet, deep down, I'm starting to worry that maybe we're not.

All I could think as I sat across from Angus, watching him flirt with me, was that it was *wrong*.

Wrong on every level. To Angus, to Theo, to me.
I'm a transparent person. I like to say what I think
and do as I feel, and dating one guy while my body
craves another just isn't my jam.

Lesson learned.

But, at the same time, this thing with Theo needs
to stop. *This has to end some time.* He said it, and
he was completely right. He's like quicksand and,
despite the boundaries we've put in place, I can feel
every spare second drawing me towards him. It's
not like I have much spare time and there are other
things and people who should be getting some of it.

I shift in the bed, pushing up on one elbow so I
can see him better. My pulse fires in my veins at his
familiar, addictive face. I ache to lean forward and
drop a kiss to his lips, but he's so peaceful that I don't.

He mentioned his brother's wedding a while back.
The idea of going to it with him is interesting. I need
to think it through a little before I commit. After all,
it will be a family affair and we're not a real couple.
It would be kind of out of place for me to attend.
Then again, people take dates to weddings all the
time. It's not like anyone there needs to know we're
just fucking.

It's a month away. I have time to consider this.

But, one way or another, that wedding is now
our line in the sand. He suggested it, and at first I
was shocked, but the more I think about it, the more
sense it makes.

The thing is, I really do want a normal life one

day. I didn't get to know my mom, and my dad never got over losing her. I always felt like a huge part of me, of my family, was missing, and I guess I want to know what it feels like to be whole again, to be part of a family that isn't damaged and grieving.

And Theo-Sexual-Quicksand-Hart ticks enough boxes that, if I'm not careful, I'll never look for anything beyond this. I'll be sixty with a red-hot career and a fabulous fuck buddy but no husband and no kids, no grandkids, no family.

This has to end and the fact we've set the date for that relaxes me. It's a kind of safety net, making it impossible for me to want more than we've got. Simple.

I pull away from the bed, grab my clothes and slink into the next room. I dress silently, risking one last peek at his sleeping figure before I go. He's smiling and he's hard. Good, he's going to hate waking up and finding me gone...

In the kitchen, I paint my lips with Garnet and press a perfect red kiss to a piece of paper near his fridge, then write:

You were too beautiful to wake. See you soon.

I hail a cab as I step out onto the pre-dawn streets of Manhattan, slipping into the back seat, closing my eyes and replaying a night that went from bad to magnificent. I was furious when I arrived but he unpicked my anger, piece by piece, until I felt only pleasure.

A few hours later, I wake to a text.

You got home all right?

My heart turns over in my chest. It's something he always does and it always makes me smile. I don't know why he thinks he needs to check, given I'm twenty-eight and have therefore spent a large portion of my life fending for myself, but his consciousness of my safety fills me with something warm and gooey.

Except it's just Theo. Part of having a God complex is convincing yourself you're somehow responsible for the safety of every mortal who crosses your path. He'll be like this with whoever he's sleeping with after me, he's no doubt been like it with every woman he slept with before me—it's not about me and it's not about us, that's just him.

Yep. How'd you sleep?

Three dots appear to indicate he's typing.

I thought you'd still be here when I woke up.

I bite down on my lip.

Sorry. Places to be, people to see etc. You know what it's like when you're busy and important.

So glad you could squeeze me into your schedule at all then.

Well, a girl has needs...

Yes, yes, you do. Speaking of which...

I wait, staring at the screen as the little dots keep dancing. It feels like it's taking him a long time to finish his message.

The wedding is in thirty-one days, in Sydney. I have to be there a few days beforehand, and I'm not back till the middle of this week. So we have about twenty-four days left. I know we don't usually see each other more than a couple of times a week but for the next month consider me fully at your disposal. Any time you have 'needs', I'm up for it.

My lips lift.

That's very generous of you.

Generosity has nothing to do with it. My offer is completely self-serving.

I smile, pushing out of bed, weary but energised all at once.

Ah, I see. Are you saying you'd like *me* to be fully at *your* disposal for the next month?

Caught red-handed.

I smile again.

If only we didn't both have full-time jobs...

If only we were both the boss...

He has a point. When was the last time I didn't work a long, exhausting day?
I don't reply and a moment later my phone buzzes.

I fly back Wednesday. I'll come to yours.

No question, no invitation, just a bald statement of his intentions. But I smile because I'm glad, and I smile because I'm happy.

Have fun in Sydney.

Then, a moment later:

But not too much fun.

Without you? Never.

CHAPTER FOUR

I HAVE A hangover to end all hangovers—I blame Holden for leading me astray—but wild horses wouldn't keep me from Asha. I knock on her apartment door, check my phone for emails and then slip it into my back pocket, right as she opens the door.

She's wearing a bright maxi dress, strapless, and her red hair is piled high on her head in a topknot.

'Hey.'

She grins. I volley it back.

'How was Australia?'

'Ridgey-didge.' I do my best Australian accent. She laughs.

'Glad to hear it.' She steps back, sweeping a hand wider. 'Come on in.'

I don't need to be asked twice. The bachelor party was pretty tame—no strippers, on Jagger's insistence. 'Grace would hate it and, to be honest, so would I.'

We played golf at the course Jagger bought about a year ago, had a few drinks, swam, played some more golf, and that was it. Or it should have been, but when we got back to Sydney Holden managed to pull me into his one-man destruction show, and I woke up feeling like I'd eaten an ashtray and drunk a brewery. I'm surprised I can still stand. The flight was good though—twenty-four hours of sleep and rehydrating so now I feel almost human again.

Ready for anything, I reach for Asha but she presses a hand to my chest. 'I'm starving.'

I lift a brow teasingly.

'For food,' she drawls. 'I haven't eaten all day.'

I look at my watch. 'It's seven o'clock.'

'I know. I had back-to-back meetings and then...' She trails off, a frown on her face.

'And then?' I prompt.

'Nothing.' She waves a hand in the air. 'Work stuff.'

We don't really talk about our lives. Not in depth. She's pushing the subject away out of habit, but I'm curious. In some way, knowing that we've set the date to end this has liberated me from our usual rules. I don't care how much I know about her now— one way or another this will end come the wedding, so what's the harm in talking to her properly? It doesn't change anything—it just makes us friends with benefits. Yeah, friends. What's wrong with that?

I put my hands on her shoulders, rubbing them slowly, her little sigh a pleasure that fills my soul. 'You're stressed?'

'A little.'

'Because...?'

'Just work stuff. Launching a new line, you know.'

'Sounds like kind of a big deal?'

'Kind of.' She reaches for my hand and weaves her fingers through mine then pulls me towards the kitchen. I pass the cookbooks I noticed last time I was here. 'I made pasta.' She nods towards something that smells impossibly good. 'You hungry?'

'I wasn't.' I grin.

Her pleasure at my compliment is unmistakable and it warms me.

'Grab a bowl. Behind you, beside the fridge.'

I pull two out and hand them to her and, despite the fact dinner is cooking, I can't resist pulling her closer, pressing a kiss to her lips. She tastes like vanilla and butter, all sweet and creamy. I ache to strip that dress from her body and taste her all over.

'So your brother obviously doesn't share your disdain for the institution of marriage?' She pulls away from me, scooping pasta into two bowls then sprinkling some freshly grated Parmesan on top. There's a bottle of white wine on the counter; she fills two glasses then hands one to me. I look around at the bench, but she shakes her head.

'Through there. It's nice out; let's sit on the terrace.'

I didn't even realise she had one—shows how much attention I've paid to the place. Through the living room, a pair of sliding glass doors open onto a deck that has a couple of sun loungers and an outdoor setting.

'It's no infinity pool,' she teases, sitting in one of the chairs, curling a leg beneath her.

I take the seat opposite, the view of Manhattan at dusk setting off Asha's unconventional beauty.

She spears a piece of pasta, her eyes holding mine. She's waiting for me to say something. That's right, she asked about Jagger and marriage.

'I think Jagger's a reformed man,' I posit thoughtfully. 'He's had his time as a marriage hater, like the rest of us.'

'But then he met—what did you say her name is?'

'Grace.' I smile, thinking of the Australian woman who didn't just steal Jagger's heart; she stitched it right back together again. I ease back in the chair, pretty sure this moment is as perfect as any could ever be—a warm summer evening, a beautiful woman, delicious food and wine, and the certainty that sex is on the horizon…easy, uncomplicated sex. 'Yeah, he met Grace, did his best to fuck it up and then went out of his way to fix it.'

She sips her wine. 'Sounds complicated.'

'Not really.' I shrug. 'She's perfect for him, just took Jagger a while to realise it—bonehead that he is.'

'Where are they having the wedding?'

'On the yacht.'

'Your brother's?'

'Yeah. It's not a huge ceremony. Sixty or so people—just how they wanted it.'

She places her fork on the table, her eyes spearing me with a warning. 'Theo, I can't possibly come if it's so intimate…'

My eyes narrow, her words the last thing I want to hear. As far as I've considered it, it's a done deal. 'I've already told them you're my guest. They'll be disappointed if you back out.'

'Disappointed?' She quirks a brow in that sexy, cynical little way of hers. 'They don't even know me.'

'But they know you're my date and, given I have a long-established hatred for the institution of dating, let's just say they're all a little curious about you.'

'But we're *not* dating.' She looks shocked.

I can't help but be amused by this. About six months ago, *Forbes* ran a piece about my brothers and me—'Hartbreakers'. Clever, right?

The gist of it was that Jagger was the sensible one whereas Holden and I were wild and untameable, cast in the image of our father—that went down well, obviously. You can imagine the words used to describe us—*bad-boy bachelors, determinedly single, rakes*—as though we were some kind of construct of a Dickens novel. Apparently women are 'tripping over themselves' to land a Hart.

But Asha isn't.

It's why this works so well. From the beginning she's been completely happy to keep this light and simple. I've never been with a woman who's so receptive to the lack of emotional complication I want. Nonetheless, her look of abject horror at the mere suggestion we're dating sparks amusement and, yeah, it knocks my ego a little, sure.

I shrug nonchalantly. 'It seemed a little more acceptable than going into details about our arrangement. Besides, I didn't think you'd like me introducing you as a friend with benefits.'

'Is that what we are?'

I grin. 'Something like that.'

Her mesmerising eyes are locked to mine, amusement and scepticism flashing in them. 'Somehow I doubt your brothers could be so easily shocked.'

She's right, of course. 'I'm a gentleman; what can I say?'

A smirk crosses her lips. 'You are very far from that, Theo Hart.'

Sparks fly from me to her, so warmth arcs around the terrace.

'Besides, you want me to come to this wedding to meet friends of yours, right? So what if I get chatting to some guy and end up dating them, or even marrying them? You don't think that will strike your family as odd?'

Something shifts inside of me. It feels a little like indigestion. I suggested this to Asha. I mean, if Angus and I are the kind of men she goes for, then she clearly doesn't have the best judgement. I mean, he's no way near good enough for her and I'm the most commitment-phobic guy in the universe.

'They'll think I wouldn't commit and you found someone who would. Or that I fucked it up somehow.' I grin. 'Believe me when I tell you that one of my relationships ending abruptly is not going to spark even a hint of surprise from any of my family.'

Curiosity crosses her features. She's weighing up her words, wondering how to ask whatever it is she's thinking. It's at this point I realise this is our first time sharing a meal together. We've feasted on delivery burgers in bed once or twice, when hunger has driven us to make contact with the outside world, but usually we're not together long enough to span a proper meal. It's more of a wham, bam, you're the best sex ever ma'am, kind of affair.

This, eating across from Asha, is different, and I notice new things about her. Like how long and elegant her fingers are, how neatly manicured are her nails. How she holds her fork mid-air as she speaks, as though she's the conductor and I'm the orchestra.

'Have you always been so anti-relationships?'

I focus my gaze on the view, a frown tightening my jaw. I don't know why but I don't particularly know how to answer the question.

'Have you always been such a great cook?' I volley back, shifting my gaze to hers.

She hesitates a moment. 'It was either that or starve.'

I lean back in my chair, silently encouraging her to continue.

'My dad couldn't cook to save his life. When we were young, we had a nanny, Mrs Bessington—Bessie. We loved her. But when she retired Dad didn't get around to hiring anyone else and suddenly the home-cooked snacks disappeared...'

'So it was sink or swim?'

'Cook or starve,' she corrects me with a wink.

'Who raised you then?'

She tilts her head to the side. 'We went away to school, and in the holidays Dad made an effort to be around.'

'Made an effort?' I prompt, curious at that.

Her smile doesn't sit quite right on her face, like her muscles are working too hard to hold it in place. 'He's always worked really long hours. I must get my insane work ethic from him,' she jokes, reaching for her wine and sipping it. 'But I guess you know a thing or two about that.'

I don't particularly want to discuss my father. 'Where did you go to school?'

'Felton Academy until I was thirteen, then I went to France for a couple of years, to a boarding school in the Loire Valley. My great-grandmother was a student there, so it's sort of a tradition,' she murmurs, spearing another piece of pasta. 'Dad's really into all that stuff.' I suspect her eyes are itching to roll heavenward.

'Did you like it?'

She laughs. 'I liked it but I'm not so sure it liked me.'

'No?'

'My rebellious phase.' She pulls her dress down a little—not far enough for my liking—to reveal the top of her breast, where a familiar line of ink is scrawled. It's cursive script and I could duplicate the text in my sleep, though I've never asked what it means.

'It's French?'

'Mmm.'

'What does it say?'

'Cendres en cendres toujours.'

Her accent is perfect. How come I didn't realise she spoke French before? Because this is probably the longest conversation we've ever had that hasn't also involved nudity—which has the habit of switching my brain off.

'Ashes to ashes, always,' she elaborates.

'Ashes to ashes? Around the time you became Asha?'

Her smile is lopsided. 'It's tragic, right?'

I laugh. 'There are worse ways to rebel.'

She runs her finger over the tattoo, a faraway look in her eyes. 'I felt so damned liberated. My boyfriend at the time did this.' She laughs softly. 'It's not as random as it sounds—he was training to become a tattooist and working with one of the best inkers in Paris. But it hurt like a mother trucker, believe me.'

I like the tattoo a little less now I know its provenance.

'But you'd know.' She nods towards my chest, where I have my own collection of ink.

'I was way too drunk to feel mine.'

'Oh, tough guy, huh?' Her laugh is like music dancing through my veins.

'Absolutely.'

'What does it say?'

'You showed me yours so I show you mine?'

'A PG version of that,' she quips.

'I think I prefer R-rated.'

'Same. Soon.' Promise sizzles between us. My cock is so hard against my pants I have to shift a bit in the seat.

I lift my shirt over my head, loving the way her eyes drop to my bare chest as though she can't help it. The tattoo is actually on my biceps so it's a gratuitous chest-reveal but I'm becoming increasingly impatient for Asha and I'm willing to play dirty to move things along.

Ποσειδώνας

'It's beautiful.'

'My chest?'

She shoots me a look of exasperation. 'And the tattoo.' She shakes her head a little from side to side and a tendril of her red hair waves against her cheek. I lean forward and catch it, tucking it behind her ear. She stills, her eyes hooking to mine, her pupils huge, her lips parted. Fuck, wanting her is going to be the end of me.

'One summer Dad engaged a tennis coach for Joshua and me. He was Greek, and super nice. He tried to teach us the alphabet but it might as well have been Sanskrit for all the sense it made. What does it say?'

Great. Now I'm imagining Asha in a tiny white tennis dress, her tanned legs all long and athletic as she runs across the court. My dick is actually painful with how hard it is.

'Poseidon.'

Her lips curve upwards. 'Like the Greek god of war?'

'That's Ares. Poseidon is the Greek god of the sea, water. Earthquakes.' I laugh.

'Is Poseidon somehow significant to you?'

'I'm Poseidon,' I deadpan.

'God complex much?'

I laugh. 'You're saying you don't think I'm a Greek god?'

She lifts her brows. 'Do *you* think you're a Greek god?'

'Hey, some women in the past might have called me—'

She shakes her head, reaching for her wine. 'Yeah, yeah, I'm sure you've had lots of women in the past say lots of things to inflate your ego. Go back to the tattoo. Or did some ex-girlfriend of yours call you Poseidon? Possy?'

My laugh is a growl. 'No.'

'You sure? It kind of suits you, Possy.'

'Stop it, Charlotte.' My voice holds a warning, but I'm only kidding.

She sips her wine, her eyes sparking with mine.

Hell, she's sexy. 'All that happens when you call me Charlotte is that you remind me of my brother, and that significantly reduces the likelihood of us having sex. Just FYI.'

'Duly noted.' Her tone is light but I know her well enough now to know there's something more beneath it.

'It was a dare.'

'The tattoo?'

'Yeah.'

'A dare from who?'

'Holden. My brother.' I gloss over the complexity of our situation, not wanting to think about the bombshell that exploded through our lives last year, nor the fact he's still reeling from it.

We all are.

'He calls you Poseidon?'

'I run our shipping business, our maritime construction, all the water stuff,' I say with a lift of my shoulders, enjoying the way her eyes follow the movement. 'Jagger's Zeus—god of the skies, because he runs our construction side. High-rises.'

She makes a cooing noise. 'This is adorable.'

I picture Jagger and Holden in my mind and try to imagine any circumstances in the world that would justify the three of us being called 'adorable'. I can't come up with any. Hell, we're the exact opposite of that.

'What's Holden's tattoo?'

My frown is reflexive. 'Hades.'

'As in hell?'

'It was his idea.' I think back to that weekend—Jagger's twenty-first—and how drunk we all were. How Holden suggested the tattoos and casually mentioned he'd be Hades. 'He runs our casinos; he used to joke that gambling was the devil's work, so...'

'Used to?'

I look at her and feel a pull to be honest with her, to confide in her exactly what a shit show the last year of Holden's life has been. But instead I shake my head. 'Still does, I guess.'

She pushes back from her chair, moving around the table towards me, perching her butt on the edge. Her fingertips trail my other biceps, where there's a more elaborate tattoo. She picks out the trident, and the wave that's washing over it. 'And here are more signs of the ocean.'

But she's so damned close and that dress is still lower than it should be. I lift my fingers up and curve them into the fabric, pulling it down completely to reveal her breasts. She smiles; there's not a hint of awkwardness in her face—and why would there be? We've seen each other naked enough times to be completely familiar with each other's bodies. It doesn't change the effect her bare breast has on me though; my blood is like fire inside me.

'You're still eating.' She looks down at my bowl, half-full.

'You're finished though, right?'

She nods slowly and moves, lifting one leg so

she's straddling me. Her hands drop to my pants, working the button and zip. I have to shift a little to give her better access, but then her fingertips brush the tip of my cock and I bite back a curse. Relief is all-consuming. She frees me from my pants, running her nails over my length, her eyes hooked to mine with a look that is faintly mocking, like she knows how crazy I am for her right now.

'Got any protection?'

'No, I came over completely unprepared. Sorry.' I reach into my back pocket and lift out a long string of foil squares.

She laughs at my sarcasm, but it's husky and summer's breeze carries it away. 'Ambitious?'

'Desperate,' I correct, ripping the top off one square and sliding it over my length. 'And presumptuous?'

'No. Spot on.' She pulls her dress up and it's only as she eases herself onto my length that I appreciate she's not wearing any underwear. Christ.

She's so tight; her muscles squeeze me and I grind my teeth together in an attempt to keep some kind of grip on my willpower because, right now, I could actually just hold her hips low on me and spill myself into her. Two thrusts of my dick and I'd be done. But I don't want that.

Hell, I've been fantasising about this for nights now and I want it to last.

She sits on my lap and I lean forward, tracing one of her nipples lightly with my tongue, causing her to make a keening noise low in her throat. I circle the dusky pink aureole of her flesh, cupping her other breast in the palm of my hand as I rock my hips, pushing deeper inside her. She moves up and down my length in small movements and I lift a hand to the back of her head, drawing her mouth down, kissing her hard, tasting wine and dinner in her mouth, aching to taste all of her.

She makes a moaning noise and I know it's a precursor to her orgasm, and fuck, I want to feel her come more than I want just about anything on earth. My tongue duels with hers in time with my cock and she's so tight around me, her muscles squeezing me until I can barely breathe, then she explodes and it's the most unbearable form of torture.

Her muscles spasm around my length. I hold her right where she is and, before she can regain her breath, I begin to move again and curve my hand around her butt, running my fingers across the crease there so she trembles a little in my lap. I shift my attention to her other nipple, this time sucking it in my mouth hard, pressing my teeth to the tip so she tilts her head back, crying out. My fingers at her rear push against her, teasing her with the promise of my complete possession.

I feel her muscles tightening again and she's rolling her hips desperately, her lips crying my name towards the sky, her body covered in goosebumps. I move back to her other breast and subject it to the same torture, rougher, harder, my teeth gliding over the sensitive tip until she's incandescent. My hand on her butt lifts up and comes back in a slap that has her crying out, my name on her lips tortured as she arches her back.

Fuck, she's so beautiful. I shove my plate aside so her back can connect properly with the table and I can see her better. Her dress is ruched over her flat stomach and her breasts are two perfect peaks. I fondle them hungrily with my hands and jerk my hips to drive my cock deeper inside of her.

She writhes, pleasure making her body frantic, frantic in a way I am completely hooked on, but it's not enough. I'm riding a wave of torturous desire. I could come at any point but I don't want to yet. I don't want to. Instead, I drop a hand to her clit and rub my fingers over her flesh, moving inside her while I stimulate that cluster of nerves.

She's swearing and crying out and I know how close she is, how wild she is. I want to taste her. It's not enough to feel her. With a guttural oath, I pull my sheathed length from her body. Her cries of protest are music to my ears—I can't be the only one driven to the edge of sanity by our coming together.

'Don't you dare stop,' she moans.

'Believe me, I don't intend to.'

I push her legs wider apart and bring my mouth to her sex so she bucks against me, her legs quivering. I hold her still, pushing at her thighs to keep them spread as I run my tongue over her length, tasting her and tormenting her until she's right back where she was, passion exploding through her.

'Please, please, Theo. God, please.'

I move my tongue deeper and then suck her tangle of nerves into my mouth and she whimpers and twists so I have to hold her thighs harder. I feel her surrender, I taste her climax and I don't stop, even as she's tumbling over the edge. It's torture, I know, but the very best kind. She rides wave after wave, her body trembling, her voice shaking, and I don't stop because in this moment all I want is this, and all she needs is me.

She's so wet, so completely wet, and my own restraint is at breaking point. She lies against the table, propped on her elbows, and fixes me with a flushed stare. 'So you're back?'

My laugh is husky. 'Apparently.'

She's moving then, bringing her body back to mine, and I wait for her to straddle me once more, to take me deep inside her, but instead she shifts off the side of the table and stands a little shakily beside me. Her eyes hold a challenge as she grips my legs and pulls me towards her. I'm big, she's not, and there's no way she'd be strong enough to move me without my help, so I do as she's asking and angle my body.

Her eyes still hold mine as she reaches between us and unfurls the condom. I frown briefly, but then she's kneeling between my legs, still looking at me as she opens her mouth and takes my cock so deep I hitch at the back of her throat.

Breath hisses from between my lips. I dig my fingers into my thighs, unable to wrench my eyes away from her as she moves her warm, wet mouth up and down my length, her eyes on mine, her possession so complete, so fucking great, that I see stars and unicorns and rainbows and pixies. Her mouth on me is heaven. Bliss. Nirvana. I tilt my head back, staring up at the dusky sky, my control slipping with every movement of her mouth.

'I'm so close, Asha,' I groan, my fingers reaching for her shoulders. She pauses at my tip, then pulls her mouth off. I reach for my cock on autopilot but she bats my hand away.

'I want you to come.'

'I'm going to.'

'Now.' And her mouth is back on me, moving up and down, my tip brushing the back of her throat, her mouth squeezing me so tight, and my hands curl around her shoulders gently now, holding on as I feel myself start to spill into her.

'Fuck, are you sure?'

Her eyes hold a warning and then she smiles around my length. I don't think there's ever been a sexier sight than this. I'm so glad she's smiled because I seriously doubt I could stop myself now. I thrust once and groan as I come hard—I'm no longer looking at the dusky sky, I'm flying through it, soaring towards the outer atmosphere. I am no longer a man, I'm something else entirely and that's all because of Asha.

I stare upwards for so long, savouring this, committing it to the banks of memory that are inviolable to time, then slowly I draw my gaze back to her, my chest tightening at the sight of her right there between my legs.

She moves her mouth then pulls away, her tongue tracing my tip one last time before she offers me the sexiest grin I can imagine and stands, her breasts still beautifully naked.

'That was…unexpected.' My voice is deep.

'Was it?' she teases, winking at me as she reaches for her dress, pulling it back up. I watch, reluctant to lose my view of her flesh.

'It was also brilliant.'

She laughs. 'So I gather.'

I stare at her, my world shifting, desire burning my veins from the inside out. The sun is still high enough in the sky to cast light and I'm glad. There's a whole night ahead of us and I intend to make the most of it. We have a finite quantity of nights like this left. The thought is almost enough to sober me, but then memories of what she just did are strong and I smile, because it's better to have had inexplicably great sex and lost it than never to have enjoyed something like this at all, right?

CHAPTER FIVE

HE'S GONE WHEN my alarm wakes me, but my bed smells of him and the ghost of his body's possession wraps around me, making me smile, making my limbs throb and my pulse gallop. I stretch then push out of bed, padding into the kitchen in search of coffee.

My day is crazy busy. I have back-to-back meetings and I'm glad because when I'm busy it's easier to keep thoughts of Theo at bay. I have to—my job demands that of me, and I don't let anything come between me and my work.

Too many people depend on me, but it's not as simple as that. There's only one person I give a shit about proving wrong, and that's my dad.

I tilt my chin in a silent gesture of defiance, focusing across the boardroom table, listening to my Asian-Pacific Sales Director's presentation.

'Luxury sales are down globally,' I murmur.

'But you'll see we're defying that in our region,' she prompts, shifting to a different slide. 'We've had solid growth and our latest point of sale research shows that consumers are migrating from rival companies owing to a perception of greater quality and value. We're seeing excellent growth in Asia Pacific, Australia in particular.'

I nod, pleased, and cross my legs beneath the table. Fire bursts inside me, desire almost impossible to ignore. Out of nowhere, I remember the way we made love on the terrace and I ache for Theo all over again. It takes every inch of my willpower to keep my mind in the moment, to focus on what we're discussing. An hour later, I have five minutes to myself and I check my phone.

There's a message from him. My pulse fires as I click into it.

Do you like Korean barbecue?

I pull a face, but a smile is twitching at the corners of my lips.

I do. Are you conducting a survey or is this an invitation?

Both. I'll correlate the data and get back to you.

My next meeting arrives before I can reply. It's three more hours before I'm done and I reach for my phone on autopilot, right as a text pops in from Theo.

I'm downstairs.

I frown.

I'm still at work.

I know. I'm downstairs from your office.

My heart-rate accelerates. I hover my finger over the keypad.

Why?

I can practically hear him laughing.

IDK...the scenery?

Now it's my turn to laugh.

If concrete's your thing...

You're my thing. Get your butt down here.

My heart slams into my ribs. I jam a stack of papers into my handbag, thinking guiltily of the fact I should definitely be reading them now instead of flirting with my fuck buddy via text message.

And definitely instead of skiving out of the office an hour or so before I should leave, just because he's downstairs and wanting to go to Korean barbecue...

I shoulder my way out of the office, flicking the lights off then calling to my assistant, 'I've got a thing. I'll see you tomorrow.'

Kevin—who is unswervingly organised and one hundred per cent the reason I can get as much done in a day as I do—frowns. 'I don't have anything in your diary...'

'It's personal.' My smile is tight and at his look of undisguised curiosity I shake my head. 'Just a thing with a friend. I'll see you in the morning.'

His disappointment is obvious. Apparently he was hoping I had some sort of romantic assignation. And even though I kind of do, I'm definitely not prepared to tell Kevin—or anyone else that. I imagine Kevin's reaction to the news I've been sleeping with the same guy for six months. He would have no end of questions and I know instinctively I'd struggle to have answers to any of them.

No, it's not serious. Yes, I know six months is a long time. Because he's not into relationships and I've spent a lifetime trying to make one man love me; there's no way I'd ever be stupid enough to sign up to that again.

But this isn't—and never has been—about love. It's not about me loving him, and certainly not about him loving me. I've finally learned that expecting nothing of anyone makes life a heck of a lot easier. The elevator whooshes to the lobby. I stride across it with my head bent, sweeping out of the sliding doors into the small drive-through area. I realise once I emerge that I've never been in his car. I scan the bays, trying to guess which it would be, then a light comes on in a sleek black SUV and he's stepping out of the driver's door, walking towards me with his trademark masculinity and confidence. He's breathtaking and, indeed, my breath bursts out of me.

'Hey.' My voice is croaky. He nods, reaching for my over-stuffed handbag, taking its hefty weight from my shoulder before putting a hand in the small of my back.

We walk side by side to the car and it's so strange because for the briefest moment it almost feels like a date. It's not, and I rush to remind myself of that, to hold onto the reality of what we are, of what I want from him.

Sex. Lots of sex. As much as possible in the next month.

No, not quite a month; it's less than that now. I ignore the blade that presses into my side.

'How did your Korean barbecue poll turn out?'

He opens the door for me. 'Two of two respondents answered favourably.'

'Wow. A one hundred per cent success rate: impressive.'

He grins, leaning into the car once I'm seated and kissing me—quickly but as though he can't help it. I smile against his mouth, curve a hand around the back of his head and hold him right where he is, deepening the kiss, sliding my tongue into his mouth to tangle with his.

His hand rests on my knee and I squirm a little, wanting him to touch me higher, needing him in a way that is almost painful.

His laugh is throaty and he breaks away from me with a small shake of his head. 'Click in, Asha.' He shuts the door and I pout because I don't love the way he was so easily able to back away from me. Not when my insides are quivering with renewed desire.

But I buckle my seat belt in place and shift my body towards the driver's seat, so when he steps into it I'm facing him. He revs the engine to life and it throbs beneath us, quiet but resonant.

'Where are we going?'

'I know a place in the Village.'

'I'll bet you do.' I cross one leg over the other and feel his eyes shift to me, to my legs, and my heart rate accelerates.

'Eyes forward, mister.'

He grins, his gaze meeting mine for just long enough to create sparks in the car and then he's looking forward again, driving effortlessly through the streets of Manhattan—something I have only attempted when absolutely necessary. I'm a good driver but these streets are such a rat race and I'd rather use my car time to get work done.

Still, there's something incredibly sexy about the way he controls the car and navigates traffic, and I find myself watching him with growing curiosity.

After about ten minutes, he pulls up at traffic lights and keeps his head forward. 'If you keep looking at me like that, I'm going to pull this car over and drag you into whatever bush I can find.'

Despite the sexy imagery, I keep my response light. 'I'm afraid there aren't a lot of shrubs around.'

'The sidewalk would do just fine.'

I laugh. 'I don't think so.'

'Then stop staring at me like you want to rip my clothes off.'

'How do you know how I'm looking at you? You're concentrating on the road, remember?'

'Something that's increasingly difficult to do,' he mutters, but when he briefly flicks his gaze to me I see the hint of a grin on his lips. My chest tightens.

Silence falls, the lights change and he drives on.

'What time did you leave last night?'

'This morning,' he corrects. 'Around three.'

'So late?'

He makes a throaty noise of assent then turns to look at me. 'You were fast asleep. I didn't want to wake you.'

'You didn't.'

'I'm glad.' He reaches over and briefly puts his hand on my knee. I swallow to bring moisture back to a suddenly dry mouth.

He pulls us into a narrow lane, parking the car halfway up the kerb. I step out and look around. It's dark. He reaches for my hand and pulls me with him, to the end of the lane and around the corner. The restaurant isn't anything like I'd expected—small, intimate, glowing golden in the early evening with a bright orange awning stretching over the footpath. As we approach, the door pulls inwards and a waitress dressed in linen dungarees and a white singlet top grins at us.

'Table for two?'

Theo puts a hand around my waist. 'Yeah. A booth.'

She spins and cuts through the room. 'This way.'

It's smoky inside, a gift from the tables that are each fitted with a barbecue grill. It's busy enough to create the kind of din that fades into white noise. The restaurant itself is rustic and intimate and somehow beautifully authentic.

'Do you come here often?' I look around, taking in the silk wall hangings, covered in brush strokes.

'From time to time.'

I curve one leg under me, propping my elbows on the table.

'You bring dates here?' I suggest, looking around once more. 'That would make sense.'

'Why?'

'It's intimate but out of the way. You're not likely to run into anyone you know. There's no press pack waiting outside.'

He grinned. 'You're wrong on all counts. I come here with my brothers, and only because the food is amazing. You know I'm not the kind of guy who bothers to date.'

His words are said light-heartedly but they set off a reaction inside of me; something shifts in a way that is unpleasant, but I've no idea why.

The waitress appears, bopping along to the music that's playing over the speakers. 'Can I get you something to drink?'

He turns to me. 'Beer? Wine?'

'Whatever you're having. I don't mind.'

He orders a couple of beers and tells the waitress just to bring the chef's selection. I don't think either of us really cares what we eat or drink. We're both seeing this as what it is: preamble. If anything, it's delaying what I really want, which is to get him back into bed as soon as possible. At the same time, there's a sinking sense of inevitability to this, a curiosity and a secret pleasure that comes from sitting across the table from him, preparing to share a meal.

'So you're close to your brothers?' I ask once the waitress has brought the beers and left us alone again.

There's the slightest hesitation before he nods. 'Yeah.'

'Are you the oldest?'

'Nah, youngest.'

'Seriously?'

'Yeah, why?'

'You just seem… I don't know. I guess you seem like a big brother.'

'What does a big brother seem like?'

'Authoritative. Confident. Always in control.'

He hooks his eyes to mine. 'I don't think I'm always in control, Asha. In fact, I have a habit of losing control completely where you're concerned.'

Pleasure bursts through me. 'I like that,' I admit.

'I'm glad.'

I sip my beer.

'Jagger's the oldest—the one who's getting married in a few weeks.' He lifts his own beer, wrapping two fingers and his thumb around the neck and lifting it to his lips. His Adam's apple shifts as he swallows. 'Holden's three months younger than Jagger.'

My eyes flare wider. 'How is that…? So he's…'

Theo places the beer back on the table and moves it around a little, watching the trail of liquid that moves in its wake.

'The by-product of an affair.' His words are clipped and I wonder what he's not saying—I'm sure there's something. Curious, I lean forward without realising I'm doing it.

'Did your mom walk out?'

'Not my mom,' he corrects. 'We all have a different mom, actually.' He lifts his shoulders. 'But yeah, it pretty much ended their marriage. I mean, Holden's living proof of Dad's inability to keep it in his pants so I'd say the writing was on the wall from the moment he turned up.'

'Wow.'

'Yeah.'

'How old was he, when he came to live with you guys?'

'Just a kid still.' He clears his throat and reaches for his beer, rocking it from one hand to the other. There's a sixth sense that keeps me quiet, and my instincts are rewarded when he leans forward a little.

'The thing is, we found out a year ago that he wasn't even my dad's.'

'What?' I frown. 'So why would he take him in? I mean, if you're going to be hanged for the crime…'

'Dad did have an affair with Holden's mom,' he says thoughtfully. 'But it ended months before Holden was conceived. There's no way he could have thought Holden was his son.'

'So why take him in?'

'Holden's mom asked him to,' he says with a lift of his shoulders. 'I think it's the one decent thing my dad did in his life, and he didn't even get that right.'

'I don't know; it seems pretty selfless.'

'Holden was devastated to learn the truth.' He shakes his head angrily. 'All his life he's been raised as a Hart and now to learn that he's not, that the truth of his parentage is lost for ever…'

'He doesn't know who his biological dad is?'

'Nah.' He shakes his head. 'My dad's on the birth certificate and Holden's mom's dead. I know Holden had an investigator looking into it but nothing's really shown up. I think he's accepted he'll never know the truth. Now he just has to work on getting over that.'

I shake my head, trying to imagine how hard that would be.

'It's really knocked him sideways. I keep telling him we're still his brothers, just the same as before, but it's not getting through to him.'

'I get that, though.'

Theo sighs. 'Yeah, I know.' A rueful shake of his head. 'But it doesn't change anything.'

'Not knowing is...' I choose my words carefully, ignoring the slight warning light going off in my brain, because I don't talk about Mom with anyone and I don't really talk to Theo about stuff. Yet my mouth moves, forming words almost without my consent.

'My mom died when I was born.' I drop my eyes to the table because it's easier to talk when he's not seeing right into my soul. 'All I know about her is from my dad and Joshua. Stories, pictures, anecdotes that don't feature me at all. I know I'm like her in some ways,' I murmur, lifting a hand to my hair and toying with it between my fingertips. 'Same complexion and smile.' I let one lift my lips for a moment. 'But nothing like her in others. She's a mystery to me. There are parts of *me* that are a mystery. It's like there's this puzzle inside me that only my mom could have pieced together and because she's not here, because she wasn't here, it will never really be the same.' I swallow, lifting my beer and taking a sip.

He's watching me. I can feel his eyes boring into me and it does something funny to my stomach. I force myself to meet his gaze and try to look normal, like I haven't just ripped a part of myself raw.

'I didn't know you felt like that.'

'It's not a big deal.' I keep my tone light with difficulty. 'I mean, I'm fine. I've had twenty-eight years to get used to not knowing her. I don't really think about it, in fact, but just talking about Holden... I mean, he doesn't have his mom or dad. His whole life as he knew it has been ripped out from under him.'

'But it hasn't.' Theo's words show exasperation. 'Jagger and I were always the biggest part of his life; we're a part of him, and we're still here.'

'Except you're not really,' I insist, reaching across and lacing my fingers through his. 'You helped make him who he is. He's been shaped by you and your brother and your father and all the people who've been a part of his life, but there are facets of himself that he thought to be reflections of your father and now he knows they're not. The biology he took for granted, accepted as a fact, is a lie. More than that, you and Jagger have a bond he'll never truly be a part of.'

He's quiet for a moment, weighing that up, and then he shakes his head. 'That's bullshit.'

'I get why you think so.' I squeeze his fingers and he frowns. 'But, for Holden, he's an outsider now.'

Theo's expression shifts, his eyes swirling with resentment and frustration—both of which I understand.

'You sound like you're speaking from experience.'

I blink, pulling my fingers away, only he holds on tighter, squeezing them in the same way I did a moment ago.

'Not really,' I respond with an attempt at airiness. 'No?'

I shift my head to the side just as a couple take seats at a table a few feet away. I watch as the guy leans towards her and she smiles up at him and I feel

a pang of something in the region of my heart: lone-
liness. I hadn't realised I felt that but, sitting across
from the guy I'm sleeping with, who'll never be more
to me than just sex, makes me realise how much I
want to be in something real, something lasting.

I turn back to Theo to find him staring at me and
my chest tightens.

'You're close to your brother?' he prompts, kicking his feet out beneath the table so they brush
against mine. Despite the seriousness of the conversation, a sensual fog winds around us, predict-
able and inescapable.

'Close is complicated,' I say after a moment. 'But
yeah. We are. I mean, we're like chalk and cheese in
a heap of ways but we're also super similar.'

'And your dad?'

I lift a brow. 'You're hoping to rattle some skel-
etons out of my family closet now?' It's an attempt
to lift the mood.

'I'm just curious.' He doesn't take the bait, doesn't
smile.

I swallow, looking down at our hands—his dark,
mine pale. 'My father's a hard man to be close to,' I
say after a few moments. 'I love him, he's my dad,
but we're not really the "sit around the table and talk
about our day" kind of family. We never have been.'

'Boarding school will do that to you,' he quips,
but with sympathy.

I nod.

'But there's something more,' he prompts when I

don't speak. And I laugh because his ability to see inside me and read my mind is unexpected.

'Why do you say that?'

He grins, a sexy shifting of his lips that makes my heart rate double. 'I can see your cogs turning.'

I shake my head, still laughing softly.

'What? You're holding something back,' he prompts.

'So? That's our deal,' I remind him. 'We don't talk about stuff like this.'

'I've just told you something deeply personal,' he points out.

'Yeah, but that was your choice.' I wink and pull my hand back right as the waitress reappears with a plate of raw meat. She places it between us and presses a button so the grill lights up. Theo stands and moves around the table, coming to sit beside me.

'Easier,' he says, by way of explanation.

I don't complain. I like him being close to me like this. Our thighs brush beneath the table. He uses the tongs to lift a few pieces of meat and places them on the grill. It begins to sizzle and I watch, almost hypnotised by the smell, the smoke, the sound.

'You know—' his voice is low, further drugging my senses '—the fact we know this only has a few more weeks left makes me kind of want to throw the old rules out the window.' His eyes hold mine and I feel in that moment the strength of this man, the charisma and the intelligence. I feel every ounce of his professional success.

'Meaning?'

'I'm curious about this stuff. It doesn't change what we are—sex is sex.'

I nod slowly. I mean, he's right. What am I afraid of? That we'll blur the lines and fall in love? Neither of us is that stupid—we know what we're doing.

I meet his lopsided grin with one of my own and tilt my face forward so our foreheads touch. 'Just remember, when all is said and done, I'm only using you for your insanely hot body.'

He seeks my lips with his. 'Deal.'

Desire flashes inside of me, hot and uncontainable. I'm hungry, but food feels a lot less important than it did a minute ago.

He pulls away and I can see from his eyes that he feels just as I do, that he wishes we were anywhere but here, in this charming, crowded restaurant in the East Village.

He reaches for the chopsticks, wielding them expertly, lifting a piece of cooked beef from the plate and bringing it towards my lips. I part them expectantly and moan as the flavour hits me.

'Oh, my God, that is amazing.'

'What can I say? I'm a talented chef.'

I let out a small laugh. 'Clearly. And the marinade is pretty good too.'

'I guess some of the credit belongs to the kitchen then.'

I swallow, watching as he places another batch on the grill then turns the full force of his attention on me. He's lifted one arm and laid it along the back of the booth so I'm in the circle of his body, surrounded by his strength and warmth, and I like it here. I really like it.

'So you were saying how you feel like you never really belonged?' he prompts and I shake my head.

'I don't think I was saying that at all.'

'Or words to that effect.'

I reach for another piece of beef, tasting it while I contemplate what I had been going to say. 'My dad never wanted me.'

He frowns so a divot forms between his brows.

'Oh, it's fine. I'm not upset about it, not like I used to be. It's nothing to do with *me*; it's just what he had planned. He and Mom knew they needed a child, an heir—he takes the whole family empire thing pretty seriously. Joshua ticked that box. My dad was done and dusted, no need for any more noisy, crying infants to destroy his peace and tranquillity.' I don't meet his eyes.

'But they changed their mind?'

'I was an accident,' I demur quietly. 'I've always wondered if maybe my mom planned it, maybe she lied to my dad to fall pregnant? I mean, maybe she chose to have me?'

'Would that have made a difference to you?'

I bite down on my lip. 'Yeah, probably.' Crap, my voice sounds shaky. I clear my throat. 'But, whatever, dad definitely didn't want another child, and he definitely didn't want a daughter.'

I feel Theo tense. 'Why not?'

'It's not like he's a misogynist. This isn't a boy versus girl thing. He didn't know what the hell to do with a daughter, and without Mom he felt like he was flying blind. I was—*am*—so different to Josh, and Dad just had no clue how to deal with that. I was like a bizarre alien or something.'

He doesn't smile, but he stares at me with an intensity that makes my skin lift in goosebumps.

'I have no experience with kids but I imagine we're all pretty much the same.'

'In lots of ways,' I murmur. 'But I was sensitive and emotional. Dad couldn't deal. Joshua has always been contained and calm, reasonable and rational. I used to fly into a rage if I didn't get my way, slam doors, stomp my feet, cry loudly, laugh until my stomach ached. I *felt* everything to the nth degree and it took a long time for me to learn that wasn't… okay in my family.'

His frown deepens. I dip my head forward, burying it in his shoulder.

'You're nothing like that now.'

I think about that. 'I probably still am, deep, deep down. But conditioning is powerful and my whole life was spent conditioning me not to act like that.'

'Self-possessed is a word I would use to describe you.'

'Sure.' I lift my shoulders. 'I've definitely learned to be that way.'

His expression shows disapproval. 'So you were

made to feel as though all your natural instincts were somehow wrong?'

Yes. A thousand times yes. But I hate admitting that to anyone. I feel disloyal and unkind. 'It's hard to distil it down to such a simple statement. My dad was grieving my mother. Her death changed him.'

'I imagine it was hard for your brother to lose her too, and for you to have grown up with no mother.'

I run a finger over my collarbone distractedly. 'Joshua missed her, though he didn't like to speak about that. As for Dad...' I shake my head. 'Grief is a difficult emotion.'

'You're making excuses for him?'

'No, but I'm conscious that I'm making it sound like my dad was some kind of a monster and that's not the case. He's fine. He's great. But he struggled with me, which meant I struggled with him. I suppose you could say that when my mother died we lost a huge part of my father too. I don't think we'll ever get him back.' I lift my face to his. Our lips are so close. I feel his breath on the side of my face and my insides squeeze in the nicest possible way. It's like a web has been spun with us at its centre.

'He must be proud of you, though?'

I lift a single brow, a twisted smile briefly lifting my lips. 'I don't think pride is necessarily in his arsenal.'

'He's proud of Joshua?'

'He's harder on Joshua.' I make the distinction carefully. 'He's always expected more of him. Joshua is the boy.' Derision at that old-fashioned notion creeps into my tone. 'He was always the one who would carry on the family name, marry well, make babies and simultaneously grow the company at an exponential rate.' I shake my head. 'My dad did that. He's formidable in business and he expected as much from Joshua.'

'And you?'

I bite into my lower lip, aware I'm running dangerously close to criticising my father—something I aim not to do. 'I think he's happy I seem happy,' I murmur. Not that Dad has any idea if I'm happy or not, really.

'You've increased Fleurs Sauvages's market share by almost twenty per cent in the last three years. Your revenue is up forty per cent on a decade ago.'

Despite the tenor of our conversation, I feel a laugh shifting through me. 'You sound like you're reading from our stock prospectus.'

He grins. 'What can I say? I looked into you when we met.'

'Did you now?' I'm not sure what to make of that. 'Why?'

A frown briefly mars his features. 'Because I've never done this before and wanted to make sure of who you were.'

His honesty floors me.

'Does that bother you?'

I tilt my head to the side. 'I don't think so.'

'Caution runs in my veins. It always has but especially after the Holden debacle.'

Sympathy is easy to feel. The shock of that discovery must have torn through each brother in a different way.

'And what else did you learn about me?'

'That you're the sexiest woman on earth?' he murmurs, reaching for the hem of my skirt and pushing it up so his hand can creep along my thigh towards my underwear. My breath catches in my throat.

'That was in our investor literature?'

'Sure was.'

I laugh softly. 'What else?'

'That you're incredibly good at what you do. That you're clever and focused and driven and industry insiders all say that, without you, Fleurs Sauvages would have lost relevance instead of the way it's transitioned to meet the needs of Gen Y.'

Heat blooms in my cheeks. 'Such lavish praise.' I tut. 'Surely you know by now flattery will get you nowhere?'

'You don't like compliments?'

'I don't need them.' I've had a lifetime without, so, frankly, they border on making me uncomfortable. I lean forward and pull his lower lip between my teeth, then kiss him hard, wrapping my fingers into his hair, dislodging it a little from the bun on the top of his head. His hand moves behind me—I realise a moment later that he's pulling steak off the grill.

'Burning,' he says by way of explanation, capturing my mouth once more.

His other hand is between my legs and he brushes

his fingers over my sex so I make a strangled, groaning sound into his mouth, earning a throaty agreement from him.

'I suddenly feel like dinner was a crappy idea.'

'You could be right. How quickly can you eat?'

'I'm not hungry.'

He pulls away and looks at me, nodding once. 'We'll get burgers delivered.'

He kisses me again, slower this time, and beneath the table his hand nudges my lace thong aside so his fingers collide with warm, wet flesh. He swears into my mouth as he slides a finger deep inside me so I buck in the booth seat, the blood in my body catching fire in a way that would rival the grill.

'Home,' I grunt, moving my body, wanting to push up and straddle him even as I'm vaguely aware that would be a really stupid thing to do in a crowded restaurant. 'Now.'

'Mine or yours?'

'Don't. Care.' I rip my face from his as though I'm pushing out of the ocean, on the brink of drowning. 'Now.'

CHAPTER SIX

I HAVE NO idea if we'll make it to either of our places. I throw a wad of bank notes on the table and pull her to standing, and then we're weaving our way through the restaurant with a lift of my hand to the waitress. In the warm, sultry air of New York, I pull her body to mine, kissing her as we step away from the restaurant and around the corner. As soon as we're in the lane I push Asha to the wall, my body hard against hers, need overpowering me.

I haven't felt like this since I was a school kid—maybe not even then. Every decent bone in my body is screaming at me to wait but I can't. I'm burning up with need. Her hands are pushing at my shirt, lifting it from my pants so her fingers can trace my flesh, feel the ridges of my chest, then she's at my pants, undoing the belt so I laugh and shake my head because with almost zero encouragement I would lift her up and take her against this brick wall, so help me God. Only the sound of passing pedestrians has me stilling, burying my head against her hair, shielding her from view of passers-by.

They walk on, but the fever is still alive between us. I half pull, half drag Asha—or is it the other way around?—toward my car, not breaking our kiss, our hands moving fervently over each other's bodies as we go. I fumble with the handle, wrenching the door to the back seat open with relief and pulling her inside on top of me.

'Thank fuck for tinted windows,' I grunt as she straddles me. It's awkward as hell and she makes a noise of impatience when her ankle connects with my knee.

Her skirt rips as she straddles me but I'm not sure she notices.

'Jesus.' I reach behind me for my wallet, unfurling it and pulling out a foil square. I slip it over my length and a second later she's taking me inside, her long, husky moan the sound of surrender and relief, of bliss and desperation. She rocks on her haunches as she takes me again and again, using my length to pleasure herself, tilting her head back, rocking on top of me as though she can't get enough. I look up at her beautiful face and then I'm dragging her head down, kissing her and lifting my hips, holding her body lower so I can drive deeper into her.

Her cries grow faster, more urgent, and higher in pitch and then she's coming, her muscles squeezing me tight, her body racked with the cacophony of her release. I want to hold off but I can't. I grip her shoulders and kiss her as silently, desperately, I orgasm, spilling myself into her, wondering if anything has ever felt this perfect before.

Our breathing is the only noise in the confines of the car. She pants and I tilt my head back so I can look at her through the veil of stars that has filled my eyes. She looks how I feel—like she's waking up from some kind of dream.

'Well, that's a first,' she murmurs, pulling a little grimace that's frankly adorable.

'Sex in a car?'

'Sex in a car.' She nods, lifting up and pulling away from me. 'Wanting someone so bad I either have to leave a restaurant or go under the table.' She turns her face to mine, smiling at me so I know that, despite the intense way we just fucked, she's okay.

'Dinner was a stupid idea,' I say with a nod. 'We're not cut out to sit across a table from each other.'

'Nope.' She lifts a hand and trails her finger over my cheek. 'No more restaurants.'

'Deal.'

She frowns. 'I can't look at you without touching.'

My chest swells with the force of a thousand and one bulls. 'Just as well I like you touching me.'

'Just as well.'

'So—' I angle myself in the seat, swiping the condom off my length and reaching for a tissue from the side door. I wrap it up and jam it in my pocket. 'My place or yours?'

Her eyes flare wider. 'You can drop me off if you want. You don't need to…'

I stare at her for so long she tapers off into nothing. 'You think once is enough?'

Pink floods her cheeks and she shakes her head, her lips lifting into a smile. 'My place. My skirt…'

'Ah.' I remember the sound of it splitting and reach down to the side seam. 'Sorry.'

'It's not your fault.'

'Not even a little?'

'Well, maybe just a little,' she agrees with a gentle laugh. 'But I'd do it all again. It's just fabric.'

Her place is only a short drive from the restaurant and I'm conscious of her the whole way there. I'm conscious of the expanse of thigh that's shown by the split in her skirt, of the way her hair is all messy because of me. I'm conscious of the fact I'll never be able to drive this car again without looking in the rear-view mirror and seeing the way our bodies came together in the back.

Fuck.

She is some kind of drug and I'm in a full-blown addiction cycle. Not for the first time, I reflect on the agreement we've come to, on the fact we've decided when this will end, and I'm immeasurably glad. Glad to have a calmly decided upon stop point, glad to know it's going to be amazing sex until we say goodbye. I've never been in a relationship like this but it's clearly the way to live.

And yet there is darkness deep inside of me, right

at the back of my mind. It's a darkness born of the certainty that in a few short weeks she'll be gone from my life, a figment of my past that I'll think of often but never again revisit. This will be over. I'll be free to live my life as I did before, and she'll be…with someone else. The idea lurches through me like a tsunami, the power of that thought inwardly knocking me off balance. Because I'm some kind of masochist, I imagine Asha smiling at some other guy, putting her hand in his, pulling him towards her. I imagine him smiling back, wrapping an arm around her body and pulling her close, nestling her into his side.

Something inside me shifts. Something that sparks pain and a total lack of comprehension. Nothing in that picture is what I want. I'm not the 'for ever' kind of guy, but with Asha I almost could be. I learned not to believe in the power of 'for ever', that it's a foolish and childish concept to ascribe to, and yet, with Asha, I could let this run for as long and as far as we could take it. I could wake up next to her every morning until it stopped being fun. I could…

But I can't. Because Asha laid her cards on the table from the very beginning. Fun, sure, but temporary. She has two reasons, and I respect both. Nothing gets in the way of her professional obligations, so the lightness of our agreement suits her perfectly. And secondly, where I was honest about not wanting to be in a bona fide relationship, she admitted she does, some day. With someone. Right from the start I've known that about her, and stringing this along for six months was totally selfish.

It's sobering and strengthening. We're doing the right thing to end this. I want her to be happy, which means I want her to meet someone else. And as much as I'm going to hate knowing I can't just pick up the phone and call her, that's life. People come, people go: nothing lasts for ever.

Her fingertips trace the tattoo, her eyes heavy, her exhaustion obvious. I should go, and let her sleep. I shift a little in the bed, watching her, and she smiles, but it's slow, lazy, her tiredness making even the simple gesture difficult.

I lift my finger to her tattoo, doing what she's just done and following the ink lines with the top of my nail. 'Does this make you think of your ex?'

Her blinks get longer, slower. 'Not really.' She stifles a yawn. 'He was a nice guy but just a part of my life back then.'

'In your rebellious phase,' I prompt, knowing I need to leave; she's tired and we both have to work tomorrow.

'Yeah.' Another small smile. Her eyes droop lower. I shift my finger to her nipple and flick it. Her eyes lift, locking to mine, heat bursting between us. If it weren't the middle of the night, if she wasn't three seconds away from sleep...

'He died,' she says, but her eyes are closed, sleep so close at hand. 'Drink driving. I was meant to be with him.' Her words are heavy, slurred by exhaustion, but I'm instantly still, my whole body on alert while I contemplate what she's just revealed. 'We were going to a party. I got sick and had to cancel at the last minute. He tried to get me to change my mind but I had a migraine. I got them a fair bit, growing up. I don't now though.' Her words are so thick with tiredness I can barely make them out. I resist an urge to wake her, to get her to tell me this story properly. 'If I hadn't been sick, I'd probably be dead too.'

A shiver runs the length of my spine. The idea of someone like Asha—with so much vitality and vibrancy—no longer being here fills me with disgust and gratitude in equal measure—gratitude that she wasn't with him that night, gratitude that she's still here.

'I'm sorry. About him.'

'Ashes to ashes,' she says prosaically, even as I hear the timbre of her voice and know it's not something she can really pass off so easily.

'Ashes to ashes,' I repeat, letting her drift off to sleep, wondering about the teenager she was then, and the woman she is now. Wondering about the man she briefly loved, who inked her breast before dying, wondering about the impermanence of life and the cruelty of fate.

Finally, her breathing becomes deeper and more rhythmic and I know she's fast asleep. I lie there for a moment, watching her, and then push out of bed, dressing as quietly as possible.

I take one last look at Asha as I shift through the door. In the light thrown through the window, the moon's fine, milky blade passing over her skin, she looks sylphlike, majestic and magical, all at the same time. I don't let myself think about what she's said, the possibility that she could have been killed, just like her friend. A world without Asha would be significantly the poorer.

I read the report for the fourth time, thinking of Theo, thinking of the way we last made love, and my body dances with those memories, dances with need, frustration, desire and a bone-deep ache.

I lift my gaze to the window and stare out at New York. The weather is sultry and warm. His pool would be heaven today, bliss. But it's only eleven in the morning; he won't be finished until much later. And my body won't wait that long. I stare out at New York and flashes of memory pierce me.

...for the next month, consider me fully at your disposal. Any time you have 'needs', I'm up for it.

A smile lifts my lips as an idea forms in my mind. I move to my desk quickly, slipping off my thong and spritzing my wrists with my signature fragrance—despite the fact Fleurs Sauvages has developed eleven perfumes in my lifetime, I always wear our signature brand, the one my great-grandmother and grandmother used to wear, the one that took our company from a small operation to a global powerhouse. I check my reflection and refresh my lipstick, then, still smiling, pull out of my office.

'Kevin? I'll be gone an hour or so. Don't call me.'

My assistant nods. 'Did you place your lunch order?'

'Emailed it last night.' I wave my hand in the air and jab the elevator button impatiently. Butterflies begin to flap their way around my belly as my car crosses Fifth.

Theo gave me a business card the first night we met. I don't know why, probably out of habit. It has his office address but even if it hadn't I would have known: Hart Towers are sort of a landmark in Manhattan. The limousine pulls up at the base of the steel monolith and I pause, taking in a breath, wondering for a moment if I should have texted him that I was coming, then dismissing the idea with another smile.

The surprise is part of the fun.

I scan the sign in the foyer, taking a guess he'll be near the top floor. 'Executive level' is the best I can do.

Foolishly, I hadn't anticipated the logistics of this. Surprising someone in this day and age at a high-security office block is not actually possible. There's a row of five receptionists and security officials. I need to pass through them before I can progress. They ask my name and double check it against their day's agenda. Obviously I'm not there.

One of them lifts a finger to me, having me wait

while she makes a call, presumably to Theo's assistant. I stand there, my desire only increasing at these hurdles. A moment later she reaches into the drawer beside her and pulls out a lanyard. She prints my name from a small machine and slides it into the plastic, passing the ID tag over to me with a nod to the end of the desk. 'Sign yourself in and out. Thanks.'

I slip it over my head and do as she said, then I have to go through the security machines, and my cheeks heat at the fact I'm not wearing underwear—fortunately that detail doesn't show up on the screen as I pass through it.

The whole way to the ninetieth floor, my stomach lurches but I don't have much space for nerves when longing and need are taking over my body. The doors ping open and I'm greeted by a bank of three assistants.

'Theo Hart,' I murmur as I approach, my eyes lifting to scan the space. It's a double-height void with floor to ceiling windows behind the reception desk. The furnishings are sparse and modern, all sleek timber and steel, and there are enormous flower arrangements spaced throughout, giving the bare environment a feeling of beauty and softness. The floor is highly polished concrete and my heels make a clicking noise as I walk.

They're forewarned of my arrival, naturally, and so is Theo. He'll be waiting for me, wondering what I'm doing here. Impatience and pleasure zip through me.

'He's just finishing a conference call, if you'd like to take a seat.'

But I'm not someone who likes being told what to do, and I have no intention of cooling my heels in Theo's reception.

'I'll wait in his office—' before she can open her mouth to object '—he won't mind.' I smile confidently and stride towards one of three doors on this level. His name is emblazoned across it in gold. With a smile, I push the heavy wood inwards. It's everything I'd expect of Theo's office. Huge, naturally, with more of the same modern designer décor as the reception. In here though, instead of flower arrangements, there are living plants. What looks like a fiddle leaf fig grows in one corner and a fern in another. And the *pièce de résistance* is a marble sculpture of Poseidon positioned beside the desk.

I smile at the piece and then my eyes fix on Theo. He's sitting at the boardroom table in the centre of the room, and his eyes lift to mine in a way that sears my soul.

A smile lifts one side of his lips, a smile of curiosity.

A voice speaks out in the room, the kind of disembodied voice heard in teleconferences. I wonder who he's talking to and how long he'll be.

His eyes continue to hold mine for several seconds and then he turns back to the screen, speaking over whoever else is talking. 'I only have a few minutes. Let's wrap this up, shall we?'

Pleasure at my ability to command his attention shoots through me. I turn away from him briefly, returning to the door and clicking the lock into place. When I turn back to him, his eyes are resting on me so my tummy swoops. I walk slowly towards the table, making sure to keep myself behind his laptop, away from the camera.

I start with my hair. He loves my hair. Lifting my fingers to the pins that have it secured in a bun high on my head, I loosen them one by one, slowly, deliberately placing each pin on the boardroom table and eventually loosening my hair so it falls in wild, tumbling curls down my back before drawing it over one shoulder.

His eyes are locked to me.

Good.

'We just need your sign-off on the plans before we can progress.'

Consternation is clear on his face as he draws his gaze back to the screen. 'I'm not going to sign off on them until they're ready. The tests I've seen show half a dozen areas that don't meet requirements.'

Flustered voices try to assuage his worries. It's so like him to be able to throw a cat amongst the pigeons, so to speak, with a few short words.

I reach for my jacket next, removing it slowly, carefully, placing it over the back of the nearest chair. Then, one by one, I undo my buttons, deliberately moving slowly down the line of my chest until my silk blouse separates to reveal a simple lace bra.

A slight hiss escapes his lips.

I smile at him as I let the shirt fall down my arms, the rustle of silk against my skin only exacerbating my anticipation. His Adam's apple jerks as he swallows. I unclasp my bra; his breathing grows heavy. I don't push it off too quickly. Instead, I savour in the removal, sliding the straps down my arms, lifting my fingers to brush my nipples as I let the scrap of lace fall to the floor.

'I need more details.' He addresses the WebEx without taking his eyes off me.

I'm not smiling now. Holding his gaze, I reach for the zip of my skirt and glide it down my hip and then the fabric rustles to the floor, revealing my nakedness to his heated gaze. His cheeks are slashed with dark colour. Someone on the other side of the screen is talking in detail and I know it's important or Theo would have disconnected the call already.

It gives me a rush of power to know I'm tormenting him. Stepping out of the skirt, I move slightly closer and then, at the edge of his desk, I cup my breasts first, letting my fingertips roll over my nipples, tweaking them slowly, imagining my fingers are his fingers, remembering all the ways he touches me there, all the ways he drives me crazy. One hand moves lower, drawing invisible circles over my flat stomach until I reach my sex.

His eyes widen and I hear a muttered curse. It silences everyone, even the people speaking.

'Look—' he stares at the screen, then at me, and

there is a helplessness in his eyes that does something funny to my insides because Theo Hart is *never* helpless '—get me more details and we'll speak tomorrow.'

'Yes, sir, but if you'll just—'

I move my fingers faster and make a tiny, muted moaning noise that has Theo standing abruptly, leaning over the screen. 'Tomorrow.' He snaps the lid down in the same motion he sweeps towards me and pulls me to his body, his lips claiming mine in a kiss that is pure white-hot desperation.

'Don't stop,' he murmurs into my mouth, ripping himself away from me just enough to see properly. Heat burns my cheeks. I tilt my head back a little as I feel an orgasm building, unmistakable, blinding, urgent.

And then his hand is on my wrist, pulling me from my body, his own fingers taking over, touching me, slowly at first, so the heat that's built ebbs and I make a moaning noise because, after two days without Theo, I don't want to wait another moment.

He understands—this is his way of tormenting me back. He drops his mouth to my throat, kissing the pulse point there, flicking it with his tongue, and then he moves his hand, bringing his hard cock against me, rolling his hips so the promise of what he can give me is right there. Christ, I want him more than I've ever wanted anything.

I push at his chest, my eyes showing wildness. 'Fuck me, Theo. Right now.'

His expression is a mask of need.

'Right now,' I repeat.

He nods once, then reaches into his pocket, his trademark protection always close at hand when he carries a stash in his wallet. He undresses quickly, so quickly, and while he does I touch myself, perched on the edge of his boardroom table. My fingers move over my clit until I'm panting with need, so close to bursting. 'Please,' I moan, but he stands there, naked, watching me, his lips just a gash in his face.

'Theo,' I groan.

He stays where he is, his arms crossed over his chest.

'I want to watch you.'

I tilt my head back, my fingers moving faster, the wave threatening to pull me under. 'I want to feel you,' I counter.

'You will.'

His promise is the striking of a match. I arch my back, heat building inside me, pleasure overtaking my every instinct until I'm flying far away from here, from him, from me, from this and us, until I'm flying above Manhattan, just air and ash, ashes to ashes, dust to dust, spirit to sky. I am a being of sensation and nothing else.

There is no time to get my breath back. Even as I'm panting, trying to make sense of the new sensual heat I find myself enveloped by, he's pulling at my legs, kissing me hard enough to push my back flat against the boardroom table, then driving his length into me, hard, his hands on my thighs holding me right where he needs me, taking me again and again until I'm twisting and turning on his board-room table, my body a thousand and one flames.

His hands possess me rather than caress me. His touch is a necessity, his fingers and palm finding every inch of me, running over it as a matter of need, not want. The same flames that burst through me are consuming him.

He drives into me and I'm tipping away from re-ality once more, but this time he's with me, his body riding the same wave. He's silent; I'm not. My cries are muted, in deference to where we are, but I can-not keep my mouth closed. I moan his name over and over, an incantation and in gratitude. I thank God for bringing Theo into my life, even for a short time. I know we're almost over but I will never forget the way he makes me feel and I will always be glad he taught me how great sex should be.

CHAPTER SEVEN

'DANIELLA CAN GO,' I murmur, scanning the email, lifting my gaze to Kevin.

He shakes his head. 'Her doctor doesn't want her flying in the third trimester.'

'Right, of course. She's pregnant.' I'm happy for her, but there's also a part of me that feels a squeeze of envy—envy at how everyone else's life seems to be following the trajectory we're told we should want, and mine is so far from that.

'Yeah, she's pregnant. You're sending her a hamper, by the way.'

I send him a look. 'You're too good to me.'

'I know.'

I shake my head. 'Can I get her a massage as well, and a really huge bottle of champagne for her once she's pushed that thing out?'

'That "thing" is a kid.'

'Oh, don't go acting all baby-mad on me.'

He grins. 'Nah, it'll be you and me, single, child-free and fabulous at sixty.'

My gut twists. I keep a smile plastered to my face but it feels false, because it's exactly the opposite of what I know I really want. 'Rocking out at a retirement village?'

'In pleather.'

'Pleather? Puh-lease.' I roll my eyes. 'What about Peter?'

'In pleather?' He pulls a face.

I smile. 'For Paris.'

Kevin's businesslike once more. 'He's in Tokyo at the trade fair.' I swear under my breath and his thick dark brows shoot towards his hairline. 'What's going on? You're usually out the door at the mere mention of Paris.'

Kevin, who's worked for me for seven years, knows me better than almost anyone, and he's completely right. Give me even half an opportunity to visit the French capital and I'm there. Paris is my soul city.

But a meeting with our production manager and warehouse team is going to take me away from New York—more specifically from Theo—and the plans we've made for tonight. 'Yeah, I know.'

'So?' he insists and I feel like my secret is in danger of slipping, so I overcompensate.

'Nothing. I just had something on with Joshua.'

'It's not in my calendar.'

'I know. Believe it or not, I do make plans without involving you.'

He stares at me sceptically.

'*Some* of the time, I make plans without involving you.'

'Well, maybe you shouldn't because this is what happens when I don't have full access to your diary. I've told them you'll be in tonight, babe.'

I wince, knowing there's no way I can get out of it. More than that, I daren't even try. I have made Fleurs Sauvages the global name it is, I have worked twenty hours a day for months at a time, several times a year, to keep us relevant, to ensure the brand's success. But failure is always only one step away, and I have no intention of failing. I have no intention of letting my dad think he was right about me, that this was too much for me, that I can't handle it.

I fix Kevin with a determined stare and nod. 'Fine. I can leave in a few hours.'

He airdrops something to my phone. 'Already booked your ticket.'

I stare at the first-class seat he's reserved, my tummy dropping down to my ankles. It's only been a matter of days—not weeks—since I went to Theo's office and surprised him mid-conference call but despite that my body is incinerating with need.

It's not that I miss him, nothing so schmaltzy as that. I just *want* him on a physical level. I need him, like I need to drink water or eat lunch. It's a physical itch that only he can sufficiently scratch.

Still, there's nothing for it.

I lift my phone out and start to type a message, then delete it. Everything sounds so formal. Instead,

I send him a GIF: a picture of a woman shaking her head in the rain. I caption it:

Rain check tonight. Something came up.

I reread the message, pleased with how unconcerned I sound, then send it.
His response is instant.

You'd better believe something 'came up'. Me. Now. No rain checks.

My heart squeezes.

Sorry, can't help it. I have to go to Paris. It's important.

He doesn't reply.

I wonder at the growing sense of disappointment gnawing its way through me. I triage my emails, then move to the wardrobe in the corner of my office, grabbing a few things out and packing them neatly into the suitcase I always keep stashed there, the distinctive 'FS' branding in shades of gold and cream denoting to the world that it's one of our premiere luxury items.

I try not to think about Theo as I pack, but it's impossible. My body aches for him, so every movement makes me hyper-aware of the fact it's been far too long since he touched me. I fold silk blouses and pencil skirts and imagine his fingers running over the fabrics, removing them from me.

I slip into my private bathroom and freshen my make-up and hair, spritzing with my signature perfume that will now always remind me, in an unwelcome and strange way, of him.

'Your car's downstairs.' Kevin's voice is piped through the intercom on my desk.

I check my reflection once more and nod to myself, moving back into my office, grabbing the small suitcase and my handbag, and my phone last of all.

I see a missed call from Theo and my heart lurches. There's a text too. Clicking into it, I have to read his message twice before it makes any kind of sense.

Venue change accepted. Meet you at JFK.

Does that mean…? Is he…coming to Paris? Or planning an airport quickie? Considering I thought I wasn't going to see him at all today, either is fine.

Excitement makes my heart thump. This I hadn't expected. I suck in a deep breath, calming myself before stepping out of my office—if I show even a hint of breathlessness, Kevin will know something's up.

'Okay, I'll message from the air,' I say, per our usual routine.

'Got it. But not too late. I have a date tonight.'

'The cellist?'

He grins. 'And her fabulous hands.'

I scrunch my face up. 'Way too much information. Have fun.'

'You know it.'

My driver is downstairs. He stows my bags and I slide into the passenger seat. It's only as we're almost out of the city that it occurs to me JFK is a pretty huge airport. Where am I supposed to meet Theo? And is he even serious?

What exactly do you have in mind?

A minute later a photo pings into my phone. It's not from today; it has to be at least a few months old because it's snowing lightly in the picture whereas today is another scorcher. In the photograph, Theo's standing in a suit and jacket at the top of a set of stairs leading to a jet that's emblazoned with 'Hart Brothers'.

Accompanying the photo are the words:

Tell your driver to go to the General Aviation facility. My jet's fired up.

Excitement buzzes inside me.

Ooh la la!

A pause, and then I get a message back:

Oui.

The General Aviation facility is set aside from JFK and the luxury of the terminal reflects the clientele that utilise it. While there's still a pretty intense security regimen to go through, everything is made easier with attentive staff and an attention to all the tiny details that make the experience a pleasure. Not that I'm there for long. I walk through the doors, someone takes my bags, including my handbag.

'We'll stow these for you, madam.'

I'm ushered to a separate room, where I pass through a security frame. 'Champagne?'

I shake my head and a bottle of mineral water is handed to me instead. My passport's checked while I take a sip then the woman comes out from behind the desk with a smile and guides me to a set of sliding doors. 'This way, Miss Sauvages.'

His jet stands like a piece of marble in the midst of the sky. Gleaming and white, and as big as a commercial jet, the stairs I recognise from the photograph lead the way to an open door. There's no carpet at the bottom, like you might expect from a film, but a pilot stands at the bottom, dressed in a navy blue uniform with a crisp white shirt with gold embellishment. 'Miss Sauvages, welcome.' His smile is friendly. 'Mr Hart is waiting for you.'

He is? Theo must have left his office almost as soon as I messaged him. How the hell did he arrange all of this so quickly?

My smile doesn't show any of my innermost thoughts. 'Great. Thanks.'

He nods and gestures for me to move up.

'Have a nice flight, ma'am.' The woman who checked my passport bids me farewell. I suspect I'll have a *very* nice flight, but neither of these two people need to know what I'm anticipating.

I move up the stairs carefully—my stilettos want to drop through the gridded holes in the steps so I have to go slowly. Once inside, my eyes sweep the space, noting the details. The luxury I had expected. Private jets are already the last word in insane wealth, so it makes sense that this one should reflect that. The seats are white leather, arranged like a lounge area, spacious and comfortable. There's a wide corridor that leads to the back of the plane. I walk down it, my eyes continuing to note the details even as I scan for Theo. I pass a bedroom and my temperature lifts, then a boardroom, and a cinema with a couple of treadmills, then a bathroom that bears no resemblance to the utilitarian décor you see on commercial planes, even in the first-class cabin. This could be in a five-star hotel—lightweight construction with pale timber, but a large shower cubicle, all luxurious and elegant.

No Theo.

I spin around and move back down the corridor in time to see him emerging from the cockpit. He probably started the day wearing a suit but, in deference to the day's heat, he's shed the jacket and tie and rolled his sleeves up to his elbows, revealing tanned, toned forearms that make my mouth go dry. His hair is in its usual bun, his hips narrow, his chest muscled, his body so familiar to me that, despite the clothes he wears, I can visualise him naked and heat pools between my legs in immediate response.

'Hey.' His grin is my undoing. So sexy. So *him*. I admit to myself how glad I am he's done this, how glad I am that our plans aren't cancelled.

'This is a surprise.' Understatement.

'I like Paris.'

I laugh. 'But…'

'No rain checks,' he murmurs, pulling me towards him, and I inhale everything about him, imprinting it on my mind, my body responding instantly, filling with need and familiarity, with comfort and pleasure. Happiness that comes not just from the expectation of physical fulfilment but from everything else— the overall sense of rightness that fills me because he's here and I'm here and suddenly this trip to Paris feels like so much more than a business necessity.

'Still—' my voice is breathy '—this is kind of overkill, right?'

'Is there any such thing?'

Is there? It doesn't feel like it. 'I guess not.'

His kiss is quick, his smile infectious. 'Sit down. We're taking off.'

He moves back towards the cockpit.

'Wait. You're not…flying this thing?'

He grins. 'Not today.'

I stare at him.

'But thanks for the vote of confidence.' His wink is teasing. I poke my tongue out and choose a seat at random. There are seat belts embedded in each lounge chair.

A few minutes later the engine purrs to life, the door is clicked shut and a hostess brings me a glass of champagne. I sip it and then Theo is back, striding out of the cockpit, taking the seat beside me with that same charming boyish grin on his handsome face. My pulse throbs.

'You do fly, though?'

'Yeah.'

'Seriously?'

'You're surprised by that?'

'You're not a pilot, so…'

'I started flying when I was just a kid. Fifteen. I was pretty obsessed, actually.'

'Really?'

'Mmm. I had a simulator installed when I was ten. It was good, but nothing beats the feeling of being in the cockpit as you take off, flying through the clouds.' He shakes his head. 'It's very energising.'

His passion is captivating.

I can't help myself. I reach out and put my hand on his knee, drawing imaginary circles. 'You didn't think about doing it for a living?'

'Nah. I get the best of both worlds now. I fly whenever I want, but it's not my whole life.'

I look beyond him, through the window, as we lift up over Manhattan. The city is picture-perfect beneath us, sheaths of glass and shimmering metal forcing their way upwards, the land such a tiny archipelago it's almost impossible to understand how it can bear the weight of such construction.

'I used to hate flying,' I confide in him. 'As a kid, I was scared to death.'

I feel his gaze on me. 'And now?'

I slide my eyes to his, a smile curving on my face. 'I grew out of it.'

'A fear of flying is perfectly normal. It's the unknown that's frightening. Once you understand the mechanics it takes a lot of the mystery out of it and makes it feel less like you're trusting yourself to fate and more like jumping on a bus.'

'You don't fly commercial?'

He shakes his head. 'Do you?'

'Always.'

He frowns. 'Really?'

I can't help it; I laugh. 'You realise ninety-nine per cent of people only fly commercial?'

'I just presumed…'

'Nah. Jets like this are bad for the environment.' I lean closer so our faces are only an inch apart. 'Look at all this space. You could fit a football team or three in here.'

'And have them ogling you? Never.'

It's just a joke but it almost sounds like that would bother him, as though he'd be *jealous*. The very idea makes my heart contort painfully, because Theo isn't a jealous kind of guy and if I ever doubted that I only need to remember that he's offered to set me up with someone 'suitable'. Hardly the action of a man who feels even a hint of possessiveness.

'I like the convenience of this,' he says with a lift of his shoulders.

I consider that for a moment. 'My assistant booked me on a flight at a moment's notice. I got a seat in first class. That's not remotely inconvenient.'

'It's lucky, though. Lucky there happened to be a seat spare, otherwise you may well have been waiting until tomorrow.'

I lift my brows heavenwards. 'Not when you were waiting in the wings...'

'True.' He grins. 'Consider me your knight in shining aluminium.'

'See? Now you've gone and reminded me that airplanes are made of the same metal as a soda can and I feel a lot less safe,' I joke.

'Seriously, the management of our planes puts commercial airlines to shame. They're refitted every six months, our pilots are all ex-military and their Continuing Professional Development is rigorous. If you're ever going to not be afraid of flying, it's when you're on a Hart jet.'

His confidence and passion scatter goosebumps across my skin. 'I'm not afraid any more. I told you, I grew out of it. I fly a lot for work, so I had to.'

He puts his hand over mine, his fingers stroking my flesh, his eyes heavy on my face. 'What's in Paris?'

I'm grateful for the conversation change. 'I have to

meet with the production manager of our Angel Pie line—it's new,' I explain quickly, because he won't have heard of it yet. 'We're launching in winter, all things going to plan. But the packaging is proving difficult to nail and some of the colours just aren't quite right.'

'You sound stressed?'

I nod. 'It's my baby,' I explain thoughtfully. 'I came up with the concept for the brand four years ago, and it's been a lot of work since then. A lot of capital too. It's a gamble.'

'But you're confident?'

I grimace. 'Can you ever be completely confident? I've done my market research. There's a huge void. Plus, the line capitalises on the global trend for embracing sustainable, ethical products. But yeah, I mean it's risky to target teenagers because they don't think in terms of their future health generally, and they're cash strapped.' I bite down on my lip thoughtfully.

'It's make-up aimed at teens?'

'Teens and pre-teens. We've got a couple of awesome celebrities lined up to engage that market, YouTubers, influencers, that kind of thing.' I wave a hand through the air and my bangles jingle against my watch. 'And it's not just make-up; it's moisturiser, sunscreen, lip glosses.'

He frowns. 'Kids wear that stuff?'

I laugh. 'Yeah, it accounts for a huge piece of the cosmetic pie. *But*—' I squeeze his hand '—the current market leaves a lot to be desired. You'd be shocked to learn how many products have been re-called because they were found to contain asbestos.'

His eyes narrow.

'There's talc, hormone-blocking *parfums*, because those ingredients are usually cheap so manufacturers tend to use them to save costs. But it's messing with kids' health, and that shouldn't be the case. There should be a way for teens to mess around with beauty and make-up without endangering their future self.'

'I had no idea.'

'Lots of people don't. So our pre-launch campaign is about awareness. We've got great position ads ready to go, mainly targeting digital media, YouTube again, then traditional youth market placement like magazines, some television ads. By the time samples go out, I'm hoping we'll have an engaged market.'

He shifts in his seat, his eyes roaming my face in a way that brings heat to my cheeks. 'I think that sounds amazing.'

'I hope so. I've had to fight so hard for it.'

'To fight who?'

I hesitate, but there's something about Theo. There are so many somethings about him, come to think of it, that I hear myself say, 'Everyone. My brother and father mainly. They're old school.'

'But you run Fleurs Sauvages?'

'It's a public company and they're shareholders. I'm as accountable to them as any other shareholder. Plus, Dad doesn't let go of the reins easily.'

'You've done amazing things for the company.'

'I know.' I don't bother to attempt false modesty. The facts speak for themselves. 'But this is a gamble. We've never targeted the teen market before and we're going against a lot of industry standards. Cheap, cheap, cheap is what's generally manufactured for that demographic, because they don't have the money necessarily and they don't look after their stuff. Plus, trends change and they want to be able to buy into *everything*. Angel Pie won't compete on price; it's a premium product, though I'm bringing our margins down as low as I can to make it appealing and accessible.'

'How does your dad feel about that?'

'Profit margins are why you're in business, Asha. We're not a charity,' I mimic, and shake my head, a rueful smile on my face. 'But I mean, when is enough money enough? We're richer than any family should ever be—okay, I know I'm talking to a Hart—but we can afford to take a small hit here. And it won't be a hit anyway. I've done the figures. It's going to be a boon for the company, but yeah, I'm reducing the price so we can get the product into more consumer hands because this *matters*. It's really important. Kids shouldn't be risking damage to their bodies because they want to tinker with cosmetics.'

'I agree.' His voice is low, gruff and something inside of me twists. 'I don't think anyone who gave you five minutes to speak your case could feel otherwise.'

I bite down on my lip. 'Dad will come around. He's just…stubborn.'

'Ah.' He moves closer and I breathe him in, my tummy twisting into a billion knots. 'And that bothers you?'

'It's the way he is.'

He shakes his head once. 'I meant that he doesn't approve of what you're doing.'

My heart speeds up at his perceptiveness. 'I spent a long time feeling like I had to prove myself to him,' I surprise myself by admitting. 'I was never going to be good enough. I'm not Joshua,' I say simply. 'It was only once I finally accepted that I'd never earn his approval, no matter what I did, that I was freed up to go in this direction, to pursue something out of left field and follow my passion.'

We're so close to one another I can see the emotions flickering inside his eyes.

'He'll never be proud of me, and that's okay.' My lips shift into a fleeting smile. 'It's not about me. It's about him.'

'It's why you've pushed yourself so hard, though?'

'At first, yeah.' I keep my voice light. 'I mean, I thought that with every good year we had, he'd finally be happy with what I was doing. And he was. I mean, he's not a monster. He told me I'd done well, but it never felt like it was enough. So I worked harder and harder and did better and better and then, a few years ago, I had this epiphany: he's never going to be proud of me in the way I want. He's never

going to love me in the way I want. And you can't
force someone to be what you want them to be. He's
my dad, and he loves me in his own way, but I was
just making myself miserable by trying to be what
Joshua is to him.' I shake my head a little. 'I launched
Project Teen—that's what I called it back then—a
week later.'

'And when it's launched?'

'I'll take a break.' I laugh. 'And maybe even get
a life.'

'Right, with your new boyfriend.' He grins in a
way that usually makes my tummy all swoopy but
doesn't right now. Instead, it makes me feel like I've
just crested over the highpoint of a rollercoaster and
I'm plummeting back to earth.

'Yeah.' I smile clumsily, because it feels like I
should. That's our deal, right? We're just marking
time now, enjoying each other's bodies, until his
brother's wedding.

His finger presses to my chin, lifting my face
to his. 'Anyone who doesn't see what an incredible
woman you are is an idiot.' I'm not sure if we're
talking about prospective dates now or my dad, but
I find it hard to respond either way.

He frowns, moving closer, and right before he
kisses me he says something no one's ever said to
me before, something that makes my gut lurch. 'You
deserve every happiness, Asha. You deserve everything.'

Out of nowhere, I wonder about him. I wonder

what he wants and what he deserves. I wonder if he thinks I deserve him. The question catches me off-guard. It's unwelcome and inappropriate so I ignore it. I surrender to his kiss—nothing else seems to matter right now anyway.

CHAPTER EIGHT

'THIS ISN'T WHAT I expected.' He looks around my place with a smile on his lips that is my undoing. God, when will I *not* crave him?

I follow his gaze, seeing this apartment through his eyes. In the eighteenth *arrondissement*, nestled a stone's throw from Sacré Coeur, this place is almost exactly as Grand-mère left it. Bright, so bright, with stunning wallpapers everywhere, sumptuous velvet furnishings, original Impressionist artwork, lamps that cast a warm glow, rugs that are hand woven from soft, beautiful wool. The French windows open onto a series of Juliet balconies, each framing a stunning view of Paris. But it's not pretentious at all. It's homely and beautiful, ultra-feminine and tactile.

'No?' He's carrying both our bags. 'The bedroom's through there.'

He lifts a brow and I laugh. 'To put our bags down.'

He grins and moves that way. A second later, I hear his laugh. 'Holy hell.'

'What?' I move into the kitchen, flicking the kettle to life.

'You actually sleep in that bed?'

I think of the elaborately sculpted four-poster with its ornate floral headpiece and grin. 'Yep. It's surprisingly comfortable.'

'Once you get rid of the hundred pillows?'

'There *are* a lot of throw cushions, aren't there?'

I make a couple of teas and reach into the fridge. As usual, Kevin's had it stocked for me; there's a range of food as well as milk, wine, juice. I finish the tea as Theo emerges.

'Let me guess,' I say at his look of bemusement. 'You have a place in Paris and it's nothing like this?'

His eyes show amusement. 'I don't think there's anything like this. *Anywhere.*'

'It was my *grand-mère*'s,' I explain. 'I didn't feel right changing it, once she died.' I look around, a fond smile on my lips. 'If you knew her, you'd understand. So much of who she was is wrapped up in this place. Coming here, it's like coming home to her. I feel her everywhere.'

'Ah.' He nods, moving towards one of the photo frames that sit above the fireplace. He picks it up, a smile on his lips. 'You?'

I nod, lifting my tea and cradling it in my palms as I walk closer towards him. 'I would have been about twelve, I think.'

'Did you come here often?'

'Most summers.'

He's quiet, but it's a silence that speaks volumes. I hear his questions, yet it's late and I'm tired. 'I made you a tea.'

He looks down at me, a smile tipping his lips. 'That was kind of you.'

'You don't drink tea?'

'Not once in my life.'

'Try it; you might like it.'

'I'm okay.' He grins, but then sobers. 'What do you have on tomorrow?'

'Meetings.'

'All day?'

'Probably.' I scan his face. 'I'm sorry you'll be here cooling your heels…'

'I'll work.' He lifts his shoulders. 'We have an office in the QCA.'

'Ah, of course.'

'But I know a great place for dinner tomorrow night.'

Something like magic steals through my soul. 'Sounds nice.'

Nice is an understatement, though. Suddenly I feel like there are no words to explain how I feel.

I wake up with a raging hard-on and a frown on my face, because there's just no way I can make the most of it in this *frou-frou* excuse for a bedroom.

'Bonjour…'

She grins at me, her eyes sparkling, her long red hair in total disarray. I imagine her on top of me, that beautiful hair draped around her shoulders. Great. That's not helpful.

'*Bonjour* yourself.'

'How'd you sleep?'

I reach for her, pulling her body close to mine. To hell with it. 'Like a log.'

'Mmm…' Her murmur is pure sensual invitation.

'I can't do this,' I grunt, shaking my head ruefully. 'I feel like your *grand-mère* is watching us.'

She laughs. 'I'm pretty sure she's not.'

I'm not convinced.

'And if she were, she'd thoroughly approve.'

At that, I laugh.

'I'm not kidding. After my grandpa died, she had quite the slew of romantic adventures.'

'Well, if you're sure…'

She makes a little noise of surprise as I pull her on top of me, her eyes flaring wide at the feeling of my cock between her legs. 'Yep. I'm positive…'

My day is long with a capital L, and all I want is to wrap it up and get back to Theo. The way we made love this morning makes my throat dry just thinking about it. But there's so much to do, so much to cover, that it's almost nine before I finally finish my last meeting, and even then it's with the promise I'll be back the next day to smooth out some of the last details.

Theo is at my place when I arrive and I pause just inside the door, staring at him for a moment, my heart in my throat at the sight of him here, in the place I feel most comfortable, most like myself.

He's wearing a suit, his hair up high on his head, his features so chiselled and strong, his face bearing a mask of intense concentration as he reads a broadsheet newspaper. He's sitting in the purple velvet chair and it's such a beautiful contradiction—him so masculine and the chair so feminine—that something inside me flutters. I want to smile, but I can't. He's just so…

'Hey—' he lifts his gaze '—whatcha looking at?'

I force a smile to my face and stamp out the direction of my thoughts. 'Nothing. Sorry I'm so late.'

'It's not late. We're in Paris, baby. Things don't get started here till midnight.'

'But dinner…'

He shrugs. 'We can go any time.'

My heart lifts and my stomach grumbles audibly.

He lifts a brow. 'Like right now?'

'Yep. Just give me five minutes.'

I push into the bathroom and smile, imagining Theo here. It's gold. Everywhere. Gold claw-foot bath tub, gold-edged mirror, marble tiles with gold details, marble vanity with gold taps.

But there's no shower, so he must have had a bath after I left this morning. Bless him. I can't stop grinning as I touch up my make-up and hair, imagining Theo Hart, all six and a half feet of him, folded into this tub.

When I emerge he's standing up, a glass of wine

in his hand. He's still looking around the apartment
with that same look of bemusement.

'I've just never seen anywhere like it,' he explains
in response to my unasked question.

'I have to admit, I've been laughing to myself
imagining you folded into the bath tub…'

'I showered at my office,' he says with a shake of
his head. 'If we come back to Paris, we might have
to get a hotel.'

I spin away from him before he can catch the
expression that crosses my features, my heart jack-
hammering against my ribcage, because it sounds
so happy and domesticated, so *normal*, but it's not,
because we won't be coming back to Paris. His
brother's wedding is only two and a half weeks
away, and that's when this ends.

I briefly imagine that we don't end it. I wonder
what he'd say if I suggest an extension to our agreement, but all the reasons for having that line in the
sand are still there.

He's quicksand and if I'm not careful I'll sink
deeper and deeper into him until eventually I find
I'm unable to escape. He's addictive and beautiful
and fascinating and there's absolutely no future here.
He's been stone cold clear about that from the very
beginning, and I have no reason to think I'd ever be
able to change his mind.

He wants this—just this—and even if I decided
to want something more, something meaningful,
that's not what Theo's offering. I reach for my

clutch purse and paste a confident smile on my face. 'Let's go.'

The restaurant is not what I expected, and I don't know why, given that the one other time we dined together he took me to an equally out-of-the-way eatery that was big on atmosphere and small on pretension. This is just like that—so charming and unique, a classic French bistro with touches of flair everywhere. It's a warm night and the windows to the sidewalk are thrown open. Chairs are lined up against the walls in the European style, but we sit inside, in another booth, this one lined with black velvet. The table between us is pale marble and a small gold lamp sits on the top, making the ambience moody. The walls are papered with a floral print; huge watercolour blooms in shades of green and pale pink pop against their creamy background. The window frames are glossy black and the floor is grey concrete.

But it's the food that takes my breath away. Delicate offerings, each beautifully arranged on the plate, without being overdone. There's seafood, meat, chicken, vegetables. We eat until I can literally eat no more, and in between I drink the fine red wine Theo has chosen.

'This is beautiful.'

Across from me, his eyes rest on my lips for a moment too long, so my heart rate kicks up a notch. Beneath the table, our feet brush and I remember we said we're better off avoiding restaurant situations—

and why. Desire is a wave inside of me, gaining speed and urgency.

'Do you come here often?'

'To Paris?'

'Yeah, and here. The waiting staff seem to know you.'

He nods. 'A friend of mine owns it, and the gin bar across the street.' He nods across the cobbled road, where I see a packed bar. It has marks of the same bohemian charm as this restaurant. His expression shifts for a moment and then he smiles, a smile that warms my blood. 'I actually thought you might be interested in meeting him.'

I sip my wine. 'Why? Is he looking for teen make-up?'

He grins. 'Nah. I meant for Operation Happily Ever After.'

He says it so easily, so comfortably, whereas his words make my ears fill with pounding blood. It's just because it's weird, that's all. Sitting opposite Theo, a man with whom I've had the closest thing to a relationship in my adult life, prosaically discussing my next partner? It's *weird*.

'What's he like?' I ask, just because he's look-ing at me expectantly, and I have to say something.

'He's a cool guy. Great surfer, likes to rock climb.'

And, despite the absurdity of this situation, I laugh. 'How well you know me.'

'What?'

'It's just…neither surfing nor rock climbing are on my "must have" list, I've got to be honest.'

'So what is?' He leans forward and his expression is analytical and watchful, so my mouth goes dry and a frown crosses my face.

'Erm… I don't actually *have* a list.'

'So make one now.'

I stare across at Theo, not letting myself populate the list with the qualities of his that I find desirable. 'Well, I guess interesting and intelligent. Someone with a social conscience. You know, not some guy who's just interested in showing off or whatever.'

'No hipsters.'

'Is this my list or yours?'

'I know you.' It's delivered deadpan but it sends a cascade of feelings through me. Because he *does* know me, and that's rare. Apart from Kevin, I keep most people at a distance in life. 'Money?'

'What about it?'

'Does he have to have it?'

I think about that a moment. 'He has to not care that I have it.' I blink away for a moment, knowing he sees everything and understands me way better than I'd like.

'That's an issue for you?'

I swallow. 'It has been.' There's no point in dissembling with Theo.

'Some fortune hunter fiasco?'

He makes light of it but I can't quite summon a smile.

'Something like that.'

'Seriously?'

I blink towards him. 'It was a long time ago.'

He swears under his breath and reaches for my hand. 'I'm sorry. No one… You should never…' He shakes his head, apparently lost for words. 'What happened?'

'You know, it was just some guy I liked, a long time ago. I thought he was The One; he thought I was his ticket to fame and fortune.' I shake my head and now my lips twist into a rueful expression. 'It was my own fault. I think I was rebelling against Dad, even then. He hated the guy, told me it would be a disaster. He was right, as it turns out.'

Theo's expression is like thunder. 'He was an idiot.'

'My dad's not… He's just…'

'Not your father,' Theo mutters. 'The ass-wipe who saw your net worth as your utmost value.'

I dip my head. 'It's probably a hard thing to look beyond, for most people. So yeah, someone with money makes it a bit more straightforward—I'd never have any doubts, at least, about why they were interested in me.'

'Done.' His expression is inscrutable. 'What else?'

'Someone who's kind, and patient. Who understands that I work long hours and gets why my work matters to me.' My smile lifts. 'Someone who makes me want to *not* work twenty hours a day.' I ignore how much of my list is a part of Theo. 'Someone who's ready to settle down, I guess, who's past the whole messing around stage of life.'

I feel like he wants to say something, but he doesn't. Instead, he leans forward so I catch the faintest hint of his masculine fragrance and my insides react accordingly. His expression is impossible to read. 'I know the perfect guy.'

'Really?' I'm sceptical, but I don't tell Theo that. I don't even want to admit as much, because I have no idea why I should be. 'Tell me about him.'

'Carrington Hughes-White. Carey. He's thirty, a financier, but he funds a charity project in Africa on the side—'

I roll my eyes. 'Because it looks good to his corporate investors?'

'No, Miss Cynical, because he understands that humanity is only as good as the way we treat those in need. He's a good guy, Asha. You'd like him.'

Am I imagining that his voice sounds raw and throaty? Probably, because his look is completely relaxed. Amused, even.

My gut feels like a stone has rolled through it. I don't want to have this conversation with him, but here I am, in the middle of what we've agreed to, trapped by it, and held in place by how completely okay Theo is with all of this. 'Okay, what else?'

'He's independently wealthy—self-made.'

'How do you know him?'

'I went to school with him. Scholarship kid.'

'And he'll be at the wedding?'

'He's like a brother to us—to all of us. Yeah, he'll be there.'

I dip my head again, not sure what to say, not sure how I feel. The wedding is still far enough away that I don't really want to think about it. And yet I lift my head and lance him with the directness of my stare. 'What's the deal with you and weddings, anyway?'

'Weddings? Nothing.'

But it's forced. I know him better than that; I understand him.

'Come on.' I reach across and squeeze his hand. 'No one's born hating love. What happened?'

His expression doesn't shift.

'Did a girl break your heart?' My tone is teasing, purposely kept light.

He doesn't respond.

'Or a guy?'

One brow lifts with mocking amusement.

'Come on, Theo. What's the deal?'

'Does it matter?'

Does it? It shouldn't, and yet... 'I'm curious.' And then my toe runs over his calf. 'Indulge me.'

'I intend to.'

My pulse races, but there's a niggle of frustration too.

Perhaps he detects that because he expels a breath as he lifts a hand, signalling for the bill.

'There's no great secret. No heartbreak. I just had plenty of opportunity to see what relationships do to people. It's not pretty. I think I was about ten years old when I swore I'd be single for ever.'

Sympathy makes my heart hurt. 'You were just a boy, though. Surely at some point you grew out of that?'

'Are you kidding?' His grin shows a total lack of regret. 'I'm not cut out for relationships, Asha. This is who I am. I grew up in a house that was constantly shaking from arguments, fights, disagreements, affairs.' He shakes his head. 'My brother Holden is dealing with the fallout of our father's bullshit decisions even now, decades later. Love makes people stupid, reckless and malicious. Why would I sign up for that?'

'Because love can also make people happy?'

'I *am* happy,' he says simply. 'There's not a single part of me that feels like I'm missing out.'

His determination is hard to argue with.

'I guess I had the opposite experience,' I say after a moment's pause, a small frown on my face. 'My dad loved my mom. He was so devoted to her. For years after her death, she was all he could talk about. My whole life has been defined by his love for her. Caroline—my stepmother—is really good about it. She never wanted to compete with Mom; she understands Dad thinks of her as the love of his second life. So I see love in all its forms—the love Dad holds for Mom, and the way he and Caroline love each other. It's the opposite of what you've described.

There's so much respect and kindness, reason and affection. And happiness, yes.'

I don't say how set apart from that happiness I am, that my father lives in a bubble and I am kept firmly on the outside.

He sips his drink, his eyes boring into mine. 'That's great—for them.'

Message received, loud and clear. He's not shifting in his opinion—but this I already knew. Why is that bothering me all of a sudden? Perhaps it's simply knowing we're nearing the end. Or maybe it's just feminine ego, like I want him to want me for ever and ever? It is weird to think he can let me go so easily, that he can set me up with a friend without a care in the world.

Could I do the same? I imagine introducing Theo to someone else. No, choosing a friend who would be perfect for him. I imagine watching sparks fly, and the thought spreads like poison through my veins.

So maybe he's a better person than I am. Maybe he's a better friend. Or maybe he's just way better at delineating sex from anything else.

I'm being stupid.

Ridiculous.

We've *both* been clear about what we want from the beginning. There's no way I'm going to ruin our last few weeks together by over-thinking everything. It was better, easier, when we didn't get too deep— sex is sex; he's right.

'Do you want to take a look at the dessert menu?' he offers.

My eyes latch onto his and I shake my head slowly, my intent clear.

'Do you want to go home?'

My nod is just as slow. I lean forward, a smile playing about my lips, 'And then I want to fuck you all night long, Theo Hart.'

CHAPTER NINE

I DON'T KNOW if it's the wine or our conversation but my body is burning up for Theo in a way I can barely contain. We get a cab back to my place—even though it's a beautiful summer night and the walk would be nice. I can't wait. I need him. There's something affirming in sleeping with him, like it reminds me of who we are and what we're doing together.

As soon as we reach the apartment I jerk the door inwards and then practically jump on him, my body melding to his, all thoughts of my long day forgotten, all thoughts of *anything* forgotten. There is only this.

'You are so fucking hot,' he groans, as though it's a complaint, his hands finding the waistband of my skirt and separating my shirt from it, pushing it up my body roughly, hungrily, desperately. I lift my arms to make it easier; he tosses it across the room then unclips my bra, his fingers worshipping the soft flesh of my breasts, his touch sparking wildfire across my body. I make a whimpering noise as he kisses me, pleasure radiating through me, but he's catching my hands and pinning them to my sides so I can't move, I'm trapped by him, as he kisses me lower, his mouth dragging over my throat, his stubble rough against my soft flesh. His bun tickles my nose and I laugh, but it's a deranged sound because pleasure is building inside of me like a wave and I need so much more, so much faster.

'I need…'

I don't finish the sentence, but he nods. 'I know. I know. Fuck.'

I hear the desperation in his words and know this is just as urgent for him, that he can wait no longer. Power rocks me because I, and I alone, am capable of bringing a man like Theo Hart to his knees. Okay, maybe not just me, but I don't want to think about him with another woman, especially not now.

He pushes my skirt down and then nudges it lower with his knee, his body surrounding mine as he guides me across the lounge room, towards the bedroom. My skirt falls somewhere on the floor, and then his hands are in my thong, pushing at the lace, holding it low enough for me to step out of. But he pulls away from me then, his eyes dropping to the scrap of fabric, a look in his eyes that sparks a firestorm in my blood.

He keeps it in his hand as he brings his mouth back to mine, kissing me so perfectly, so achingly exactly like I want it. His tongue is duelling with mine, his other hand—the hand that doesn't hold my underwear—is lifting up to cup my cheek then moving behind my hair, dragging me to him, holding me right there so he can plunder me. I whimper against him and then I'm lifting my leg, wrapping it around his waist, trying to bring him closer.

Damn it, he's still dressed. 'Way too many clothes,' I mutter, the words panting out of me.

'Yeah.' His own voice wobbles; he laughs huskily then strips out of his shirt, revealing his chest to me. I'm so hungry for him and yet I lift a hand to his naked chest, stilling him, slowing things down. I stare at the ridges created by his muscular definition, tracing each one with my fingertip, dropping my mouth to his collarbone. I run my teeth along it, delighting in the way his breath snags in his throat, in the racing of his pulse that I can feel beneath my lips. I move my hand, laying my palm flat over his pec so every rapid thump of his heart resonates inside me and my own answers it. In that moment my heart beats for his, and the speed of his. We are matched.

He growls, pushing at his boxers, no longer able to wait, and I understand, but God, I just want to savour this. I'm conscious time's running out for us and I want to remember every little detail. I trace his tattoo with my tongue, smiling as I imagine a young Theo going to get inked, aligning himself with a Greek god. Though, to be fair, he wasn't wrong.

There is something Greek god-like about him—didn't I think that the night we met? A shiver runs down my spine as I remember the first time we made love when he was new and I had no idea what to expect. His power and strength, his skill and attentiveness.

'You really are so good at this,' I whisper, moving around to his back, pushing his boxers the rest of the way, cupping his naked bottom, the muscles there making it firm beneath my touch.

He spins around, pinning me with his arms, and a second later his mouth is on mine, my gentle exploration at an end as he ratchets this up, his need palpable. He wraps his arms around my back and pulls me to him so his arousal slams against my belly, hard and insistent. I reach between us, cupping my fingers around him, smiling against his mouth as anticipation fills me.

'Turn around.' It's a guttural command.

I lift my face to his for a second but he flashes me a tight smile—tight, I think, because he can barely hold on another moment—and then he's bending me forward towards the bed.

'Stay there.'

Another command, and this time I obey it without question. I lie with my wrists on the bed and when he comes back I hear the tell-tale noise of protection and then his hands are on my thighs, spreading my legs wider. He mutters something in Greek and then he drives himself into me, his possession from behind so deep, so all-consuming while his hands on my hips steady me as pleasure blinds me momentarily.

'Theo...' His name on my lips is a curse and a

prayer. I dig my nails into the bed, holding on for dear life, fully aware I'm at risk of losing myself and not sure I care. 'God, Theo.'

He moves his hands to curve around my rear, and all I can do is feel—I feel every shift of his body, every thrust, every breath that whooshes out of him. I feel the balmy night air breezing through the half-open window, I feel the softness of the bed beneath me. I feel Theo in every pore of my body. I squeeze my eyes shut as I come, pleasure bursting over me like a dam wall at breaking point.

I don't realise I'm screaming until his hand curves over my mouth and a husky laugh emerges from him. 'You're going to wake all of Paris.'

'Don't. Give. A. Shit.' I press my face to the bed, my cheeks warm, my eyes foggy. It's too good. Everything about this moment is mind-blowing. But then he brings a hand around to my clit and begins to rub my sensitive flesh as he moves deep inside me and I can barely hold myself together. I bite down on my lip to stop from screaming so loudly but God, this feels good.

He is an expert at my body, an expert at *me*.

I feel another wave building but, before it can crash over me, his hands are chasing mine, catching the wrists, holding them completely still.

'I want to tie you up,' he murmurs, so my heart rate accelerates and I am beyond speech for a moment. 'What do you think?'

My mouth is dry. The image of being at his command is intensely erotic. 'Do you have any cable ties?' I joke, but my voice is airy and thin.

'Something better.' He slaps my butt lightly and releases my hands. 'Hop up.'

He pulls out of me and I climb up onto the bed, moving to the centre. His hands catch mine once more and his body comes over me, his gaze locked to mine as he presses my fingers to the ornate wrought iron bedhead. It takes me a second to realise he's using my thong as a restraint, weaving it in and out of the metal and around my wrists.

'Seriously?'

He grins. 'Innovative, right?'

'Genius.'

His eyes hold a warning and then he kisses me once, hard, fast, before lifting his face and staring down at me once more. 'Let's see if it'll hold.'

I don't realise what he means until his tongue is on my sex, running over my flesh, tormenting me and delighting me. I cry out and buck my hips, jerking on my arms but they don't move. They can't. I'm effectively trapped.

'Theo!'

His laugh is warm against my flesh and then his tongue is at my clit, his fingers separating me and sliding inside so my whole body is filling with warmth and heat. 'Fuck!'

He laughs again, a gravelly sound.

'This isn't…fair…'

'Do you want me to untie you?'

I push up to stare at him. 'No!' It's a whisper. 'I want you to…'

'You want to come again,' he teases, enjoying this.

I fall back to the bed, my pulse racing. 'Yes.'

'And you will, Asha. I'm going to make you come so many times you black out.'

A smile curves my lips. 'Is that a promise?'

Somewhere after the fourth orgasm I feel like I could actually faint. Pleasure has crested through me and I have no idea how I'll ever feel sane again. I'm living in some kind of euphoric world, all bliss and pleasure and hedonism.

'I want to stay like this for ever,' I groan, my body heavy with delight, my nipples tight and sensitive, my blood languid after rushing through my body for over an hour.

His control blows my mind. He is still so rock-hard. I feel his cock against my thigh as he flicks my nipples with his tongue and I shiver because all I can do is feel, and I feel almost too much.

'I like having you as my prisoner,' he murmurs, the words dark.

'Even though I can't touch you?'

'That's part of the appeal.' He pushes up onto his elbows, his eyes linked to mine. 'Do you want to touch me, Asha?'

I nod slowly. I do. I stare at his body hungrily.

'What do you want to do to me?'

I bite down on my lower lip, thinking about that, wondering which of my dozens of kinky fantasies I'd like to play out. The truth is, he's made all mine come true, and yet there's still so much more I want. A lifetime of exploring Theo's body wouldn't be enough.

I push that thought—that dangerous incursion into my pleasure—to the back of my mind.

'I want to go down on you,' I say honestly, my mouth dry at the thought. 'I want to climb on top of you and take you deep inside me.' A grin lifts my lips. 'I want to tie you up.'

He laughs and shakes his head. 'Done, done and no way.'

'Huh.' I pout. 'So what's good for the goose isn't for the gander?'

'In this case, yeah.'

'That doesn't seem fair.'

'Are you complaining?'

I shake my head slowly. 'Not even a little bit.'

'Good.' He brings his mouth closer to mine, brushing a light kiss over my lips. 'You are the sexiest woman I've ever known.'

The praise warms me all the way down to my toes.

'What an honour,' I tease him, but really the admission means something to me. In a relationship defined by sex, being the best he's ever had is important and flattering and worthy of holding to my heart.

He reaches above me, untying the makeshift restraint. I flex my wrists, grabbing for the underwear and laughing when I see how stretched out it is. 'I don't think I'll wear it again.'

'I like you without underwear anyway.'

Heat flies through me.

'In fact, I'm just going to imagine you naked beneath your clothes from now on. Deal?'

I reach up and push at his chest. 'Deal.' But, before he can speak, I drag my mouth to his cock and remove the condom, because I want to feel him inside me, all of him.

I take his length deep in my mouth, my body exulting in the power of this, tasting the promise of his release. His hands on my shoulders are tight and I hear his guttural cry.

'You need to stop,' he implores me quietly, his hips lifting a little, his hunger understandable after God knows how long of driving my body to the edge again and again.

In response, I flick his tip with my tongue. He swears, a hiss from between his lips, and then his hands are in my hair, his fingers tangling in its length as I move my mouth up and down until I taste more of him.

'You need to stop,' he repeats. 'I can't hold on.'

'Don't hold on.' I lift my eyes the length of his body and stare at him for a brief moment before taking him deeper, moving faster now, curving one hand around his base and cupping him, squeezing him, as I take him all the way to the back of my throat.

He cries my name as he comes and I hold myself where I am, my mouth low over him, and then I begin to move again until he's spent and his voice has silenced. Only the sound of his husky breathing fills the air. I let go of his cock and pull up, smiling at him and his passion-ravaged face.

'Now imagine how much better that would have been if you'd been tied up.'

He reaches for me, pulling me towards him, snuggling me into the crook of his arm. 'I beg to differ, Asha. Nothing could ever be better than that.'

Her fingers stroke the geranium petal reflexively. It's a gesture born of idle thought, not intent, and yet my eyes latch onto the repetitive motion and my body stirs. Light breaks across Paris, golden and warm, and Asha shifts a little, her eyes moving to mine, her irises such a rich shade of green, like the ocean, or the leaves of the geranium.

'You're awake.' Her smile is like sunshine after the storm. But what storm? With Asha, it's always sunshine. My body is in a permanent state of nirvana. I am alive with sensual heat, rock-hard with desire, heavy with satiation. It's revolutionary to me to experience something like this. Maybe I've been wrong all these years, preferring to hook up with women for a night or two at most. The *ongoingness* of this, without any emotional complication, gives me the best of all worlds.

We know each other intimately and with that knowledge comes the kind of pleasure you don't get from a one-night stand. I'm going to miss this. And her.

The realisation is like a lightning bolt in my mind, briefly slashing through the warm pleasure of my thoughts. Because I *can't* miss her. It's not allowed, it's not what we've agreed. Sex is sex and once Asha's out of my life I'll find someone else to have sex with, someone who'll agree to these exact same terms. Even when I don't want to? That thought doesn't bear examination. We have a plan and I have no intention of breaking it, even when there's something moving through me, something selfish and hungry that just wants more of this, always.

I know, even as I reach for the geranium in her fingertips, that there is no one like Asha. I might find someone different, someone who fits with me in other ways, but Asha is unique.

'Where did this come from?'

'The windowsill.' She smiles, more sunshine.

'Have you been up for long?'

She makes a noise of assent. 'Jet lag.' The word is said with a smile but there's a depth to her tone that has me studying her face thoughtfully. 'I was thinking about my *grand-mère* too.' Her eyes shift down, shielding her thoughts from me.

Curiosity flexes inside of me. 'When did you lose her?'

'A long time ago.' She lifts the geranium to her nostrils, inhaling its scent, a wistful smile changing her expression now. 'She loved geraniums. All flowers, really. When she was a little girl, they didn't have a lot of money. She used to tell me about her life in the Loire Valley, filled with abundant beauty and a permanently empty belly.' She lifts her eyes to mine and my breath rushes out of me at the sparkling depth in her irises. 'My great-grandfather was in the War and when he came back he would collect flowers for my great-grandmother every morning. *"I never thought I should see colours like this again. I never thought I would smell their intoxicating fragrance".*'

Her expression assumes a faraway look.

'He was a chemist by training, so it wasn't a big step for him to move into perfume production. He distilled several flowers, over months, years, blending their essences until he created the exact fragrance he wanted, the scent that had kept him going while he was away. It reminded him of my great-grandmother and life in the little village they called home.'

She smells the geranium again and I am struck by how elemental she is, how like the stunning geranium—strong and vibrant, beautiful.

'And that's how the company was born?'

'Mmm.' She smiles. 'He called it Fleurs Sauvages. Our name—Sauvages—means 'wild', and while he was at war he used to say that was just how he felt. Wild and untamed, feral, surviving on instinct alone. But, coming home, he saw beauty in the wildness, beauty in the flowers that grew through the cracks in the village walls, little escapees seeking only sunshine and water.'

Her laugh is a soft pealing bell. 'I spent a lot of time at his knee, listening to his stories. Can you tell?'

'And he liked to talk?'

'Oh, towards the end, yes, he lived for these memories. They're a part of our company ethos now, a part of our institutional memory. He's eternal because of the business.'

'How did he start selling the perfume?'

'He was an ambitious man. War had made him hungry too, and he had a daughter to feed. He was very clever, associating the brand with wealth and aspiration from the beginning, so Fleurs Sauvages was the only perfume anyone wanted to wear.'

I stroke her arm and she smiles at me, so unguarded and relaxed, my chest expands. I like making her smile.

'I used to love coming here.'

'To this shrine to colour?' I tease.

Her smile is wistful and a rueful expression touches her features as she looks around the room. 'To France. I grew up in America but France is so much a part of me. I hear their voices in my head while I work, my grandparents, my great-grandparents.' Her smile is reminiscent now.

'Did you come to stay with your grandmother after your ex died?'

The smile slips. 'For a time.' She moves in the bed, turning back to face me. She is naked, just how I like her. I reach for her, drawing her closer to me, wanting to kiss the smile back into place.

'I think he'd be proud of you.'

Her eyes are huge in her face. I brush my lips over hers and feel her sigh. 'Do you?'

It's so strange, that she wouldn't immediately see that as an indisputable fact. I catch her face in my hands, one on each cheek. 'Hell, yeah, Asha. Of course he would be.'

And I kiss her to show her how honest I'm being. I kiss her as though my life depends on it. She tastes like vanilla and raspberries; her skin is warm like sunshine. She is a wildflower brought to life, with her bright hair and soft skin.

My very own *fleur sauvage*. I push up, my body over hers, an insatiable need to possess her driving my movements now. I reach across the bed, pulling a condom from the bedside table and rolling it in place. She stares up at me, her hair like a jewel across the bedlinen. I kiss her as I thrust deep inside her, moving quickly, desperately, hungrily, my body knowing how to give pleasure and take pleasure all at once.

She arches her back, her moans calling to me. I drop my head, taking one of her beautiful nipples into my mouth, my hands on her hips revelling in the feeling of her, of this. I remember the way she looked tied to the bed, the way her hair spilled across the pillow and I remember the way she went down on me, taking my cock deep in her mouth until I tipped my seed into her throat.

Fuck. She is hotter than anything, anyone, anytime. I make her mine, as I've done countless times since we met, and she welcomes me as always, meeting my passion with her own, answering my needs as I answer hers.

It's only much later, when she's dressed for her day, making coffee in the kitchen, that I realise we crushed the geranium into nothing. I pick up its broken, fragile remnant and hold it in my hand for a moment before discarding it on the bedside table.

Nothing lasts for ever. Ashes to ashes.

CHAPTER TEN

'ASH. WAKE UP.'

I blink slowly, a fog of disorientation making it hard to think straight. Where am I? There's a noise, low and soft, like the hum of a car. No, not a car. A plane. I'm on the Hart Industries jet. We left the States last night, bound for Sydney. Is it morning? Travelling multiple time zones always throws my body clock out of whack, or maybe it's some kind of self-preservation technique because, a month after my abortive date with Angus Fienes and our subsequent deal, the Sydney weekend is here and that means one thing: this is over. The end. No more Theo.

'We're nearly landing. Come and see.'

I look towards the window to my right. All I can see is blue sky.

'Not yet. I'll show you.' He's like a little boy at Christmas. Pushing aside the last vestiges of sleep, I step out of the bed and heat suffuses my cheeks as I remember how we spent a good portion of the flight. It turns out there is something special about the mile-high club after all.

I place my hand in his without thinking and follow him through the plane. At the door to the cockpit he surprises me by spinning around, pressing a kiss to my lips then grinning again, the same look of happiness on his features.

I return his smile but it feels dredged from deep within me. My dream is hot on my heels, grabbing hold of me, and I remember it piece by piece as Theo opens the door.

I was in a maze, one of those huge mazes made of pine trees, thick and dark, and I couldn't find Theo. I knew he was there because I could *feel* him but I couldn't find him. And as I took each turn, looking for him, the maze corridors grew thinner and darker so they were pressing down on me and against me, the needles sharp, hurting my skin, the air thin, making breathing difficult. There were no stars in the sky but it was night, and it was neither cold nor hot, just heavy. The air was oppressive. I shiver as the dream rushes through me.

Theo doesn't notice my expression.

'Have a seat.' He gestures to a fold-down chair behind the captain. 'Asha, this is Major Andrews.'

'Hey.' I remember him from the last flight.

'Good morning, ma'am.'

I don't tell him to call me Asha. What would be the point? I'm probably never going to see him again. The thought rushes through me like an icy wind. I've made my peace with this—or thought I had—but the truth is, the reality of what I have to get through in the next seventy-two hours is enough to make my insides shudder.

This is the end.

Inescapably, inarguably, and probably for the best. Since we left Paris I have seen Theo almost every night. We didn't consciously agree to that, but the impending cessation of our relationship filled us both with an insatiability, and indulging it seemed not a question of desire so much as a necessity. I have no idea how I'll draw breath when Theo isn't a part of my world and yet I must, because soon that's the reality in which I'll find myself.

I imagine my future and know how important this is. I want everything he doesn't; I want what he can't give me. This has to end, even when that feels like ripping my arms from my body.

Theo takes the co-pilot's seat. His hair's down, and it falls about an inch beneath his shoulders. The ends are much fairer than the top, but it's not because of any chemical intervention or vanity, just the sun's natural effect on him. He's wearing a white T-shirt and a pair of jeans but he looks like he belongs behind the wheel—er...controls—of this thing. And there are about a billion controls. Tiny dials and wheels, switches and buttons. I watch, awestruck, as he and Major Andrews move side by side. It's like some kind of ballet, perfectly choreographed. Despite what Theo says, he looks so at home here. I imagine he could well have chosen this as his career.

'Wait for it,' he murmurs, turning around to face me, his smile so beautiful I can't help but return it. The plane dips a bit and the clouds wrap around us, grey and thick, woollen. It's impossible to see, but then, flying's not like driving. They're relying on their instruments to direct them.

The plane wobbles a bit as we pass through more clouds, but here, at the front of the plane, it's barely a dip.

'Wait for it,' he says again, and now Major Andrews turns around to grin at me, apparently amused at Theo's excitement.

A few seconds later and the plane is out of the clouds. Sydney opens up beneath us like a tiara against the ocean, all sparkling silver high-rises, white waves, golden sand.

The distinctive Opera House and bridge are visible as the plane circles lower, and I crane forward in my seat.

It's a spectacular city and this view of it is unrivalled. The plane drops lower and I keep my eyes on the view, marvelling at its beauty as conversation between Theo and Major Andrews turns quiet and serious. They're focused now on the business of landing the plane.

I watch as they run their fingers over the dials and then the airport comes into view, the runway long and straight beneath us. Theo grips the controls and the plane lurches lower, and lower, and my stomach flops because seeing a plane come down like this is unnerving, actually. I'm not worried, just awestruck; it's breathtaking.

Lower and lower. There's a noise as the wheels drop and then we're in a proper descent and the plane touches down. I let my breath go, smiling as they apply the brakes and the plane slows down quickly, the wings offering resistance to help bring the plane to a halt. Theo unbuckles his seat belt and turns to me, standing before the plane has stopped moving. Major Andrews is steering it now, using the instrument panel to bring the bird into a hangar a little distance from the commercial planes.

'So?' Theo grins, his hands on his hips. 'What do you think?'

What do I think?

I think seeing him fly an airplane is incredibly hot. I think Sydney is beautiful. I think *he* is beautiful. I think a thousand things and then I think a thousand that I shouldn't, and in the back of my mind is my dream, the darkness and oppressiveness of it threatening to eclipse the happiness of that moment.

'I think that was pretty cool,' I say lightly, careful not to give away even the slightest hint of the thoughts that are hounding me.

He grins. 'I'm glad.' His kiss is light and over before it begins. He pulls away from me and I watch as he walks along the plane, bracing himself on a chair as he nears my handbag. He lifts it up, then grins.

Not a hint of concern.

No beetling of his brow.

Nothing.

It's almost the end, and he doesn't care.

I tell myself I don't either.

Sydney in September is beautiful, and warm. I stretch against the sun lounger. The pool makes a gentle lapping noise at my feet. The harbour is right beneath us, sparkling and pretty, filled with boats— big old ferries but nimble, elegant speedboats too.

I don't hear the doorbell to the penthouse but Theo does. He pushes up, his hands trailing my feet as he moves past me. 'The door,' he explains at my quizzical look.

'Oh.' I stay where I am, my eyes heavy. Since we arrived in Sydney yesterday, all we've done is sleep, eat, swim and make love. There is euphoria in this, but also the ever-present feeling of disbelief, of bracing for impact, like I'm in a train that's heading towards a broken bridge and there's nothing I can do to stop it, nor to avert disaster. But I'm being melodramatic, aren't I? It's not as though I've never had to overcome anything in my life, and I'll overcome this too.

A moment later, voices break through my slumberous state. Two male voices and that of a woman. I blink my eyes open just as they step onto the terrace.

'Ash...' Theo smiles but I feel something in his

expression. Frustration. Guilt? It makes no sense. I reach for a towel, wrapping it under my arms.

'This is my brother, Jagger.' He gestures to a man—handsome, with fair hair and white teeth. 'And my sister-in-law-to-be, Grace.' He comes to stand at my side but doesn't touch me. It's noticeable only because he's barely stopped touching me all morning.

'This is Asha Sauvages, a friend of mine.'

Grace's eyes flick wide. 'As in Fleurs Sauvages?'

'Uh-huh.'

'Wow. I love your products.'

I'm glad, because I've brought a shedload of cosmetics as a wedding gift for her. 'Thanks.'

Her smile is genuine. There's something about her I find myself warming to. 'We only popped in to say hi,' Grace explains, flicking her gaze to Jagger. 'We won't keep you long.'

'It's fine,' I rush to reassure her. 'We're just losing time here by the pool.'

'Did Theo mention my hens' night?' she prompts, pulling her long blonde hair over one shoulder.

Jagger reaches for her hand once she drops it to her side, his fingers lacing through hers. She lifts her face to his, smiling naturally, kindly, and the strength of their connection is palpable.

'I hadn't yet, no,' Theo responds.

Grace rolls her eyes then shoots Theo an impatient look. 'It's tonight. You're invited.' She reaches into her pocket and pulls out a small card. It has the name of a restaurant on it. 'Sorry about the late notice. I told him about it a couple of weeks ago...'

He lifts his hands in the air. 'I forgot. What can I tell you?'

'Yeah, yeah.' Grace grins, so it's obvious she's not really annoyed. 'It doesn't matter. You can make it?'

'Yeah, of course.' I nod after only the slightest hesitation, thinking of time away from Theo with true regret. 'I wouldn't miss it.'

'Great. I'll see you there. Eight o'clock.' Then, after another pause, 'Do you want me to send a car for you?'

'No, Grace! You're the bride. That's sweet of you but the last thing you should be doing is worrying about me. I'm really flattered you've even invited me.'

'Of course!' She says it like it's the most natural thing in the world. I feel like a total intruder. This is a private family event and I'm no one to any of them. Not really. Jagger drops Grace's hand and pulls her close to his chest, dropping a kiss to the top of her head. I can't help but contrast their easy familiarity with the way Theo and I are standing a couple of inches apart, carefully not touching.

'Are you excited?' I ask Grace, drawing her a little away from Theo and Jagger. We move towards the door by silent, unspoken agreement.

'Yeah. Nervous too,' she whispers. 'Not about the marriage but about the wedding. So many people, all looking at me.' She shakes her head. 'I didn't realise I was nervous about that kind of thing until recently.'

'Oh, you just have to fake it,' I say with confidence, putting my hand in the small of her back and guiding her into the house. 'Come with me. I have something for you.'

She frowns. 'For *me*?'

'You are the bride, right?'

'Yeah, but you didn't need to do that.'

'It's fine,' I rush to assure her. We walk towards the bedroom and I'm grateful AF that the maid service has been because a few hours ago the room bore clear evidence of how we'd spent the night.

I push in and lift my suitcase from the wardrobe, unzipping it and removing a couple of heavy-duty shopping bags. A bounty of FS products sits inside each one.

'Oh, wow.' Grace stares at them, shaking her head. 'Asha, this is way too generous.'

'Don't be silly. It's my company, you know.' I wink at her and she smiles, a beautiful smile that lights up her eyes.

'That's really kind of you.' She throws a look over her shoulder to make sure we're still alone. 'So you and Theo…?'

Her curiosity is natural but it makes something inside me sting. How did he introduce me? As a friend, that's right.

'Just friends,' I say, the hole in my chest hurting all the more for the fact that, at its heart, the statement is true. We're friends who sleep together, nothing more. And we never will be more.

'That's what he said.' She shakes her head. 'That's a shame. I kind of liked the idea of him settling down.'

My heart skids to a stop, then rushes back into action. 'I don't think that's going to happen anytime soon.'

Grace's eyes narrow and I have the strangest feeling she's trying to read my mind. Then she lifts her shoulders as though it doesn't really matter. 'You're probably right. Thank you again for this. It's way too much…'

'Nonsense.'

Inexplicably, and out of nowhere, my throat thickens with the threat of tears. I shake my head to clear them, forcing a smile to my face. 'I'll see you tonight.'

I throw the Scotch back, staring out at Sydney with a growing sense of unease. Asha and I formed our deal weeks ago, and it makes sense. She wants things I can't give her. I can't monopolise her body, her time, just because I love making love to her, when she wants to settle down and have kids. What we're doing feels great right now but what if she wakes up in a year's time and resents me for holding her back?

We made this agreement and it's the right thing to do, but, fuck me, now that we're in Sydney and the wedding is just around the corner, I can't quite believe we're nearing the end of this. I try to picture my life without her in it, and I know how I'll cope with that, I know I'll find someone else to sleep with as quickly as I can, just to prove to myself that she doesn't mean more to me than I'm comfortable with—

But shit, right now, the idea of fucking someone else is like drinking acid.

The idea of not seeing Asha again is like a dagger through my gut.

I hear the door click open then slam shut and turn towards it, taking a moment to sum up the situation. She wore a simple green maxi dress to the hens' party. It's emerald in colour, picking out the depth of her eyes and the translucency of her skin. I stare at her for several seconds, at the way she's styled her hair in big, loose waves, tumbling down her back, and a deluge of wants and needs overtakes me.

But then she stubs her toe and swears under her breath and I realise exactly what I'm looking at.

'You're drunk.' I can't help it. I laugh. Asha is 'tiptoeing' through the penthouse, but with all the grace and stealth of a baby rhinoceros.

She turns to me, her eyes huge in her face, and lifts a finger to her lips. 'Shh…'

I laugh again, a deep, rumbling sound, as I move quickly across the room and put an arm around her waist. It's an arm designed to steady her but, holy crap, just having her so close to me makes my body harden, awareness throbbing through me.

'Did you have a good night?'

'I had the *best* night.' Her voice is the loudest whisper I've ever heard. I steer her towards the kitchen and lift her easily, plonking her on the edge of the bench while I grab a bottle of still mineral water.

'Grace is so nice. And her friend Penny is nice. They're all so nice.'

She dances a little on top of the benchtop, wiggling her hips and lifting her hands in the air. 'But I'm hot.' She frowns, pulling at her dress, her frown deepening when she can't get it off.

'Hang on—' I laugh '—it's zipped up.' I come around behind her and run the zip the length of her body, fiercely telling my cock to settle down because Asha is in no condition to have sex.

'That feels good,' she murmurs, apparently not getting the memo.

I step away from her, not looking at how gorgeous she is, not looking at the delicate lace of her bra that reminds me of the thong I used as handcuffs that night in Paris.

I hand her the mineral water. 'Drink this.'

'I'm not thirsty.' Her voice is a purr.

Great. She's doing her level best to seduce me and I've decided to go all honourable and not sleep with her because she's drunk? What the fuck is wrong with me? Then again, that's not new. Sleeping with someone who can barely walk has never been my thing. But Asha's Asha. We're different.

'Do you know what I don't get, Theo?' Her voice is a little slurred, her eyes heavy. She drinks the mineral water and smiles at me but her eyes are troubled, as though she's hurt. The idea of that—of anyone hurting Asha—brings all my masculine protective instincts to the fore.

Something inside of me shifts. 'What's that, Asha?'

'Jagger is so madly in love with Grace. I mean, he's crazy for her. He even showed up tonight—'

'What?' I interrupt, pulling a face.

'Yeah. He said he didn't want to go a whole night without seeing her.'

I bite back a derisive comment. That brother of mine has got it bad.

'How come he wants to be normal and you don't?'

I know what she's asking but it's easier to make light of her question than it is to answer it honestly. 'You don't think I'm normal?'

She rolls her eyes and winces as—I can only presume—her head aches in response. I spin away, grabbing a couple of paracetamol. 'You know what I mean.' She's frowning when I turn back to her.

'Nope.' It's a lie. Guilt shifts inside of me. Sober, Asha is sharper than a blade. I doubt I could win an argument with her to save my life. But, after God knows how many glasses of champagne, she's blurry and foggy and I'm ashamed to say I'm taking advantage of that.

'They're so in love.' She shakes her head then winces. I press the tablets into her hand.

'That's good, given that they're about to get married.'

'You know what I mean.' She lifts the paracetamol tablets to her mouth and puts them in, then sips her water. 'His dad is your dad and Jagger's getting married.'

Something in the region of my chest tightens, like a band is being strung around me.

'Mmm.' It's non-committal. 'You should go to bed, Ash. You're done.'

'Don't do that,' she mumbles, her eyes lifting to mine, and there's something in them. Accusation and sadness. My gut rolls.

'Do what?'

'Don't make a joke out of this. I'm asking you seriously. Why?'

'Why what?'

'How come he's getting married and you're...?'

I expel a sigh. 'Jagger and I are different people. We want different things.'

'You both want to be happy,' she counters.

'But it doesn't follow that the same things will make us happy.'

'But he's not afraid of marriage.'

'How do you know?'

Her eyes flare wide.

'Maybe he's afraid but he loves her enough to do it anyway.'

Something shifts in her expression. She's foggy and drunk and so the words don't seem to settle properly for several seconds. 'You mean he's met the right person,' she says with a frown.

I feel danger all around me, alarm bells pealing, and yet I nod slowly. 'Yeah. He was married before. It didn't turn out great. So he must love Grace a shit-load to be trying again.'

She nods, contemplating this. 'So he's met the right person, and you never have.'

More alarm bells. That's not what I meant. But doesn't she have a point? Kind of. 'It wouldn't matter who I met, I'm not interested in marriage. Nothing and no one is going to change my mind.'

'Maybe you just think that now,' she whispers, frowning as she wriggles away from me and jumps off the bench. Her legs are wobbly; she has to steady herself on the edge to stay standing. 'Maybe you'll meet someone one day and decide you want—'

'No.' I press a finger to her lips, knowing how important it is that she believes me. 'There is no one on earth who could interest me in marriage. I will never want that, Asha. Not with anyone.'

'I do.' It's a simple statement but my heart breaks. For her?

'I know that.' A gravelled admission.

'I was looking at Grace and Jagger and I just felt so… I don't understand how you don't want that.'

'Everyone's different.'

Oh, Jesus. A sheen of tears fills her eyes. I hate myself right now, I really do.

'You might change your mind one day?'

'No.' I stare at her for several seconds so she understands the truth of my words. 'I know myself. I won't. Ever.'

'Even for me?'

Her words shock me, galvanising me and paralysing me at once so I'm a contradiction of instincts. 'Asha…'

My voice holds a warning. She stares at me, her expression inscrutable.

'I've told you…'

'But since then,' she insists, her voice a little slurred, but her meaning crystal-clear, 'haven't you started to feel…anything?'

Have I? I shake my head, knowing that feelings are dangerous, hurt is inevitable. And I don't want to hurt Asha. 'No.' A firm denial, ringing with finality.

She blanches, spinning away from me, lifting a hand to her head. 'I'm tired.'

'Yeah.' My voice is stony. 'You should go to bed.'

CHAPTER ELEVEN

I WATCH THE wedding with a smile plastered to my face but the whole time I'm conscious of Theo up there, looking so handsome in that tuxedo, and something inside me is hammering hard against my ribs.

Tears are clogging in my throat, because I feel like I'm sinking or drowning or being forced off the edge of a cliff.

All I can think about is our conversation. I've barely seen him since—he was involved in wedding preparations yesterday and he spent last night with his brothers. Or maybe he was just avoiding me?

I was pretty tipsy after Grace's bachelorette night, but not so tipsy I can't remember what I said, and what he said. Not so tipsy that I've forgotten what I want and need from him, or how empty I felt when he didn't offer it.

Not drunk enough to anaesthetise the pain at my own stupidity.

I've fallen in love with Theo. I think I've known it for weeks, maybe even months, but this last week has crystallised those feelings into certainty. Seeing Jagger and Grace together was the final piece of the puzzle. Yes, I love him, and my life will never be the same again.

I draw in a breath and his gaze jerks sharply to mine as though, even at this distance, he's attuned to my every movement. His eyes run over my face. I keep that tight smile pinned to my lips but inside I'm falling apart completely.

And suddenly I'm not here in Australia on the deck of this sublime yacht in the shade of the Sydney Opera House. Suddenly I'm nine and it's my birthday and my dad is drunk, really drunk. He doesn't know I'm sitting under the piano—I used to love that place, so out of the way and quiet, away from anyone's notice. I hear him on the phone. I don't know who he's talking to. *'She looks so much like her but, God help me, I hate her sometimes. I hate her, I hate her. How can I feel anything but?'*

My eyes sweep shut and for a moment my smile drops. When I open my eyes Theo's looking at me from where he's standing beside his brother, his expression showing concern. I look away, swerving my eyes towards Grace.

I'm in love with Theo Hart and, just like my dad, he'll never love me back. Just like my dad, he's not capable of that. I suck in a painful breath and my blood hums with self-recrimination. I knew this all along. I had a thousand warnings and I heeded none of them. This was always within my power to control and I didn't.

I've been so stupid, so reckless. I deserve to feel this soul-splintering ache. He warned me. At every step of the way, Theo has warned me. He has no problems with our relationship ending; he doesn't want me. Just like my dad.

Memories of boarding school run through my mind, the awful knowledge that I was being sent away because he couldn't bear to have me in his home a moment longer. I had no home, not really. Not if home is a place where you're welcomed and loved.

I've been alone for as long as I can remember and being alone is what I loved about this situation with Theo—at first. Initially, we were like two people who were on parallel paths. We had sex but neither of us impacted too significantly on the other's life. He was no threat to me. I felt safe. Somehow that changed and now he's in every facet of my life, just like he's in every cell of my body.

And I'm in none of his.

The wedding is short but, to me, it drags. I stare at Theo and I accept that I have to walk away from him. Not later tonight, not tomorrow. Immediately. It's going to be the hardest thing I ever do but I was right all along—he's quicksand and I'm already in so deep. Up to my neck at least. If I don't leave now, I'll drown.

I harden my resolve, keeping a smile pinned to my face even as my heart is dying. This is what I have to do. Not once have I let my dad see my grief. Not once have I shown him how much his rejection hurt me. My pride forbade that, and that same sense of pride shapes my plan now.

I'll go without a backwards glance and not for a second will I let Theo know the reason. It wouldn't be fair on him. He's never promised me love, and it's not his fault I've broken the rules we agreed to. None of this is his fault.

'What do you mean, "gone"?'

I stare at the waiter and that old adage 'Don't shoot the messenger' screams inside my brain but I can't help it. I look at the man as though he's just told me the sky is about to fall because everything Asha said after Grace's bachelorette party is right there in the forefront of my mind and my sense of foreboding is impossible to ignore.

'Gone where?'

'Miss Sauvages asked me to explain, when the official photographs were completed, that she had an urgent situation at work. She sends her apologies and best wishes.'

'What else did she say?'

'I'm afraid that's all, sir.'

I glare at the waiter and then nod tersely, something pushing at my gut. I pull my phone out and type a text.

Where are you?

No answer. It's my brother's goddamned wedding so I can't leave, but something feels strange, despite the explanation the waiter gave me. I just can't imagine what emergency would have required her to leave then and there.

A little before midnight, I send another text.

I'll be back at the apartment soon. Hope everything's okay.

No answer. And, for no reason I can think of, a sense of unease grows within me. I leave as soon as I can politely do so, disembarking and getting straight in a limo, heading back to the penthouse with a dozen questions tumbling through me.

'Hey, babe? Is everything all right?' I ask loudly as I push the door inwards. The apartment is pitch-black.

'Asha?'

I move from room to room, my mind slow to accept what's patently obvious. I leave my bedroom until last. When I step inside, it's empty. Devoid of almost everything of Asha's except for two things. Her beautiful floral scent lingers in the air so if I close my eyes I can imagine she's standing right in front of me. And there's a note on the edge of the bed, her handwriting unmistakable.

I pick it up with an inexplicable sense of trepidation, unfolding the paper and reading it with my jaw clenched.

Theo,
Sorry to leave so abruptly. I had an urgent
work thing come up and didn't want to pull
you away from the festivities.
  Pass on my best to Jagger and Grace.
Thank you for everything.
Asha

I stare at her words, written in that beautiful cursive script of hers, with a squeezing in my gut. I feel like I'm on a rollercoaster and I can't slow it down. The note is so formal, so businesslike.

This is my fault. I knew she was upset with me; I'd planned to talk to her but there was no time yesterday. Or perhaps I didn't want to make the time. I knew she was still upset this morning, and I knew it when we got to the wedding and I said goodbye so I could go stand with Jagger. She was so tense it was as though she was holding a part of herself back from me. I pretended it didn't matter but, Christ, now I see. She was hurting, even then. I hurt her.

I call her number. It goes straight to voicemail.

I try again ten minutes later. Nothing.

I send her an email. No response.

I try calling a little while later, then reread the note, slamming stuff in my own bag as I skim the words.

This makes no sense. I load up a new text message.

Where are you?

It's a while before she finally replies.

Just landing in LAX.

Nothing else. Nothing more.
I stare at it and shake my head. It doesn't make any sense. Nothing makes sense.

Can we have dinner when I'm back? Day after next.

She doesn't reply for several hours, by which point I'm ready to get straight on a jet and fly myself directly to her apartment building. When she does finally get back to me, it's brief.

That's not a good idea. It's been fun, but I think it's best if we leave it at that. Take care of yourself, Theo.

Hell, to the no. No way is she ending it like this. After everything we've shared? My mouth forms a grim line on my face. We agreed to end it, she's right, but it was never supposed to be without a proper goodbye. I deserve at least that, don't I?

Running away was a really cowardly thing to do. I knew it as soon as the plane took off and I expelled a huge sigh of relief. I knew it and yet I didn't change my course, or my mind. It was a matter of survival or something.

And now, three days later, I lie in bed, staring

at the ceiling, listening to the pounding at the door without moving. Because I'm being cowardly still.

I know it's Theo. Who else would it be?

Sure enough, my phone buzzes a moment later and when I look at the screen his face buzzes up, larger than life. It's like being the victim of a drive-by shooting. I hadn't expected to see him, and not this photo, the one I took so many months ago when things were simple and I was the happiest I've ever been. Salt fills my mouth. I slam the phone down and stare resolutely at my ceiling.

A moment later, a text pings in.

We have to talk.

There's a tiny burst of hope that flares inside me. What if he doesn't want to lose me, to lose what we are?

But I know Theo too well to let that hope last long. He's stubborn and determined and he's not going to let anyone or anything change his mind. The whole time we were sleeping together he was adamant we would only ever be about sex. And on that last night in Australia I basically told him I loved him. I begged him to love me, just like I have begged my dad, over and over, and his response was just the same. Rejection. Resounding, soul-destroying rejection.

He's right, though. Running away after everything we've shared isn't right; he deserves a little more of an explanation, a proper goodbye. But not like this. It's going to be hard enough to face him without feeling like I've been hit by a bus. I sit up in bed and stare at my reflection. My eyes are red-rimmed, my skin pale, my hair a complete disaster. Reaching for my phone, I begin to type.

Sure. I can meet for a quick drink tonight. Six p.m.?

As soon as I send it, I feel better. Empowered.

Where are you?

I ignore his text, my heart pounding. A moment later, another message.

Fine. Four Seasons?

I don't know why he's chosen there as a venue. It reminds me of the night we agreed to end this, the night things shifted between us, and the feelings are like torture.

Asha?

Okay. I'll see you then.

I don't sign off with an X and I switch my phone to flight mode afterwards. It's rare for me to be out of contact but I just need some time.

How much time? God knows.

I dress with care that evening, choosing a pair of black leather pants and a beige sweater shirt that falls off one shoulder. It's a confidence thing, but it doesn't really help.

I have to pause outside the bar to get my breath, and then I stand in the doorframe, a little to the side so I can see in without being seen. I recognise his hair from across the room and a visceral ache spreads through me. I'm so tempted to turn around and walk away. It hurts like hell to see him, to feel like everything's shifted between us.

But I've already ghosted him once, I don't intend to do it again. This is going to be the hardest thing I've done in my whole darn life.

I grind my teeth and step into the bar, moving through it with my head dipped, sliding into the seat opposite before he sees me and before he can stand up.

I regard him, carefully keeping my expression blanked of anything, my eyes holding his for just long enough to be polite.

'Hey.' My smile is tight. 'How's it going?'

I sit there, staring at him, waiting for him to say something, but for a long time he just stares at me as though he's trying to make sense of a math problem.

'How are you?'

His question lands right between my breasts. I swallow back an acerbic rejoinder and try to remember the line I'd prepared. 'Fine, thanks. I'm sorry about leaving the wedding so abruptly. I had something pop up and—'

'What's going on, Ash?'

My stomach swoops. He knows me too well to be fooled by my lie. 'We agreed the wedding would be the end for us.'

'We agreed I'd help you meet someone else.' He pauses, a frown on his face as he searches for something else to say. 'The wedding was neither here nor there.'

Something flares inside of me. 'This might come as a surprise, but I think I'm pretty confident I can find my own dates. Thanks all the same.'

His expression shifts, a look of frustration drawing his brow downwards, but before he can speak a waitress appears, a bright smile on her face.

'Hey! What can I get you?'

Theo drags his eyes away from me. 'A beer. Asha?'

I feel like I need a drink but I want to get out of here as quickly as possible. I order a single shot of Scotch.

The waitress disappears, leaving us alone once more. I notice everything about him. I look at his hands and the memories of them on my skin are visceral and shocking.

'I wasn't pimping you out to my friends.' His voice is raw, like it's being dragged from deep inside of him. 'I just wanted to know you'd be with someone who deserved you.'

Theo looks away from me for a second and I study him for several moments, my eyes resting on his face, my heart twisting painfully in my chest. God help me, I love him. I love him so much that sitting across from him is a form of agony and torture because I know he doesn't love me, that he won't ever love me. He loves sleeping with me and, if I played my cards right, I could make it so that we keep doing what we were doing, mind-blowing orgasm after mind-blowing orgasm. But then what? For how long?

I have to get away from him.

'Look, Theo, this has been great. I've had a lot of fun with you, but I think it's pretty clear it's run its course.'

He turns to face me slowly but is forestalled from answering by the reappearance of the waitress. She places our drinks down and slides the bill between us. Theo takes it without looking up, placing his black credit card on the tray then passing it back to her. 'Start a tab,' he murmurs. I think it's just to get rid of her.

'Yes, sir.'

'I won't be staying long.'

'Why not?'

I frown.

'Why can't you stay?' He doesn't give me a chance to answer. 'Why do we have to end this?'

My stomach squeezes.

'Australia was just an arbitrary line in the sand. I don't want this to be over.'

'I do.' I'm surprised to hear the truth ringing through my voice.

'Why?'

I grind my teeth together. 'We want different things.' I stand up, reaching for my bag and jamming it under my arm. I have to get out of here. He's as much quicksand as ever. 'This isn't enough for me.'

'I know that.'

Somehow, his agreement angers me even more.

I don't want him to be placid and reasonable. I want him to fight with me. I want him to fight *for* me. But he doesn't.

'All I want is for you to be happy.'

I turn my head away, looking towards the door of the restaurant. 'And then what, Theo?'

'What do you mean?'

'You find someone else to fuck senseless whenever the mood strikes you?'

I can't identify the emotions that dance in his eyes, but I think I see shame there.

'And how long does that go on? The rest of your life? Is that really all you want?'

A muscle jerks low in his jaw. 'I want you.'

My stomach squeezes. I take a step back, uncomprehending. 'What?' It's just a whisper, a pained, hoarse word.

'I want what we have. I don't want it to end. I want more time.' He stands up too, hip to hip with me, his eyes holding mine, his sincerity so palpable it hurts. 'I want another month. Two. Three. However long you can give me.' His hands lift up and cradle my face and I feel more than his sincerity, I feel his sadness. I know how our end is hurting him, just like it's hurting me. My throat is raw with unshed tears.

'I can't do it.'

'I won't hurt you,' he promises, dropping his head forward so our brows touch and I taste him on my breath. 'I would never hurt you.'

I sweep my eyes shut. 'You already have, Theo. You can't help it.'

'Don't say that. I've tried so hard to do the right thing by you...'

'It's not your fault,' I promise, not moving, breathing him in for as long as I can because I know this now, right here, really is the end. 'Do you know what I liked about you? Do you know why I wanted to hook up with you that night at the gala event?'

He's silent.

'I'd had a terrible day. It was my birthday.'

He opens his mouth to say something. He hadn't realised. He doesn't even know my birthday—that's how shallow this is.

'Which means it's also the day my mom died. And I spent the day with my dad and all that guilt he lays at my feet and I just wanted to forget. I chose *you* to help me do that because I knew you were like this.' I gesture to his chest. 'You're a bachelor. In fact, you're famous for it. I knew what I was getting myself into. I just forgot that, somewhere along the way.'

A muscle jerks in his square jaw. 'Tell me what I can do to make this work. Just for a bit longer.'

'Nothing.' I pull away from him then, straightening, pushing against my sore, aching heart. I reach for his hand and squeeze it in mine. His strong, capable hand—hands that have promised me the world even when his heart never had any intention of following through with that.

'Look after yourself, Theo.'

I turn and walk out with my head held high and my heart smashing into a billion pieces. I don't think I'll ever be the same again.

CHAPTER TWELVE

'Asha, wait.' I run after her, catching her as she reaches the street corner. It's September. It shouldn't be cold but, out of nowhere, rain has started to fall. Just lightly, but the air has that smell of cooling asphalt and lightning. I grab her arm and spin her around. She's crying. Everything inside me grinds to a halt.

'Christ. What is it?'

'Nothing!' She glares at me with undisguised anger.

'I'm sorry, okay. Tell me what I can do to fix this.'

She shakes her head and laughs, but it's a sad laugh, a sound rich with disbelief. 'You don't get it, do you? All along you've told me what you want and I thought I was okay with that but a few weeks ago, that night with Angus, I started to feel... I guess it was like opening a box inside of me. I realised how much I wanted to be in a relationship, how important it is to me to have a family one day, but the answer was never about meeting someone else. I don't want anyone else. I just want you.'

I stare at her with intense frustration. 'Then how come we're both standing here in the rain arguing about this? I want you and you want me. It seems pretty damned simple to me.'

I drop my mouth to hers and the kiss is like coming home again. Fuck. I have never felt so whole as I do in this moment. I kiss her, pushing her body against the building, my back being doused in rain that has started to fall more heavily now, and I lose myself in the magic of this perfection. I breathe her in, tasting her, my body cleaved to hers, and I believe, in this moment, that everything's going to be okay.

'No!' She rips her head away, pushing at my chest, glaring at me and then she sobs, a sound that's akin to ripping my heart out of my chest. 'No.' Softer, but somehow more desperate.

'What is it?' I demand, but with desperation because we're so close to working this out. I just need her to tell me clearly what she needs from me and I'll do it. I'll give it to her. Anything.

'We don't want the same thing. We want precisely the opposite thing.'

'You're crazy.' I shake my head. 'We've just covered this.'

'I want you in my life in every single way. Not as just my lover, but as my boyfriend, my friend, my confidante. Everything you've been this whole time without realising it. I want you in my life for as long as we both shall live. I want you to be my partner, my husband, my everything. I want you to be the father of my children.' The last sentence is broken, filled with grief.

Her words are shelling down on me, harder than the rain, harder than anything. I listen to them with a growing sense of panic, my breath burning through me, and shake my head without realising I'm doing it. Everything she's saying is the exact opposite of what I want, except in one way. I don't want marriage, children, for ever, but I do want Asha. I want her, but not like she's described. I can't offer her those things.

'And you just want me in your bed—' her eyes are squeezed shut '—for a few more months.'

The insufficiency of what I've offered slams me like a freight train. We're looking at each other from two sides of a ravine. It's impossible to cross it.

'I want you to be happy,' I say quietly. 'And I think I can make you happy. For a time, at least. I think you're hurting now and you don't need to be.'

She sobs softly.

'I think you are beautiful and brave and that if I was ever going to question my approach to life, if I was ever going to change my mind about relationships and marriage, it would be for you.' I need her to hear that, to know it's the truth. 'This is who I am, and I can't change. I won't change. But if you let me, I will give more of myself to you than I ever have to another soul, and I will make you happy again, I will make you laugh, and I will be there with you until you're ready to walk away.'

She stares up at me and I have no idea how she

feels, no idea if she's going to agree or disagree, but I know I need her to say yes. So I keep going, taking her silence as an opportunity at least.

'Look. The whole "setting you up with someone else" thing was dumb. It made it seem like I could let you go without a thought, and that's not it at all. I just thought I could find someone who'd give you what I can't, someone who could make you happy because you deserve to be happy. But you're not, and it's my fault, and I want to fix it.'

I move closer to her again, pressing my body to hers, reminding her of the one way we can make sense of everything, of the way we can fix whatever's broken in both of us.

'Can we just pretend Sydney never happened?'

The idea comes to me from nowhere and it feels pretty fucking perfect, to be honest. Because before Sydney we were happy and everything was easy.

She lifts a hand to my chest but doesn't push me away. 'It wasn't just Sydney. I've had this feeling—' she taps her other hand to her chest, pushing it between her breasts '—inside me, here, for a long time, I just didn't understand it. But there's nothing worse than loving someone who will never love you back. I know what I'm talking about—I have lived my whole life with this feeling, knowing that my dad doesn't love me and that, no matter what I do, he never will.'

My heart breaks for her.

'You don't love me, right?'

God. You have no idea how badly I want to contradict that. To say what she needs to hear, just to make her smile. But lying to her is worse than anything else, so I don't.

'I like being with you.'

She flinches.

'I love spending time with you. I love how you make me feel.'

'But you don't love me.'

I look past her, to an old flyer on the door.

'Just say it, Theo.'

Fuck. 'No, Asha. I don't.' The world is dropping away from me. I feel as though I'm falling into the pit of fire at the centre of the earth's core. 'I'm sorry.' I feel a thousand things for Asha but none of them is exactly what she wants. 'I wish I'd been clearer about this.'

'You were plenty clear,' she murmurs, sidestepping me, moving directly into the rain. 'I should have left it as a one-night stand. I'll always wish I'd done just that.'

And the warmth in my heart turns to ice as disbelief fires through me at her statement. 'I'll never be sorry,' I say urgently, moving through the rain and pulling her into my arms. Her tears fall and my self-directed anger grows. 'I will never be sorry for a second we spent together except for one thing— that you were hurt by me.'

She nods, and lets out a small sound of agreement. Her tears mingle with the rain. I drop my face to hers, kissing her again, slowly, but I taste the salt in her mouth and it stirs something up inside me. I have to let her go. This is so selfish of me. She's told me how she feels and what she wants and I can't stand here toying with her emotions when I have no intention of offering it to her.

'I will always remember you as one of the best things that's ever happened to me.' I force myself to smile, to make it sound relatively upbeat and simple.

We stare at each other for several seconds, the rain lashing us, and I ache to do something, some small thing to make this better. 'My car's around the corner. Let me drive you.'

'No.' A whisper, but loaded with strength. 'It's fine. I'm fine.'

She's not. Fuck. 'Asha…'

She shakes her head. 'Don't. There's nothing more to say.' She swallows hard and looks away. 'Just… I don't know. Take care of yourself.'

She says it like her life depends on mine. Is that what love is? How the fuck would I know?

She turns and walks away and I ache to go after her, to run behind her until she stops walking and listens some more. But what do I say? What do I offer?

Nothing. I can offer her nothing and so I let her go. My father's legacy is one of pain. He hurt everyone who was ever foolish enough to care for him, and the memory of Asha's tear-stained face makes me realise I'm just the same. No matter how hard I tried to fight that, I've picked up the mantle and run with it. Out of nowhere I think of that geranium in

Paris, crushed by our passion, and the symbolism is impossible to ignore. I have destroyed something special and rare inside of Asha and the only answer is to let her go now, and hope she forgets all about me.

I watch her walk away and know I will not chase her. I'll never see her again, and the only gladness I can wring from that certainty is that I am doing what's right for her—finally.

Two months after that night in the rain, I shoot a look of sheer disbelief at Holden. His grin makes me want to punch him. 'Turn it off.'

'What? I thought she didn't mean anything to you?'

I clench my jaw, looking back to the TV. I feel Jagger and Grace watching me and want to storm out, but I don't because they're waiting for me to say or do something and I have no interest in cluing them in on how much I fucked up with Asha.

So I look at the TV even as it feels like a line is being sawed down my middle and my organs wrenched out. Christ, she looks so beautiful. Her hair is styled in braids, wrapped around her head like a crown, and she's wearing a sand-coloured jacket, tailored so it shows off her curves in a way that makes my insides pound, with an oversized scarf that's a shade of green perfectly complementary to her eyes.

'The bump in share price is gratifying, naturally.' She smiles in a way that makes my heart turn over

in my chest. The reporter, sitting across from her in
one of those TV sets that's mocked up to look like
a lounge room, nods encouragingly. I note the way
he looks at her and feel a rush of possessive heat.
It's completely inappropriate. It's been eight weeks
since I last saw her. I sent her a few texts for the first
week or so, tried to call to make sure she was okay,
but she didn't answer, didn't respond. Eventually I
got the message: *leave me alone.*

'But, more exciting than that, Cliff, is the market
response we're seeing to the launch of this range.
Angel Pie has sold out in four of the seven coun-
tries we launched into. Our mailing list and social
media accounts for this brand alone have seen tre-
mendous growth.'

'Is it too early to talk us through the P&L for the
launch?'

It's one of those business programmes that straddles a chatty news breakfast format, hence the em-
phasis on the business side of the range.

I lean a little closer without realising it.

Asha's smile is pure charm. My hand forms a fist
at my side.

'Way too early.' She laughs. 'But, as you know,
launches come at a cost. We have R&D to cover, but
I expect at this rate we'll be in the black for Angel Pie
within six to eight months. It's tracking incredibly well
amongst our expected demographic but we've found
an unexpected lift in a market we hadn't expected—
those with skin issues or recovering from aggressive

medical treatments like chemotherapy. The products are all so gentle and naturally formulated that...'

'She talks the talk.' Jagger speaks over her so I don't catch the rest.

I turn to face him, my face feeling all tight and hot. 'She believes it. This is her passion, man. She really cares about this.'

Just like she really cares about me. Guilt incinerates me.

Grace nods. 'It's true. We talked about it at my hens'. I think she's amazing.'

I turn back to the TV. She's laughing at something the interviewer has said and her life is such a fragment of my soul that for a second I feel like I've come home again. But I haven't; I'm not. Asha is a thousand miles away, or might as well be. I spin away from the television, stalking towards the bar.

'I mean it, Theo. She's really amazing. Are you sure it's over for the two of you?'

I grip a tumbler in my palm, staring at the wall behind the bar. I see Asha as she was on that last day, standing in the pouring rain, so beautiful, so fucking heartbroken, and all because of me. 'Yeah. It's over.'

'Do you...?' Her voice trails off into nothing.

I spin around to face her, sloshing some Scotch in my glass. 'Do I what?'

'Would you like me to talk to her?'

'No.' I laugh, a dismissive sound. 'You think if you call her up out of the blue and ask her about me she won't hang up on you?'

Grace narrows her eyes and her voice is the closest to haughty I've ever heard it. Gone is the light banter she usually reserves for me. 'It's not out of the blue, and I had no plans to call her up and ask about you. I'm having lunch with her tomorrow. I thought you might come up in conversation is all.'

Every cell in my body begins to screech. 'You're what?'

'Catching up with her tomorrow.' Grace speaks more slowly, as though I've developed a hearing problem.

'What?'

'They're friends.' Jagger's grin is broad, like he's enjoying this way too much. I shoot him a look of impatience.

'Since when?'

'Pretty much since we met,' Grace interjects.

'Convenient, right?' Jagger bounces back, twisting the knife in.

'Why?'

Grace lifts a brow, looking beautiful and somehow more vibrant than normal, which is saying something. 'Erm...because she's really lovely?'

My gut strangles.

'Is that a problem for you?' Grace asks gently, a frown crossing her face.

Jagger's grin drops and now his face holds a warning.

'Nah,' I lie. 'Suit yourself.' I throw the Scotch back.

'Anyway...' Grace's voice shows she's a little uncomfortable. 'We actually stopped here on our way back to Sydney because we wanted to talk to you both.'

My ears prick up. 'It sounds serious.' Holden's body is similarly poised. We've had enough bad news for a lifetime, enough unpleasant discoveries.

'It is.' Jagger puts an arm around Grace.

'What's going on?'

Then Grace's smile spreads across her face and she presses a hand to her stomach at the same time Jagger says something loud and excitable that sounds a lot like, 'Grace is pregnant'.

'You're for real?'

Grace nods. 'I'm three months along. We knew at the wedding but wanted to wait…' Her eyes fill with tears. 'We've just been so blessed… It felt a lot like tempting fate to tell you guys any sooner…'

Holden's the first to react. He stands and wraps Jagger in a massive bear hug, then folds Grace in. Her eyes meet mine over Holden's shoulder and it spurs me to act. I cross the room and pull her away, hugging her, then shaking Jagger's hand.

'This is great news.' And I mean it. I see how happy they are and for the first time in two months I remember the noble sacrifice I've made—Asha wants exactly what Grace and Jagger have. She deserves that. She deserves *this*. But I'm not the guy to give it to her.

Much later, on the terrace, when it's just Jagger and me, I turn to him, a tightness on my face. 'Listen.' I force a smile to my lips. 'I'm happy for you, man. I really am.'

'Sure you are.' He laughs.

'What?'

'It's just you and Holden are giving off a similar aura these days.'

I grimace. 'We're really screwed then.'

'Why don't you just call her?'

My body tightens. I reject his suggestion. 'Call who?'

He laughs, a gritty sound. 'The woman you can't stop thinking about?'

I don't pretend to misunderstand. 'It's been two months. Whatever we were is completely done.'

'So you're seeing someone else?'

I recoil from that very idea. 'Nah.'

'So you're celibate for the first time in your adult life and you're trying to tell me it has nothing to do with Asha?'

I shift my view, looking out at Manhattan. 'What's her due date?'

'Thirtieth of May. Why don't you call her?'

'Grace?' I purposely misunderstand.

He reaches across and punches my arm. Not hard, but not playfully either. 'Damn it, Theo, you're being an ass.'

I grind my teeth together, not one hundred per cent convinced he's wrong.

'What happened between the two of you?'

'We were just sleeping together,' I say, hating that

I'm talking to him about Asha but also realising how desperately I need to talk to *someone* about all this. Because two months after she walked away from me I can't get her out of my goddamned head.

'Sure you were.' He nods. 'Except Grace says Asha was completely in love with you.'

'She talked about me to Grace?' I jerk my head around to Jagger.

'Not in so many words. Grace is good at all that touchy-feely stuff.'

I shake my head, letting my eyes dance across the skyline. 'Asha wants the whole marriage and babies thing. She wants what you have.' My smile is tight.

'So?'

'So? Look at who you're talking to, man.'

Jagger's eyes drag over me. 'What's your point?'

'Come on.' I drag my toe over the grout. 'I'm glad you've got Grace and that you're all happy and shit but you know, you *know*, better than anyone, how unlikely that is.'

He nods, slowly.

'Dad really did a number on us.'

'It's not just Dad.' I shake my head. 'It's you and Lorena. It's Asha and how hurt she was by me. It's everyone. It's fucking Holden. All my life I've seen what "love" does to people. It's not pretty. It's not for me.' I drag a hand through my hair. 'Life is so complicated. I just don't get why you'd make it even worse by getting involved with someone. By getting married.'

Jagger's smile shows sympathy, and I hate that.

'The thing is, when you meet the right person, it's not that complicated at all. It's the easiest decision you'll ever make because you just can't live without them.'

It's weird how Grace and I have stayed in contact, and now become friends, but we have. It has nothing to do with Theo. I had to make her swear, right from the outset, not to talk to me about him. It was the only way I could move forward with my life; I needed a clean break.

But sitting across from her in this impossible-to-get-into sushi bar, I feel the question tripping out of me at every opportunity, so I basically have to bite my tongue to stop from asking how he is.

Some time after our second pot of green tea, she volunteers the information anyway.

'He's doing okay, you know.'

My eyes lift to hers, trepidation in my voice when I answer. 'I'm glad.'

'Are you?'

I swallow. 'Sure. I don't wish him any harm.'

She smiles, a small smile. 'And you, Asha? Are you okay?'

I nod, pasting a smile on my face. 'Never better.'

'Liar.'

'Why do you say that?'

'Because I know what heartbreak looks like.' Her eyes grow moist and she reaches over, putting her hand on mine. 'I'm so sorry.'

What else can either of us say?

I smile bleakly but it's something.

'Tell me something happy,' I urge. 'Cheer me up.'

'I do have good news, in fact.' She leans forward, her eyes bright. 'I'm going to be a mom.'

I walk around the city for a few hours after lunch. I just need to clear my head and I can't think straight at my place, where Theo's ghost seems to hang out, waiting to blow memories into my brain. I can't escape him. He's everywhere. Even now, eight weeks after I ended it, I feel his presence and I want to… I don't know. I stop walking and press my back to a building, closing my eyes.

'You all right, lady?' A guy in a backwards-turned baseball cap approaches me.

I nod. 'I'm fine.' Then, belatedly, 'Thanks.'

But I'm not fine. I wind up back at my office, not my home. It's the one place Theo never came to, the one place I can be without imagining him. Here, at least, there's a modicum of peace, albeit fleeting.

I lose myself in my work, just like I have done every day for the last eight weeks, and I do everything I can to push Theo from my mind, just for a moment, just for a bit.

CHAPTER THIRTEEN

IT'S AFTER JAGGER and Grace have gone back to Australia that I find myself thinking about them, thinking about their marriage and their life, the baby that's on the way. I find myself remembering the way they are together and contrasting that to the way Jagger was with his first wife. Holden and I hated Lorena from day dot—she was using him and it was patently obvious to everyone *except* Jagger. So when I first heard Jagger was getting married again I was wary for him. Hadn't he learned his lesson?

Hadn't we all?

But seeing them together…it's so different. They're so different. Jagger and Grace are nothing like Jagger and Lorena, nothing like Dad and his wives. It all seems so natural and easy between them.

It *felt* natural and easy between Asha and me. Everything about her made me happy, made me smile. Why couldn't we just keep going as we were?

I stalk towards my bedroom window and stare out

at Manhattan, drawing in deep, strangled breaths. The sound of my lungs pumping fills the room.

Seeing what 'love' did to my mom, my stepmothers, to Jagger, to anyone and everyone, leaves me in little doubt that I did the right thing. I don't want any part of that world, and never have done.

But I do want Asha. I want her with every single part of me.

Enough to put my own doubts aside?

The sky is grey and bleak, rain threatening. I stare out at it, my eyes scanning the skyline, and then I imagine Asha, as I often do. What's she doing? Where's she at? Manhattan is massive so I'm not surprised we haven't run into each other, but it doesn't stop me from looking for her everywhere I go.

Fuck.

It's been ten weeks. Seventy days. When the hell am I going to stop feeling like a fire's been lit in my chest? I'm hollowed out, barely recognisable as the man I used to be.

I feel…

I feel…

I don't know.

I've never felt anything like this before. My life is tied to hers, I know that. I'm so sick of waking up and knowing I won't see her. That I won't get a text from her. That I won't hear her voice or be able to make her laugh.

I'm so sick of this.

That night we met for a drink, the night we broke

up, I told her I just wanted her, and it's true. I do. I want Asha. But enough? Enough to put aside years of telling myself love is the devil itself? Enough to admit to myself that what we were—what we are—goes way beyond sex?

Fuck.

I pull my hair up into a bun, jerking an elastic around it hard, frustration evident in every line of my body.

I can't see that future. When I think about marriage and everything Asha wants, a part of me closes up like a vice. But when I think about Asha, when I imagine I'm with her again and everything's fine, I can breathe, I can finally breathe.

But I can't go to her and ask her to take me back unless I'm willing to offer her every damned thing she wants, and I don't know that I am. I just know I can't keep going like this. I just know I need to see her, to hell with what makes sense, to hell with the fact it's selfish and ill-advised.

I need to see Asha like I need air and water, and I can't ignore that for a moment longer.

It doesn't occur to me for even one second that she won't be feeling as crappy as I do. I imagine we're two sides of a coin, both tortured by our separation, both made miserable by not being together. I imagine she's in hell, just like me.

So when I see her walking towards her apartment with a huge smile on her face and some beefcake guy at her side, it's like having the ground ripped out from under me. I'm glad I'm partially obscured by a lamppost. It gives me longer to watch unobserved. It gives me a chance to leave without letting her know I came here.

But I don't leave. It's like watching a head-on collision. I'm rendered silent by my shock.

They stop walking and I hold my breath, waiting to see what happens next. Is it a date? Maybe he's just a friend.

She puts a hand on his forearm, leans forward and says something quiet. His eyes widen and he laughs, wrapping an arm around her, then pulls her towards the front door of her apartment building.

My heart is pounding inside me. I stare at it, unable to make any sense of what I'm seeing.

It's a frigidly cold day but I stand there, staring at the apartment, as though with the sheer force of my will I can bring them back down, as if I can make him disappear out of her life.

My pulse is slamming through me and whatever indecision I've been toying with, seeing Asha so completely moved on with her life makes me realise how much I haven't. And why.

'I told you, it's the best cheesecake ever, right?'

Kevin takes another bite, closing his eyes exaggeratedly, and nods. 'Your heartbreak is terrible for my waistline, though.'

I don't bother to deny that's what I'm feeling. I've looked on the internet. I know it to be true.

heartbreak/ˈhaːtbreɪk/
noun: heartbreak
plural noun: heartbreaks
example: what Asha feels without Theo

I don't know what I expected. Probably that I'd start to feel more like myself again, but I don't. I feel like I'm floating on a turbulent ocean with only my job to anchor me. And Kevin, who's been some kind of godsend.

The thing is, for all the pain I feel, I never doubt I did the right thing to walk away from him. It would have been so much easier to stay. So much easier to ignore my needs and exist only in that heaven of his creation. But I have known this pain too well, this ache to be loved by someone incapable of offering it, and I cannot submit to it again. With my father, I have little choice. He's my dad, I'm in his life by biological necessity. I have a choice with Theo and I refuse to spend any more time knowing myself to be unwanted.

I just want you.

Not enough. Never enough.

We take the cheesecake and a bottle of Prosecco into my lounge and put on The Fashion Channel, and every time a Fleurs Sauvages product is name-checked Kevin makes us do a shot of Prosecco, so I'm pleasantly light-headed when he leaves an hour later.

Not light-headed enough, though. The blissed-out feeling only lasts as long as it takes for me to be alone, and then it's back, along with the ghosts in this apartment; Theo is everywhere I look, everywhere I stand.

I lie down on the sofa and stare at the ceiling. I don't cry. I did a lot of that in the first couple of weeks but now I'm simply numb.

The door buzzes a minute later.

'Hang on.' I make my voice extra cheery in the intercom for Kevin's sake, before buzzing him up, looking around to see what he's forgotten. There's nothing I can make out, so I wait with the door open an inch.

My smile drops when the elevator pings and Theo steps out, a look on his face I can't possibly interpret. I stare at him, my mind going blank, my mouth going dry, my belly flopping all the way to my toes. My fingers begin to shake and my legs don't feel strong enough to support me.

He stares at me when he reaches the door and his eyes are so tortured, so haunted, that I immediately forget my heartbreak and anger, my confusion, and say, 'Is something wrong? Is it Grace? The baby?'

He shakes his head, his eyes sweeping over me. When he drags his fingers through his hair I see they're shaking too.

'I waited for him to leave.'

It takes me a second to realise he's talking about Kevin.

'I don't know why I'm even asking this, but I just

need to hear you say it. I need to know. Are you see-ing that guy?' He swallows, a look of distaste on his face, his voice gruff. 'Are you fucking him?'

My intake of breath is harsh. It's none of his busi-ness, but it is, because I'm Asha and he's Theo and our lives will always be the other one's business. Denying that is stupid and unfair.

'You have no right to be here,' I say instead, shak-ing my head, holding the door firmly in my hand.

'I just need you to tell me and then I'll go,' he de-mands, and then, softer, 'Please.'

I swallow, the plea bringing tears back to my eyes. 'What are you doing here, Theo?'

His eyes bore into mine, his expression like stone. 'I came to see…if you're happy. And I saw that you are. I saw it with my own eyes.' He rubs his hand over his face as though he can erase whatever he thinks he's seen. I mentally replay my afternoon, and all I can think is that he watched as Kevin and I entered my apartment building. I try to see it from the outside, from the perspective of someone who doesn't know that Kevin is a long-time friend and employee, and yes, I can definitely understand what conclusion Theo's leaped to. 'I just need you to say the words. Tell me you've moved on.'

I nod slowly, even when none of this makes sense. 'And will that make you happy?'

His laugh is completely lacking in humour. 'Yeah. It'll make me ecstatic.'

I bristle at his sarcasm.

'I'm sorry.' He closes his eyes, and his voice is raw. When he opens his eyes I see so much in his expression that my heart begins to twist painfully in my chest.

I open the door a bit wider. 'Did you want…to come in?'

He shakes his head. 'I can't.' A muscle jerks in his jaw and I know him so well that I understand what he really means. He can't come into my apartment when I've just been—in his mind at least—having sex with Kevin. His misery is completely unreasonable, given that I told him I was in love with him and he let me go, but it's so patently clear that he's in some kind of agony right now.

'Why did you come here?' My voice emerges as a whisper.

'It's complicated,' he says. And then shakes his head, rejecting that. 'No, it's simple. I can't… I don't want to live without you, Ash.'

Disbelief sweeps through me.

'I've been so dead set against marriage, relationships, the idea of the whole fairy tale happily ever after crap, but when I think of you, all I want is to hold you tight and never let you go.' He glares at me with a swirling torrent of emotions.

'I fucked up. I really, really fucked up. I treated you like you didn't matter, when you're *all* that matters to me. I acted like we were just sex when sex is… I mean, I love sleeping with you, but I love being with you so much more. I love talking to you and laughing with you, eating with you, walking with you. I love listening to you talk about your company and your passions, I love holding your hand and running my fingers through your hair. I am so in love with you, and I have been fighting that because I thought loving you would mean losing you, and losing you badly, like I've seen happen time and time again in other people's lives and marriages. But I've already lost you. I've already lost you in a way that's killing me inside, so what the hell am I so afraid of? Nothing can be worse than this.'

He swears under his breath. 'Nothing except coming here to tell you this, ten weeks too late.' He takes a step away from me, pressing his back against the wall opposite. 'Nothing except finally realising how I feel about you and seeing you with someone else.'

He closes his eyes, breathing in deeply, and I stand right where I am, staring at him, unable to look away, transfixed by the appearance of him at my apartment and the words he's saying, and the fact that I hear his sincerity and I understand, completely, how he feels. I expel a soft breath and something like warmth flows through me. A warmth I haven't felt since before we left for Australia.

A warmth that promises spring and fresh growth, *fleurs sauvages* and sunshine. But pain has made me cautious.

'What did you expect me to say when you showed up here?'

He lifts his eyes to mine and he is so bereft, so

lost, it costs me to stay where I am, to stay here when he's there and my heart is already straining towards him.

'I don't know. I think I hoped…but how could I hope? After everything I put you through.'

Still, I stay where I am. 'So why come here?'

'I needed to see you.' He shakes his head. 'I needed to *tell* you. Because even if you've moved on, you deserve to know that I get it. That I was wrong, and that I'm sorry. I need you to know that I love you, irrespective of how you feel now.'

His words tumble through me and I close my eyes, breathing them in. In my mind I see a dandelion, the seeds flying away on the breeze. I am free.

'I look at our relationship and see the myriad ways I let you down. And still you loved me. Still you stuck by me and tried to explain. God, Asha, I'm sorry.'

I nod, because he's right. He hurt me. But none of us exists in a void. His life, his childhood, the wounds that were inflicted on him, are all part of who Theo is today.

'You saw what heartbreak does to people.' I step into the corridor, towards him. 'You saw your mom being hurt again and again by your dad, and as you grew older you heard how your dad had done that to Jagger's mom and Holden's mom. You saw so much hurt and you decided relationships can cause only pain.' I press a hand to his chest and feel his good, solid, beating heart. 'And then you met me, and you fell in love, and even though you tried to fight it, you realised that there is good in relationships too.' I press up onto the tips of my toes and brush my lips over his. 'With the right person, there is so much more good than bad. And the bad is worth putting up with to get all the good.'

He's frozen still, his breath trapped inside of him.

Standing so close to Theo, I feel like a part of me that was missing is being returned, stitched back into the foundation of my soul. But he's still hurting. He doesn't see the full picture.

'That's my assistant, Kevin.' I wrap my arms behind Theo's back, smiling as his eyes widen and he exhales for the first time in a long time. 'He's taken on cheering me up as his mission in life.'

'So you're not…he's not…'

'I love you,' I say simply, loudly, clearly. 'And always will. There's no one else.'

He drops his head then, pressing our brows together, and I hear his ragged breath, like he's run a marathon. My heart bursts.

'I love you.' Because he needs to understand that. 'I can't promise you that we're not going to fight from time to time, that's life, and people don't always agree. But you're not your dad, and I'm not your mom. We're us, and what we have, what we share—' I press my hand to his chest again '—this is the real deal.'

'I know,' he groans, lifting his hands and cupping my face. 'God, I know, I just can't believe it took me so long to wake up and see this clearly.'

'It doesn't matter.' I shake my head urgently. 'You did wake up, and today is just the beginning for us.'

'The beginning of what?' he murmurs, but he's lifting me up, taking me into the apartment and kicking the door shut.

'The rest of our lives.' I kiss the words into his mouth and he laughs, a sound of sheer delight.

He pulls his head away for a second, his expression serious, his eyes holding mine intently. 'For as long as we both shall live. Okay?'

My heart turns over in my chest. 'Yep.'

'You know what I was thinking?'

I turn to face him, the moonlight casting a streak of silver over his handsome face.

He draws circles on my flesh, his eyes following the action. 'When we get married, if you take my name, you'll be Asha Sauvages-Hart. And I was thinking how much that suits you... Asha Wild Hart.'

Speaking of hearts, mine is about to explode.

'I think you've tamed my wildness, though,' I point out with a broad smile, shifting a little and putting my head on his chest, so I can listen to the rushing of his pulse. It thunders through his body and it thunders just for me—and always will, of that I have no doubt. He's left no room for doubt: there is only Theo and me and the love we hold for each other, wild, full of heart and never-ending.

* * * * *

COMING SOON!

We really hope you enjoyed reading this book. If you're looking for more romance, be sure to head to the shops when new books are available on

Thursday 16th April

To see which titles are coming soon, please visit

millsandboon.co.uk/nextmonth

LET'S TALK
Romance

For exclusive extracts, competitions
and special offers, find us online: